Porch Lights

Porch Lights

Dorothea Benton Frank

HARPER LUXE

An Imprint of HarperCollins*Publishers*

FIRST HARPERLUXE EDITION

HarperLuxe™ is a trademark of HarperCollins Publishers

Library of Congress Cataloging-in-Publication Data is available upon request.

ISBN: 978-0-06-212835-5

12 13 14   ID/RRD 10 9 8 7 6 5 4 3 2 1

For all the brave men and women who
serve our country in every branch of the
armed forces, especially in Afghanistan

I stand amid the roar
Of a surf-tormented shore,
And I hold within my hand
Grains of the golden sand—
How few! Yet how they creep
Through my fingers to the deep,
While I weep—while I weep!
O God! Can I not grasp
Them with a tighter clasp?
O God! Can I not save
One from the pitiless wave?
Is *all* that we see or seem
But a dream within a dream?

—Edgar Allan Poe, "A Dream Within a Dream"

Contents

1

This island is a very singular one. It consists of little else than the sea sand, and is about three miles long. Its breadth at no point exceeds a quarter of a mile. It is separated from the mainland . . .

—Edgar Allan Poe, "The Gold-Bug"

Meet Jackie McMullen

I will tell you *the* one thing that I have learned about life in my thirty-something years that is an absolute truth: nothing and no one in this entire world matters more to a sane woman than her children. I have one child, my son, Charlie. Charlie is barely ten years old, and he is the reason I get up in the morning. I thank God for him every night before I go to sleep. When I was stationed in Afghanistan, I slept with a T-shirt of his wrapped around my arm. I did. Not my husband's. My son's. It was the lingering sweet smell of my little boy's skin that got me through the awful nights while rockets were exploding less than a mile away from my post. I would fall asleep praying for Charlie. And, if

I had known what would happen, I would have petitioned harder for my husband, Jimmy's, safety in those same prayers. I should've prayed harder for Jimmy.

Now I'm driving south on I-95 while Charlie sleeps, slumped in the seat next to me, and I wonder: what the hell was the matter with Jimmy and me? Why did we think we had the right to be so cavalier about what we did for a living, pretending to be bulletproof and fireproof and thinking nothing could happen to us? Sure. Me—an army nurse doing three seven-month tours in a war zone—and Jimmy answering the firehouse alarms, rushing out to save what? The world? No, my Jimmy died trying to save a bunch of low-life crackheads in a filthy, rat-infested tenement on the Lower East Side of Manhattan. He fell to his death when the floor beneath him collapsed. How do I tell my Charlie to make any sense of that when I can't make sense of it myself?

Ah, Jimmy McMullen, there will never be another man like you. Nope. Not on Earth and not in Heaven. You were one of a kind. Here's to ya, blue eyes, wherever you are. I took a swig from my water bottle.

I was pretty certain that wherever Jimmy was couldn't be too far away because I could feel him, watching over me, over us. And when the world grew still, deep in the night, I could literally feel enormous regret gushing from his gorgeous big Irish heart, regret about leaving us. But I'd never believe it was his fault for one minute. He'd been stolen from us, ripped out of our lives like a bad tooth. Jimmy's death was another victory for the Dark Side. Plain and simple. At least that's how it seemed to me. I mean, I was not some crazy religious fanatic at all, but I believed in God. And the God I believed in would never sanction such a senseless, violent death for such a righteous man.

Jimmy McMullen *was* a righteous man who loved his church and never missed Sunday Mass unless he had a fever of a hundred and three. On his days off, he took Charlie and his toolbox over to the rectory and hammered loose boards back in place or unclogged a slow draining sink or put a coat of paint where it needed to go. Father O'Quinn would ask Jimmy if he could help him out on Saturday at nine in the morning, and Jimmy would be there at eight thirty with a bag of old-fashioned doughnuts and a disposable cardboard tray, two large cups of coffee wedged in the holder. That's what he did in his free time when he wasn't taking Charlie to a Yankees game. That was just the kind of guy he was. Faithful to his family, his church, and his word. And generous to a fault. You would've loved him. Everyone did. Charlie idolized him, absolutely idolized him. And Charlie's despair was the cause of the deepest, most wrenching concern and worriation I have ever known. No matter what I said or did, I just couldn't seem to bring him around.

It was completely understandable that a child of his age would be traumatized by the loss of a parent, even depressed for some period of time. But the changes in Charlie were alarming and unnerving. After two months or so I kept thinking he would somehow make peace with our new reality because life goes on. He did not. Jimmy's Aunt Maureen was the one who made me see that something had to be done.

"This child is severely depressed," she said. "He's not eating right or sleeping well. We've got to do something, Jackie. We've got to do something."

"I know," I said. "You know, in Afghanistan when a child loses his father he's considered an orphan. They're sent to orphanages, where the boys outnumber the girls about ten to one."

Aunt Maureen looked at me, unblinking, while she quickly calculated the whys and wherefores of such a radical policy—without a husband the woman sinks into poverty, without government intervention they would literally starve, little boys are valued more highly than the little girls . . . what happens to all the little girls? Human trafficking? She knew exactly what I wasn't saying.

"Dear Heavenly Father, there's so much wrong with the world."

"You're telling me?"

"You must have seen terrible things."

"Yes. Yes, I have."

"Well, God bless you. And look, Charlie has us, such as we are. At least he doesn't have to worry about being sent to an orphanage."

"I thank God for that."

"Amen," she said. "Amen."

Aunt Maureen, unmarried and in her sixties, was Charlie's secondary caretaker while I was overseas. There's no question that she was cut from the McMullen cloth in terms of understanding and fulfilling obligations, but unfortunately she didn't exude the warmth that seemed to flow endlessly from the rest of Jimmy's clan. Not even a little bit. She wore sensible shoes, no makeup, and was . . . well, in a word, dowdy. And prim. Yes, Aunt Maureen was prim, a throwback from another time when domestic life was governed by a hard-and-fast set of rules. Rules that had consequences when they were not followed to the letter. She'd always been that way, seemingly uninterested in the opposite sex, the same sex, or sex. Or in having her own family. Maybe the idea of a house filled with a gaggle of noisy children frightened her, which even as a parent of only one child was not a concept beyond my grasp. Every woman I knew with a husband and little ones would have said that raising children is as scary as the day is long. But putting aside her appearance, demeanor, and domestic aspirations, she was a good woman. A fine woman, in fact. Each time I was deployed she appeared like clockwork, standing in the hallway of our apartment with her heavy suitcase and a shopping bag of treats for Charlie, comic books and other things, ready to do her duty. And she always brought me a bag of things she knew I'd miss: dried fruit, power bars, Snickers, and two pounds of my favorite kind of coffee, ground for drip.

She gave Charlie her all; it's just that some pretty shallow waters flowed in the river of her emotions. It didn't matter because Charlie understood her nature and he was fine with it. They had an arrangement. When Aunt Maureen was in residence, she slept in Charlie's room and Charlie slept on the pullout sofa in our living room. Jimmy cooked dinner, and Charlie washed and dried the dishes with her. Jimmy made lasagna, meat loaf, and chili like no other, but show me an FDNY fireman who couldn't cook, right? That's what they did down at the firehouse when they weren't fighting fires—they cooked. They cooked and they ate, they watched television and ate snacks, they lifted weights, and then they ate some more. I used to tell him that his ladder company should have had its own show on the Food Network. Or at least a guest spot on *Throwdown! with Bobby Flay*. Can't you see all these good-looking, ripped guys showing Flay where the bear goes in the buckwheat when it came to meat loaf?

We had a good life, Jimmy, Charlie, and I. We owned a co-op in a stone building in the Cobble Hill section of Brooklyn. It was built in the 1930s, nice but not grand and near where Jimmy's parents used to live. I mean, the kitchen was reasonably new but there was no room for a dishwasher because we chose to use that space for a washer/dryer stack. I had a germ thing about using washers and dryers that were used by everyone else in the building. Who knew what nasty horrors they put into them? There's no need to paint a picture. Funny, the laundry service on base in Kandahar was fine, except for my disappearing underwear, but a public washer and dryer stateside made me gag. My mother has this weird idea that living in Brooklyn is like that movie *Fort Apache, the Bronx*. But then she has a lot of weird ideas.

Anyway, our kitchen had a nice big window, and that seemed like fair compensation to us. I could watch the birds in the morning while I scrambled eggs or flipped pancakes, and that always made my heart a little bit lighter. The living room also served as our dining room, and our air-conditioning consisted of window units. We had two bedrooms and two bathrooms and the use of a small backyard, which was a luxury.

The day that the terrible news came, Aunt Maureen was there in a flash. She picked Charlie up from school and stayed with him until my mother arrived. Then they kept vigil until I could get home on bereavement leave. Aunt Maureen had called my mother and asked her to come at once. To her credit, Mom was literally in my living room six hours later—not an easy feat considering she lived nearly a thousand miles away.

Before I get too far ahead of myself I should tell you a little about my mother, Annie. Basically, she's the antithesis of Aunt Maureen. She's rock steady like Maureen, but she's got this other side that, well, let's just say that a little bit of Momma goes a long way for some people. She's just too much. You know what I mean? She's too effusive, too dramatic, too fussy about the superficial and not fussy enough about other issues—for example, she still wears red lipstick, she drives a Sebring convertible, and she thinks she can interpret dreams. Okay, maybe that's a lame indictment, but what I'm trying to say is that she says and does these things all the time that make me cringe. And how did she let my father just walk out of the door after twenty-something years of marriage? There was no history of screaming fights, no tears were shed, and no marriage counselors were brought in to help. They just split. Yes, that happened the day after I got married. It was all over the fact that Dad's fishing tackle was left on the back porch and she had company coming. At my mother's house, the back porch is the main entryway. God forbid someone tripped over a smelly cast net. It is the single dumbest story in my family's history. And I'm a little embarrassed to admit that for a long time I thought it was a dramatic move on her part to steal some thunder from my wedding weekend. Now I can see that Dad had simply had it with her, her rules, her house, her everything. I understand. I escaped too.

They've been living apart now for almost eleven years. I know they're lonely without each other, but wow, are they ever stubborn. They're like two mules. At least I *think* they're lonely, and they must miss each other. Dad has never been out with another woman, to the best of my knowledge, and Momma has never dated either. If anybody's stepping out on the other I don't want to know.

When I have asked him why he doesn't just go home, he says he's waiting for Momma to cool down. For eleven years? Hell, volcanoes cool faster. When I ask her how Dad's doing, she says Dad's just gone fishing up in Murrells Inlet and she imagines he'll come home when he's had enough sun. I know, I know. It's their business, but when Jimmy died, I needed my parents. Both of them. And so did Charlie.

So Momma came to Jimmy's funeral and Dad stayed home because Momma said she couldn't be in the same room with him. She said the thought of having to look at him made her nerves act up. She always said that as though her nerves were a separate entity with a will of their own. How could I forget that? I'd been walking on eggshells around her my whole life, living in fear of making her nerves act up. Isn't that great? I was in such a state of disbelief and anguish over losing Jimmy that I didn't object, but it was typical of her to think of herself and her nerves first and to never give a thought that maybe I needed my father too. Here we have a fine snapshot of the differences between us.

Momma stayed for a week and a half. The first thing she did was ask me with a smile when was the last time we had pushed all the furniture away from the walls to clean. Was she implying we lived in squalor? Didn't she realize how long I'd been away? I just let her take over and do whatever she wanted. As if I could have stopped her anyway. Annie Britt was a whirling dervish with paper towels in one hand and a sponge in the other. She reorganized all our closets, packing up most of Jimmy's clothes for Goodwill, something I was loath to do. I kept his sweaters and a few other things, like neckties and his FDNY uniform, that I thought Charlie might like to have one day. Next she cleaned the bathroom and kitchen until they glistened. Have at it! She filled the freezer with single-serving containers of soups, stews, and pasta sauces, and she helped me write thank-you notes for all the flowers and cakes that people brought and brought—to her surprise, as though people in the North didn't offer condolences like people in the South.

"We mostly bring hams and pound cakes," she said. "I mean, how much baked ziti can a person consume?"

"The same amount as ham," I said and thought, Oh, brother.

Charlie's toys were dusted and rearranged on his shelves, and all the while she dusted and rearranged them, Charlie sat on the side of his bed telling her in fragmented mumbles what each one meant to him. As he spoke, he was so subdued that my heart ached for my little chatterbox to reappear.

The week after she left, Charlie's troubles mushroomed. He seemed to have lost interest in everything. Even his skateboard, the one physical activity he was crazy about, stood by the door, abandoned as though the idea of fun belonged to his past. I had to argue with him to go to school. Maureen was right. He wasn't eating enough for a boy his age. He didn't even want to take a bath. He began having nightmares about terrorists and burning buildings. Then he dreamed that I died and that he was all alone, lost somewhere in a place like Central Park surrounded by strangers and no one to help him. After one of those horrific episodes, he would appear at the foot of my bed sweaty and shaking. I'd get up, throw my arm around his shoulders, and lead him back to his room. After a few nights of putting him back to bed, not once but many times, I let him bring in his comforter and sleep on the floor next to me. Obviously, I knew Charlie sleeping in my room could become a bad habit, but I didn't care. My poor boy was just as distraught as I was, and we were both exhausted from grief and lack of sleep.

Every night after we lost Jimmy, I'd lie in bed in the pitch-black dark just thinking. It wasn't that I couldn't accept his death. God knows, I'd seen plenty of death in the hills of Afghanistan—men, women, and children, torn apart and literally blown up by the insanity of their own countrymen. And what happened to the Americans was just as bad and sometimes worse. Hell, I'd seen the Taliban use children as suicide bombers for the promise of candy. No, it wasn't about death per se.

It was that I was just completely and utterly heartbroken; that's all.

The day I married Jimmy was the happiest day of my life, next to the day when I held my newborn Charlie in my arms. Our love and the love I felt for our little family pulled me through a war. Overseas, I was so careful all the time because coming home to them was always on my mind's front burner. Charlie was my sweetheart, and Jimmy McMullen was the only man I had ever loved. I would never get over the horror of losing him. Never. And now I worried that maybe Charlie wouldn't either.

I tried so hard not to get upset in front of Charlie, knowing it wouldn't do him any good and believing I had to be strong for him. But alone in my bed at night, tears would come, memories of the three of us by the score would come rushing through my brain in some kind of a landslide of scenes, skipping from last Christmas to the summer before, Charlie's first day of school, holiday programs, another summer preceding it, telling Jimmy I was pregnant, on and on. By some godforsaken hour I'd sleep again in fits and starts, only to wake up once more and remember again that he was gone. In so many ways, Jimmy's death *was* unbelievable. I'd stare at the ceiling, waiting for the alarm to ring and worrying about what would become of us. Intellectually, I knew that eventually I would somehow adjust. Eventually, I *would* adjust. But what about Charlie? How deep was his wound?

Finally I called my father, and the next thing I knew I was weeping as though the news were brand new.

"I'm getting on a plane today," he said.

Dad arrived that night to assess the situation and to offer what comfort he could. He worked his grandfatherly magic on Charlie, and for a little while it seemed that my boy was perking up. Dad took him to the Museum of Natural History one day and on another to the Yogi Berra Museum out in Montclair, New Jersey, where Yogi Berra himself happened to be that afternoon. He signed a baseball for Charlie that he carried around with him wherever he went, including the dinner table. They went out for ice cream every night after all the dishes were washed and put away. Dad told Charlie stories, wonderful stories about how he used to churn peach ice cream when he was a kid, and Charlie marveled at the fact that you could actually make your own. They were still talking about making ice cream when they came home one night.

"It's a heckuva lot better than what you can buy in the stores," Dad said with a laugh.

"Can you teach me how to make it?" Charlie asked.

"You betcha booties, baby! You can count on it! Get your momma to bring you down south to see me, and we'll make ice cream every day."

"Even blueberry?" Charlie asked.

"Even blueberry," Dad said.

"You still have that old churn?" I asked.

"It's somewhere under your Momma's house," he said. "You bring Charlie and we'll find it."

Dad's magic had a shelf life with an unfortunately short expiration date. Within just a few days of his departure, I began to see all the signs of Charlie's depression returning. God, I felt so impotent and so deeply sad to realize there was so little I could do for him or for myself that could change a thing. And feeling that useless made me more depressed. But hell would freeze before I would tell my mother. She'd have me in a shrink's office in five minutes.

Who was I kidding? It was right after the Fourth of July. I knew it was time to head south, shrink or no shrink. It wasn't that I didn't have enough love to take care of Charlie on my own. It was anything but that. It was that I thought he needed to be buoyed by the love of everyone. Maybe the love of my parents, the friends of our family, and the island old salts would fill the air, he would breathe it in, and my little boy would be restored.

He was half sleeping, slouched against the window with his pillow bunched in between his shoulder and his cheek. His DS was in his lap, never too far from him. I know every mother in the world feels this, but my heart was so filled with love for him at that moment I thought it might burst.

I looked over at him for another moment and whispered, "Love you, baby."

He grimaced a little, not liking being disturbed, and then he reached out and put his hand on my arm. It was a proprietary touch but also one seeking for reassurance that I was still there.

A few minutes later, he sat up rubbing his eyes with his fists. "Mom? Where do you think Dad is?"

"Heaven," I said. "Don't you?"

"Yeah, but you know, it's like he's still around. But not in a creepy way."

"How do you mean?"

"Well, like when before the end of the school year, I'd be studying for a hard test? It was sort of like he was there, telling me to keep at it, not to give up. Do you know what I mean?"

"Yes. I do know. And you want to know something else?"

"What?"

"It makes me feel a little better."

"Yeah, but not for long enough."

"I agree with you, but you know what? I think it would be mighty strange if we weren't sad right now."

"Yeah."

"One more thing: you don't have to be sad every minute of the night and day, you know. And you can talk to me about it anytime you want."

"That's two things."

"Right."

I sighed then, realizing we were little more than two hurt birds flying back to the mother nest to heal. I hoped I had made a good decision. A long vacation of salted breezes, hammocks to while away steamy after-noons, building sand castles, and making ice cream with my sweet dad—all those things could go a long way to mend our broken hearts. I hoped.

2

Near the western extremity, where Fort Moultrie stands . . . is covered with a dense undergrowth of the sweet myrtle . . . attains the height of fifteen or twenty feet . . . burthening the air with its fragrance.

—Edgar Allan Poe, "The Gold-Bug"

Meet Annie Britt

Frankly, we had precious little to say to each other, *but* because he actually took his Old Man and the Sea hand off his fishing rod long enough to call me, I spoke to him. I had not heard from my estranged husband since the funeral. Of course, I was very polite to him. If I hadn't known better I'd have said the spirit of James McMullen was conspiring to have us kiss and make up, but I don't believe in that kind of nonsense. Well, not as a general rule. And that's not why he called anyway. Buster, as he was known to all, had been to visit our daughter, Jackie, and our adorable grandson, Charlie, way up the road in Brooklyn, New York, and he didn't like what he found. Like I had? Who in the world would be happy to see their daughter and her little boy struggling under the weight of that kind of traumatic and horrendous loss?

I mean, I don't want to sound judgmental, but Buster's not exactly the expert of the world on the hearts of women and children. *Apparently* there had been a recent conversation between Jackie and Buster, and *apparently* Jackie had cried him a river. Weeping is not my daughter's style. At all. She's a soldier, for heaven's sake! But everyone has a limit of what they can endure. His call truly alarmed me. Truly.

She told Buster that she's very, very worried about Charlie. He wasn't coping well. He was having terrible nightmares, he was lethargic and not eating well. Oh, my poor dear little grandson! And just the idea of my daughter sobbing made my chest tighten. Buster, unsure of how to handle her, did the right thing. He brought the problem to me. *As! He! Should! Have!* After all, I was *still* the mother of the family, even if our child was a military nurse, toting a loaded gun around the world and even though her father preferred the waters seventy-seven miles to the north.

I called Jackie immediately and pleaded with her to spend the balance of the summer with me on the island. Maybe beseech is the better word because it was more begging than pleading. Oh, she hemmed and hawed around for a while, and suddenly to my astonishment, she gave in, making me swear on a stack of Bibles not to spoil Charlie rotten. I promised enormous personal restraint and thought, Gosh, that wasn't nearly as difficult as I thought it would be, which was an indication of how worried she must be. And if she was that worried, maybe she needed to stay here for longer than a few weeks. There was no reason I could fathom for her to go back to Brooklyn. Why would anyone want to live in a place like that anyway? Glory be to God! All that noise? And it's so cold in the winter! And you take your life in your hands every time you cross the streets with cars and taxis and ambulances zipping all around you like madmen! And the subway? Let's just say I'd rather walk ten miles in the pouring rain than go all the way underground just to get across town—I'd be underground for good soon enough.

She could practice nursing at the VA hospital right here in Charleston, and Aunt Maureen could visit anytime. I liked Maureen. Not spoil Charlie? Let me tell you this: if you were ever caught in those enormous blue eyes, flashing from behind his stick-straight black bangs that longed for a trim (in my estimation), you'd open your heart and your wallet and give the boy everything in the world.

I knew I drove my daughter out of her mind some of the time. To be honest, she drove me a little batty too. She internalizes every blessed thing and broods, while I like to think of myself as liberated from the shackles of social convention, you know, undaunted by anything life throws my way and unafraid to speak from my heart. She thinks I'm too dramatic, which is patently ridiculous, and I think she's not dramatic enough. Cleopatra was dramatic. Holly Golightly was dramatic. Lady Gaga is dramatic. I was perfectly in control of my personal theater, but the truth? I was very excited they were coming.

Even my house was buzzing with anticipation as though the floors and walls and windows knew that Jackie and Charlie were coming home. The sun was shining, and gorgeous breezes drifted from room to room, laced with the smells of the sea. It was Saturday and a perfect summer day, barely a drop of humidity and somewhere around seventy-five degrees. Who needed air-conditioning? I hardly ever used it unless the temperature was over one hundred degrees.

Jackie had called just an hour before to say that they were north of Columbia and if the traffic continued moving along she would be home in time for lunch. She used the word *home*. I didn't know if she meant it to mean her home or my home, but that simple word *home* coming from her was so wonderful to my ears. And I hoped with all my heart that she still believed this *was* her home.

I had done everything within my means that I could think of to set the right tone. My largest pot was filled with okra soup, simmering on the back of the stove, and my rice steamer with warm fluffy white rice. Not an hour before, I had pulled a pan of brownies and a pan of corn bread from the oven, and they'd filled the kitchen with the delicious smells of butter and chocolate. The table was set with a cheerful tablecloth. I'd even cut some flowers from my garden—oh, all right, they were sprigs of white oleander that I rinsed to baptize the bugs away—but I put them in the middle of the table in my mother's small Fiesta ware red vase and the mood was set. All there was left to do was pour the iced tea, drop in a lemon wedge, and put a blessing on it all. Soon I'd be sharing a meal with the two very dearest people in my world. Buster didn't know what he was missing.

Oh! What an old fool I was to worry so. A ten-year-old boy didn't give two figs about how his bed was made, but I made and remade his trundle bed three times. Three times! But you know, in view of his nightmares, I wanted that bed to look so comfy that he'd curl up under those covers, forget about his worries, and sleep the best sleep of his life. The quilt was new and had puppies all over it. Maybe we would name them together. Plus, I put fire escape ladders in every bedroom closet to ease any anxiety he and Jackie might have.

For fun, I bought him a stack of new comic books and a new yo-yo, a book on the history of baseball and another one packed with true stories about the pirates that once sailed the waters around Charleston. Then in a moment of whimsy I picked up a crazy Hawaiian-print bathing suit for him—the young people call them board shorts—and a T-shirt from the Charleston RiverDogs plus a schedule of their ball games. Would Buster come down and take him to a game? I hoped so, and if I had the occasion to speak to him again in this lifetime I would drop the hint. Diplomatically. If he wouldn't go, I would, even if it was a hundred and five in the shade, which it usually was this time of year. We could eat hot dogs together and whatever else they had. Lord! I haven't had a hot dog in years!

Lastly, I found a miniature picture of Jackie taken on the morning of her First Communion, reframed it, and placed it on his night table. It was such a precious photograph. There was Jackie in a beautiful white organza dress, her veil billowing in the breeze and her two front teeth gone missing. I remembered that morning like it was yesterday. It was good for a child to be reminded that his parent was once a child too.

I gave a gentle yank to the smiling ceramic shrimp that was attached to the cord hanging from the ceiling fan to circulate the air slowly like the breeze of a waltz. From the doorway I appraised it all for the tenth time. Charlie's room, which was right next door to Jackie's, had never looked more inviting.

Jackie's room had been her bedroom when she was a little girl, but it had long been turned into a guest room. After Buster went off fishing I had our Charleston rice poster bed moved in here, because frankly, I was getting too old to be climbing up bed steps to go to sleep. What if I woke up in the middle of the night to use the bathroom? If I wasn't fully conscious I could fall and break a hip. I would be found three days later by my neighbors, dehydrated and in agony. So I pushed Jackie's twin beds together in my bedroom and had GDC Design Center make an upholstered headboard so it looked like I had a king-sized bed, which I needed like another hole in my head. Still, it was better than being found in an undignified heap on the floor. It wasn't that I worried about osteoporosis. Thankfully I had the bone density of a much younger woman; I was a true Steel Magnolia. It was more like I just worried about everything, but I worked very hard not to let my anxieties show.

Jackie's room looked rather amazing too, if I said so myself. I dressed her bed with all white linens and lots of pillows, including two antique European squares trimmed in hand-crocheted lace. I carefully folded my mother's delicate handmade quilt over the foot. I had mended and repaired that quilt more times than I could count, but it was still so beautiful to me. The pattern was a mosaic of flowers in a large basket. Naturally all of the flowers were faded with age, but I could imagine how vivid they must have been when the quilt was presented to my mother as a wedding gift from her great-aunt. That was back in the day when a young girl learned to sew at her mother's knee and grown women put great stock in the quality of their needlework. A wave of nostalgia washed over me. There were very few quilting bees around town these days, and it would be an extremely rare occasion to see generations of women gathered around a hearth doing needlepoint. These days young women play Bunko, drink white wine, and furnish their homes with a bed in a bag from some discount retailer. I know this because that's how I acquired Charlie's bedding and I did love to play Bunko and have a glass of wine myself. But still! What has this world come to?

Before I left the room, I smelled the inside of her closet. It was musty, like any closed area of a beach house can be. I opened the doors and hurried to my linen closet for a sachet of potpourri. Yes, I keep extra potpourri on hand because I make it myself from lavender that grows in a hedge of buzzing weeds in my yard. Besides, a sachet makes a wonderful hostess gift. And bumblebees love lavender.

Yes, I make lavender sachets. And yes, I am fast turning into, Heaven save me, my mother.

I pulled the cord of Jackie's ceiling fan to get the air moving. I rolled the sachet between my palms to release the oils in the seeds and slipped the ribbon over the neck of a hanger, deciding to leave the door open. She would probably think the room was too fussy. I doubted they issued her lace-trimmed sheets in Afghanistan, but I wanted her to know that I cared about her so much that I'd use my very best everything for her. I put an assortment of new (well, okay, gently read) novels on her nightstand along with a bottle of some fancy Italian water and a pretty glass. On her dresser I left a waterproof canvas beach bag filled with an assortment of magazines, a tube of suntan lotion, new flip-flops, and a visor that said SULLIVANS ISLAND across the brim. I had done my best.

"Anybody home?"

PORCH LIGHTS · 27

"Yes, yes! I'll be right there!"

It was the voice of Deb, my crazy wonderful neighbor. Deb ran the Edgar Allan Poe Library down the island and had for years. Until I took early retirement, I taught English and history for eons at the Sullivans Island Elementary School right next door, secretly specializing in South Carolina's illustrious past, especially stories about the pirates and naturally, Edgar Allan Poe. Poe lived on Sullivans Island while he was stationed at Fort Moultrie right before the so-called Civil War. Anyway, Deb and I had known each other all our lives and she was the very best friend I'd ever had. And her husband, Vernon, well, he was another story. Let's just say that Deb believed that once you got married, you stayed married. In fact, I bought her a needlepoint pillow that says a retired husband is A WIFE'S FULL-TIME JOB. True story.

She was standing on the top step of the stairs I descended every morning to walk the beach with her, wearing a broad-brimmed straw hat I hadn't seen before. The crown was covered in a psychedelic bouquet of artificial flowers, and it was about the wildest thing I'd ever seen. But then Deb was my most flamboyant friend, the complete opposite of the stereotypical librarian. She made me seem conservative.

"Hey!" she called out our traditional island greeting.

"Hey!" I flipped the latch on the screen door and held it open for her. "Come on in and tell me this instant where you got that hat! It's gorgeous!"

"I got it at Belk. Big sale. Want to try it on?" She handed it to me.

"Indeed I do," I said, plopping it on my head and checking myself out in the hall mirror. "I look like an ass in hats."

"No, you don't!" She gave me a friendly hug. "Is Jackie here yet?"

"No, but almost. She called from Columbia a while ago."

"Gosh, I can't wait to see her, Annie. The poor thing. How's she doing?"

"I guess she can't be doing too well, or she wouldn't be coming here."

"Stop! She loves you! You're her mother!"

"It's complicated, and you know it. Glass of tea?"

"Lord, yes. I'm parched like the Sahara."

Deb followed me into the kitchen, where I took two glasses from the cabinet and filled them with ice from the freezer of my Big Chill jadeite green refrigerator that looked exactly like my mother's from the 1950s.

"Here we go," I said and handed her a glass.

"I still can't believe you spent that much money on a refrigerator."

"Some women lust after hats and others lust after appliances."

"You're so crazy. Is this sweet?" She pointed to her glass.

"Aren't you sweet enough?" I arched an eyebrow in her direction.

"You know it, girl." She giggled and peeked inside my pots, her hundred enameled bangle bracelets tinkling like a wind chime as she lifted the top. "Smells divine."

"Stay. Stay and have lunch with us." It was a half-hearted invitation.

"No, darlin', thanks, but I have to be at my Zumba class in less than an hour. But we can sit on the porch for a few, if you want. The breeze is heavenly."

"Let's do."

Inside of a minute we were settled in the old weatherbeaten Kennedy rockers that ran the length of my front porch. There was a Pawleys Island hammock in the far corner, positioned there to catch the crosscurrents of air when the weather was stifling. But it was a lucky afternoon. The rising tide carried enough air to rustle the palmetto fronds and to blow our hair around.

"I still can't believe what-all kind of horrors your daughter has been through," Deb said. "You *know* she's seen some sights."

"No doubt about it. But she's a daredevil. And James was a daredevil too. This is what can happen when you sign up in a seriously risky profession. I always secretly wished she had married a doctor. I mean, I loved James like a son, but, you know . . ."

Deb sat up straight in her chair. I knew I had annoyed her.

"Annie Britt?"

Here it comes, I thought. And here it came. I tightened my jaw and tilted my head to the side.

"Now, you listen to me, and hear me good! If I hear that you said 'I told you so' to Jackie, I will hunt you down and cut off your tongue!"

"Oh, I won't *say* it, but you know she's dying for me to, so she can rant and rave. The whole blessed time I was in New York she kept taunting me."

"Rubbish. You're paranoid. She's not a teenager anymore, Annie, pushing your buttons and all that. She's a fresh widow with a little boy."

"Humph!" I said and added, "I'm still her mother, you know. I am well familiar with her situation. Just to reassure you, I want you to know I have given this a great deal of thought. I will be the last person on this planet to give her one iota of anything to complain about. You won't believe how well behaved I can be. Just watch."

"Humph!" she said. "You'd better be! I still can't believe you didn't get your picture taken with Mayor Bloomberg. He's a good-looking devil, isn't he?"

"Yes, but it wasn't exactly the right time and place. I mean, a funeral at Saint Patrick's Cathedral? And what a funeral it was! You would've thought Elvis died."

"He did. Remember? Years ago."

"Oh, shush. I know that. I'm just saying it was a funeral for a movie star. Bagpipes with all that mournful music. Limousines. Television cameras. Streets closed. Unbelievable. All his friends were there in their formal dress uniforms, walking beside the truck. They even put the darn casket on the top of his fire truck. I've never seen anything like it in my life, that's all. Those firefighters have a real brotherhood."

"That's probably part of the appeal that makes them sign on in the first place."

"I'm sure you're right."

"Well, I'm sure I would've cried my eyes out even if I didn't know the man who died."

"Absolutely. And the honor guard at the wake? They had a fireman in full dress positioned on either side of the casket, standing as still as those Beefeater guards at the Tower of London. The whole thing was some spectacle."

"Golly, I imagine it was. And how is Charlie doing?"

"Not so hot. He idolized his father."

"Poor thing. I'm sure we've got a book at the library on children and how they grieve. Would you like me to bring it home for you?"

"No, but thanks, though. I think I just want to be with them a little while, and then I'll figure out what to do."

"Keeping them both busy is probably the best thing."

"Probably. You're probably right."

We were quiet for perhaps maybe twenty-three seconds and then Deb leapt right into our other most favorite topic. The gorgeous single doctor next door. Steven Plofker. "I saw Mr. MD's porch light on until after midnight last night. Then he went out in his car. He was alone."

"So did I. I saw the whole thing, sitting on my porch in the dark, enjoying the ocean rolling in and out. I could almost smell his cologne wafting through the oleanders. Mother McCree. I went to bed and couldn't sleep for hours, tossing and turning."

"Ooo, honey! You've got a thing for him, Annie. You got it bad, girl!"

"Don't be ridiculous. I'm old enough to have been his babysitter. Besides, I'm a married woman." It was a game; didn't Deb know that?

"Only on a technicality. How many years have I known you?"

I could feel blood rising in my face. I had two hormones left. Benedict and Arnold. "Hush. I'm just curious, that's all. Just like you. What do you think he was up to? A midnight house call? Hmmm? A little late-night delight?"

"Who knows? He's a man, isn't he?"

I sucked my teeth. I loved Deb, but I didn't love that she was implying that Steve Plofker was just like any other man, on the late-night prowl for a skirt. Wait! I had implied the same thing. But somehow it sounded very different coming from me. I mounted my high horse.

"Deborah Ann Jenkins. He's a doctor, for heaven's sake! Maybe there was an emergency."

"He's a dermatologist, Annie Britt. You think there was a midnight outbreak of contagious acne? Do you think we've got a poison ivy pandemic on our hands?" Deb giggled and I shook my head. She was a hopeless giggler, but she made me laugh.

"Would you listen to us? We're turning into the Snoop Sisters."

"Well, when the day arrives that you find something better to do than monitor the comings and goings of the George Clooney of Sullivans Island . . . you'll let me know?"

"We're pathetic."

"No, we're not. We're curious. You said so yourself. Anyway, I think he's gay. I've always thought that."

"You just say that because he flirts with me and not you. Besides, he was married."

"Yeah, to some woman who didn't have the sense not to go out on a boat during a thunderstorm."

"Bless her heart. She was on her way back to the dock when she got struck by lightning and the boat capsized. Not her fault."

"Here's to barometers, right?" Deb took a long drink of her tea, draining her glass. "She should've checked the weather."

"Amen. Anyway, he's got to be lonely, don't you think?"

"If you say so. So far I haven't seen any women around his house, have you?"

"Nary a one. But he's probably still grieving."

"Maybe Jackie will like him. We should introduce them."

"He's too old for her."

"But not too young for you! Ha! Mercy! It's almost one! I have to go, or I'm gonna be late. I wish you'd come with me, Annie. It would do you so much good."

"Do me good. Humph. I walk the length of this island every day of my life. That's plenty of exercise for one woman. Besides, I'm too old to be jumping around."

"Oh, come on! It's fun!"

"Maybe another time," I said, wishing she'd get on with the business of leaving. I could feel my nerves starting to act up. Jackie and Charlie could arrive at any moment, and I wanted that moment for myself. If that sounds selfish, you haven't longed for your child like I have.

"Okay, then, Mrs. Robinson. I'll see y'all lay-tah! Tell that precious Charlie I'm baking him a blueberry pie."

"That's his favorite! He'll love it! How did you know?"

"Because I actually listen when you ramble on and on!"

"Oh, you! Stop!"

I blew her a kiss, and the screen door closed behind her.

I sighed hard and leaned back in my rocker. Then I rocked forward and stood, moving to the edge of the porch to have a good look at Steve's house. His very charming cottage was nestled in the dunes about ten yards from mine. Deb was jealous because she lived two houses on the other side of him and her house was positioned in a way that denied her a direct view of his deck and porch. And, although she wouldn't admit it, his bedroom. I had the *ideal* view. Yep. I did. I saw plenty, and yes, I looked on purpose. Seriously? I would've used my binoculars except I was afraid he'd see me. And if you're thinking I'm a peeping Thomasina, this was a very different affair from sneaking through the bushes in the dark and peering into random windows. It was specific and enjoyed from the safety of my own property.

Most of the island houses like ours were built of clapboards, perched high on stilts because of the occasional flooding tide from a hurricane. His, like mine, had louvered shutters that actually worked when we needed them closed to protect our windows from things like branches that took flight in high winds. His tin roof was red, and mine was silver. His house, which bore the misleading name of "The Dew Drop Inn," was painted bright white with red and black trim. It looked like a greeting card for a real estate company in all its optimism, but the fact was, he wasn't the kind of fellow you just dropped in on for a visit without calling. Or maybe I wasn't the kind of woman who just went willy-nilly knocking on a single man's door, especially one like him, whom I had no business visualizing in any other capacity than a nice neighbor. Good luck with that.

I often wondered what kind of casseroles he liked. Chicken divan? Probably not. No, he seemed like a man who liked heartier things to eat. Lasagna? I made a passable lasagna. I wondered then if I could ask him to show me how to use the rotisserie on my grill, the fancy one I bought Buster for his birthday that he never used. Buster preferred his Big Green Egg. But figuring out the machinations of my grill was a reasonable excuse to call on Steve.

I had been watching the Food Network too much, which led me to thinking about chickens, marinated in tons of herbs, lemon zest, garlic cloves, and olive oil, turned slowly on the spit, and basted until they were so tender that the meat nearly fell off the bones. I wanted to watch him eat with his hands. Lick his fingers. Moan from the sheer pleasure of a perfectly roasted bird. Okay, there you have it. I'll admit that I was a little caught up in my silly fantasies. Why shouldn't I fantasize about a good-looking man within pitching distance of my porch? I wasn't dead quite yet.

Of course, there were many moments when I wished Buster had not left, but there were just as many moments when I wished there was a nice man around to say something sweet to me. I could not recall the last time Buster had paid me a compliment. Steve would say that my hair was really pretty if we bumped into each other at the mailbox or that he really liked my dress. Was it new? He'd help me carry my bags of groceries or my dry cleaning into the house. He was a gentleman.

Buster, who was the living embodiment of an overgrown boy, never did any of that. It was always Buster and Jackie just standing back and letting me do all the work. But who was going to manage our lives if I didn't? So keeping things neat and orderly had made me single? I knew what people said, that I had nagged my husband out of my life. Listen, I was tired the day after that wedding ceremony, I mean, bone tired. I didn't have a single joint in my body that didn't ache like holy hell from standing in high heels for hours on end the day before, smiling and thanking people for coming, moving mountains of gift packages to help keep things tidy, to . . . you name it, I did it. Anyway, the morning after the wedding I was slicing ham and baking biscuits and setting the table while Buster sat there in his boxer shorts like a postbinge Hemingway watching golf on the television while his fishing mess was strewn all over the back porch as the minutes ticked by, closer and closer to the hour of the arrival of our guests. It seemed like the grass had grown five inches overnight from the rain, which meant there would be mosquitoes eating our out-of-town guests behind their knees, and I just sort of lost my mind.

In between wiping away the spots on my champagne flutes and lining them up in a perfect triangle on the dining room table, I asked him three times to please, for the love of God, to clean up his gear. He pretended not to hear me and kept on watching Tiger Woods or whoever was playing golf, the most boring sport in the universe. There isn't a grown woman alive on this planet who doesn't know what I'm talking about. I was so frustrated I was about to scream, and if I'd had the strength I would have. To my surprise, when a string of advertisements came on, he got up, called me a fussbudget, and walked out. That's what happened to my marriage, and there's not much more to tell. Fussbudget? Nice. Thank you very much. Go to Hell, please. And stay there.

Maybe walking Jackie down the aisle of Stella Maris Church freaked Buster out, you know, his job was finished and his game was over? I've heard that happens to men. Or maybe he just didn't want to be married anymore? Or—and the thought of this stung like a jellyfish—maybe he really didn't love me anymore and had not loved me for years? Or maybe he was worried about his own mortality. The obituaries were filled with men of his age who dropped dead from natural causes. Anyway, it was terrible to think that the father of my only child was all done loving me or loving our little family enough to try and sort out whatever the differences there were between us.

So kill me. Ever since he moved in next door, I've thought about Steve to cheer myself up. The welcoming look on his face made me feel alive and attractive and like I still had some worth in the goings-on between men and women. What's the matter with that?

Ah, mercy me. Steve's cottage may have been next to mine, but in the sober light of day the differences between us were as blatant as the differences between our homes.

My hundred-year-old cottage, "The Salty Dog"—an undignified name bestowed by Buster and one that I despised—was a creaking box with a porch, sort of a metaphor for me and my abdominal muscles that, when left unharnessed by the miracle of elastic, had settled into something of a relaxed, slightly protruding, cushiony state. Over the years my house had been painted probably every pastel you can name except mint, which is in sync with the pantheon of my changing hair colors. Presently the Salty Dog was pale yellow with accents in white and Charleston green, which for my money was black. But it creaked like my knees and it had seen better days, as I had. And no matter how much and how often I renovated it or myself, we were both still getting on in years. Fat old bald men can have pretty women as young as they pleased, but it seldom works that way in reverse. Maybe I *was* too old for romance or a new love. But I refused to completely believe such a depressing thought because of Deb. She says that on the day you stop believing in love you may as well lie down and die. I think she may be right.

To be frank, it wasn't like Steve was knocking down my door. And I wasn't knocking down his. We merely enjoyed coincidental meetings by the mailbox, the occasional glass of wine on my porch, and discussions of what was being done right or wrong by the town fathers. From his deck to my porch, we would call out to each other, remarking on sunsets, agreeing that they were the singularly most spectacular ones on the earth. He waved to me as I watched him jog the beach with his goofy spaniels. When we ran into each other at High Thyme and Poe's Tavern, we exchanged hellos like old friends. It was enough for me. If it was meant to evolve into anything more, it would. I still believed I could handle Dr. Love. That's why the good Lord invented dimmer switches. There comes a time when we're all better off in the dark.

3

"Ah, if I had only known you were here!" said Legrand, "but it's so long since I saw you; and how could I foresee that you would pay me a visit this very night of all others? . . . I lent him the bug. . . . Stay here to-night, and I will send Jup down for it at sunrise. It is the loveliest thing in creation!"

—Edgar Allan Poe, "The Gold-Bug"

Jackie

"Charlie? Don't—"
      SLAM!
"—slam the car door."

"Sorry, Mom. Wow, I feel like I'm still moving."

We got out of the car. I put my hands behind my waist, arched my back in a stretch toward the sky, and yawned.

"There's a name for that sensation, but I'm so tired I can't think of it. It's worse with boats. Wait! Sea legs. That's it." I unlocked and raised the back of my SUV and thought, Ugh. We could unload the car later. I wanted to say hello to my mother and have a look at the ocean.

"More like I-95 legs. Huh?" Charlie said.

"Yep. You're right. Come on. Let's go find Glam-ma."

I heard a thwack, and I looked up toward the house. There she stood on the top step of the Salty Dog, positioned in the bright sunlight looking not like a middle-aged woman on the high end of that scale but like someone mythical who could sprout gossamer wings any second. My mother was still a beautiful woman, as pretty as she had ever been in my entire life. How she maintained her looks was another mystery. Just the sight of her, the house, the smells, and music of the ocean just beyond the dunes, I swear, it made me literally weak in the knees. I was twelve years old again, all my troubles thrown out somewhere into the future where I couldn't see them yet or even know about them. I was home. And safe. At least for that moment.

What was it about this crazy little island? Why did it always feel so far away from the rest of the world? How did that work? Was there some invisible wall at the foot of the Ben Sawyer Bridge built from the magic bricks of a pied piper? But it was true enough that once we crossed that causeway and that funny little bridge, the whole world shifted and we sighed in a gush to be back on Sullivans Island. It happened every single time.

In the moments that followed, I was swept into my mother's arms, fully appraised with a smile of deep love and relief. We had arrived safely, and she didn't have to say any more novenas to protect us from that sleep-deprived maniac who would plow us down with his runaway eighteen-wheeler. A kiss was planted on top of my head. Then Charlie was eaten alive in one huge bite by my mother's blue-gray eyes, brimming with tears of happiness. This visit was so horribly emotional for me. So many things had happened in such a short period. In addition to losing Jimmy, I was waiting for my discharge papers because reenlisting had become impossible. What was I going to do with myself? What about money? I had Jimmy's benefits, but would that be enough in eight years to put Charlie through college? I had no idea.

I knew Charlie thought of this trip as a summer vacation because that was how I had framed it to him. But it was no vacation for me. I was exhausted. From life. From death. I wanted to collapse on the ground and weep, but I would do no such thing. I had made a vow to myself that once I arrived here there would be no more tears. Crying wouldn't bring Jimmy McMullen back to us. Crying wouldn't fix the problems of any of the women and children in Afghanistan. No, I could cry buckets of tears and they wouldn't change a single thing.

We stepped into the house, and I could smell my childhood—the good parts. My mother had been cooking.

"Okra soup?" I asked.

"Yep," she said. "And rice and corn bread. I made brownies for dessert. Y'all hungry?"

"I'm starving!" Charlie said.

"Boys are always starving," I said, happy that he had an appetite. "Go wash your hands, sweetie." I gave him a love swat on his backside, and he hurried from the room. "Can I do anything to help, Mom?"

"No, honey. Everything is ready. Come, let's sit."

"Do you have anything he can drink besides tea? Caffeine? Not good."

"Diet Coke?"

"I'll just give him iced water."

"Humph. You grew up drinking iced tea. So did I."

"Yeah, well, all the pediatricians say it's bad for kids."

"Whatever you say!"

Thank you, I thought. I washed my hands in the kitchen sink and dried them with a paper towel. I took my old seat at the table, the one where I'd sat for years, daydreaming about adventure while my mother complained about the most trivial details of her life and my father listened with the patience of a saint.

Daddy? How do you stand it? She's never happy.

Don't criticize your mother, Jackie. Remember the Fourth Commandment? Besides, she cooks like an angel.

Charlie returned, we said grace, and in minutes we were eating like starving animals. It was delicious. Call me a pain in the neck to mention this, but the corn bread had been baked in a pan that shaped the bread into ears of corn. For some reason it irritated me. Why in the world did she waste money on silly baking pans like that? Maybe I was wrung out from the long drive, but all I could think about was Afghani women trying to prepare a meal in an old dented pot on a piece of sheet metal over an open fire. It probably wasn't fair to draw the comparison, but I couldn't help it. Maybe my hard drive was overloaded.

"Can I have more?" Charlie asked.

"You can have as much as you'd like!" she said and got up to refill his bowl.

"Sit, Mom. He can help himself, right, Son?"

"Yes, ma'am."

"So how was your trip?" she asked. "Y'all must be ready to fall over!"

"Pretty much. It was long, but you know it's a straight shot down 95, so it's more of an endurance contest than anything else. And I've got a GPS, so I couldn't get lost if I wanted to," I said, hoping I sounded congenial and not like I felt.

"What's a GPS?" she asked.

"Global positioning system," Charlie said. "All you do is punch in the address where you want to go and it tells you how to get there. Would you pass the corn bread, please?"

"Just like that?" Mom remarked, smiling at Charlie's manners and passing the basket to him.

"Yep."

"Yes, ma'am," I said, correcting him.

"Yes, ma'am," he said. "Just like that. I can show you if you want to see."

"Absolutely!"

"Charlie's my copilot," I explained.

"My word," Mom said. "You're growing up so fast!"

"You can even switch it to a man's voice if you want to," Charlie said and stuffed his third ear of corn bread into his mouth.

"You mean to tell me that this global thing talks to you?" She looked at me for verification.

"Well, it wouldn't be safe to use it if it didn't. I mean, the earlier versions would just make a *bing* sound when it was time to turn right or left. But basically reading the screen is just as dangerous as texting while driving."

"Texting?" she asked.

Charlie and I looked at each other and laughed. "Oh, Glam-ma! We've got to bring you into the twenty-first century!"

It did me so much good to hear Charlie laugh again. Maybe coming here wasn't such a bad idea after all.

"I guess I don't get off this island often enough," she said, looking wistful.

"I'm not sure all this technology is so wonderful." I reached over and patted the back of her hand. "Lunch was wonderful, Mom. It was just what we needed."

"Well, good. I'm glad y'all enjoyed it. Now, who wants a brownie?"

"I guess I could eat a brownie," Charlie said with so much seriousness that we all laughed again.

"And then you'll help me unload the car?" I said.

"Better make that two brownies," he said. "I need to build up my strength."

Mom washed dishes while Charlie and I pushed and pulled our suitcases up the back steps and into the house.

"Same rooms as last year!" she called out to us as we passed by her.

"Okay!" we called back.

I dropped my things right inside my door and went to Charlie's room to help him get unpacked. Naturally, Mom had accessorized our rooms to a fare-thee-well,

Charlie's especially. It was like a visit from Santa on a smaller scale. She had promised not to spoil him. Didn't she remember that?

"Look at this comforter," he said in a whisper. "Does she think I'm still, like, five or something?"

"She means well, Son," I said. "You know she went to a great deal of trouble."

"Yeah, I know. Look at this whole stack of books and all this other stuff. And this bathing suit? Wow. Is this how guys dress down here?"

"I guess."

He opened the yo-yo and let it unroll. "What's this thing supposed to do?"

"I'll show you later."

"I should've brought my skateboard. I forget how flat the island is."

I perked up at that. Maybe he was coming around a little if he wanted his skateboard.

"Well, I could call Aunt Maureen and ask her to send it. But it would probably cost the same to put it in a box and ship it as it would to buy a new one. I don't know. We'll see."

"I could do the research on my laptop."

I took that as a good sign too, and a tiny smile crept across my face as I put a stack of T-shirts into a drawer.

"Okay. Get the facts and then we'll make a decision." Jimmy always said any problem you could solve with money wasn't really a problem. That was true, but only if you had endless resources.

"Okay," he answered.

I turned to see him lying on the bed in the kennel of idiotic, grinning puppies, flipping through the pages of a comic book.

"Wait," I said, "let's see if I've got this right."

"What?"

"Please. Don't say 'What?,' say 'Yes, ma'am?' "

"Yes, ma'am? What?"

"You're going to lie there reading a comic book about pirates while I do all the unpacking?"

"Guess not, huh?"

"You got it. Come on, young man. Gimme a hand here."

We finished up in short order, creating some rhyme and reason to where we put his clothes and rechargers and gadgets. I went to my room to unpack my things and called back to him over my shoulder, "Don't forget to thank your grandmother for all the loot."

"No worries," he called back.

I pulled up the Venetian blinds and let the full force of the breeze rush in. My old room, like my mother's room, faced the ocean. I stood there for a moment to take in the view. It was simply astounding to have the entire Atlantic Ocean right in front of my face not five hundred yards away. It was so vast. The only thing that separated us from the water was a front lawn, choking under the proliferation of dollar weeds, and a string of sand dunes. All across the white mounds of sand, honey-colored tall grasses grew in clumps, sprouting here and there. They moved like hula skirts swaying in the air. Beyond that, seagulls squawked their crazy birdsong, swooping down across the rippling water that glistened in the sun like broken glass. And in the far distance, a container ship riding low in the water under the weight of its goods slowly made its way across the horizon toward Charleston harbor. Enormous clouds that looked like thick cotton candy rolled by. It was a magnificent scene, and it reinforced the reasons why my mother had always lived here. Anyone would be hard pressed to find a place more beautiful. Or peaceful. This could be very good for me and for my boy. Yes. Very good indeed.

I lifted my heavy suitcase and was about to swing it around and throw it up on the bed when I saw the quilt. I staggered a little, not quite believing my eyes. It was on *my* bed. That old quilt was one of my mother's greatest treasures, besides some dishes and a couple pieces of Waterford crystal. When I was a kid if I touched it without permission I got screamed at so loudly that I was sure the whole island heard. And now it was on *my* bed? What did that mean? And her antique lace pillow-cases were on the bed too. Was she giving them to me? Or was she just trying to make me feel better? Then I saw the books and the water bottle and tote bag with the visor and all the other things she'd put in the room for me. I stopped and thought about her generosity. I wouldn't be caught dead in a pink visor and I wasn't particularly a fan of her choice of reading material, but she couldn't have known that. She was just trying to protect my eyes from the glare of the blasting sun and give me something to occupy my time. It was nice of her, as were all the things she had bought for Charlie. But it was also a little overwhelming. I didn't want to be in her debt. I didn't want to be in anyone's debt. And a lifetime of experience in dealing with her had taught me how she operated.

If I seemed gloomy, she would say, "Well, what else on this blessed earth can I do to make you happy? What do you expect from me?" And then I would seem like the Ungrateful Child and probably say, "Well, what do you want from me?" Then she would tell me that I had to snap out of it for Charlie's sake and I would say I was doing my best but I missed my husband. Then she would stare at me wondering why I had married a fireman in the first place, and I would be infuriated. You see, there's a big part of my mother's lofty opinion of her social position that I think she stole from Lady Astor. She had no reason to think she was some high-falutin socialite, but she did. And I had no apologies to make about living a middle-class life without pretension. We were polar opposites when it came to those things, and that's all there was to that.

I turned around to see Charlie standing in my doorway. "What's up, baby?"

"My stomach hurts," he said.

"Ate too much?" I asked.

"Yeah. I hate okra."

"I used to, but now I can eat anything. You should see some of the stuff I had to eat in Tikrit. It looked like dog food. Or maybe it *was* dog."

Charlie gagged. "Gross. Maybe I'll just go lie down for a little while."

"Good idea. Try and get a nap."

"Yeah, maybe. Okay."

I thought, Great, now my son is an emotional eater. He stuffed himself at lunch just to please my mother. She was an awfully good cook; I mean, she was a much better cook than I'd ever be.

I put the quilt on the chair and began to unpack. I didn't need to be a great cook. It seemed to me that people who cooked like mad just made work for themselves.

I looked at the sorry clothes I had thrown into my suitcase. Mostly I had brought shorts and T-shirts, bathing suits, and a couple of things I could wear to church or out to dinner if we felt like going somewhere else to eat. I figured that if we didn't have something we really needed we could buy it. It wasn't like Sullivans Island was deep in the jungle or something. Downtown Charleston was only minutes away, and Mount Pleasant was loaded with stores.

I could hear Charlie groaning from his room, so I stuck my head in his door. "You feeling a little green around the gills?" I asked. "Want me to see if Glam-ma has something to settle your stomach?"

He sat straight up, and his face was filled with panic. "No! Don't say anything!"

"Why not?"

He whispered to me, "Because I don't want her to think her soup made me sick."

"Oh, honey. I don't think it was the soup. I think it might have been the quantity."

"Whatever! Just don't say anything, okay? I'm fine!"

"Okay. I won't say anything. Why don't you relax for a bit, and then we can take a walk on the beach? How's that? Say, half hour?"

"Sure," he said. "Sounds like a plan."

The half hour came and went, and when I went back to his room he was fast asleep. Poor thing. He was worried about my mother's feelings. He would do without something to ease his distress rather than risk bruising her ego. Even at ten years old he already knew not to upset her nerves. It just wasn't worth it. I'd pick up something for him at the drugstore when I went out. It wasn't a bad idea to have our own first-aid kit anyway. Then if I needed a Band-Aid I'd know where to find it without having to explain every nick and splinter.

I took off my jeans and pulled on a pair of shorts. I didn't want to go to the beach without Charlie, but I wanted to feel the sun on my legs. I picked up a magazine from the stack in my room and wandered out to the front porch. Mom was sitting there deeply engrossed in one of the many romance novels she loved. I knew it had to be a hot one because it had a calico print cover over it, like something she might have picked up at a craft fair to disguise the erotic promise of the cover's art.

"Whatcha reading? Are things bulging and bursting?"

I startled her.

"What? What did you—? Bulging?" She took her reading glasses off and narrowed her eyes at me. "You listen to me, young lady. You know I only read these books for the history!"

"Oh, I see." I giggled, and so did she. "And where is this historic saga placed?"

"Tenth-century Scotland! The ladies of the Castle MacDougall are in hiding because the lord of the manor has gone insane from a terrible fever. He's running amok with a hammer, threatening to bludgeon anyone whose shadow crosses his. Pretty exciting stuff. Come sit with me."

"Does he have black flashing eyes?" I sat in the rocker next to hers and flipped the pages of my magazine. Who cared about all those stupid movie stars anyway? They were all twenty years old with fake boobs and fake long hair and too many real tattoos. You could swap one for another and never know the difference. "And a thick mane of hair to match?"

"Of course! And his shirt has come free of his kilt and—"

"What's he wearing under that kilt anyway?"

"You know I cover my eyes when I get to that part."

"Of course you do. I know that. I would too."

Mom laughed, and I thought at that moment she was the most benign creature in the world.

"I'm so happy you're here," she said.

"Me too."

"Where's Charlie?"

"Snoozing. He's completely fried."

"I imagine so. That's a long trip for a kid. And with everything else . . ."

"Yeah, I'm thinking just let him find his schedule, let his body get the rest he needs for his brain and his bones. Have you heard from Dad?"

She bristled. "Certainly not!"

"No, I mean, he told Charlie he'd come down and see him, show him how to make ice cream."

"In what? That old churn under the house?"

"Yep, that's the one. You know where it is?"

"Of course I do! Glory be! That nasty old thing is probably filled with bugs and snakes!"

"You think I'm afraid of bugs and snakes?"

"No, dear." She shot me an anti–GI Jane look of dubious support and continued. "But better to go over to Haddrell's and buy a new one. You don't have to churn anymore. Now you just flip a switch. Electric. On my momma's soul, there's a new gizmo every five minutes. But I have such sweet memories of turning that old crank with my momma . . . and with you when you were a little girl."

"I think I like the old-fashioned way better," I said, "maybe because it's a sweet memory for me too."

With those simple but heartfelt words, we found our first moment of solidarity. I suddenly realized that I wanted Charlie to have the memory of churning ice cream the old-fashioned way. Solidarity was sure to come and go over the coming weeks, but we were united in one purpose. Charlie.

Don't ask me what else we talked about, because I think we talked about everything in the world that afternoon, everything that wasn't too heavy, that is. We took turns checking on Charlie, who was sleeping soundly, which pleased both of us to no end. We probably drank a gallon of tea while the sun moved from east to west and finally began to set. She told me about Deb and her Zumba classes and she told me about the hot doc next door, saying I should meet him in case I wanted to fill some time at the VA hospital or at the medical university downtown. She didn't want me to get bored, and she was more than happy to see about Charlie.

On an odd note, she became animated but very circumspect when she talked about this Steve Plofker fellow. Her voice went up an octave, which led me to consider that perhaps she had a crush on him. The thought of that sort of rocked my brain, but I tried very hard to maintain a poker face because it was one of the rare occasions when I felt like she was talking to me as a girlfriend. Besides, the truth would reveal itself in its own good time. I wondered if Daddy suspected any competition. Probably not. I wondered if he would care. Of course he would. His ego would get up on its hind legs and start bellowing like Tarzan. Funny. I'd never thought about my mother's needs in the romance arena. Probably because I have never had a single thought about my mother *being* in the romance arena.

We probably would have spent the whole night on the porch, just swapping old memories and stories and reliving easier days. I wasn't even hungry because lunch was on the late side and I had eaten a lot more than I usually did. I guess I was sitting there in that rocker just time traveling back to my childhood. Maybe I was too exhausted to get up. Maybe I thought Charlie would just sleep through the night. I never expected what happened next.

Mom got up to go to the kitchen to pour us a glass of wine and to get a box of Cheez-Its, which are my personal devil to resist and she knew it.

"Do you want me to flip on the porch light?"

"No, I think I like it like this. Check on my boy, will you, please?"

"Of course!" she said and closed the screen door gingerly.

Slamming screen doors, car doors, cabinet doors—doors slamming was a shared pet peeve. Anyway, a few minutes later Mom reappeared with Charlie at her side. Even in the dim light I could see that he had been crying.

"Sweetheart! Come here! What's wrong?" I held out my arms to him, and he climbed up on my lap, burying his face in my shoulder. "Tell me, baby. What happened? Did you have a bad dream?"

"No . . . I was just . . . listening to him . . ." Charlie choked up and began to cry in earnest. I could feel him shudder, and with each sob my heart broke a little more.

"Oh, my poor sweet boy! Tell me, honey. Tell me who you were listening to."

"He was listening to his voice mail," my mother said, holding up his cell phone. "There's a long message on here from Jimmy."

"It was the last time he called me," Charlie said. "I just don't want to erase it."

"You don't have to, sweetie. You don't ever have to."

It was then that I realized that no first-aid kit in the world could fix this. But at least I didn't have to worry about Charlie working Mom's nerves; he already owned her heart.

4

Nonsense! no!—the bug. It is of a brilliant gold color—about the size of a large hickory-nut—with two jet black spots near one extremity of the back, and another, somewhat longer, at the other. The antennœ are—

—Edgar Allan Poe, "The Gold-Bug"

Annie

Well, I don't have to say this, but I'm going to say it anyway. When I found Charlie listening to his father's voice mail, it just about broke my heart into a million and one pieces. After I pulled myself back together and I could really see just how off kilter Jackie was, I decided I simply had to step in and take over. I was going to keep the boy's mind busy. And I was going to find plenty for Jackie to do too. My mother always said, "Idle hands are the Devil's workshop." The same thing applied to brains. Mercy! Was that the truth or what?

So at seven thirty the next morning, while the house still slept, I called Deb. "You up?"

"Of course I'm up! Already worked the word jumble and read Dear Abby. What's going on?"

"Can't walk with you this morning. I'm throwing you over for a younger man."

She whispered, "Dr. MD?"

I sighed. "Unfortunately, no. Younger. Charlie."

"Oh! Well, I guess I'll live. How'd the first day go?"

"A little rough. But they'll be all right in time. They just need time."

"What can I do?"

"Nothing. But thanks. I'll call you later."

I went to the kitchen, put on a pot of coffee, and started making a batter for pancakes. I heated some syrup and blueberries in a small pot with some butter and put some bacon in a pan to fry. I knew the smells of maple and bacon would rouse them and then we could all launch our day. I was going to ask Jackie to wipe down all the windows that faced the ocean because they were covered in salt spray and I was taking Charlie out to discover what treasures had floated to shore overnight.

Within fifteen minutes they both wandered into the kitchen, rubbing their eyes.

"What smells so good, Glam?"

"Come give me a smooch and I'll fix you a plate!" I said. Charlie obediently gave me an antiseptic peck on the cheek and plopped into a chair. "Be a good boy and pour some OJ for all of us, will you, hon?" I gave a nod to the juice glasses on the counter.

"Sure," he said. He got up again, opened the door of the refrigerator, took out the carton, and began shaking it.

"Shake that over the sink, Son," Jackie said, filling a mug with steaming coffee. "Morning, Mom. We got any half-and-half?"

"Here it is," Charlie said, putting the carton on the table.

"Hi, sweetheart." I blew her an air kiss and said, "Oh wait, Charlie! We don't put the cartons on the table."

"We don't?" he said.

"No, baby. We pour the juice right into the juice glasses and the half-and-half goes in my special cow." I took my white ceramic cow from the cupboard and filled it through the hole in its back. "Now watch this." I began to pour the cream in a trickle into Jackie's mug. "Moooooooooooo!" I said in a low-pitched bovine voice, and Charlie looked at me with eyes the size of saucers like I was out of my blooming mind.

"Glam likes a side of theater with her breakfast," Jackie said, rolling her eyes.

"Oh, come on," I said, "let's lighten up around here! It's a beautiful day!"

We were all finally seated, and I said, "Should we put a blessing on this?"

Charlie said, "Sure!"

"Do you want to say grace, sweetheart?" Jackie said.

"Okay. Um, bless this food, Lord, and us, and thanks . . . uh, amen."

"Amen," I said and cut into my pancakes with the side of my fork. "That blessing of yours sounds a little rusty, sweetheart."

"Yeah, well, back home, Aunt Maureen always says the blessing, and boy, does she go on and on and on . . ." Charlie made a face to reflect the extreme suffering he endured for the sake of a sanctified meal.

"And let's see. You're sitting there and the food's getting colder by the minute and your stomach is growling like you haven't eaten anything in months?"

"Exactly!"

"Well," Jackie said, "Aunt Maureen is very devout and she means well. The pancakes are so good, Mom."

"Thanks, hon. Well, Charlie, I think there's real merit in thanking the good Lord for a nice meal, but I agree with you, it's the intention that matters, not the length of the prayer. How *is* Aunt Maureen?"

"She's great," Jackie said. "The whole world could use a dose of Aunt Maureen's heart. I mean, she's picking up our mail while we're gone and sorting it in case there's anything important. And she's watering the plants so they don't die. I mean, she just can't do enough to help us."

"Isn't that grand?" I said, hoping I sounded genuine. Yes, I was a little jealous of their obvious affection for her. I couldn't help it. "I wish she'd come and visit me some day."

"She should get out of Brooklyn once in a while," Charlie said. "I don't think she ever goes anywhere on vacation except to Chicago to see her relatives who are so old and smelly they can't even get out of bed."

"Charlie!" Jackie said. "That's not nice. Maureen has to go see about them once in a while. She's the youngest member of her family by at least ten years."

"How *is* the rest of Jimmy's family? I haven't heard about them in ages."

"Nursing homes. All of them. Except for Uncle Thomas and Aunt Ellen. Uncle Thomas is the one who was a priest? He lives in the archdiocese's retirement home. And Aunt Ellen, well, she's just not the same as she was."

"What happened to her?" I asked.

"She's got signs of Alzheimer's," Jackie said. "She needs to be in assisted living, but she won't go. She wants to stay in her own home. She goes nuts if anyone tries to talk to her about it."

"What's Alzheimer's?" Charlie asked.

"It's the meanest disease in the whole world," I said. "Would you like some more, Charlie?"

"Uh, no thanks. But it was delicious!"

"Alzheimer's is a terrible illness that makes you lose your memories a little bit at a time until you don't know who anyone is," Jackie said.

"Oh," Charlie said and drained his juice. "Gross."

"Charlie? Sweetie? Why don't you put your dishes in the sink and let's you and me go for a walk on the beach?"

"I don't feel like walking the beach," Jackie said.

"You never did," I said with a forgiving smile. "I was just thinking that it might be nice to spend some time with my grandson. That's all."

"That's actually a great idea," Jackie said. "I'll clean up the kitchen."

"Thanks! Let's get out of here, Charlie." We started out of the room and I stopped. "Jackie?"

"Hmmm?"

"Listen, remember how we always wiped down the front windows?"

"I'm all over it, Mom. Y'all go have fun!"

In minutes, we were on the other side of the dunes. I slipped off my sandals and left them at the bottom of our steps. Charlie was barefooted. We were heading toward the lighthouse. Within twenty yards of our walkover, Charlie spotted a horseshoe crab.

"Wow! Look at the size of this! It's a monster."

Without any trepidation, he kicked it over with his big toe. It was predictably empty.

"Probably a female," I said.

Charlie looked at me with the most curious expression and then a devilish grin. I knew what he was thinking. Where, exactly *where*, were the genitals?

"How do you know?"

"Because, my young scholar, this shell is easily twenty inches long and males don't get this large."

"But it's got this long thing . . . doesn't that make it a boy?"

"No, that long *thing* you refer to is a tail spine, not a tallywacker."

"*Tallywacker?*"

"Yes. And you know exactly what I'm talking about too! But it's probably best not to tell your momma I said that word, okay?"

"Sure. Then what's it for? Defense?"

"Well, defense against its own habitat, I suppose. You see, sometimes a wave can flip them over on their backs. They stick that tail of theirs in the mud and flip themselves back over on their stomachs. Pretty cool, huh?"

"Yeah. Way cool. Can I keep it?"

"Of course! Why don't you run it back up to the house now before someone else comes along and takes it." Charlie was gone in a shot. "And makes a lamp out of it." I was talking to myself and lost in the moment of watching my grandson filled with the joy of discovery. Oh, he had seen horseshoe crabs on this beach before, but this was the first time he had touched one without thinking twice. He was growing up. Before I could think about the tide or the dogs on the beach Charlie was running back. What energy little boys have! I thought.

"I put it on the deck to catch the sun!" he called out.

"Good, because if it's not completely dried out—"

"I know, I know. It draws ants. Meanwhile, I got the biggest crab shell in the world!"

We picked up our walk, moving to the water's edge so the incoming tide would wash over our feet.

"The horseshoe crab isn't really a crab, you know."

"It isn't? Well, then, what the heck is it?"

"It's an arthropod. Related to the scorpion and spiders in general. Hasn't changed a thing about itself in two hundred million years!"

"For real?"

"Yep. People call them living fossils."

"Wow." Charlie was quiet for a few moments before he spoke again. "So what else do you know?"

"What else do you *want* to know?"

A flock of seagulls was wandering around the shore, and they began to scatter and fly away as we approached them. Charlie, as any little boy would, ran toward them waving his arms and growling like a crazy lion. When the remaining few took off in a panic, he laughed.

"Dumb birds. A lot of stuff. Like what's the story on that lighthouse?"

"The lighthouse?"

"Yeah. It's really weird-looking. Aren't they supposed to be round?"

"Well, they usually are, but a triangle is a stronger shape. See the way the edge faces the ocean? This one has survived hurricane winds over 125 miles per hour. But I agree with you, it is weird-looking."

"Can we go in it? I mean, not right now. But sometime?"

"Oh, I think I could get us an invitation for a tour."

"Sweet. Totally sweet."

"Ah, Charlie, there are so many wonders here, just waiting for you to find them."

"Like what?"

"Well, Charleston's very historic. I mean, even this island has its share of important history that happened right on this very sand."

"History is a snore. Boooor-ing!"

"Really? Really? Do you think pirates are a snore?"

"Oh, please, Glam. All that baloney is just made-up junk."

"Pretty cynical for ten years old, aren't we?" He shrugged his little shoulders, and my heart melted. "How about Blackbeard? He was here all the time. Did you know that?"

"Come on."

"No, *you* come on! Grandmother never lies. I'm going to give you a book to read that will tell you all about Blackbeard and Stede Bonnet and all those characters. Their very real lives of danger and mayhem were a huge influence on Edgar Allan Poe, you know."

"Who's Edgar Allan Poe?"

I stopped dead in my tracks, grabbed my blouse over my heart, and gasped long and loud for effect. "What? You don't know . . . he was *here*! Stationed at Fort Moultrie before the war!"

"Which war?"

"The only one that mattered, dear heart. Poe is the father of the detective novel and a pioneer of science fiction . . . oh, Mother McCree! I can see I have my work cut out for me!"

By now Charlie had his arms folded across his chest and was staring at me through his bangs. I caught a glimpse of the man he would become, strong-willed and determined, but the stubborn little devil was caught in my snare. I had him right where I wanted him. So rather than lecture him, I began to walk again, making him beg me to tell him stories. He was amazed to learn that Robert Louis Stevenson's *Treasure Island* was actually Poe's "The Gold-Bug," just re-imagined.

"I read *Treasure Island* last year in a comic book! But I never even saw a copy of the bug book."

" 'The Gold-Bug.' I'll give you my copy if you'd like," I said. "There's even a Goldbug Island right over the Ben Sawyer Bridge!"

"Really?"

"Yes. Most people think 'The Gold-Bug' takes place on this very island because it is also believed that Blackbeard and a lot of other pirates used to bury their loot here. And they made maps to come back and find it. Pity the poor fellows who had to dig the holes to bury the booty."

"Why? And Glam, booty isn't a nice word either, you know."

"What?" I could feel my face turn red. " 'Booty' means 'treasure.' Anyway, because the captain would throw them in the hole with *the treasure!*"

"You mean, they were buried alive?"

"I imagine they shot them first. But being buried alive was a recurring theme in a lot of Poe's work too."

"That is some seriously creepy stuff, Glam."

"Well, it could never happen today, but back in Poe's day they didn't have funeral homes who prepared bodies for burial. So the family would see about all that. And sometimes people in deep comas were accidentally buried alive. You should read *The Fall of the House of Usher*. I'm telling you, Poe was like Stephen King!"

"Stephen King? The guy who wrote that movie *Carrie*? It's Mom's total favorite."

"Really? Well, Stephen King wrote the book on which the movie was based. If there is one, you should always read the book before you see the film."

"Why?"

"Why? Oh, my dear . . . because a book lets your imagination soar and a movie makes all the decisions for you. A book is almost always, but not always, a far richer experience than a book turned into a movie. But I think it's probably a real challenge to condense a whole book into an hour and a half or two hours on film."

"Wow. Mom says books are better too, but now I know why."

I smiled. If I had done anything right with Jackie, I had given her a love of reading. We walked and walked, talking about pirates and treasure maps and all kinds of things until we were finally walked and talked out.

"Let's go home," I said. "It's long past lunchtime."

"It is?"

"Charlie? Look at the position of the sun."

I gave him a quick lesson on the sun and shadows, and he was simply amazed. What did they teach these kids in school nowadays? How to write poetry in Mandarin? Phooey on that.

"And," I added, "you're going to notice that when the thermometer gets to around one hundred degrees, around four in the afternoon, the skies will get very dark and then we'll have a great thunder boomer for about half an hour. When it's over, the skies turn blue and the sun comes back out."

"Wow, this is like being in a rain forest or something, isn't it?"

"Some people consider us to be semitropical."

"Semitropical."

"Yep. Semitropical."

Later, at home over a fast lunch of tomato sandwiches and cups of leftover soup, Charlie regaled Jackie with all the things we talked about on our walk.

"She knows all this *stuff*! I mean, *amazing* stuff! Can I have some ketchup, please?"

"She is the cat's mother," I said with perfect timing, but neither one of them reacted. I was so sleepy then, I would have given a front tooth to just close my eyes for an hour. Charlie had flat worn me out, and it was barely three o'clock.

"You're telling me?" Jackie said and handed him the bottle of ketchup, which he used to thoroughly douse his sandwich. "She's my mother, you know."

"I know! But how come you never told me any of these stories?"

"I don't know . . . I guess because you never asked?"

"Well, children, if you'll clean up, the cat's mother is going to take her book out to the porch and read for a while."

Finally they stopped talking and looked at each other.

"The rule is," Jackie said, "you're not supposed to refer to Glam as *she*, especially when *she*'s right in the room. It's considered disrespectful."

"Oh," Charlie said. "Sorry. I didn't know."

"It's okay, precious," I said. "Have a brownie."

I was lost in tenth-century Scotland's social machinations and what the lassies and laddies did in the dark when Jackie and Charlie joined me. I quickly closed my book, not that there was anything to be ashamed of in the pages, just a few bees and a couple of birds.

"So what are you up for this afternoon?" Jackie asked. "I was thinking I might take Charlie to the aquarium. You want to go?"

"Oh, no thanks. All those sharks give me nightmares."

"Sharks?"

"Charlie, you *know* they have sharks there. How many times have you been to the aquarium?"

"Not since I was a baby."

"Really?"

"Yep. I still have that stuffed turtle in my room at home, though. It's a baby toy covered in crusty baby slobber. Smells like sour milk."

"What?" I said with a grimace. "Nasty!"

"Your nose is growing, boy," Jackie said. "I've washed that thing a hundred times. At least."

"Well, that was from the last time I went. Hey! Look at the dogs!" Charlie said, squealing in excitement.

Stella and Stanley, Steve Plofker's chocolate-colored Boykin spaniels, ran across our dunes and right up to the edge of our deck. They were sniffing around his horseshoe crab shell. Charlie ran down the steps to ward them off, and moments later Dr. Love appeared to retrieve his pets. From where we stood up on the porch we could hear him call out to Charlie.

"They won't bite," Steve said. "Go ahead, you can pet them. Who are you?"

"I'm not allowed to talk to strangers," Charlie said, acting nervous. He looked up to the porch. "Glam? Mom?"

"It's okay, Charlie. Well, hello, Dr. Plofker! Got the day off?" I called out. "Come say hello to my daughter, and that's my grandson, Charlie."

He was all sweaty, and it was obvious he'd been running, getting his daily exercise. He was wearing shorts. Nice legs.

"Hi, Charlie. Watch my dogs for a minute?"

Charlie was already on his knees on the ground, scratching them behind the ears. "You bet!"

"Great! Thanks!"

Steve ran up the steps, opened the screen door, and said, "It's Sunday. That's why I'm not working."

"Merciful Mother of God! In all this excitement, I forgot to go to Mass!"

"It's okay, Mom. We all forgot."

"Well, we'll just have to go twice next Sunday," I said. "Would you like a glass of iced tea?"

"Sure . . . actually, just water would be great. Thanks."

"San Pellegrino, Evian, or island *eau naturel*?" I said, thinking there was no end to my cleverness and that suddenly I had as much energy as a young woman. "Say hello to Jackie. Jackie, say hello to Steve."

"Anything's fine, Annie. It's nice to meet you, Jackie. I've heard a lot about you and Charlie, and well, I'm so sorry for your loss. I'd shake your hand, but I'm pretty sweaty."

Yeah, you're sweaty, I thought, and you smell like something irresistible out of tenth-century Scotland.

I left them on the porch, and, as fast as it was humanly possible, I poured some Evian over ice in a glass and rushed back. Steve was leaning against the banisters, and they were talking about Afghanistan. It was probably prudent for him to be made aware that my daughter was handy with a gun and that she knew her way around an operating room too. Might as well get all that unfeminine but necessary weapons expertise business out in the open, right? I handed him the glass, leaned in discreetly, and took a good whiff. Wow.

"Thanks," he said.

"Oh, honey, it's nothing. Why don't you stay and enjoy the rest of the afternoon and then have some supper with us?"

Steve looked at Jackie as if he was waiting for her to second the motion, but she shifted her attention to Charlie and Steve's dogs.

"Oh, I probably shouldn't. I don't want to impose, I mean . . ."

"Cute dogs," Jackie said. "What time are we going to sit down, Mom?"

"Thanks," he said.

Steve cracked a smile. Apparently Jackie liked him well enough to let him come to the table with us. She'd had him worried there for a moment. How did she do that?

"Oh, I don't know . . . around six thirty? Or as soon as the sun passes over the yardarm? How does that sound?"

"Great! That gives me time to make myself presentable. I'll see you ladies later."

"He's a hottie," I said, watching him as he crossed our yard. "Isn't that what they say these days?"

"I wouldn't have the first clue what they say these days," Jackie said.

"Well, then what does 'booty' mean these days in the parlance of the young people?"

Jackie laughed then, and I loved the sound of it. "Um, it's what you shake on the dance floor, Mom. Why are you asking me that?"

"Because I used it to describe pirate's loot, and Charlie nearly choked. He told me I was using a bad word. Imagine a ten-year-old correcting his grandmother? I just corrected him right back."

"I'm sure you did, Mom."

"Well, excuse me!"

Jackie laughed again. "It's okay, Mom. You can correct him all you want. But you talk like you're a hundred-year-old woman!"

"Humph," I said, "I think I still have a whole lot of living left to do, if it's okay with you and the rest of the world!"

To my surprise, Jackie gave me a hug. "I think . . . if I lost you? I don't know what I would do. You know that, don't you?" she said and took a big sniff as though she was going to turn on the waterworks any second.

"Well, now, come on, let's not get all sentimental . . . I'm not going anywhere for a long time! Besides, we have a lot to do! We have a gentleman coming for supper!"

5

"Well!" I said, after contemplating it for some minutes, "this is a strange scarabœus, I must confess: new to me: never saw anything like it before—unless it was a skull, or a death's-head—which it more nearly resembles than anything else that has come under my observation."

—Edgar Allan Poe, "The Gold-Bug"

Jackie

A gentleman coming for dinner. Great. Actually, on second thought, it might be nice to have a diversion at the dinner table, especially for Charlie's sake, although Charlie seemed to be pretty fascinated by my mother's tutorial about all things pertaining to the Lowcountry. I should tell you that in that short span of time since Steve had left to take a shower, she seemed to have had a total nervous breakdown. You would think Prince Harry was dropping by tonight for a barbecue with the way she began flitting around. She dashed out to the grocery store and came home with ten bags brimming with food. In between paring potatoes, trimming asparagus, and baking bread, she put new candles everywhere and a candy bowl on the buffet, and she even put a scented votive candle and fresh flowers with sprigs of lavender in the bathroom. It wasn't a bad thing to be excited about having company, but her sweet spot for the boy next door made me a little uneasy. Someone probably needed to tell Daddy, but I did not want to be that someone. It was usually best to stay out of other people's business, and she probably didn't even realize how transparent she was.

I knew she was standing at the door to my room because she arrived in a cloud of perfume, and when I turned to look at her, there were those infamous red lips. Yikes, I thought, don't be so obvious, girlfriend. But my mother's heart had always been worn on her sleeve.

"Hi!" I said. "Do you need a hand with dinner?"

"What? Are you going to wear that T-shirt? I mean, it's fine, but I was thinking you might want to wear something pretty?"

I narrowed my eyes into the smallest slits possible and scowled at her.

"Oh, dear! I'm sorry, Jackie. I've offended you. I just . . . oh, listen to me, will you? Going on and on. It's just my nerves acting up. Wear whatever you like. Of course. Wear whatever you like."

"Thanks." I was still annoyed. "So, um, is there anything I can do to help?"

"Oh, would you be a dear and set up the bar on the porch? I was thinking it would be nice to sit outside until it gets dark. Just gin and vodka and tonic and the vermouth, of course, and a shaker, and oh, some lemon peels and olives? Oh, and lime wedges. And maybe a little bowl of nuts? Obviously, we'll need an ice bucket . . ."

"Mom? He's coming at six thirty and it doesn't get dark until nine. We'll get completely hammered if we sit around drinking for that long."

"Oh! My goodness! You're right! Ha! I didn't think *that* one through very well, did I? Well, anyway, we need little napkins too. I've got some adorable ones in the buffet drawer that I bought . . ."

My mother was a connoisseur of paper cocktail napkins that proclaimed popular wisdom and witticisms.

"I got it, Mom. Why don't I set it all up and then you can check it out. How's that?"

"Perfect!" she said, then added in a whisper, "Wait until Deb hears that Steve's coming for dinner! She'll just die! She's got a little crush on him, you know."

"She does?" Like you don't, I thought.

"Yes, she most certainly does. She'd deny it, of course, but I know that woman like the back of my hand. I'm going to set the table now. I think I'll just use the every-day bistro dishes because we're having steaks. I don't want steak knives cutting on my mother's good china."

"God, no." Bistro dishes? What qualifies a plate as *bistro*?

"I know what you're thinking," she said. "You're thinking I'm an old fussbudget, but when you inherit my mother's china and it's in mint condition—"

"You're right! I'll appreciate the care you took of it."

"That's right!"

"I knew this Italian girl in my building, and she used to call her mother a pignoli."

"You mean those little nuts you use in pesto?"

"Yep. It's Italian slang for fussbudget."

"Well, it's not nice to call your mother a nut!" she called out, as she scurried away like a little mouse that had just caught a whiff of cheese.

I ran the brush through my hair one last time and looked at myself in the mirror. I looked all right. I didn't need a flowered sundress and prissy little sandals to prove anything to anyone. Earlier, Mom had coyly dropped the bomb that Steve was a widower, which was too bad, but what was I supposed to do? Get all gussied up like Ruby taking her love to town? I don't think so. Besides, Mom was the one who had it going on for him, not me.

I gathered up all the bottles of liquor and wine, glasses and setups, and arranged a bar on the weathered old trestle table on the porch. After I satisfied myself that it looked just fine, I spent a few minutes lost in the panorama of the nearly deserted beach. Its personality was constantly changing. In the morning's rising sunshine, high-energy dogs and joggers were at play. Later, the sun worshippers arrived en masse, stretched out on blankets or chairs, reading novels and prone for hours, cooking their skin, soaking in the song of the ocean and all the vitamin D they could absorb. But the end of the day was the time I liked best, when the sand cooled, the light changed to a softer rose hue, and a kind of peace settled all over the island. It was nearly six o'clock, and farther down the shore, the last stragglers of the day were gathering up their towels and coolers, making their way toward home. Tomorrow they would go back to their jobs and resume their lives. It suddenly seemed as though everyone belonged somewhere except me. I was in an actual limbo. So many decisions needed to be made about my future. Was I really finished with my military career? I thought, Yes, I am. I never wanted to be that far away from Charlie again. I decided then not to dwell on it too much. It was too soon. Like Scarlett, I'd think about it another day.

Maybe the future would present itself like a limousine. A brand-new white stretch would mysteriously pull up to the curb; I could just climb in, slide across a beautiful leather seat, and go for a ride along the years. That was a cowardly thought if I'd ever had one. Since when had I ever invited someone or something to take over my life? But in that moment, the thought of not having to worry about every single detail of every single day held some mighty powerful appeal. And *that*, I reminded myself again, was why I had come home—to not worry so, if only for a while. If Jimmy were alive, I wouldn't have a thing to worry about. We'd be in our home in Brooklyn watching the news and making supper. It was so hard to accept that even such a simple daily act like watching the news and making supper together could never happen again. I wasn't so sure then that I even wanted to live in that house anymore. Without Jimmy it was ruined. And all wrong. Wasn't it?

It was still very warm. Though the heat of the day was broken, the night would become sultry as the tide rolled in. I could already feel the rising humidity as my hair and skin grew damp. And my heart felt heavy, as though something in my chest was sinking. Jimmy had loved the island too. I missed him something awful.

"Hey, Mom?"

Charlie appeared. His hair was wet combed and slicked back. My mother's fingerprints were all over that one. He looked adorable. And miserable. It was impossible not to smile.

"Well, hello there, Handsome!"

"I hate my hair. She trimmed my bangs too."

"She?"

"Whoops. I mean, Glam," he said and rolled his eyes.

"That's better. Well, Son, they needed it. Your bangs were over your nose."

"I just hate cutting my hair."

"I know this about you."

"So, Mom? What am I supposed to call the doctor? And can I have a Diet Coke?"

The screen door opened, and my mother came out to the porch and joined us.

"Call him Dr. Steve," I said and handed him a cold can. It was decaffeinated. Mom must have bought them for Charlie.

"Deb calls him Mr. MD," she said, and I winked at Charlie. She scrutinized every detail of the self-service bar and gave it a passing grade. "This looks very inviting."

"Mr. MD? That's silly," Charlie said.

"Thanks," I said.

We heard a door close somewhere in the distance and my mother said, "That's him. He's coming. Get ready!" She shook her hands in the air. Her nerves were acting up again.

Sure enough, I looked up to see Steve walking toward our house. She even knew the sound of his door closing?

"Get ready for what?" Charlie asked.

I looked at my mother and caught her eye. She was embarrassed.

"What?" she said. "Why, get ready for a wonderful night at the Salty Dog, that's what!"

"Such a silly name for a house," I said.

"You're telling me," she said.

As he climbed the steps and came onto the porch my mother's excitement was nearly palpable. Then, for some reason, I gave myself a mental kick in the pants. Maybe she was just lonely. She probably was. What was the matter with me? I was so suspicious of her. From the time I'd been a teenager, I'd always thought she had an ulterior motive in everything she did because many times she did have one. But, shame on me, I could see from her face that she just wanted to have a nice evening, and I was ready to run and tell Daddy that Mom was being unfaithful to him. I was being just as ridiculous as she was overenthusiastic.

Steve, who smelled very nice, handed her a bottle of wine.

"Oh! Thank you, Steve! Not necessary but always appreciated! Would you like a cocktail?"

"Well, I think that's a wonderful idea. Can I make one for you?"

"Why not? I think I'd like a gin and tonic. Jackie? Would you like a drink?"

"Sure," I said. "A glass of white wine would be great."

"Got a corkscrew?" Steve asked, holding up an unopened bottle of sauvignon blanc. Then he dug into his pocket and pulled out a Swiss Army knife. "I have this if you need one."

"No, we've got one. Right there on top of the napkins," I said. "It makes a good paperweight too."

"Smart girl!" my mother said.

"Can I see how that works?" Charlie asked.

"Sure. Step over here, young man," Steve said. "You see, you take this curlicue end and wind it down into the cork—"

He was fixing my drink before he fixed my mother's. She was visibly irked. Mom needed poker lessons. But this Steve fellow spoke to Charlie in such a nice way. He didn't just dismiss him like so many adults dismiss children. I liked that.

"Here, why don't you let me do that so you can get Mom's drink," I said.

"What? Oh, I'm sorry! Sure." He handed me the bottle of wine and picked up a highball glass. "Did you say vodka, Annie?"

"Gin. But I'll have whatever you're having. It doesn't matter, really."

"Let's both have a gin and tonic," he said and turned back to the bar.

"That sounds delightful!" Mom was so pleased that he wanted to have what she was having that she actually clapped her hands together in glee. I was glad he missed that. My poor mother was starved for affection. Why had I not realized this?

"Okay, Charlie baby. We're gonna pop this cork together. What do you say?"

"Sure!"

I turned the corkscrew deeply into the cork, sat in a chair, and held the bottle between my knees. "Now, I'll hold the bottle and you hold the bar good and tight, and pull it out straight."

Charlie took the top of the corkscrew in hand and pushed against the bottle with his other hand, making all the appropriate noises that accompany manly exertion, and after many such grunts we had a *pop!*

"Good job!" Steve said and handed Mom her drink. "Can I pour for you?"

I passed the bottle to Steve, and he half filled a goblet.

"None for me," Charlie said, and everyone laughed.

The evening was under way, and the conversation was easy and friendly. Every now and then I would catch Steve looking at me in the way that men look at women when they are interested in what's under the skirt, and I would respond with an expression of disapproval. What the hell was he thinking? The last thing I wanted was to get tangled up with anyone, but especially him.

At some point while we were refilling glasses and Mom was engaged in an animated conversation with Charlie about tide clocks and how they worked, Steve offered me his condolences.

"Your mother told me all about your husband's passing, and I just wanted to say how sorry I was to hear it. I mean, I know I said it earlier but . . ."

"Thanks." I didn't make eye contact but kept my attention on the wine bottle and how much I was pouring. "Yeah, it's devastating for me and for Charlie. I think this is going to be one of those awful losses that you just never get over."

"Yeah, I hear you. You know, I lost my wife in a boating accident a few years ago. Lightning. She was struck by lightning. So stupid."

"Mom told me. I'm sorry."

"Thanks. Yeah, I thought that by the time I reached this age I'd have a family. At least you have Charlie. He's a great kid."

"Yep, he's the real deal. All boy. Great heart. Smart as a whip."

"Yes, he seems so. I gotta say, though, I never expected to find myself back on the market, did you?"

I don't know what it was that he said that made my blood run cold, but it did.

I stared at him. "I've been a widow for a total of eight weeks. I hardly consider myself to be on the market." Just as quickly as I had let my mouth run away with itself, I realized how rude I had been. "I'm sorry. That was rude. I apologize."

"No, I apologize. I'm an insensitive Neanderthal."

"I know all about Neanderthals," Charlie said. He was obviously eavesdropping while pretending to be mesmerized with my mother's pedantic, repetitious, and very long-winded lecture on the formation of sand dunes.

"Well, do you know anything about grills?" Mother asked with a wide smile. The gin was doing her some good, as her facial muscles were less taut and she seemed to be relaxed at last.

Steve raised his hand. "I do. Back home in Cincinnati, they call me the Grill Meister. Can I light it for you?"

"That would be such a blessing!" she said. "Grills make me so nervous. Leaking gas and all that scary stuff."

Steve gave her a pat on the arm, and I thought the old girl would swoon.

Over the next half hour, the grill was heated to the temperature Steve thought was the exact level to prepare a perfect steak. And the steaks were gorgeous, just as Mom said they were. They were rib eyes, thick and marbled, and the smell of them on the fire was divine. I guess Steve's dogs thought so too, because they started to howl at the top of their canine lungs.

"Glory be! What a mournful sound," Mom said. "They sound so pitiful!"

"Don't mind them," Steve said. "I'll just run home and put them in the den. I shouldn't have left them on the porch where they can smell the meat."

"You'll do no such thing!" Mom said. I was very surprised to hear her speak to him in such an emphatic and stern tone, but I thought, That's the gin talking. "You'll bring Stella and Stanley right over here. They're precious."

It was a landslide victory for the *love me, love my dog* club.

A-rooooo! Ar Ar Ar-roooo! Rooo a rooo a rooo! Their frantic howling continued in earnest.

"Wow! Listen to them!" Charlie said. "You want me to go get them?"

"Are you sure?" Steve asked Mom.

"Absolutely. I'll make them scrambled eggs. Hurry, Charlie, before the neighbors call the authorities! And turn on the porch lights so you don't break your neck. They can sit right next to me."

Porch lights? It wasn't dark. Wait. Scrambled eggs? My mother had never allowed a dog into our house, much less made them eggs. I wanted to ask her if I should set two more places, but she wouldn't think I was funny. I wasn't going to say one word. Nope. Not one word. But I was mystified.

Somehow we made it to the table and Steve's dogs settled down by our feet, kept quiet by Charlie's continuous scratching behind their ears and, after they devoured their Swiss cheese omelets, by slipping them bits of steak. I was positive that Mom knew that Charlie was slipping them treats in exchange for their silence, but she said nothing. Feeding dogs from the table is verboten in most cultures because it turns them into beggars. But on that night my mother was so light-hearted that almost nothing could darken her mood. And I wasn't about to correct Charlie for his transgression. On certain occasions our family motto was it just didn't pay to be right. This was one of those occasions.

"Supper is delicious, Mom. Thanks."

"Yes! To the chef!" Steve said.

"To Glam-ma!"

"Oh, y'all. You're welcome. I only made the potatoes gratin and the asparagus almondine and the baked goat cheese and Boston butter leaf salad with the pomegranate vinaigrette and baked the olive bread and whipped up a mousse au chocolat." She stopped, took a deep breath, and smiled for effect. "It was *Steve* who grilled the steaks, and they are absolutely perfect! And this wine is delicious too. Here's to you!"

We all raised our glass in Steve's direction, and he smiled. "Glam-ma?" he asked.

"Short for glamorous grandmother," I said.

"She only cooked up . . . a storm! No! A hurricane!" Steve said.

"She is the cat's mother," Charlie said, and I nearly choked.

"What?" Steve said. "Well, no matter. I say, here's to Charlie, our dog whisperer!"

"I wish I had a dog," Charlie said. "But we can't have one because we're not home all day. Mom says it's not fair to have a pet without giving them company."

"Oh, Charlie, come on now," I said, feeling like The Evil Parent.

"Well, Charlie, your mother's right. I mean, I feel terrible when I go to work in the morning and I have to leave Stella and Stanley alone all day. They turn into crazy maniacs when I come home. They start jumping and whining to run up and down the beach and chase a tennis ball or Frisbee or anything."

"I could play with them while you're at work," Charlie suggested, his blue eyes pleading.

"Now, Charlie, let's not impose," I said.

"No, wait, Jackie. That's brilliant!" Steve leaned over and looked at Charlie, quickly making a plan. "Okay, I have an idea. Let's make it a business deal. What if you walked my dogs twice a day, made sure they had water and kibble, and played with them for a bit? I can pay you, say, five dollars a day? How long are y'all going to be here?"

"I don't know, but yeah! I can do that! Wait. Mom? Is it okay for me to take care of Stella and Stanley?"

"Well, sure, why not? It's not like it's a terrible commute." I smiled at Steve then. What a nice offer for him to make to a little boy who had just lost his father. It could only be a good thing. "Now, Steve, Charlie's never had a job before. Is there a problem here on the island with child labor?"

"None that I'm aware of," Steve said, feigning seriousness. "Ever since they broke up that ring of murderous babysitters . . ."

"Oh, stop, you two! You'll scare my grandson!"

"Sorry." So our Dr. Plofker had a decent sense of humor. Well, that was nice. "Look, I think this is actually a wonderful idea. It will teach him responsibility."

"And then you can see if you really like taking care of a . . ." Mom said, her words trailing off at the sound of the doorbell. "Now who in the world is that?"

Mom started to get up when Miss Deb just walked right in.

"Hey, y'all! Isn't some handsome young man going to take this blueberry pie from me? It's still warm. Well, lookie who's here!"

Her face flushed and I thought, Well, maybe *both* of them really do have a crush on Steve. Only Miss Deb would bring a pie in a sweetgrass basket with a lid to keep it warm. Sweetgrass baskets were the Lowcountry equivalent of Fabergé eggs.

"Blueberry! Sweet!" Charlie, who was for the moment the island's most heralded child, hopped up, took the pie from her, and hurried it to the kitchen.

"And then he'd better come back here and hug my neck!" Deb called after him. "I'm sorry, I didn't mean to interrupt your supper. I didn't know you'd still be at the table. I saw the porch lights and thought—"

"Please! Don't think a thing about it!" I got up and gave her a hug.

"Look at you, darlin' chile. It's so good to see you."

Her eyes were brimming with sudden tears. I squeezed her shoulders. "It's okay. Thanks," I whispered.

"You are my best friend in the world, Deb Jenkins. You can walk in my house twenty-four seven!"

Mom was pleased with herself for throwing "twenty-four seven" out there like a younger person might have done.

"Dr. Plofker," Miss Deb said, nodding to him as he pulled another chair to the table for her to join us.

"Ms. Jenkins, how are you this evening?"

"Doing just fine, thanks."

"Are you hungry?" I said. "We've got mountains of food. Can I fix you a plate?"

"Oh, no thanks. I got my supper early because I had to take Vernon to the emergency room. His blood pressure shot up, and he got all wiggy on me. The poor old sweet thing. Sometimes I'm not so sure that retirement is good for him."

Miss Deb's husband of a million years was something of an agoraphobic hypochondriac who stayed home in his La-Z-Boy recliner watching reruns of *Little House on the Prairie* around the clock. Miss Deb took care of him but also went on with her life.

"Poor dear," Mom said. "Would you like a glass of wine?"

"*Oh, my word!* We're drinking wine from a *bottle*?" Miss Deb said. "It's not even Saturday night! I'll *definitely* have a glass!"

"*Hush!*" Mom said under her breath.

"How do you usually drink it?" Steve asked, pouring a glass for her. "From a shoe?"

The Good Doctor was overhydrated. Miss Deb looked at my mom, and they dissolved into giggles like a couple of schoolgirls. Then my mother cleared her throat, trying to regain her composure.

"Ahem! Ahem!" she said. "Well, truth? Deb and I take a drive out to Costco once a month and stock up on that white wine that comes in a box. It's easy to store. And you see, if you get it *really* cold you can't tell that it's well, you know . . ." My mother was clearly embarrassed, her face turning every shade of red.

"Cheap! Now you know our secret," Miss Deb said without a shred of shame. "Cheers!"

"Cheers!" we all said.

Steve looked at me and arched his eyebrows as if to say *aren't these two old birds funny?* I was not about to agree with him. Anything that segregated my mother and demeaned her in the slightest was not okay with me, especially knowing how much effort she had put into the night. And I could see the lights go out in his eyes. He knew he was off base.

"Mom is prudent, not cheap. There's a difference," I said.

"That's right," she said. "And it's an important distinction."

"Wine is wine, isn't it?" Charlie asked.

"No, baby," I said. "Not all grapes are created equal. For example, hamburger is beef, but it isn't nearly as delicious as the steaks we just had."

"Got it," Charlie said. "Gosh. You learn something new every day."

We all had a good chuckle then.

"Charlie? You sound like an old man," I said. "Can I cut y'all some pie? And I can put some mousse on the side. And Mom, don't even think about lifting another finger tonight. The dishes belong to me."

After dessert, Steve tried to stay behind to help, but I finally managed to shoo him out to the porch with Mom and Miss Deb. It wasn't that I would not have appreciated the extra pair of hands, because to tell you the truth, my mother had used every pot and pan she owned. It was that doing the dishes was something Jimmy, Charlie, and I had always done together. The sight of Steve with a dish towel in his hands made me so uncomfortable—the happy trio washing up the supper dishes? I just felt sick all over as though even an act as small as letting him dry glasses would be a betrayal to

Jimmy. Yeah, Jimmy and I had become such creatures of habit. After dishes, he'd check the locks, I'd turn down the lights, and we'd pull down the bed together. Sometimes we'd watch the late-night news and agree on how terrible and corrupt the world had become. Sometimes we'd read in bed. But we had always been in sync, and I missed him. I missed him so badly I could have cried just thinking about him then, but no. No more tears.

Later on, Steve stuck his head back in the kitchen to say good night. "See you in the morning, Charlie?"

"Sure. What time?"

"Eight o'clock?"

"Sure! Hey, Mom? We got an alarm clock?"

"Cell phone."

"Right!"

Steve gave me a friendly nod and left. Things had gone okay between us once the ground rules were established, but I knew he was taking home some awkward feelings. Basically the rules were these: one, be really nice to my mother, and two, don't try to hook up with me. For the first time in my whole life I felt protective of her. But I saw things in her that night I had never seen before.

Later still, as Charlie and I were drying the last of the silverware and dropping it into the drawer, Miss Deb came sailing through to say good night.

"That breeze out there on that porch is something else!"

"It always was and ever shall be thus—especially on high tide," I said. "If we could bottle it, we'd all be filthy rich."

"Thanks for the pie, Miss Deb," Charlie said. "It was so good."

Charlie's hair was back in his face by then, and he looked just like who he was—a very vulnerable little boy who ought to be up to some mischief but instead carried the weight of the world all over his face.

"Anytime you want a pie you just let me know, okay? In fact, have you ever had a chocolate pecan pie?"

"No, ma'am."

"Well, then, that's next. When this pie plate is empty, you let me know, all right? Night, y'all."

"Thanks," Charlie said. I could hear how tired he was in his voice. My poor baby.

I walked Miss Deb to the door and gave her a hug. I watched her go down the steps, and she stopped halfway, turning back to me. I could see she wanted to say something, but like most people trying to offer encouragement in the wake of disaster, she was at a loss for words. So I said it for her. "We're gonna be all right, Miss Deb. I don't want you to worry."

"Of course you're going to be all right. You have to be. Besides, this island cures what ails you."

"This island and a slice of your pie. I hope we're right. Thanks again, huh?"

She nodded her head and turned again, this time making it to the bottom of the steps. I watched her as she crossed our yard and made her way toward her house. She was thoughtful and kind. There was a lot to be said for those qualities.

When I got back to the kitchen, Charlie was arranging our dish towels over the oven handle to let them dry. Show me another ten-year-old boy who did that, and I'd show you one who was imitating his parents' behavior. I rinsed the sponge out again, thinking about how hard Jimmy and I always tried to set a good example. It was amazing what stuck and what didn't. I wiped down the counters for the final time of the night.

"Mom? Can I go to bed now? I have to go to work in the morning, you know."

Priceless. How old was he?

"Of course. Go kiss Glam good night, and I'll come tuck you in."

"Okay."

I turned out most of the lights, and a few minutes later I wandered to his bedroom and found Charlie under the covers. Mom was perched on the side of his bed. She was telling him a story about Edgar Allan Poe and how back in his day there had been illnesses that caused deep comas that resembled death. Sometimes people were accidentally buried alive, so they put little bells in the coffin that could be rung by the breath of the not exactly deceased.

"You're kidding, right?" Charlie said with a mounting panic in his voice.

"Why, no. But it was a long time ago and—"

"Charlie! Did you brush your teeth?"

He jumped in surprise, not having known I was there until that moment. "Yes."

"So if I go touch your toothbrush, it will be wet?"

He shimmied out from under the covers and ran to the bathroom.

"I'll just go check," he said and slammed the bathroom door. "Sorry!"

"Mom? What are you doing?"

"What do you mean? I'm putting my grandson to bed."

"And telling a little boy who hasn't slept right since we buried his father a story about people being buried alive? I mean, do you really think this is a good idea?"

"Oh, honey, Charlie's old enough—"

"You are unbelievable. Do me a favor? How about we don't tell him any more stories like that for a while?"

"Really, Jackie, you're making a mountain out of a molehill."

"Okay, I'll tell you what. When he gets up ten times in the middle of the night, I'll send him to you."

I turned and went to my room. And this time *I* slammed the door.

6

"In supposing it to be a bug of real gold" . . .

"This bug is to make my fortune," he continued, with a triumphant smile, "to reinstate me in my family possessions. Is it any wonder, then, that I prize it?"

—Edgar Allan Poe, "The Gold-Bug"

Annie

She was wrong. Charlie slept like a stone. But I felt so perfectly horrible about what Jackie had said that I was up half the night myself checking on him and checking on him. I knew that Charlie had been having trouble sleeping, but I hadn't realized he was so impressionable or I never would have told him anything at bedtime that might have frightened him. Never in a million years. Why, I wouldn't hurt a *hair* on that child's head. Didn't Jackie know that? Lord, this was giving me some terrible anxiety. The worst part was that she was probably right. Oh, hells bells. No more death stories from me!

It was getting on to seven when I called Deb. "You ready to walk off some pie?" I asked.

"Sweet Mother of Mary! Am I ever? I ate for two people yesterday. I'll meet you at the bottom of your beach steps."

"Sounds good."

I tied my walking sneakers on, and minutes later we were off at our usual pace, that being walking as fast as we could while still being able to carry on a conversation. There were clusters of dog people at Station 26, Station 22, and farther down the beach. (Station numbers were a carryover from when we had a trolley car on the island, which was way before my time, thank you.) It seemed that the same dogs showed up every day but I never recognized their owners, probably because they changed clothes and, after all, two lively chicks like Deb and me traveled at a pretty spritely clip.

"I did something really stupid," I said.

"What?"

I told her about Poe and his obsession with people who were accidentally buried alive, and she shook her head.

"It's simply a literary fact," I said.

"Yeah, one better imparted in the light of day. You have to watch yourself with kids."

"Well, he slept just fine, but now I've got an issue with Jackie."

"You worry too much, and anyway, Poe was a crazy nut," she said.

"People think that, but it's really not true."

"What? You gonna tell me that he wasn't a drunk?"

"No, of course not. He was a bit of a binge drinker. The poor thing had that kind of genetic structure that when he took one or two drinks he was trashed."

"That *is* unfortunate!"

"Right? Awful. Anyway, he certainly had good reasons to become a drunk if he wanted to, but he didn't drink himself to death like the world thinks he did."

"Like what? God, this is a beautiful day, isn't it?"

It was a picture-perfect day, as though it had been ordered up by the Department of Tourism—blue skies, sparkling water, nice breeze, what else could you want?

"Gorgeous. First of all, his parents both died when he was just a toddler. They were actors and actually performed at the Dock Street Theatre downtown! Isn't that funny? Anyway, right away he was separated from his siblings and made to live with this man John Allan and his wife, Fanny. All the Poe children were left destitute. Now, the Allans? They were Yankee Protestants, *if* you know what I mean."

"No, actually, I don't have a *clue* what that means."

"Well, they lived a very stern and strict Calvinist life of emotional deprivation—"

"Emotional deprivation? What in the world is that? You mean they didn't love him?"

"Well, Fanny loved Edgar, but the old man was brutal. He was this great big hulk of a guy who believed that hard work and sacrifice should rule the day. Frankly, little Edgar was as soft as a grape and wanted to be a poet from the time he knew what poetry was."

"Soft as a grape? Annie? You're speaking in code. Do you mean he was gay?"

"No. Well, maybe. There's no hard evidence of it, but he was extremely effeminate and had almost courtly manners, I guess a bit like an Oscar Wilde kind of character? Anyway, he was terribly affected, which was the kind of thing that would have driven his macho stepfather right up a tree."

"Jeesh. Hard to imagine Edgar Allan Poe as effemi-nate. Peculiar, yes. But not girly."

"Want to talk about peculiar? He married his thirteen-year-old first cousin, but there's no reason to believe it was ever consummated, which is probably a good thing."

"Ew. Just the thought . . . I mean, this guy wrote some dark, scary stuff. How is it that I run a library named for him and never knew all of this?"

"Because you read novels and I live, eat, and breathe history and biographies. It's no crime. Just a difference in preferences. Anyway, do you know that he—"

"Probably not, Miss Poe Expert. And don't tell me you don't read novels. I've seen some of your books with those covers."

"So shoot me, but listen to this. With all the stories that he published he only ever made six thousand dollars from his writing in his whole life."

"What? That's crazy! So how in the world did he support his child bride and himself?"

"And her mother, who was both his aunt and his mother-in-law."

"That is so nasty."

"Yep. It sure is. Literary criticism. Basically, he skewered other writers his whole career and it earned him puh-lenty of enemies. I'll get you a copy of his obituary. You won't believe it! The guy who wrote it said no one would care if Poe was dead. It's the meanest thing I ever read. But sorry, I could go on for hours yakking about his screwed-up life."

"Hey! You know what?"

"What?"

"You should! We could do a lecture series at the library to raise money. Would you do that? Talk about Poe, I mean? I could get some of the ladies to make sandwiches and cookies, and we could have a tea. What do you think?"

"Really?"

"Why not? They do it at the library downtown all the time. It would probably be better to start after Labor Day. You know, when everyone's back from vacation and settled back into their routine?"

"That sounds like fun to me. Yeah, I think I'd really like to do that."

I thought about it more and realized it would give me some purpose that I felt like I'd lost when I retired. It would be awfully nice to be recognized as a qualified-but-not-exactly-an-expert on something even if my reputation was limited to just our little island. I wouldn't be merely a retired fussbudget, I'd be a *guest lecturer.* Would Steve come? What would he think?

"What are you thinking about, Annie?"

"Well, I was wondering what people would say if I stood up in front of the whole world and gave a talk on Poe. You know how this island is, Deb. All the old biddies will say, 'Oh, she thinks she's so smart.' You know how they are."

"You listen to me, honey, not them. If Thomas Edison had worried about what small-minded people thought when he was trying to invent the lightbulb, we'd still be in the dark."

"You're right. I need to just gather up some courage and take the plunge."

"That's the spirit! Now, you haven't told me. How did our Dr. Plofker wind up at your dinner table last night?"

"Because earlier in the afternoon he took one look at Jackie and practically invited himself. I think he was attracted to her."

"Oh, don't be silly. He was just being nice. Shoot, Annie, they've both lost their spouses and they're both young. Jackie's only thirty-five, right?"

"Yes. And he's forty-three, I think."

"He probably feels a kindred spirit with her, don't you think? I mean, I've decided that he's definitely not gay. But I don't think he's interested in anyone."

"No. He's got the total hots for Jackie. I caught him looking at her with that stupid expression men get when they're thinking about dicky dunking."

"Honey, the frost ain't on the pumpkin quite yet. And how do the total hots compare with the partial hots? On fire versus a little sizzle?"

"Oh, you! Stop!"

"I'm just saying, from what I saw? Nobody's got the hots for anybody. Y'all just looked like three grown-ups having fun. And besides, he's the kind of guy who knows how to make people feel good."

Part of me hoped she was right, and the other part, shame on me, hoped she was wrong.

"Probably why he became a doctor in the first place. Isn't that what they're supposed to do? Anyway, I don't know if you caught the part about him giving Charlie a little job watching his dogs?"

"Yeah, Charlie told me about it while y'all were talking. Listen, boys need dogs for a whole lot of reasons. I think it will do him wonders."

"That's what I'm hoping. And it won't hurt to have a man in his picture either."

"I was thinking that too, but what's going to happen if Charlie gets all attached to Dr. Wonderful and then Jackie takes him back to New York? Wouldn't that be painful for him?"

"We're putting the cart a mile before the horse here."

"Right."

"Charlie has yet to even walk his dogs one time, and he only just met Steve yesterday. Anyway, I have to cut our marathon short this morning. I promised Charlie blueberry pancakes again. And I've got to get his adorable bahunkus out of the bed."

"No problem. I have to take Vern to see that cute physical therapist in Durst's office. We've got a nine thirty, and I should've started getting him ready yesterday if I wanted us to be on time. The poor devil moves so slowly these days."

"Okay. Let's hustle!"

We did a U-turn and waddled back as fast as we could. Just to clarify what I mean by "waddle," I mean that power-walking thing fast walkers do, slightly slower than a jog. When we got to my steps, Deb kept going without missing a beat, calling out "See you tomorrow!" I threw my arm up and waved at her over my head, feeling very lucky to have such a reliable friend.

I went straight to Charlie's room as it was twenty minutes before eight. He was already up and in the bathroom, and lo and behold, his bed was made. Jackie was in the kitchen pouring coffee. She was wearing what appeared to be men's boxer shorts and an old ill-fitting T-shirt. The backs of her thighs were as smooth as a baby's bottom, and I wondered for a fleeting moment how mine would stack up next to hers. Probably just fine. All that walking had to be good for something besides endorphins and catching up on the news.

"Good morning, sweetheart," I said, keeping my voice light and chipper, hoping she wouldn't bring up last night's discussion until I had something to eat. "How did you sleep?"

Wrong question! Wrong question!

She looked up at me with that *look,* the one that said, "How can you even ask that when you *know* I never slept a wink, thanks to you and your Poe story about coffin bells!"

Well, it was a new day, and I was having none of it.

"Listen, missy, for your information, Charlie slept soundly all through the night and I happen to know that you did too." I took my favorite mug from the cabinet and filled it. "I know this because I was up almost every hour."

"How do you know I was sleeping?"

"Because, baby girl, you snore like a man."

"I do not."

"Would you like me to record it tonight and play it for you tomorrow?"

"I don't snore."

"Surely you're not calling your mother a liar, are you?"

"There would be no value in that."

"Well, I'm just trying to tell you that I think you might be acting like an old worrywart about this one. Edgar Allan Poe is one of our most fascinating residents in the entire history of Charleston's citizenry, and there's no reason why Charlie shouldn't learn everything there is to know about him."

"Okay. Truce. Just tell him the dead people stuff in the daylight, okay?"

"Fine. Now, can I make a plate of pancakes and crispy bacon for you?"

"Sure. No bacon, though. Too fattening."

"I buy that center-cut bacon that only has seventy calories in three strips. Then I nuke it for two and a half minutes. Honey chile? There ain't a lick of fat in 'em when I'm done. Now, you want bacon or what?"

"Really? Okay, I'll have bacon. Want me to fix it?"

"Yes, please. Use three paper towels. Two on the bottom and one on the top. And pour the juice too, please. There's no time to waste this morning. We've got to get a workingman off to his new job!"

You see that? I could still delegate and produce an impressive showing on the breakfast table and settle a difference of opinion without bloodshed, all at the same time. I had not lost my touch.

Charlie bounded into the room with the kind of energy clearly wasted on youth, wolfed down six pancakes, God only knows how much bacon, and two glasses of milk and orange juice, and bounded back to the bathroom.

"Brushing his teeth?" I asked.

"Yeah, he knows I'm the toothbrush police," Jackie said, absorbed in reading *The Post and Courier*.

I picked up the dishes and put them into the sink to rinse. There were two mourning doves outside of my window, the exact same color as a pair of soft gray suede gloves I once owned. The little darlings were cooing, presumably to each other, and so sweet to watch. I paused for a moment, feeling sentimental, thinking about how they mated for life. I liked to imagine that they cared about each other. Maybe they did. Didn't *National Geographic* or someone do a study that showed penguins had actual affection for their mates? Well, it was lovely to think of the animal kingdom falling in love and living happily ever after. It couldn't be nearly as complicated as what went on between humans. If Mrs. Dove got fussy about her nest, would the mister call her names and go off fishing for eleven years? I doubted it.

"Did you hear what I said?" Jackie asked.

"What? Oh, no. Sorry, sweetheart! I was lost in Bird Land."

"Oh. I said I'm just going to take Charlie over to Steve's since it's his first time. You know, just to make sure he's comfortable going in an empty house. Steve said he was leaving the key on top of the mailbox. I want to make sure he gets in."

"Oh, yes! That's a good idea."

"Should I bring the dogs back over here? I mean, what about these dogs?"

Well, now I was in a nice pickle, wasn't I? I hated having dogs in my house, and Jackie knew it. No matter how nice they were, they shed and did all sorts of things that dogs do, like sniff and squirt their calling card, and what if they decided to have a nap on my bed? Please! But there I was last night like a damn fool making them omelets and treating them like long-lost family. If they hadn't belonged to Steve Plofker, I wouldn't have let them in my kitchen for beans. What to do with the dogs? Great. I was about to get caught being a hypocrite. I hated that. So I dodged being the bad guy with the age-old trick of answering a question with a question.

"Gosh, what do you think we should do?" Throw the ball in her court, Annie. Good one.

"What do *I* think?" She paused for a moment. "Well, let's see how they smell," she said, "and then we'll make the call."

"They smelled fine last night," I said with all the innocent benevolence of Doris Day, circa 1960 Hollywood.

"Yeah, but who knows? They might have found a raccoon or a skunk and rolled around with it. Ick."

"Well, I'll let you decide, then. If they pass the smell test, I'm thinking they might enjoy the front porch. What do you think? It's nice and cool."

"Yeah, I'll get Charlie to take them for a run on the beach, and then we'll come back here. Maybe we have something they could use for water bowls?"

Sure, what about my mother's Limoges vegetable dishes? For the record, I did *not* say this aloud.

"I'll find something," I said. "You and Charlie had better get moving."

"Right! See you in a bit! Thanks for breakfast!"

She blew me a kiss and was out the door with Charlie on her heels. Well, she seemed reasonably happy, and given the situation, that was more than I had hoped for. People always said that dogs had a way of lightening the mood. I put the last of the breakfast plates into the dishwasher and turned it on. It was time for me to grab a shower.

I had one of those nylon poufs that comes with my antiaging, extra-moisturizing, slight-exfoliation body wash, and as soon as I got under the hot water I took it to task, scrubbing every inch of my body I could reach, and used a washcloth and contortion to reach the areas I could not access any other way. Well, if there was ever to be another person in my shower, maybe the epicenter of my back would get the polish it deserved, but we all know that was looking less likely with each passing year. So what? I continued. I washed my hair until it squeaked and then gave it a small amount of conditioner, rinsed it out, stepped out onto my ultra-plush bath mat Deb brought me home from a trip to Istanbul, and wrapped myself in a towel sheet. Why Deb went to Istanbul is anybody's guess. Nothing but a bunch of hooligans over there, I expect. Everything I need is on this side of the causeway.

But back to the last vestiges of my youth? I will not go down without a fight, I thought as I rubbed moisturizer into my upper arms. I will try to remain as attractive and young-looking as modern cosmetics will allow—no knives, thanks. I had my cache of secret weapons. That cute Dr. Duke Hagerty downtown gave me a little shot of youth in my forehead from time to time to make the creases disappear. I'd used Latisse on my eyelashes and had regrown them to the point that I had to trim them. Can you imagine? And Julie Nestler down at Beauty and the Beach worked a little magic on my hair and eyebrows every two weeks and no one was the wiser.

But still the nagging question was the same: was I too old to be attractive to someone like Steve Plofker? Or anyone? Even with my daily exercise and watching what I ate, I could see undeniable signs of aging in my skinny but sagging upper arms. That deeply saddened me because I knew there was nothing to be done about it; but the bazillions of little crepe lines in my neck horrified me. Was I headed for an old age of wearing long-sleeved high-necked getups like Katharine Hepburn in *The African Queen?*

Hell, no! I would approach this as I approached other dilemmas. It was time for the ultimate test: a naked evaluation in a full-length mirror in broad daylight. Assess the situation and then make a plan. So I bravely stepped into my dressing room, where the mirror faced east. It was still morning, and the light was as heartless as it was unrelenting. Did I really want the truth? Could my battle-beaten ego really bear the truth?

"Don't be ridiculous!" I said to no one. "You must do this!"

I held my breath, sucked in my stomach, dropped my towel, and looked straight into the mirror. (Results were lower than expected.) Then I exhaled, turned around, and, with a hand mirror, I looked at my backside and the backs of my thighs and the backs of my arms. (Dimples belong on faces.) Then I sucked everything in and up and looked at myself sideways. (Sigh.) In conclusion, may I just say that the jury did not indulge in a long deliberation and found that truth is wildly overrated. Extremely and wildly overrated.

It was no time for self-forgiveness and misplaced optimism. It was time to take action. I read somewhere, in *Southern Living* magazine, I think, that there was a woman in Charleston who did miraculous makeovers. *What was her name? What was her name?* Did I keep the magazine, or did I throw it out in one of my manic recycling purges? Margaret. Margaret something . . . something with a D. Oh, hells bells, I'd Google her. Maybe I didn't know anything about GPSs and texting, but I could Google with the best of them.

I threw on a sundress of red tulips and sandals to match and brushed my hair back from my face, pushing it behind my ears. I gave the old face a quick coat of powder and a few strokes of blush and applied a bright rosy lipstick. Then I looked in the full-length mirror again, blowing myself a kiss. Well, maybe I'd never be breaking hearts at thirty again, but I didn't look like fifty-eight, whatever that looked like. Now, where did I leave that issue of *Southern Living*? It was the one with all the casserole recipes in it. I'd turn the house upside down until I found it.

7

"Jupiter and myself are going upon an expedition into the hills . . . in this expedition, we shall need the aid of some person in whom we can confide. You are the only one we can trust." . . .

. . . "but do you mean to say that this infernal beetle has any connection with your expedition into the hills?"

"It has."

—Edgar Allan Poe, "The Gold-Bug"

Jackie

O nly eight in the morning, and it was already as miserable as the weather in Afghanistan. At least we didn't have the infernal dust and swarms of flies. And I could wear flip-flops instead of boots.

"Come on," I said to Charlie.

We crossed the yard and slipped through the oleanders that separated Steve's property from my mother's. His Expedition was in the driveway, and his BMW was gone. Why one person needed two cars was beyond me. Just as we took the key and heard the metal move in the lock with a distinctive click, we could hear Stella and Stanley hurrying to meet us, barking happily. We opened the door and one of them, Stella, I think, jumped up on her hind legs, threw her paws on Charlie's shoulders, and licked his face over and over. Her culinary benefactor had returned.

"I think she likes you, Son," I said, marveling at the love and enthusiasm of the dog and, not surprisingly, Charlie's. Stanley, obviously the better trained of the pair, sat at my feet. "Good boy." I scratched his head.

"Yeah. Okay, now. Down, girl. Okay, now. That's enough," he said, rubbing Stella's side. "I've got this handled, Mom. You can go."

"Well, it's your first visit inside a strange house, and I thought it might be a good idea if I came along."

The real reason I had come with Charlie was to be sure Steve Plofker had not left his porn collection all over the place, if he had one, that is. I know that sounds very cynical, but I had known the man for less than twenty-four hours and for all I knew, he did. And my mother wouldn't know a sexual deviate from a turnip truck, so don't go there.

I went down the hall to where I thought I might find the kitchen and the dog's leashes. The entire hallway was lined with photographs, obviously taken by Steve or his late wife, from vacations and trips all over the world. There were pictures of them together and of each other in front of temples in Thailand, castles in Scotland and Ireland, a volcano somewhere, riding camels in Egypt, fly-fishing in someplace that looked like Montana or Wyoming, on the beaches of various islands—they must have really loved traveling. And the pictures were beautiful. Really gorgeous. She was too. Was this a memorial to her? It softened my heart a little toward him to think it might be. My next thought was that if I had to look at a wall of pictures of Jimmy I'd probably spend the rest of my life wallowing in some massive pit of depression.

What was his wife's name? I had not asked him. He knew Jimmy's name. Well, I would ask the next time I saw him. It was something I should know.

She was very pretty—long blond hair, big eyes, perfect smile, thin, toned, probably tall too. She didn't look stupid either. And she was stylish. I'd probably have hated her guts if I'd known her. And Lord pity the poor woman who tried to fill her shoes.

The leashes were on the kitchen counter with a note to which was attached a crisp five-dollar bill. I handed it to Charlie and we read it together. It said:

Dear Charlie,

Have fun with my crazy dogs. They get one cup of dry food and cool water to drink. No chocolate

*treats ever. I tell you this because they will eat any-
thing and chocolate is dangerous for dogs and I
didn't know if you knew that. And bad news, you
have to scoop their poop. That's what the little bags
that are attached to their leash are for. Make sure
you get them off the beach by ten! The dog police
will arrest them and give me a ticket.*

See you tonight!
Dr. Steve

"Sweet! Five bucks! The easiest money I ever
made!"

I had to laugh. He made it sound as though he'd
been gainfully employed for decades. For some reason,
maybe because I was feeling at home, I opened the
refrigerator.

"Mom! What are you doing?"

"You can tell a lot about someone by what they eat,"
I said.

"Oh. To me it looks like you're stalking, but what do
I know?"

"Let's keep this between ourselves, okay?" There
was nothing in the refrigerator besides a large container
of a sports drink, some boxes of coconut water, diet
beer, and skim milk. The freezer, however was another

story. It was loaded. Loaded with labeled containers of blueberry cobbler, peach cobbler, and other sweets all identified with labels in Miss Deb's handwriting and other containers of chicken divan, beef stew, spaghetti sauce, and chicken soup that were labeled by my mother. Did the pastry chef know what the savory chef was up to? Suddenly I doubted it.

"We'd better get out of here," Charlie said.

"Just doing a little reconnaissance, Son."

"Whatever," he said.

We hooked the dogs up to their leashes and left the house the same way we'd come in. I locked the door and Charlie was off, running behind Stella and Stanley as fast as his ten-year-old legs would carry him. I decided not to worry for the next thirty minutes. I would not worry that a giant shark would leap from the waves and grab my boy or that he would step into the hole of a sand crab and break his ankle. Nope, I was going to be Grace Kelly's official portrait of Her Serene Highness until he got back.

Mom was waiting on the porch with a pitcher of iced water laced with lemon slices and cucumber spears, some magazines, and of course her novel of dubious literary worth.

"Well, he's off and running," I said, closing the screen door behind me.

"Yeah, I saw those dogs take off. It's hard to tell who's exercising who!"

"Truly. Well, I'll tell you another good thing about this job. It keeps him off that stupid DS of his."

Mom removed her reading glasses and looked at me. "GPS? DS? Somebody needs to help me with all this newfangled jargon."

I poured myself a glass of iced water and pulled out a spear of cucumber. "It's this really annoying handheld electronic game device that half the kids in New York are addicted to that keeps them from using their brains and gives them mangled thumbs. Well, I'm not positive about the thumb problem. It's just that I hate electronic games. They're an awful waste of time."

"I play solitaire on my laptop."

"Oh." I wasn't taking her bait. "That's different. Solitaire is a classic. And I doubt if you play for hours on end. What's the lemon and cucumber for?"

"They're a natural diuretic. And sometimes the evening can slip away while I'm battling the Angry Birds or playing Words with Friends."

"Still. You're an adult. You're making an informed decision." The idea of my mother in this wonderful house, lonely, turning to computer games for company, gave me a knot in my stomach.

"So tell me," she said in almost a whisper, "what does the inside of his house look like?"

"Don't you know? I mean, haven't you ever been over there and gone inside?"

"Are you out of your natural mind? Don't you know that if I went over there the monsignor of Stella Maris Church would have the Ladies' Altar Society sew big fat red As on all my clothes?"

"Oh, God, you are so funny sometimes. Really, Momma! You are!"

"Well, are you going to tell me, or do I have to drag it out of you?"

She was serious. Oh, man. Mom and Miss Deb both had a crush on the man next door.

"It's okay. Very tidy. And there are about a hundred pictures of his late wife plastered on the walls."

"Really! Oh, my. The poor thing."

Before she could gain steam on the subject of the widower, Charlie ran by us and waved from the beach. We stood up and waved back. I was happy for the diversion.

"He's adorable," she said, and we sat down again, rocking slowly.

"Thanks. I think so too. I just worry about him. You know?"

"Why? He's a perfectly healthy, perfectly normal boy."

"Yeah, but you know, he doesn't exactly know his way around the world. In New York he's got a little street savvy, but this is foreign territory. Now suddenly it seems like he wants to spread his wings and fly all over the island. It just makes me very nervous. I mean, look! Look at the ocean! It's huge! It looks like it could roll up here and swallow us all up!"

"Oh, Jackie. My dear child. You know, I know you've been through a terrible thing, losing Jimmy, and what you witnessed over there in the desert and mountains I can only barely imagine."

"Enough blood to give you nightmares for the rest of your life. Let's start there."

"Let's not. Mercy! Baby, you've got to let him be a boy. You have to teach him well and then trust him a little. He's got a good head on his shoulders. He's not going to do anything foolish. All the boys on this island run and play. It couldn't be safer."

"You don't understand, Mom. He's been very protected all his life. I mean, he's not allowed to even walk to the bodega down on the corner without adult supervision."

"What's a bodega?"

"Oh, um, it's the urban equivalent of a little convenience store. You know, they sell milk, eggs, sandwiches, lottery tickets—that kind of stuff. Like Mr. Gruber's Wishing Well used to be."

She nodded and said, "Now it's the Co-op. And he *really* can't walk to the corner on his own? Why?"

"Because someone might grab him. Remember that story about that poor kid in Brooklyn last year?"

"Dear Mother of God, how could I not remember? Horrible."

"He was just walking to school. It was the first time he was going alone."

"Well, I happen to have it on good authority that there are no registered sex offenders on this island, and if we have any serious weirdos they must be on their meds."

"How do you know that?" I said.

"Because between Stella Maris Church, Deb's Zumba classes, my Bunko group, and the beauty parlor I hear everything. There are no secrets on Sullivans Island. Remember that."

"Like I have anything worth hiding?"

My voice had a definite edge to it. She became quiet for a few minutes.

"You know, sweetheart, you might find some value in yoga. They give all sorts of classes right over in Mount Pleasant. And meditation too."

"Yoga? Are you serious?" Was she implying I had lousy judgment? Would yoga straighten out my brain? Meditation? Really? I could feel the heat rising in the back of my neck, and she knew that now I really *was* getting pissed.

"Yes, I'm serious! It's supposed to be very good for your stress levels, and Lord knows, honey, you've got a lot on your plate right now."

"And you think I'm not handling it very well. Is that right?"

"No! Good heavens, Jackie! Don't get on your high horse with me! I'm on *your* side!"

I could see Charlie approaching us. I wasn't going to let him catch me bickering with my mother. That would be poor form, as I did not allow him to bicker with me.

"You're probably right. I should look into it. Who knows?"

"There, that's my girl. Oh, look! Here come Charlie and his furry friends! I have to get them water. Try and see how they smell, will you, dear? I'll be right back."

Mom went inside to the kitchen, and I held the screen door open for Charlie and the dogs.

"Can I bring them in? Really? Glam said it was okay?"

"Only on the porch, kiddo. They have to stay out here. But it's shady and cool so they should be fine."

Charlie led them in, unhooked their leashes, wound them up, and put them on the trestle table. Before he could finish pouring a glass of water for himself, Stella and Stanley had already curled up on the floor. They smelled salty and earthy, as dogs coming in from the beach are supposed to smell.

"Whew!" he said after draining his glass. "These dogs have a lot of energy!"

"But you had fun, right?"

"I had a total blast! Oh! There are some kids having a sand castle–building contest down the island. I'm gonna go back and see what they're doing. But I think I'm going to get in the hammock first. You know, catch my breath."

He plopped himself into the hammock with such force that it was only by God's holy grace that he didn't flip over and land on the floor of the porch, knock out his teeth, and break his nose.

"Whew! They love to run!" He stuck his foot out to push off from the porch bannister. "I'll go check them out later."

"Who?"

"The kids. The ones with the contest."

"Right. Well, when you go, let me know. I might take a walk with you."

"Sure! Okay!"

Mom came back out carrying two plastic food storage containers of water and put them down on the floor next to our new charges. They looked up at her gratefully and rose to have a drink, slurping so loudly that we all laughed.

Already bored with swinging in the hammock, Charlie got out and made an announcement. "I'm gonna go put on my bathing suit, and then I'm gonna go see what those kids are doing."

Mom looked at me, and I looked at her. She could see that I was getting extremely nervous, and then it struck me. I had inherited her nerves! What? Could it be? It was the worst possibility of the gene pool come to life. The thing I hated, no, *despised* about her was now present in *me*! Well, I wasn't going to let anyone see me sweat. Especially them.

"Of course, Charlie! You go ahead and have a good time! But don't go in the water. And if you do, don't go over your knees. Is that a deal?"

"Your mother's right, Charlie. You might get stung by a jellyfish. It's almost August, you know, and jellyfish come in great swarms during the A months."

"Wow," he said, considering the news. Then he saluted us. "Aye, aye, captains!" He ran inside to change.

"Thanks for backing me up there, Mom."

"I've always got your back, baby."

"I know, I know. It's just that I couldn't live if anything ever happened to him. I just couldn't stand it. Did you ever worry about me like that?"

"Are you kidding? Worse. The first time you went on a date in a car with a boy I had to take five milligrams of Valium and a strong drink of gin. Maybe two. Then I went to bed and made your daddy stay up to listen for you."

"Really?"

"Yes, really. And how do you think it was for me when you went into a war zone?"

"But Mom, that's my passion. And I'm trained to handle it. You know that. Besides, I Skyped with Jimmy and Charlie every chance I had. You knew I was safe."

"Yes, I know. But what I'm saying to you is that there will never be a time that you don't worry about Charlie. Just as there will never be a time when I don't worry about you. It's the very nature of motherhood. And sometimes it's really hard to deal with it because you know you sound like an old fool to everyone who hears your concerns. The good news is that it's normal."

"And the bad news is that it never stops."

"That's right. But you get used to it. And the older he gets, the less you'll panic."

"Because he'll get smarter?"

"No, because he won't be home with you. He'll be away at college and then out into the world, and hopefully he'll find a nice girl who will fret and wring her hands over him. Then you'll have someone else besides me to share your burden."

"But then they'll marry and have children."

"Yes, and another generation of people to obsess over will come into your life. Isn't that awful?"

"Oh, Mom." We smiled at each other then.

"It's just how it is, baby. It's just the way it goes."

"I guess. Anyway, sometimes everything seems to conspire against you, doesn't it?"

She looked at me hard, and then she refilled our glasses. Just then Charlie came running through the screen door in the crazy board shorts Mom bought for him and Stella and Stanley jumped up.

"You can't come, guys!" he said to them. "It's after ten!"

Apparently the dogs understood English and they returned to their spots, curling up on the floor, resigned to their incarceration, which was still better than staying home alone.

He was about to leave when I stopped him.

"Young man?"

He screeched to a halt, complete with sound effects, and backed up. "Yes, ma'am?"

"Sunscreen? Towel? T-shirt?"

"Uh . . . do I really need that stuff?"

"Well, no," Mom said nonchalantly, "but only if you don't mind getting skin cancer. Or having sand inside your bathing suit in a terrible place. Didn't I buy you a beach towel?"

"It's nearly a hundred degrees!" I said. "You don't want to fry yourself, do you? Sunburns hurt like the devil, remember?"

"Uh . . . be right back!"

He ran back inside, slamming the screen door.

"Don't slam—" we called out, and before we could add "the door" he called out, "Sorry!"

Mom and I shook our heads with a smile.

"He seems to be having fun today," Mom said.

"Yeah, he does. I was surprised to see him wearing that swimsuit. He's usually so conservative."

"All the boys wear them," she said.

She was right. They did. The pattern of one boy's bathing suit was wilder than the next.

He came back through the porch again, not slamming any doors, white traces of sunscreen all over his face and arms and a towel over his shoulder. I had a vision of what he would look like at sixteen, and my heart tightened for the briefest moment.

"I'll probably be back in an hour," he said.

"What station are you going to?" I said.

"Just Twenty-six."

"Well, come home for lunch," I said. "Have fun!"

"Look out for sharks and jellyfish!" Mom called out as Charlie disappeared over the dunes.

"Sharks and jellyfish. Great," I said.

"Well, where else would they be? It is the ocean, you know."

"It's just one more thing to worry—"

"Jackie, sweetheart, listen to your old momma. I've done a lot of living, and I've learned a few things in my day."

I was about to be on the receiving end of her wisdom, which would most likely prove useless, as it usually was. I don't mean that to sound disrespectful, but my mother and I were two completely different people.

"Listen to me, here's something to think about. You know how you can lie awake at night worrying about something that seems so terrible but then in the morning it seems like just about nothing?"

"Well, some of the time that's true but not always." She was right again.

"Well, holding in worriation is stupid. You staying up at night for no good reason. Sometimes if you just say the thing that's got you all scared it's not as bad as you thought it was. I mean, the telling of your troubles can lessen them. That's why shrinks make so much money."

"Boy, is that the truth. Look, beyond the obvious, that is to say my widowhood and my fatherless child, there's the business of my commission with the army. I'm not reenlisting because I have to take care of Charlie. And even if I go back to work stateside again, who's going to take care of him? Maureen? I mean, I can only impose on her so much."

"You can impose on me," she said quietly.

I caught my breath and actually gasped. "What do you mean? That I should move back *here*?"

"Why not?"

"Well, in the first place, Charlie would have to change schools, and he's got his friends, you know?"

"Kids adapt."

I was quiet. Kids were the most resilient members of the human race. But was I ready?

"Yeah, but then what would I do with myself?"

"Jackie, there are so many places that need good nurses right now that it's not funny. What about the VA hospital? You could take care of wounded men and women coming home from Afghanistan."

"Maybe."

"Who would better understand their stories than someone who had been there and seen it all firsthand? Why not volunteer over there to check it out?"

"Maybe. I don't know. But, Mom? I just can't see it. I mean, I can't see my future right now. I can't *see* me here. Remember when I was a little girl? I could always see the next steps coming. Like riding a train, going down the track from one station to the next. All I had to do was look out of the window and see the changes coming. Right now I can't see anything."

"It's okay, hon. You just need some time."

"Look, Mom, I know you always thought I was crazy to make some of the choices I made, and I might have been, but I always chose the future I could see. And now I can't have it anymore. It's all been taken away from me. What did I do to deserve to lose everything?"

"Oh sweetheart," she said, "you didn't lose everything."

"I lost the love of my life," I said, choking up, and a few traitorous tears slid down my cheek.

"Yes, and it probably won't help to hear this at this particular moment, but you *had* the love of your life. Most people never do."

She reached into her pocket and handed me a tissue. She always seemed to have a tissue when I needed one.

"Well, now I don't know what to do," I said and blew my nose. "I'm sorry. I promised myself I wasn't going to cry anymore."

"Oh, screw that, honey. That's a dumb vow. I'm your momma, and you can cry with me anytime you feel like it. And you and Charlie are welcome to stay here for as long as you'd like."

"At some point I have to enroll Charlie in school for the fall."

"Jackie, try to trust the good Lord a little more. You know this yourself: one door has to close for another one to open. Maybe the good Lord really does have a plan for you."

"Maybe. Maybe I should drive up to Daddy's and see what he thinks."

"Fine. That's probably a good idea. You leave Charlie with me. He can go next time. And do a favor for me, will you?"

"Sure."

"Ask Mr. Britt if he still considers himself to be married?"

"What? Oh, no! That's not for me to ask! That's your business!"

"Humph! That man," she said and stood up. "Well, would you look out there?"

Over the low dunes she had spotted Charlie, building a sand castle that was already above his knees. Three other kids were watching from the sidelines until he waved them over. The next thing we knew, they were digging and adding height to his creation, and then they began to dig a moat all around it. As soon as the moat was finished, they dug a channel to the water's edge, which, as soon as their digging met the water, filled with water over and over as the remains of each incoming wave trickled in. We stood there watching as they dripped bits of mud all over the castle, making it look like the melted wax that made its way down the side of a candle stuck in the neck of a Chianti bottle. Over and over they dripped handfuls of mud until it was all covered. They stuck a piece of tall grass into the top and attached shells to its sides. At last they stood back to admire their work. Then they all ran to the water to rinse away the sand.

"He's having a wonderful time," I said.

"Um-hum," she said. "He sure is."

"I know what you're thinking," I said.

"Really? Tell me what I'm thinking."

"That he can't do this in Brooklyn."

"I never even had an inkling of such a thought," she said, lying like a professional right through her rosy red lips. "Don't you think he's hungry by now? Should we make sandwiches for all of them?"

My mother had hit the first of many, many home runs.

The afternoon continued like that, with Charlie and his new friends devouring peanut butter and jelly sandwiches, juice boxes, and so many green grapes I knew I'd have to go to the store before supper. They ran up to the house to use the bathroom and then back to the beach, after giving Stanley and Stella a cursory scratch and a few words. His new friends were three siblings from Greenville, renting a house just two houses on the other side of ours. They seemed awfully nice, and for once I didn't worry about who their parents were and what they did for a living. I didn't have to because the youngest, a boy named Jojo, told us all we could ever want to know about his family. His momma was a history professor at Furman University and his daddy was a lawyer who specialized in bankruptcy law, which, according to Jojo, was quite lucrative these days.

"He's rolling in it," Jojo offered.

"Is that so?" I asked, watching him polish off the last cookie in the house.

"What's he rolling in, hon?" Mom asked.

"Why, dough! Duh. What else do grown-ups roll in?"

I looked at my mother and she looked at me, and we knew it was probably best not to tell the little darling that grown-ups roll in lots of things.

For many reasons, I was so glad that Charlie had found some nice kids to play with for the afternoon. Between the dogs and the Greenville contingent, the mood was profoundly lighter. Before long, Dr. Steve's hot little bachelor car was pulling up into his driveway. By that time Charlie was showered and reading a comic book and we had all assembled on the porch to welcome the close of what had turned out to be a steaming hot but perfectly lovely day.

"You'd probably better take Stella and Stanley home," I said. "Dr. Steve is going to wonder where they are."

"Aw, let the guy go through his mail, don't you think?" Charlie said.

Go through his mail, indeed. Charlie didn't feel like getting up. But before I could tell him to move it, there came Steve through the oleanders. He looked a little tired.

"He's coming over," I said. "Should I set up the bar?"

My mother leapt from her chair, almost taking flight to her dressing room. "What? Oh! I have to brush my hair! I must look awful! Where's my lipstick? Quick! Jackie! Get a bottle of wine and some glasses!"

She was gone. I didn't need another single sign to know my mother had feelings for Steve.

"Hi, Jackie," Steve said, opening our screen door and stepping on to the porch, looking at me, wondering what I looked like naked. God, some men were so easy to read. But his look still caught me off guard. Mom liked Steve. Steve wondered about me. It gave me the creeps.

Sorry, but when I got to Murrells Inlet, I was telling my father. I didn't want to start trouble, but my poor mother had been lonely long enough. If you asked me.

8

. . . ascending the high grounds . . . Legrand led the way with decision; pausing only for an instant . . . to consult what appeared to be certain landmarks of his own contrivance upon a former occasion.

In this manner we journeyed for about two hours . . .

—Edgar Allan Poe, "The Gold-Bug"

Annie

It was early, I had just returned from my early beach walk with Deb, and I was grating a growing mountain of extra-sharp cheddar cheese into my biggest mixing bowl. The day was so still it could have been postapocalyptic. Even the bugs weren't chirping, and honey, when the bugs quit chirping you'd better be looking for a piece of shade! We were in for a scorcher. Life didn't sit so well with me when the thermometer climbed over ninety-five, especially when the humidity was high too. I could practically feel Spanish moss growing in between my toes. But Deb? Nothing seemed to ever bother Deb. You couldn't do anything about the weather, she always said, so it was better to worry about other things. Maybe I should take a page out of her playbook.

I'll tell you, that woman was just a bundle of energy, and she had such a positive outlook about everything. I mean, if my husband was as peculiar as hers I don't know that I wouldn't be lacing his oatmeal with little doses of arsenic. But Deb wouldn't mash a bug. She was nothing but goodness through and through. Wait. My husband *was* peculiar. I mean, isn't it peculiar enough to qualify as peculiar if you leave your wife of how many years without telling her if you're ever coming back? All he does is send money and show up stag for disasters.

I imagine some women would envy my position. Some might even say it was a perfect marriage. There's always cash in the bank, not a bottomless supply but enough to get along nicely. I don't have to make dinner unless I feel like it. I don't have to do his laundry. I don't have to clean up his mess. No snoring. No freezer filled with nothing but fish and fish bait . . .

This internal litany of bonus points continued until I noticed that Jackie had come into the room.

"Oh! Morning! There's coffee," I said. "You feel like an omelet or French toast or what?"

"I'm good," she said and took a mug from the cabinet. "I think I'm just going to have a bowl of cereal."

She gave me a peck on the cheek, filled her mug, and went to the pantry to forage.

"There are bananas in the wire basket. Have one. It's expected to hit a hundred degrees before noon. You need the potassium in hot weather. And don't you roll your eyes at me. Bad girl."

"Sorry. But how do you know I rolled my eyes? I'm facing the shelves."

"Because I know you. Don't you know when Charlie rolls his eyes? How'd you sleep?"

"You have enough food in here to feed us for a year. I slept like the proverbial dead. I don't know what it is but when my head hits the pillow . . . must be the salt air."

"Or the curative powers of being in your mother's home? Hmmm? The Salty Dog?"

"That's probably it," she said and smiled at me. "What are you making?"

"I'm making a pimento cheese ball. Remember those? You take grated cheese, mayonnaise, a little garlic powder, cayenne, and onion and then you mush it together with chopped pimentos into a baseball and roll it in pecan pieces? Yummy!"

"Is somebody coming over?"

"Not that I know of, but I was so embarrassed last night when Steve came in and we didn't even have any kind of cocktail food besides stale peanuts. I just don't want to get caught empty-handed again."

"Oh, Lord. Please don't tell me that he's going to be coming over here every single night. I mean, I didn't come the whole way down here to look at his face every five minutes. Not to be rude or anything—"

"I *don't* expect that he'll be over here all the time. And these cheese balls can last until Christmas. Which, speaking of Steve, we'd better get Charlie up. It's dog time."

Did she really think she was going to dictate who came and went and how often?

I pointed to the kitchen wall clock that, in addition to offering the minute and hour of the day, depicted a scene from Napa Valley that Deb gave me for my birthday a few years ago after, you guessed it, a trip to learn about California wines. Now, that's someplace I might like to go, I mean a destination over the causeway that's worth the effort.

"Righto. I'll be right back."

She hesitated and then did not pour the milk over her cereal, which I took to mean that she was going to walk Charlie over to Steve's again. I was right. Before she left the house I called her over to the side to have a private word. "Look to see something for me, will you? I have a bet going with Deb, and you're the only one who can settle it."

"Look to see what?"

"Boxers or Superman. Just take a fast look."

"What? What are you saying? Gross! I can't do that, Mom! Besides, Charlie is like right there under my feet."

"Right! Okay. Wait. I knew that. Okay. Check the hamper! Just take a quick peek."

"You and Deb are terrible. I'll do no such thing."

"Yes, you will."

"How do you know?"

"Because now you want to know too!"

She looked at me with the strangest expression and said, "If you think I care for one split second what kind of underwear another man wears, then you don't know anything about my marriage to Jimmy."

I thought, Oh Lord, here we go again. This was my Jackie, who might have slept hard but hadn't slept well, and it was too early in the morning to canonize anyone.

"Jackie? Sweetheart? You've got a little chip on your shoulder. I know you adored Jimmy and that you always will. I loved him too. He was a wonderful husband and father."

"Sorry, I don't know what is the matter with me."

"All right, then. Let's not worry about this anymore. What's twenty dollars? I bet on boxers."

"You bet *twenty dollars* on Steve's u-trou?"

I nodded. "I know. Pretty silly."

"I'm not letting you lose twenty dollars. If it's boxers, I get ten."

"Done!" I said and we shook on it.

Sometime during the next half hour, they went next door, Jackie clinging to her coffee mug and Charlie rushing ahead. I watched as Charlie bolted from Steve's house like a shot fired down the beach with Stella and Stanley, the dogs' tongues flailing in the wake of their own breeze. Yes, I stood on the porch watching him, waiting for Jackie to return, thinking how I loved seeing my grandson running so fast, going where Steve's beautiful pets would lead him. I wished I could see Charlie like that every day for the rest of my life. Carefree. So young. So beautiful. I wished I could somehow freeze that moment in time and put it in my pocket like a talisman that would always bring me a moment of happiness.

Finally, when Charlie was long out of sight, Jackie climbed our steps and came in.

"You owe me ten bucks," she said.

"Yay! We're rich. Hey, I thought of something. How will Deb know we're not lying?"

"I took a picture with my phone. See?"

She clicked here and there on the keypad of her cell phone, and suddenly there was a picture of men's boxer shorts. In living Black Watch tartan color. So? He had a thing for Scotland too? Another thing we had in common.

"My. My! You're a genius, Jackie. Glory! I'll tell you one thing," I said, "technology is a marvelous thing."

"Sometimes it is and sometimes it isn't. I'll print it for you."

I had no idea what she meant by her comment, but I was fast learning that when it came to anything technical beyond my laptop, it was best for me to simply nod my head.

By ten o'clock Jackie was on her way to Murrells Inlet and the breakfast dishes were humming away in the dishwasher. The dogs were curled up on the front porch, snoring softly, snoozing after their morning run, and Charlie was sitting at the kitchen table playing his electronic game, which had him so hypnotized that it irked me just as it irked Jackie.

"So, old fellow? What shall we do today? Would you like to go on a picnic?"

"A picnic? To where?"

"Well, wherever you'd like to go. I was thinking we might take the ferry out to Bulls Island. Or maybe we'd just have us a walk out to the back beaches and I can show you millions of little fiddler crabs and how they dance. What do you think? Or we could save the picnic for another day and just go to Poe's Tavern. They make pretty good fish tacos."

"You mean Poe like that guy you were telling me about?"

"*That guy* indeed. I can see I'm going to wind up having to buy you the T-shirt."

"Awesome! Let's go there."

"Only if we walk there on the beach?" It was just too hot to walk on the street.

"That's cool with me."

"All right, then. Give me about half an hour, and then we'll meander our way down the island and see what we find."

I attended to some household business, namely doing a load of laundry, running a dust cloth across the furniture, and wiping down the bathrooms. Then I consolidated all the garbage and had Charlie haul it out to the bins.

"Make sure you always close the tops tight! Raccoons!"

"Got it!" he called back to me.

Then there was the boring business of recycling. I began gathering up all the magazines, and don't you know that right away I put my hand on the issue of *Southern Living* that ran the profile article on the makeover queen of Charleston? Fate! I immediately sat down and flipped to the page: "Margaret Donaldson Makes Miracles!" The subtitle read "Look Ten Years Younger!" I tore the article out and put it aside. Not that I had an apostle's faith in that sort of thing, but as soon as I had a private moment, I was going to call Margaret the Miracle Maker and give her the challenge of her career. I wasn't all *that* possessed by my appearance (okay, maybe I fussed over myself more than the average girl), but I wouldn't mind if, on occasion and in the right lighting, people took Jackie and me to be sisters. Maybe that was asking too much. Or not. But I definitely needed a haircut. Well, we'd see what she said.

It wasn't long until Charlie and I were walking the beach. I brought along a plastic bag from the Bi-Lo grocery store in case he found shells or coral or anything else that he wanted to bring home. Now, I worried about my carbon footprint with the best of the tree huggers out there and did not use plastic bags as a general rule, but tossing some salty wet carcass into my canvas tote bag, a premium I received from a donation I'd made to the Spoleto Festival, would have ruined it, as would a package of chicken that dripped water and traces of blood.

When we finally reached Poe's Tavern, it was bulging with people, locals and tourists. Charlie was as quickly sucked into people watching as I was. Every kind of person in the world was there. Pretty young girls in sweet sundresses had his attention, and so did the teenaged girls who seemed to be showing too much bosom and bottom for my money.

"Your mother never dressed like that," I said. "I would have killed her."

Charlie covered up his mouth with his hand and giggled. "I'll bet!"

After waiting for fifteen minutes or so we got a table, and as soon as he was finished reading the menu, he was ready to talk. I, on the other hand, was feeling indecisive and had already drained my glass of water.

"What should I have, Charlie?"

The waitress, or maybe they call them servers these politically correct nowadays, stepped up to our table, refilled my water, and rattled off some specials. I looked at Charlie, shook my head, and shrugged my shoulders.

"She's gonna have the Annabel Lee burger, and I'd like to have the Gold-Bug chicken sandwich with a side of fries, Edgar's Drunken Chili, and extra cheddar cheese. And we'd like some chips and salsa for the table. And extra ketchup? And a Diet Coke. Whatcha drinking, Glam?"

"Why, I think I'd like a Diet Coke too!" I sat back in my chair and looked at my grandson, who had just simply stunned me by the way he'd just taken over. "Heavens!"

"I'll get that order right in for y'all," our server said and scurried away.

"Charlie! I have to say you sure handled that one. How did you know I liked the Annabel Lee sandwich?"

"Because it's a pretty name and you like pretty things. Besides, someone had to be the man, and I was the only man at the table. So tell me some more about Poe."

"Well, I have to tell you, Charlie, your momma isn't so keen on me dwelling on Mr. Poe with you. She thinks he's too creepy."

"My mother treats me like a baby," he said. "If she ever read my comics she'd probably faint. They're as scary as all you-know-where."

"I see. And this you-know-where would be some-place that's even hotter than this island today? Mercy!"

"Exactly! Anyway, she worries way too much about every single little thing."

"Look, even though your momma is a grown up with a son who's a big boy, she's still my baby and I worry about her all the time. It's the number one spe-cialty of mothers all over the world."

"Well, tell me about Poe, and I promise to downplay it with Mom. How's that?"

I narrowed my eyes at him and clenched my jaw. Could he be trusted with the really dark and sinister material? Absolutely not.

"All right," I said against the advice of that nagging little voice in my head that told me I was heading for trouble. "In 1827, he was stationed here at Fort Moultrie for thirteen months under another name."

"What name?"

"Edgar Allan Perry."

"Why did he use a fake name?"

"Well, no one is really sure about that, but usually when somebody uses a fake name, it's because they want to avoid discovery. And Edgar was extremely poor and in debt, so I imagine he was trying to elude his creditors."

Over a basket of warmed nacho chips and salsa verde, we discussed Edgar's brief military history and why he'd grown up with such a thorny personality.

"Apparently it didn't take too much to get his temper going," I said.

"Having a bad temper gets you nowhere fast," Charlie said.

"Yes. You're right. How do you know these things?"

"They're what my dad always used to say."

We ate our lunch and I tried to stick to the topic of Poe, but it was clear that Charlie's mind was wandering as he ate.

"We could talk about Poe long into the night because there's so much to know about him and his work. But why don't we tackle his famous cryptograms?"

"What's a cryptogram? Do you want a bite of chili?"

"Sure. Thanks!" He pushed the bowl to my side of the table, and I scooped some out and put it on the side of my plate, thinking that chili with jalapeños might come back to haunt me. "It's like a puzzle you make up to do secret writing in code. For example, if you substituted numbers for the letters of the alphabet, using one for an A and two for a B, you could write a message in code. Like 'The treasure is buried under the magnolia tree!'"

"Wow! That's more fun than writing computer code, that's for sure!"

"What do you mean, computer code?"

"You know, Glam, you use it to write a program for your computer."

"Oh, *that* computer code! Oh yes, of course." The child appeared to be speaking English, but I had no idea what he was talking about. "Anyway, cryptograms, buried treasure, and the famous Captain Kidd are at the heart of Poe's well-known story called 'The

Gold-Bug.' I think you're mature enough to read it, but the language is very old. It might be fun if we read it together. What do you think?"

"I think definitely! Didn't you tell me that we have a copy at home?"

"Oh, me! My brains are going to mush! Anyway, cutie, I have his complete works!"

"Sweet!"

"Yes, it's pretty sweet. Poe was a dark and deeply peculiar little man, and many people thought he was crazy."

"Maybe he was. This is so good!"

"Good! Well, actually at the end of his life he was completely mad. Most people thought he lost his mind due to excessive alcohol, but just recently they found out he had a brain tumor the size of a lemon."

"How'd they find that out?"

It was simply impossible to talk about Poe without going to the macabre.

"Well, they exhumed his corpse to give it a more prestigious location in the graveyard—"

"You mean, they dug him up?"

"Uh, yes. Gross, right?"

"Uh, duh!"

"Well, it's just too bad that he was never recognized as the genius he was during his lifetime." I was trying to switch the conversation away from death to the achievements of Poe's life.

"Neither was my dad."

I heard a crack in his voice and looked down to see his eyes filling up with tears. So I stopped, leaned over, and put my hand on the side of his face. I could feel the heat of his distress.

"Baby, it's okay to be sad. Tell me how your daddy was a genius."

"Because he could do anything and anything he did, he did it so great."

Charlie spoke quietly, so quietly that I could barely hear him. Obviously he didn't want to make a scene, but he couldn't hold back his tears either. Bless the little fellow's heart. Bless his dear sweet heart.

"And he knew what I was thinking before I even said it. And he could read Mom's mind too."

"That's because he loved you and your momma so very much, Charlie. His mind was perfectly in tune with y'all's." Big tears flooded his face. I reached up my sleeve and produced a tissue. I held it over his nose and said, "Blow!"

Charlie blew so loudly that he honked like a goose.

"Glory be!" I said.

He laughed then, looked up at me with those impossible eyes of his, and said, "I just miss him, you know?"

"I know, sweetheart, I know."

I paid the bill and bought him a T-shirt with the likeness of Poe on the front. Charlie was thrilled. On the way out of the restaurant we spotted the family from Greenville.

"Hey! Y'all going to the beach later?" Charlie said. "I got the T-shirt!" He waved it in the air.

"Oh, great," their father said, "now I get to buy three!"

"See you later at Twenty-six!" they said in a chorus.

As soon as we left the restaurant and were back on the beach he stopped, pulled off the T-shirt he was wearing, and pulled the new one over his head.

"How do I look?" he said.

"Don't you want me to wash it first?"

"Wash it? What for?"

"Oh, never mind. Let's get moving. It's already two o'clock. What do you think you might like for dinner? Do you still like fried flounder?"

"Love it! Can you still make hush puppies?"

"I imagine I can!"

We walked together but at a distance from each other. Charlie was too old to hold hands, and even if he'd wanted to there was a certain self-awareness about him that was surprising for his age yet would have prevented him from doing anything that smacked of *babyish*. I'd never raised a boy, and perhaps that was normal. He had mentioned again that he felt like Jackie treated him like a baby. Pulling away was part of growing up. That was true enough. At least he wasn't too old to be tucked in at night or too old to be read to by his grandmother. That was welcome evidence that his childhood still existed.

I watched as he stopped now and then to examine something that had washed ashore. He'd lift a specimen from the sand, give it a hard look, and if it was broken he'd hurl it high into the air, over the dunes. If it was worthy of his growing collection of found artifacts, he would bring it to me to put in the bag.

"Is this a conch shell?" he asked.

"Actually, it's a whelk. But it's a very nice one. Should we bring it home?"

"Definitely! What kind of a whelk is it?"

He thought he had me on that one.

"Well, it's a knobbed whelk. The Latin name is *Busycon carica*. And you can tell it's a knobbed whelk by its coloration but also by the nine little knobs on the shoulder of its body whorl. See? Count them."

He touched each one with the tip of his finger and counted. "Yup. There're nine all right."

"So how do you like them apples? Does your Glam-ma continue to dazzle her perfect grandson?"

"Uh, yeah! Wow! Did you like study shells or something?"

"I guess so. I mean, not in school but on my own. I like to know these things."

"Me too," he said.

"I'll give you a shell guide when we get home," I said.

"Cool," he said and ran off to see what else he could find.

I couldn't get his tears out of my mind. Of course he missed his father. What he didn't know was that he always would and that in all those important moments that were yet to come to pass in his life, there would be a searing wound. Over time the wound would grow smaller, but it would never disappear. Jimmy would never see Charlie graduate, become an adult, and marry. Jimmy would never know Charlie's children. He would never be there to herald Charlie's successes or to offer comfort or advice when it was needed. No, Jimmy was gone and Charlie had been robbed. People believed, and I had also been brought up to believe, that there was a Heaven and someday we would be reunited with our loved ones. Well, that's nice, but death tears a hole in your life and losing someone you love is horrible. Especially for a child.

I hoped then that Jackie would marry again. Although she was understandably in the worst frame of mind possible to even slightly entertain the notion. I got *that* message almost every time we spoke. Lord, she was so restless and churlish, but I imagine she just couldn't help herself. The entire life that she and Jimmy had built had just imploded. She needed a lot of time to adjust. Maybe she had a bit of post-traumatic stress disorder. That made sense.

I hoped she was having a good visit with Buster up in Murrells Inlet. He would help her heal. He was really a precious old devil when he wanted to be, and God knew, he had a sweet spot for his daughter. Wasn't he the one she'd called crying? This was not the time for stories about me and Mr. Sea Hunt; it was about getting Jackie back on solid emotional ground. Hopefully, Buster would sit her down and get her to talk. She needed to unburden herself of her grief and every single other thing she was worried about. Maybe the reason she wasn't telling me much was that she didn't want me to see her as weak.

When I reached the house, Charlie had already gone inside, having sprinted the last hundred yards. It must have been a thousand degrees then, because if even the slightest amount of blazing hot white sand slipped into my sneaker, it burned. I stayed alive (slight exaggeration) by thinking of a cool shower and a nice big glass of iced water.

I pushed open the screen door. Charlie was on his knees on the porch, hooking the dogs up to their leashes, and the telephone was ringing inside the house.

"Gotta take them out for a bathroom break," he said.

"Right! I'll get it," I said.

Be still, my heart, it was Dr. Steven Plofker on the caller ID.

"Hello?" I said as calmly as I possibly could.

"Hi! Annie? It's Steve. Am I catching you at a bad time?"

"Oh, heavens, no! What's going on?"

"Well, Mike Veeck, one of my patients who's covered in poison ivy welts and can't tolerate the sun for a few days, just gave me two tickets to the RiverDogs game for this afternoon. He's an owner of the team. And I thought, Why not? I don't have any appointments after four. And I wondered if Charlie might like to go with me? He told me how much he loves baseball. Should I ask Jackie?"

"Sure, but Jackie's up in Murrells Inlet with her father, the man formerly known as The Husband. What time does the game start?"

"Let me see here. Um, it looks like it starts at five. And according to my Mike, one of his other partners, Bill Murray, is supposed to be at this game."

"Really! Well, I'm sure Charlie would love to go!"

"Great! Tell him to be ready at four thirty. I'll pick him up."

"That's awfully sweet of you, Steve."

"Hey, I'm a sweet guy, and besides, what fun is a ball game without a kid?"

"You're right! I'll make sure he's ready. And Steve?"

"Yeah?"

"Thanks for thinking of Charlie."

"Sure. See you soon."

I went out to the front porch and once again filled my eyes with a beautiful scene of Charlie at play with Steve's dogs. I wished then, as I had secretly wished so many times since their arrival, that Jackie and Charlie would stay forever. Shouldn't families be near each other? New York had had its chance with them, and I deeply believed I was entitled to a turn. Jackie needed me, didn't she? And wasn't Charlie just blooming? In no time at all, he was turning as brown as a berry, not that I'd ever eat a brown berry but I'm pretty sure that's how the saying goes. Anyway, why wouldn't you want to surround yourself with people who loved you?

He was heading back toward the house. I couldn't wait to tell him the news. "Hey! Guess what?" I held the screen door open for him to come inside.

"What?"

"You're going to a RiverDogs baseball game with Dr. Steve!"

"I am? When?"

"In about two hours. And guess what else?"

"What?"

"Bill Murray is going to be there! You do know who Bill Murray is, don't you?"

"Duh! *Ghostbusters, SNL,* and *Groundhog Day* Bill Murray?"

"The one and only."

"What's he doing there?"

"Well, apparently he has some money invested in the team."

"Do you think I could get his autograph?"

I could almost see Charlie's heart pounding against the face of Edgar Allan Poe on his shirt.

"Well, I don't know, but I'm sure if you asked Dr. Steve he might be able to figure that out. And Mr. Murray is supposed to be a prince of a guy. He's got kids."

"How do you know that?"

"Because, Little Mr. Inquisitive, he used to live down the island."

"*What?* Are you serious?"

"I never lie! Now, go get a shower."

"Oh, my Lord!" I like to think the young one exclaimed in a prayer of Thanksgiving. "This is the coolest vacation ever!"

Steve was prompt, Charlie was ready, and the dogs were happy to see Steve.

"Y'all are so spoiled!" he told his dogs.

"They're delightful!" I lied.

"Sorry about reading 'The Gold-Bug' together, Glam. We can start tomorrow?" Charlie said as he pushed his hair back from his face. "I got a little pad of paper, just in case, you know, in case we see him."

"See who?" Steve asked.

"Bill Murray," I said.

"Well, we'll likely see him if he's there because we're sitting in the owners' box."

"I'm gonna faint," Charlie said.

"Don't faint," Steve said. "So you're reading 'The Gold-Bug'? That's a tough one."

"That's why we are going to read it together," I said.

"Use my e-reader," Steve said. "It's probably public domain. You can download it in, like, two seconds and when you don't know the meaning of a word you just highlight it and it gives a definition. Couldn't be easier to read old books and classic works. I'll leave it on the table for you tomorrow morning. How's that?"

"Awesome!"

"We'd better get going, or we'll miss the opening pitch!"

"We're outta here!" Charlie exclaimed. He opened the screen door and hung on it, waiting for Steve.

"What time do you think y'all will get home?" I said.

"Oh, probably by dark. Here's my cell number if you need us."

Steve reached into his wallet and handed me his card.

I started getting nervous then. What if Charlie got lost in the crowd?

"Oh, no worries! Y'all just go have fun! Behave yourself, young man! And make sure you don't lose sight of Steve for one minute. You know how crazy crowds can get."

"Don't worry, Annie. I'll keep an eye on him the whole time. Should I take Stella and Stanley home?"

"Oh, no. They're so comfortable here. And they're good company."

They left and I thought, Oh, hells bells, Jackie is going to come home and kill me dead. And she just about did. She came waltzing in around seven thirty, just as I was sliding a nice piece of flounder into the grease.

"Hey! You hungry?" I asked, trying to sound like Mrs. Blithe Spirit. "I've got a ton of flounder."

"Sure. I'll just go wash up. Where's Charlie?"

"Oh, Jackie! The most wonderful thing happened!" I had practiced the story over and over since Charlie and Steve left. "Steve had tickets to the RiverDogs game to sit in the owners' box with Bill Murray! Isn't that grand? Charlie was beside himself with excitement! They should be home any time now because the game started at five."

"You did what?"

"I told you—"

"You told me you let my only child go off alone with a near-perfect stranger and you didn't even call me to ask if I thought that was all right?"

"He's not a stranger, Jackie. I know Steve very well, and he has a wonderful reputation. Pristine, in fact. There's no reason to think that there's a thing to worry about."

"Really? What if something *does* happen to him?"

"Since when don't you think you can trust your own mother's judgment? Now, you go wash your hands and come back in here and apologize to me. I'm losing patience with your paranoia, Jackie. It's not right, and it puts unnecessary stress on Charlie."

Well, that shut her up for the moment. We ate dinner in relative silence until we heard the car door slam. Charlie came bursting into the room, practically floating.

"Guess what? The RiverDogs won by one point, I sat with Bill Murray the whole time, I have five of his autographs—I'm gonna sell four on eBay—and he gave me a T-shirt and a baseball and a hat and he signed them all!"

Steve was standing by the door smiling, pleased as punch that he had done a very nice thing for Charlie and that it had worked out so well. Jackie's face was bloodred with embarrassment.

"And I ate four hot dogs, I got to go in the dugout and meet the team, and then I threw up, but only once. And I'm fine now. And I'm starving. Is there any more fish?"

9

. . . the tulip-tree. . . . Embracing the huge cylinder, as closely as possible, with his arms and knees, seizing with his hands some projections, and resting his naked toes upon others, Jupiter, after one or two narrow escapes from falling, at length wriggled himself into the first great fork . . .

—Edgar Allan Poe, "The Gold-Bug"

Jackie

So spank me, I was wrong. My mother might be right. Maybe I am paranoid. So what? If she was in my situation, wouldn't she be a little freaked out? I think she would be. I'd seen children beaten to within an inch of their lives. Children who'd been raped. I'd seen atrocities so horrible that they registered in my mind as something I'd seen on a screen on film, not in real life. And listen, that said, I don't want to be that mother who won't let her kid go places until she has the life history and ten references on the person who wants to take him somewhere either. Pick up any newspaper. News flash!

The world is crawling with perverts! Clergy, coaches, and politicians! Who can you trust anymore? I know, I know, I overreacted. But sorry, anyone who doesn't believe horrible things happen to innocent children should spend some time in Kandahar. She should've given me a heads-up. I mean, that's just common courtesy. Isn't it?

It was barely six o'clock in the morning, but I was still smoldering, tossing and turning in my sheets and self-righteous indignation. I decided to get up, go out for coffee, and buy myself a copy of *The New York Times*. Maybe that would lighten my mood, to read some news from the big world out there, like maybe Jane Brody's health column. I'd always liked her so much, and since I'd been in the Middle East I'd missed a lot of other things that made it worth the expense and aggravation it took to live in a major metropolitan area like New York. Like great pizza and the chance to see the Statue of Liberty anytime I felt like it. The Macy's Day Parade on Thanksgiving morning and the Bronx Zoo. The Cyclone roller coaster on Coney Island, Chinatown, Little Italy, and so many other things and places . . . Central Park, Radio City and the Rockettes, on and on. It would kill my mother if I told her this, but I really loved New York.

Everyone was still sleeping, so I left a note on the kitchen table: "Gone out for a newspaper and a cappuccino. Be back soon. On my cell. Xx"

I got into my car and backed out of the yard, headed toward the Ben Sawyer Bridge. It was too early for the bookstore to be open and it was the only place I knew of that sold the *Times* in its café. So I went in the other direction, remembering Page's Okra Grill, where I could sit and read and amuse myself with the paper until a decent hour and a better mood rolled around. While I was in nursing school I'd spent hours there, studying for exams. I wondered what Dad would have to say about what Mom had done. Maybe I'd call him. He'd side with me. I was sure of it. Of course a great deal of planning had gone into how he was going to see Charlie without Mom going nuts. Mom was just going to have to suck it up.

I bought my paper, saw that Page's Okra Grill had moved to the location where Alex's used to be, and went there. I was getting reacquainted with Mount Pleasant whether I wanted to or not.

It was not even seven, but Page's already had customers. I went in and took a seat against the back wall at a table for two. The waitress, a mature woman whose name tag said LIBBY, was there in moments.

"Mornin', hon! Can I start you out with a cup of coffee?"

"Thanks."

She filled my mug and asked, "Juice?"

"No, thanks."

"Fine. Well, here's our menu. Have a look, and I'll be back in a few minutes."

I had no intention of ordering breakfast, preferring to eat later in the morning with Charlie, but after watching steaming plates of fluffy scrambled eggs and sausage patties pass within smelling distance, I was weakening to the point that if I didn't get some breakfast I was going to start crying. Well, not really crying, but I might whimper if the next plate going by wasn't for me.

"So, did y'all decide?"

"Yes. I'd like two eggs over easy, grits with no butter, sausage patties, and a biscuit with no butter."

Libby stared at me like *Who are you kidding? Have the butter.*

"Watching my cholesterol. You know. Gotta watch that stuff."

"Uh-huh. Well, would you rather have egg whites and turkey sausage?"

"No way. Isn't it enough that I gave up butter in my grits?"

"If you say so. I'm just pointing out the fact that you have options. Personally? I agree with you. You couldn't pay me folding money to eat turkey sausage.

Pretty little skinny thing like you doesn't have to worry about all that mess. You're too young!"

"I'm a nurse, and I've seen the horrors of blocked arteries."

"Oh. Well, I mix up my eggs in my grits so as I don't miss the butter."

"That's exactly what I'm intending to do. That's what we always did around here when I was a kid."

"Oh? You from east of the Cooper?"

"Yeah, I grew up on the island, but I've been gone for a long time."

We always said "the island" to mean Sullivans Island. If you were from the Isle of Palms you said "Isle of Palms," and more recently people had begun referring to it as the IOP.

"Uh-huh. I can hear a teensy bit of a Yankee accent, but that's okay. My ex-husband is a Yankee, and so are a lot of my friends."

"Well, that's nice." She didn't say it like "Some of my best friends are lepers," so I didn't take offense. "I've been living in Brooklyn for a dozen years."

"Oh, so you're here visiting?"

"Yeah, I just got out of the army."

"Oh! So you're an army nurse? Where did they send you?"

"Afghanistan."

"Afghanistan! Wow! Let me just put your order in, and I'll be right back. I want to hear this."

I poured two tiny containers of nondairy half-and-half into my coffee and stirred it, looking around at the scant population of early risers. Some were retired men who probably came here every morning to discuss whatever it is that old men discuss—health and money, I guessed. Some were tourists dressed in crazy outfits obviously on their way to an early-morning tee time. There was a table of two people, an older man and a younger man. The older man was being interviewed and it didn't look promising because the younger man looked very ill at ease. Some looked like construction workers, and others, older ladies, probably had doctor appointments or were on their way to the grocery store or to Mass. Everyone in the restaurant had a story, and I was sure that every story had its share of joy and pain, regrets and ambitions. I wondered what they thought my story was or if they wondered about me at all. One thing was certain about my mother's assessment of life: what my mother had done last night did not seem so horrible as the morning light continued to grow. Maybe the night brought out something feral in me that needed to howl at the moon. The night was when I thought about the enemy or any enemies of my family and what I wanted for us. I was good under the cover of night. Very good. Maybe I really was being overprotective of Charlie.

Libby returned with my biscuit and said, "The rest will be up in just a minute. So tell me, what in the world were you doing in Afghanistan?"

"Taking care of the injured and trying to understand the culture. Trying to figure out how to make it better for the women and children without getting our heads blown off."

"Wow. My ex-husband, Raymond, did four tours in Vietnam. He was a son of a bitch, between us girls. Came home as crazy as a loon."

Was I as crazy as a loon? I didn't think so. Just jittery.

"Yeah, boy. He got liquored up all the time and went down the dock to shoot fish with his hunting rifle. That wasn't any kind of a life for me! No, ma'am! So are you going back over?"

"I can't. I lost my husband last month, and I have to stay stateside because we have a son who's just ten."

"Oh, hon! That's terrible! I'm so sorry! Y'all still got family here?"

"Yeah, my mother. She's still on the island. And there's my dad, who's up in Murrells Inlet."

"Oh, they're divorced? I'm sorry. I always say I'm sorry when I hear news like that. I mean, maybe it is the best thing for them *both*, but it's still sad when families fall apart."

"Well, they're not divorced. They just can't seem to work out their differences. Not that they've tried very hard, that I know of anyway."

"And you'd like to see them back together, I imagine?"

"Of course. Who doesn't want their family to be intact and happy?"

"I hear you, darlin'! Let me go check on those eggs for you."

Libby returned a few minutes later, put the plate in front of me. I had inhaled my biscuit. She lingered as though there was something she wanted to say. When she couldn't seem to find her words, I spoke up. "So I guess you're divorced, then?" I cut into the egg white, scooped up some grits with it, and ate it. It was so damn delicious I couldn't believe it.

"Yeah, but it's all right. I met a nice guy. Mike is his name. You know, I was thinking, why don't you just tell your daddy he needs to come home? Daddies always listen to their little girls."

"Well, I'm not so little anymore, and I'm afraid I did something worse than that. I rode up to Murrells Inlet yesterday and told him that the man next door was flirting with Momma. He didn't like that much." I took a deep sip of my coffee and cut another bite of egg, letting the yolk fully integrate with the grits. I couldn't get it into my mouth fast enough. "Actually, the truth is that my momma's flirting with *him*. But you know, my dad's been gone for eleven years and I can't blame my mother, really."

Libby stood back and swallowed hard. Then she narrowed her eyes. "Hold on, sister. You *told* on your momma? You're kidding, right?"

"Well, it wasn't exactly like that. Besides, my mother is well, taking grandmotherly liberties with my son—"

"What do you mean—liberties?"

"*Oh, no!*" I could tell by the look on Libby's face that she had the completely wrong idea. "No, last night she let him go to a baseball game with a friend of hers. It was a RiverDogs game, and he went without my permission—"

"While you were off seeing your daddy?"

"Right."

"Wait a minute, you didn't even know all that when you were up the road telling your daddy about this man flirting with your momma, did you?" Libby's face was incredulous.

"No. I mean, you're right. One thing has nothing to do with the other."

"Uh-huh. You want a piece of advice from a tired sixty-three-year-old waitress who has seen it all?"

"Sure."

"Love your momma, honey, and try to treasure every minute you spend with her. Forgive her everything she does. She's not out to aggravate you. I'd give every last tooth I have left in my head to have my momma back for just ten minutes. I'm not lying either. She was the best friend I ever had, and well, I didn't know it until she was gone. Cried a river."

"Oh, I know she's my friend. I mean, I usually know. Just lately, things have been rough."

"I'm sure, losing your husband and all."

"Yeah, especially because he died in a fire. He was a fireman with the NYFD. Pretty gruesome."

"Great God in heaven! I'm gonna pray for your whole family. Oh, I'm just so sorry."

"Thanks." Why was I telling this old woman the story of my life? But, on an odd note, she was honestly moved by my story.

"Now, as far as your daddy and the man next door? Let the two roosters work that out. Listen to old Libby. I've seen it all. Don't get involved. Just sit back and see what happens. You done planted the seed."

She stepped away, got the coffeepot, came back, and refilled my mug. "I'm gonna get you another biscuit.

On the house. I saw them pulling fresh ones out of the oven a minute ago."

"Thanks," I said, thinking I couldn't swallow another bite.

But somehow I did, and that biscuit disappeared as well. I needed to join a gym.

The truth was that Charlie had not been kidnapped, that Steve Plofker was probably an extremely nice man, and that I was obviously a wall-licking lunatic when it came to Charlie's comings and goings. Old Libby might have made a donation of most of her molars to no purposeful end, but I knew she was right. And I needed to get a serious grip on my emotional judgment. This was the Lowcountry, for heaven's sake, and the last serious crime on Sullivans Island had been committed by some local breaking curfew by riding around on his golf cart after dark. And my mother was the most well-intentioned person I'd ever known. I mean, Aunt Maureen was great, but nobody loves you like your mother loves you. I needed to give her a break. I needed to give Aunt Maureen a call. And I needed to calm down.

When I got home, Charlie and Mom were just cleaning up the breakfast dishes.

"There's still coffee if you want some," she said, and I detected a chill in her personal atmosphere.

"Okay," I said. "Charlie, baby? Did you pull up your bed?"

"Uh—"

"So why don't you run and do that, and I'll help Glam finish up the dishes."

"Sure!" And he was off and running.

And at the same time I shouted, "Don't run in the house!" Mom mumbled, "I can do my own dishes, thank you."

She *was* annoyed.

"Mom, I'm really sorry about losing my temper with you last night. I don't know what in the world is the matter with me. You are so nice and so thoughtful, and I am the daughter from hell. Anyway, I'm sorry and I love you and I promise to try and, I don't know, control my temper. Are you still mad with me?"

I watched her shoulders rise as she held on to the side of the sink as though she needed it for balance. Then she turned her head to one side, looking out of the window. Finally, after what I imagined she thought was the appropriate amount of time to leave me dangling seemed to have passed, she turned to face me. Her face was resolute.

"Of course I'm not mad with you. You get your nasty disposition from your father's side of the family, although he is usually a pretty passive man. Way too passive, in fact. All that repressed anger is going to kill him one of these days. The Britts were always renowned for their hot tempers. Anyway, come here to me."

My mother put her arms around me and hugged me with all her might. "There now," she said, standing back and looking at me. "Have a little faith in me, Jackie. Let Charlie believe my judgment is the same as yours. Then you can relax a little more. And we can all enjoy our time together if we're not worrying about you losing your cool over every darn thing. Right?"

"I know. You're right."

"You know, it occurred to me this morning that you're probably used to a pretty rigorous exercise regime in the army and all. I mean, you're all muscle!"

"Yes. We worked out every day. It was good for stress."

"Aha! You see? That's what you need!" She reached in the pocket of her apron and pulled out a newspaper clipping. "Here, look at this. I cut this out from the *Moultrie News* for you. Kickboxing classes! You can go kick the, pardon my expression, *crap* out of something, and that's bound to make you feel better, don't you think?"

I hated to admit it, but I had been so foul-tempered since my arrival that it was becoming clear, even to me, that I needed some outlet for my anxiety. And to burn off those biscuits. Kickboxing might just be the ticket.

"I'll check it out."

"Good! Now tell me about your visit with your father."

"Well, it was good, you know? We hung out and talked, trying to figure out my future. For now he thinks I should go over to the VA hospital and volunteer. I think it's a brilliant idea. I can't just sit around like this all the time." I looked at my mother's face and wondered for a moment why she looked so stung. Then I remembered that she was the one who had suggested it in the first place. "Just as you suggested a few days ago."

The sting on her face dissolved into satisfaction. "Well, it's nice to see that he and I still agree on something!"

"Yeah. Anyway, I'm going to take a ride over there today and see what's going on. Do you want to go with me?"

"Oh, thanks, sweetheart, but I have so many things to do today. So tell me, what's his house like?"

"Dad's? You haven't been there?" Mom cocked her head to one side and looked at me. "No. Huh?"

"Hardly."

"Well, it's a new house, not particularly pretty, pretty drab in fact. And it's filled with blah furniture and a big-screen television. There's a nice front porch with a swing and a couple of rockers. But you can tell it's really just a man cave. There are no rugs or pretty towels. It's very basic. You wouldn't like it."

"Humph. I'm sure I wouldn't. But you had a good visit with him, I hope?"

"Yeah. It was really good."

"What did y'all talk about besides volunteering?"

"We talked about Charlie."

"I see. Well, that's good. I haven't told you this, but I have some news. I'm pretty excited about it."

"What?"

"Tomorrow I have an appointment with a woman named Margaret Donaldson downtown. She was all over *Southern Living* last month."

"Why?"

"Because she's going to bring my appearance into the twenty-first century. She's a makeover professional."

"Why in the world do you want a makeover? You look fine!"

"How would you like to look *just fine*? That sounds like someone wearing sensible cardigans and ortho-pedic shoes. God, Jackie, I'm only fifty-eight. I'm not dead yet, you know."

"Mom, maybe I didn't say this correctly. I mean, I wouldn't change a thing about the way you look because you are so pretty for any age. I'm the one who probably needs a makeover."

"Maybe. I mean that in the nicest way, honey. You're a beautiful girl. And I know it's beach casual and all that, but you know, looks are important."

"To who? God, Mom! You know I'm not looking to attract anyone!"

There I went again. I was on the express train to Crazy Town again.

"Take a deep breath, Jackie. I only meant that a pretty nurse would certainly cheer a wounded veteran faster than one who didn't give a hoot about how she looked. Happiness produces endorphins. You should know that. And you're a beautiful young woman who might have fun with it. That's all. Now, where's Charlie? It's way past time to go get the dogs."

"He's already off down the beach with them."

"He is?"

"Yeah. I decided he's old enough to do this on his own. And there's something I haven't told you."

"What's that?"

"Daddy's coming down tomorrow to make ice cream with Charlie."

"He is? Well, that's very nice. And I shall not be at home to receive him, shall I? Kindly ask him to stay out of my bedroom and my medicine cabinet, will you? He can use the guest powder room if nature calls."

She turned on her heel and left the room. Once again, I couldn't really blame her. And I wondered for the fiftieth time what it would really be like if they got back together again. He really was an old salt, and she really was a glamour puss. But didn't Hemingway, who was an authentic old salt if ever there was one, marry all those glamorous women? And weren't they gorgeous in the blazing heat of Key West? I'd seen plenty of pictures of him with his wives in enormous straw hats and beautiful gauzy outfits and Katharine Hepburn–style high-waist trousers with pleats and cuffs and pockets. It could work. *They* could work. What could I do to make them see that their love wasn't dead?

Healing seemed to be the central theme of my life. I was thinking about Charlie and me and how broken we felt, but what we felt was nothing compared to the devastation suffered by the veterans at the VA hospital. I spent a few hours there going around with the nurses and administration staff, and they had more jobs for me than I could have ever imagined. I could work in the pharmacy or registration or any number of places. What I really wanted to do was practice nursing because that was what I was trained to do. I filled out applications, and they said they would call me in a day or two.

I had no doubt that they would because they seemed overwhelmed. But I didn't feel overwhelmed because after Afghanistan it would take something pretty riotous to rattle me in any hospital setting.

The next morning arrived, Mom said her good-byes, Charlie took off with the dogs, and I cleaned up the kitchen.

"Good luck!" I said and gave her a smooch on her cheek.

"I can't wait to hear what Ms. Donaldson has in store for me."

"Well, for the record, I think you're nuts, but hey, if it makes you happy? I say go for it!"

"Aren't you even curious what it would be like to have someone make you look ten years younger?"

"No. Because that would make me twenty-five."

"Well, tell your father I said hello or kiss it or something."

"I'll think of something to say."

"Okay, then. I'll see you when she's all done with me!"

My instincts told me that she sort of wished she was going to stay home because it was one way she could spend a day with him without taking responsibility for him being there. Daddy was coming at my invitation, and I knew he was pretty nervous about it too. I didn't know when the last time was that he had been in the house, but I imagined it had to have been years. Mom and Dad were not mortal enemies by any definition. She simply held him at arm's length and he deferred to her wishes. It was all right with me when older people who had been married for decades got to the point where they simply wanted different things. Pursue them, for heaven's sake. But did they have to live in separate houses? Couldn't they figure out a way to live together, even if it was only as friends?

And what if Mom came home while he was still here? We would have a colossally awkward situation. Hopefully she'd call first.

I heard the screen door close on the front porch and went out to remind Charlie to put fresh water in the dog's dishes. It was not even ten o'clock and already eighty-five degrees. Needless to say, it was humid enough to swim from one room to another. He was in the hammock with an e-reader.

"Where'd you get that?" I asked.

"Dr. Steve. He said I should use it to read 'The Gold-Bug' because it has a dictionary in it and some of the words are words I never heard of."

"Like what?"

"Huguenot? Coppice? Manumitted? Do you know what they mean?"

"Well, we have Huguenots in Charleston whose families came over three hundred years ago. They were French Protestants, and I think they followed Calvin's teachings."

"Who the heck is Calvin?"

"Why don't you Google him and see? You can use my laptop."

"Yeah, maybe later. But look at this." Charlie put the cursor over the word *coppice* and a definition popped up. *Thicket.* "What's a thicket?"

"It means a densely wooded area, the kind you'd have to hack through with a machete."

"Wow. Cool."

"Yeah, cool. Listen, your grandfather is going to be here soon, so I hope you've got your room picked up and that the bathroom can pass inspection. And be careful with that thing. They break if you drop them."

"No worries, Mom. It's all good."

"Okay, then, I'm going to go make iced tea for Guster and me. I'll bet we drink it all."

"Probably. I'll just be right here," he said. "I'm going to make a map."

"That would be a good exercise for the old bean. What kind of map?"

"To find hidden treasure!"

"Well, of course! Why else?"

I went inside, put a large saucepan filled with water on the stove to boil, took four tea bags from the pantry closet, pulled off their labels, and tied the strings together. I wasn't thrilled that Steve had taken another oh-so-cavalier step into Charlie's life by allowing him to use his e-reader. For one thing, they were expensive, and if Charlie dropped it, I'd have to replace it. And I wasn't too happy that he was reading Poe. I knew "The Gold-Bug" was benign enough, but if he liked it, he'd surely move on to the more grotesque stories by Poe.

When the water began to boil, I pulled the pot off the burner and dropped in the tea bags, thinking that ten minutes ought to do it. I heard a car door slam and went out to the back porch to see who was there. It was Dad. Dad with his curly salt-and-pepper hair and muscular arms and little paunch. He wasn't a large man, only five foot nine, maybe, but he was adorable in his Hawaiian shirt and tortoiseshell Ray-Bans and Top-Siders. He was carrying an old wooden ice cream churn under one arm and two bags of groceries with his other hand.

"Hey! Wait! Can I help you with that?"

"Yeah, take a bag and give your old man a smooch!"

I planted a noisy kiss on his cheek and took both bags. Gosh, he smelled good, I thought, and it was in that moment that I realized he was considerably better groomed than he had been yesterday. Just seeing him brought a smile to my face. He stopped at the bottom of the steps.

"Is *she* here?"

"No, the coast is clear, and I think she's going to be gone most of the day."

"Humph." He almost seemed disappointed. "Well, it's probably best. Where's Charlie?"

"In the hammock, that's where he pretty much lives now. That is, when he's not chasing after our neighbor's dogs or building sand castles with some kids in a rental house down the road."

As soon as we got inside the house, I called out for Charlie and he came running. "Guster!" He threw his arms around Dad's waist, and Dad hugged him back.

"Well, would you look at you? You've got a regulation Lowcountry boy suntan! How about that?"

"Yeah, I've been going to the beach every day, and I got a job, you know. Did Mom tell you?"

"Yes! Yes, she did. Are those puppies on the porch?"

"Yep! Come on! I'll show you!" He grabbed Dad's hand and hurried him out of the room. "I have so much to tell you! Did you bring the ice cream machine?"

"You know I did! It's a genuine White Mountain ice cream freezer that's made by hand. It makes the finest ice cream in the entire world! And I brought all the

192 . DOROTHEA BENTON FRANK

things we need to make some first-class blueberry ice cream." Dad turned back to me. "I'll be on the porch."

"I gathered as much. You boys go have fun."

And the afternoon passed like this: Charlie talking nonstop about his job and the RiverDogs through lunch of egg salad sandwiches and Charlie chattering away like a magpie about Poe and "The Gold-Bug" and hidden treasure while they turned the crank on the ice cream freezer and Charlie bending Dad's ear over sand dune formation and jellyfish while they gobbled up all the ice cream until, from the heat of the afternoon and the energy it took for him to remain focused, Dad fell asleep in his chair.

"I think he's snoozing," Charlie said to me in a whisper.

"Let's let him rest, baby. Why don't you take the dogs out?"

"Okay."

I looked over at my dad. He was four years older than Mom, so that made him sixty-two. Sixty-two wasn't old by any measure, but I'd noticed yesterday that he seemed to be slowing down a little. I couldn't remember him falling asleep like that in the past. It must have been the heat. But what if he got sick? Who was going to take care of him? Would Mom? If he *was* sick, would he even tell her? I was in no shape to be thinking about his mortality or anybody else's for that matter.

After about twenty minutes, Dad sat up straight and said, "Oh, my! I was fast asleep!"

"That's okay. It's hot as hell anyway. Want another glass of tea?"

"Sure. Where's Charlie?"

"He just took the dogs out. He'll be right back."

I went to get his drink, and when I returned I found Dad standing up and looking out over the dunes. The afternoon sun glistened and sparkled on the water, and pelicans and seagulls were everywhere, flying, squawking, and swooping through the sky.

"I've always loved this view," he said, and there was a certain wistfulness in his voice.

"Me too."

"Don't let Charlie go in the ocean tomorrow."

"Why not?"

"There's a hurricane coming our way. Not much of one, but they can cause rip tides."

"Got it. I'll watch the news too."

Charlie returned in the next few minutes and brought the dogs up onto the porch, where he unhooked them from their leashes. Stanley and Stella had a few slurps of water and then settled down in their spots.

Dad said, "Charlie? I'm getting old, you know."

Charlie said, "What do you mean? You're not old!"

"Well, I'm old enough to forget that I bought you a special gift that's in the back of my SUV. You want to go get it?"

"What did you do, Dad?"

"Oh, it's just a little something I think he needs. That's all."

We followed Charlie through the house and down the back steps. Charlie looked through the back window of Dad's GMC Denali and started jumping up and down.

"Unlock the car! Unlock the car!"

Dad started laughing and unlocked his SUV with a click of his remote. "It's open, Charlie. Just watch your head!"

Charlie lifted the back and pulled out a brand-new skateboard. "Oh, my God!" He was practically hyperventilating. "It's a Sector 9 Vagabond Longboard!"

"There's a helmet in there too! Put it on!" Dad called out. Then he turned to me. "I was riding over to the Whole Foods to get the berries, and I passed the Parrot Surf Shop on Coleman. I thought to myself, I wonder what they've got in there that Charlie might like."

"Anything and everything!" I said. I gave Dad a little kiss on his cheek. I really didn't like Charlie being showered with gifts every time I looked around, but he wasn't spoiled by them. At least not so far.

We watched as Charlie strapped on his helmet, dropped the board to the street, put his weight on it with his foot to test the flexibility, and turned back to us. "See y'all later!"

We were as happy as Charlie.

Just as Charlie came around the block for the third time, Steve pulled into his driveway. Charlie was going for a fourth lap.

"Wow!" he said as he got out of his car. "Look at Charlie go!"

"Steve! Come say hello to my dad!"

Steve, poor unsuspecting Steve, came forward with a smile to shake Dad's hand.

"I'm Buster Britt. Annie's husband." *Not her ex-husband* was what he really said. Dad's face could have been hanging on the side of Mount Rushmore then. I thought for a moment that he might punch Steve.

"Yes, nice to meet you, sir. I'm Steve Plofker."

Dad bristled at Steve's deference to his age. "So you're the next-door neighbor who was nice enough to take my grandson to a ball game and give him a job to boot?"

"Yeah, but the favor works both ways, you know? It's great for my dogs to have company because it keeps them from getting lonely and neurotic. And what fun is it to go to a baseball game without someone to talk to? Charlie is a really fine young man. We've had a lot of fun together since we met."

"So I've heard. I'm a baseball man myself," Dad said, probably thinking he wouldn't mind sitting in the owners' box.

"Really? Well, I'll see what I can do about some more tickets, then. You around for a while?"

"Oh, yeah. Just ask Jackie where to find me. I've been up at Murrells Inlet for a bit."

"I hear the fishing's pretty good up there," Steve said and winked at me.

He actually winked. Please. Well, I thought I might gag, but I was pretty sure that Daddy saw it too and had an instant suspicion that Steve's attentions were directed toward me and not Mom. I was afraid of that.

"You like to fish?"

"I've been known to drop a hook in the water. Now and then."

"Well, when you get a day off let me know. Been getting some bodacious flounder. I like to go gigging too."

"That sounds great," Steve said, nodding his head like a bobblehead figurine. "Dogs on the porch?"

"Yep," I said.

"Would it be okay if I just go get them?"

"Of course!"

Steve went inside, and Dad turned to me and said, "You're pretty trusting to just let that guy walk in your mother's house like that."

"He's a doctor, Dad, and FYI, that house belongs to you too."

"Still," he said.

"Ya gotta learn to trust, Dad."

"Humph," he said. "Trust. Look who's talking. Humph. I gotta get on the road. And FYI to you? That sonofabitch has his eye on you, not your mother."

"Then he's dreaming."

"Let the poor schnookle dream. He's got a funny-shaped head."

"Yeah, well, there are a lot of brains in there."

Why in the world would I come to Steve's defense? Daddy looked at me and harrumphed again. "Tell my grandson not to wear a rut in the road with that skate-board. I'll call y'all tomorrow."

I threw my arms around my dad's neck. "You're the greatest, Dad, do you know that?"

"You're still my little girl, Jackie, and you're the apple of my eye."

He kissed me squarely in the middle of my forehead and got into his car.

"Be careful!" I called out, and I waved and waved until he was out of sight.

It was almost six when Charlie came home, sailing through the house, calling for me. "Mom! Mom!"

"Out here!"

You'd think we were a bunch of shut-ins with the amount of time we seemed to be spending outdoors, but frankly with the broiling heat and ferocious humidity the most comfortable place in the house was the porch, where we had breezes coming at us from three sides. I was sitting in a rocker, enjoying the end of the day, finishing reading that morning's paper. These days people said "What do you read the paper for? You can get the news instantly on the Internet." Well, I'd say to them, there's a lot more in the paper than news. There are feature articles and opinions and announcements. I loved getting newsprint ink on my hands and clipping out different articles for friends. How many pie recipes had I sent Miss Deb over the years? And how many articles on growing lavender and other useful herbs to Mom?

"Whatcha doing?" Charlie asked.

"Just reading. How's the new skateboard?"

"Completely totally awesome. I mean, *totally* awesome!"

"So you had a good day with Guster?"

"Amazing. Mom, I have to talk to you about something."

"What?"

"Well, I've made a decision."

"And?"

"I'm staying here."

I sat up straight as though someone had knocked the wind out of me. "No, you are not!"

He held his hands up in the air. "Hear me out! Just hear me out!"

"This had better be good."

"Okay, look. I never get to see Glam and Guster, and they're both here. That's one thing. And number two, I've been gone for over an hour and you didn't have to come with me. It's safe here. And three, I love it here."

"Look, Charlie, I understand, and I don't entirely disagree with you. But we have a home in New York. And there's Aunt Maureen and all your friends at school. Why don't we try and come here more often? I mean, there's no reason why we can't spend summers and holidays here."

"You don't get it, do you?"

"Charlie, your daddy's buried in Brooklyn."

Charlie's mood fizzled right in front of me. He didn't want to go home to our house in Brooklyn. But that was where we belonged. He had had a few terrific days, and I could understand why he wasn't anxious to return to the old grind.

"Look. We still have a few weeks before you start school. Let's just try to enjoy ourselves."

"I hate it when you talk in *we* because then I know the answer is going to be a big fat no. Like when you say, 'Let's eat our Brussels sprouts. Come on now! We don't have all night!' It's better here, Mom. For all of us."

10

. . . into the ground, at the precise spot where the beetle fell, my friend now produced from his pocket a tape-measure. . . . Legrand begged us to set about one to digging as quickly as possible.

—Edgar Allan Poe, "The Gold-Bug"

Annie

Margaret Donaldson was a goll-dern certified Houdini/Svengali/Einstein, and I *know* that's not very ladylike language, but I cannot be emphatic enough without strong words. I worship her. Not literally. But I think you get my drift. I could not pass a mirror, a window, or a stainless-steel appliance without taking a look at myself. Dang, sustah!

Buster's car wasn't there. I had missed him. Oh, well, too bad for him! At least I told myself that. There had not been such a dramatic change in my appearance since the day I threw off my peasant blouse, stepped out of my cutoff jeans, and slipped on my wedding gown and veil. It was only natural that

I would wonder what the only man I had ever loved would have said if he could see me. And to be completely honest, I wanted him to see what he was missing. No such luck.

I waltzed into the house to find the kitchen empty and no supper on the stove. Good! Let's take the new and vastly improved Annie Britt out to dinner and see what happens. I was ready to go break some hearts—if I could find a live one, that is.

Charlie and Jackie were on the porch reading. I swung the screen door open, stepped out, and let it slam behind me. It was that kind of a moment for me.

"Ta da!" I sang out to announce my arrival. I struck a glamour-girl pose and asked, "So what do y'all think?"

"Glam-ma! You look . . . amazing!"

That precious child was so generous and kind. And smart.

"Mom! Holy cow! It's the new you!"

I had spent most of the day at Ms. Donaldson's studio. She'd brought in Hailey from the Allure Salon to do my hair and two of her assistants to redo all of my makeup. Then we'd taken a ride over to Gwynn's, where a wardrobe specialist had sold me three new outfits, from head to toe, including foundation garments that worked one miracle after another. It was too warm to be mummified in elastic, but I looked the best I had looked in a very long time. Like my momma used to say, "Pride knoweth no pain."

"I'm thinking crab cakes tonight at Station 22 Restaurant. Anyone care to join me?"

"Sounds great to me," Jackie said. "You look way too fab to stay home."

"They have flounder and hush puppies?" Charlie asked.

"Yes, flounder, no, hush puppies, but they have awesome coconut cake. How's that?"

"Sweet! Good sub!"

I was simply going to have to dust off my deep fryer and make that skinny little angel a mountain of hush puppies.

"Go wash your face, Charming Charlie, and let's go show off your gorgeous grandmother."

Within the hour we were climbing the steps to the dining room at Station 22. I was wearing all white linen with lots of turquoise jewelry, and my salt-and-pepper hair had been shortened by at least five inches into an angled bob that gave it lots of bounce and movement. The only thing I wasn't thrilled about is that they had confiscated the three red lipsticks in my purse and made me swear to never wear red again, using some nonsense about it running out into the little lines around

204 • DOROTHEA BENTON FRANK

my lips. Now, if that was really happening, wouldn't I have known it?

To be dead honest, I really couldn't say that I looked younger, but I certainly was more contemporary and I felt, well, elegant in a casual kind of way.

We were greeted by Marshall Stith, the proprietor, whom I had known since childhood.

"Mrs. Britt? Can this be you? Not that you needed to change a hair on your lovely head, but my dear, you look fantastic!" He spun me around to take a 360 view of my new look, and all the guys at the bar, whom I had known since the sandbox, whistled and applauded. Men are so silly. "And here's Jackie and young Charlie. Charlie, where are you going to college, son?"

"Charlie? Tell Mr. Stith what grade you're in," Jackie said.

"Aw, come on! I'm only going into fifth grade," Charlie said and laughed.

"I'm sorry for your loss, Jackie. What a terrible tragedy," Marshall said.

"Thank you," she said.

Well, we got to the table and had started looking at the menus when the first drink arrived. "Mark Tanenbaum and Larry Dodds wanted you to have this cocktail to salute your new persona. It's a Cosmopolitan, which I think they meant to be an opinion," Marshall said. "Can I get you something, Jackie?"

"White wine would be fine. Thanks. And a 7Up for Charlie, please?"

"Sure thing!"

Their drinks were delivered almost instantaneously, and we touched the sides of our glasses. "Cheers!"

I waved at Mark and Larry and blew them kisses. Jackie cleared her throat. It was a very small glass, which was a good thing, because by the time we ordered our flounder, crab cakes, and mahimahi, there came Marshall with another cocktail.

"This one is from Johnny Disher and Bill Roettger," Marshall said and leaned in to whisper in my ear. "It's called Sex on the Beach." He put another glass of wine in front of Jackie. "Your wine is from Steve Reeves. He's a very nice man." She had barely made a dent in her first.

"Really?" I giggled and whispered back. "Tell those old goats they'd better look out! I just might take them over the sand dunes—one at a time, of course!"

"What am I missing, Mom?"

"Nothing, sweetheart. Just my old friends being goofy." I waved at the guys and blew more kisses.

Jackie gave them a small-fisted wave, then groaned loudly, which only made me blow more kisses and

I thanked goodness Charlie had left the table to put money in the jukebox. Apparently, according to my prude of a daughter, grandmothers were not supposed to behave in any manner that approached the outskirts of flirting.

"So Dad was here all day. I'm sorry you missed him."

"Well, I'm not."

"Well, if he'd seen you he would've fainted."

"I seriously doubt it. He probably wouldn't notice a thing. So did he ask about me?"

"Of course!"

I could tell she was lying, but I let it go.

"That's nice," I said. "What did he say?"

"Oh, you know, 'How's your mom? Where is she?' You know, that kind of thing."

"Um-hum," I said thinking, Yeah, sure, he probably said, "Is the old bag home?"

"You should've seen him with Charlie. He's really mellowed."

"You know, with him it was always all one way or the other. Either he was so mellow that you felt like sticking a compact mirror under his nose to see if he was still breathing. Or when he didn't like something he was so sarcastic it made me want to curl up in a corner and cry. I don't miss that part at all."

"I don't remember him ever acting like that."

"Then, my dear, you have a very, very selective memory."

It did not serve anyone well to remind her of all the times her father had insulted her in public to voice his displeasure instead of taking her aside and speaking to her with respect.

"Maybe. Well, he was a doll today."

"No one could be happier to hear that than I am." I drained my glass.

Charlie returned right as they put our food on the table. "What are y'all talking about?" he said.

"About your day with Guster," I said. "So y'all had a good time?"

"It was the best possible day, Glam. It really was."

Just as Charlie was about to launch into a recitation of everything that had happened that day, Marshall appeared with yet another cocktail.

"Don't worry! This one's considerably weaker."

"What is it?" I asked.

"Well, it's from David Kenney and Mike Richardson. It's a Salty Dog."

"That's the name of Glam's house!" Charlie exclaimed. "What's in it?"

"Well, it's got some vodka and some grapefruit juice and some salt around the rim."

"How do you get the salt on there like that?" Charlie asked.

"When you're all done with dinner, you come and find me and I'll show you! How's that?"

"Cool," Charlie said and began to scoop his fish away from the bones and eat it with gusto. Marshall's flounder was always exceptionally fresh and sweet. "Can y'all pass the ketchup? I could eat flounder every night of the week."

"Me too, sugar," I said.

I waved and blew more kisses to my old childhood friends, and Charlie caught me.

"Glam?" He looked toward the bar and then back to me with the funniest expression on his beatific little face. "Are those decrepit old dudes flirting with you?"

"No, darling, we are *pretending* to be flirting," I said.

"Yeah, and they just pretended to send you three cocktails!" Jackie said and rolled her eyes.

"They're some of my oldest friends on this island and would never step one toe over the line of propriety."

"Oh," Charlie said, and I think he got the gist of it. "So they're just fooling around?"

"Exactly!"

After dinner, Charlie got a lesson in how to sugar or salt the rim of a glass, Jackie went to the ladies' room, and I gave every one of my old friends a good smooch. Lord have mercy on my soul and body, there's nothing like a native island prince to make a girl feel good.

It didn't take long to wind up dinner and return to our porch. Charlie was so full of flounder and cake and so tired from the day that he put himself to bed. When Jackie and I went to his room to tuck him in, he was already fast asleep.

"I doubt if he even brushed his teeth," she said.

"Oh, phooey on that. His teeth aren't going to fall out tonight!"

"You're right," she said. "I'm too rule-driven."

"You said it, not me."

"I get that from you! Come on. Let's sit outside for a bit."

The tide was changing, and there was a nice breeze as we settled into our rockers on the porch.

"Let's leave the lights off so we can see the ocean," I said.

It took a few minutes for our eyes to adjust to the night, but soon we could see brilliant stars and the silver sparkling of phosphorescence all over the water. The birds were asleep, and all there was to hear was the occasional music of the rustling of palmetto fronds against one another and the lazy water washing the shore. It was as idyllic a paradise as even a honey-mooner could want.

"So tell what else your father had to say for himself," I said.

"Well, he met Steve."

"Oh, really? How did that go?"

"Okay, I guess. Daddy practically invited him to go fishing on the hope of getting invited to a RiverDogs game."

"Well, that's typical. Always trying to get something for nothing."

"Whatever. And he's got some lame idea that Steve has his eye on me, which is the biggest waste of time in the world if he does."

I realized right then and there that it was true. Not only was Buster no longer interested in me, Steve *was* attracted to Jackie. Without a thought in the world that the news might upset me, she'd confirmed what I already knew. I could feel myself blushing, and I was grateful for the darkness.

"Maybe I'd like a glass of wine. Can I get something for you, Jackie?"

"No, thanks. If I want something, I'll get it."

"Okay."

I went inside quietly, and in the kitchen I poured myself a goblet of some kind of Merlot that I found in the pantry left over from the other night. I stood at the sink and took a long sip, wondering if I would be able to redo my makeup the same way in the morning. Probably not. What did it matter anyway? There was no one to look at me for any other reason than basic social pleasantries. Oh, it had been fun at Station 22 to have all my old pals hoot and holler and buy me drinks, but they were either still married or divorced and dating someone half their age, and besides, we all knew one another too well for romance. Not to mention, even if it was only on a technicality, that I was still legally married to Mr. Britt.

I heard a car coming. I looked out the window and saw Steve pulling into his driveway. There was someone with him. A woman. I hurried back out to the porch.

"Jackie?" I was almost whispering. "Want to see something? Look over there."

By then they were in his kitchen, and because we were in the dark we could see them through his windows quite clearly. She was tall and blond and young, perhaps even younger than Jackie. My heart sank, and for the umpteenth time I reconciled myself to the life of an old crone whose womanly worth was negligible to the world, a trifling thing unworthy of notice by the opposite sex, a burden to society. It could be worse, I thought. In many cultures, women my age were already dead.

"Holy crap!" Jackie said.

"What?"

"She's a dead ringer for his dead wife."

"Really?"

"Yeah, really."

"That's probably normal," I said. "I wonder how old she is."

"It's hard to tell, but I doubt if she's even thirty. She has really thick hair."

In our family, thick hair was a coveted attribute.

Suddenly the lights in his kitchen went out, and moments later they were outside on his deck. He turned off his porch lights and lit the candles in two of the big lanterns that bordered the edges of his deck, probably so that she wouldn't go walking off the edge and break a leg.

"Well, isn't he the Casanova with his mood lighting and all that," Jackie said. "Next thing we know he'll have Sinatra streaming."

I imagined that streaming meant playing.

"And here I thought he was lighting the lanterns for safety reasons. Shows you how far out of the loop I am."

"Oh, Mom," Jackie said in sympathy. "We've got to do something about your romantic life at some point, don't you think?"

"I'm afraid that's a hopeless cause," I said. "But that's okay. I have you and Charlie to fill my heart."

To my way of thinking there was nothing less dig-
nified than a middle-aged woman crying the blues
about men.

We continued to watch them. They were standing
together with a glass of something. He was pointing up
to the sky, showing her some constellation or a UFO.
Then they turned around and appeared to be walking
in our direction.

I crouched down in my chair a little.

"God, Mom, what if they see us?"

"Oh, so what if they do? Steve Plofker doesn't own
the beach any more than I do."

They did not notice us. Steve sat in one of his deck
chairs and she stood behind him, massaging his shoulders. I watched as she leaned down and kissed him on
his head. Even though I knew it was an inappropri-
ate thought, something in me ached to slap the hell out
of her.

"Well, look at that," Jackie said.

"I thought you had no interest in him," I said.

"I don't, it's just . . . look how she's acting!"

"Hush! They'll hear us. You know how voices travel
on night air!"

But it was true. She was a no-good low-down
depraved animal. They were standing, and she laid one
on him that would've made Hugh Hefner gasp in shock.

The next thing we saw was her leg crawl up around his hip and he put his hand squarely on her backside.

"Get a room, you two," Jackie whispered in disgust.

As though they read her mind, they stopped and went inside. Were they going to his bedroom? Just as the lights went on, they went off. Steve and his harlot left the house, got into his car, and drove away.

"He's taking her home, and he should be back in less than an hour. You can get to anywhere in Charleston and back at this time of night in less than an hour. Otherwise they're having a little screw."

"I'm gonna go with *big* screw, and who cares?"

Jackie looked at me with a kind of sad face. Did she think that I was disappointed to see Steve with someone more age-appropriate and presumably legally available than I was? Did she think I had gone through this makeover for him? Well, I was and I did and it was pathetic, but at that moment I didn't care. I had never uttered one word about him I couldn't defend, and there was nothing wrong with trying to feel good about myself.

"I'm going to go check on Charlie," she said. "You want anything?"

"No, now that the lovebirds have flown the coop, I'm just going to sit here and enjoy a little more of this beautiful night."

She went inside and left me to marinate in my sullen soup.

What was it about daughters that they could practically smell your thoughts? Of course I could feel her confusion about her feelings toward Steve. It *was* too soon for her to get involved with someone else. That would destabilize Charlie's entire existence. But she was attracted to Steve in an odd kind of way. She didn't even know it yet. Lord knows, Steve was the opposite of Jimmy McMullen. Jimmy had been a rough-and-tumble man's man. Gregarious, clever, resourceful, generous—he was the kind of man who made you feel protected and safe. And somehow, at the very same time, the Devil danced all over the place in his beautiful eyes. You never knew what kind of surprise he had for you, just to make you laugh. He was not above the occasional placement of a whoopee cushion.

Steve was, well, serious. But he was a dermatologist, and his entire orientation to the world was naturally reserved, methodical, and more cerebral, because that was what was required to practice medicine. I had often observed his restraint to speak up or tell jolly stories about his practice or his childhood. He always wanted to hear your story, your news, your concerns. Steve's eyes were not filled with merriment and caprice, but they were the kindest eyes in the world. Our doctor next door held his cards close to his chest, which, of course, made him that much more interesting.

It was time to turn in for the night, but I just didn't want the day to end quite yet.

Jackie reappeared with a glass of water.

"Seafood makes me thirsty," she said and sat down next to me. "Or maybe it was the fries."

"Salt."

"Probably. What's up for tomorrow?"

"Hopefully another day like this one. Hopefully that storm turns and goes out to sea. Did you check the weather?"

"No, but I will. Whatcha thinking about?"

I stood up, stretched, and walked to the edge of the porch to look out over the dunes. "I was thinking, well, I was thinking what I always think when I'm standing here on a night like this."

"Which is?"

"That this must be the most beautiful place on Earth. Don't you agree?"

"I think this island has bewitched us all, Mom. I really do. Come on, let's lock up the house."

In the morning I began the impossible process of trying to duplicate the face I'd had the day before, and I decided at least I'd gotten my money's worth with my hair. My hair was still looking very good. I decided to forgo makeup until I got back from my walk with Deb. I put on an old pair of Bermuda shorts and a baggy old T-shirt and called her.

"You ready to rock and roll?" I asked.

"Oh, Annie, I've got to take Vernon to the emergency room. He's having chest pains."

"Lord! Don't tell me this! Do you want me to come with you? What can I do?"

"Not a thing. He's already in the car. Listen, you and I know it's just the low pressure from this silly storm, but what if I'm wrong? Anyway, I'll call you when I get back. I'm sure he's fine."

"All right. I'll say my magic novena."

"Thanks."

We hung up, and I thought about how the low pressure of hurricanes seemed to make so many babies come into the world early and how many poor souls depart unexpectedly. I didn't know if there was proof of it, but if you asked any OB-GYN or geriatric nurse, she would nod her head in agreement. I hoped Vernon would be all right.

I poked my head inside Jackie's and Charlie's rooms. They were sleeping like logs, which is a stupid metaphor if there ever was one, but you get the picture. I decided to make a nice breakfast for everyone, and afterward maybe I could convince my grandson to take a walk with me. We'd bring the dogs and have fun.

I decided to make watermelon juice and French toast from a loaf of brioche and fry up some extra-thick bacon I'd bought to make red rice. And for some reason, maybe I had seen it on some cooking program, I decided to add a sprig of rosemary and a cinnamon stick to the coffee grinds basket. Once the water started to drip through the coffee, the whole room smelled divine. The bacon was sizzling in my cast-iron skillet, and the French toast was ready to turn.

It wasn't long before Jackie straggled in with her arm around Charlie's shoulders.

"Jeez! What smells so good?" Charlie asked.

"Please don't say "jeez," Charlie. It sounds like you're taking the Lord's name in vain," I said and looked at Jackie for backup.

"Everything smells good, and Glam is right," Jackie said, inspecting all the pans. "Mom, if this doesn't stop we're going to gain fifty pounds!"

"Portion control! It's all about moderation," I said. "Charlie? Do you know how to use a blender?"

"Sure," he said.

"Say, 'Yes, ma'am,' Charlie baby."

"Yes, ma'am!" Charlie said, like a good parrot.

"Well, let's get those chunks of watermelon lique-fied! Here, I'll show you!"

"Don't have to, Mom. He used to make frozen mar-garitas for us all the time," Jackie said.

"*What?*" I was horrified!

"Mom! I'm kidding! I'm kidding!"

"That's not funny, missy! Don't you make me go cut a switch! You're not too big for me to turn over my knee, you know."

"I'd like to take a picture of that!" Charlie said. "I make milk shakes in the blender all the time."

"Aha!" I said.

We had a good chuckle, and the mood in the room was just right.

"Well, I lost my walking buddy for today," I said, putting plates in front of Jackie and Charlie. "Deb had to take Vernon into the ER again."

"Blood pressure?" Jackie said. "This looks deli-cious, Mom."

"Thanks. No. Not this time. He's got chest pain," I said, sliding a piece of soggy bread into the skillet for myself.

"This *is* delicious, Glam," Charlie said, inserting a man-sized forkful into his mouth.

"Hmmm. Chest pain's not something to mess around with," Jackie said.

"Maybe someone else wants to comb the beach with me this morning?"

"I would, but I have to be downtown by eleven. I'm meeting the head of Human Resources at the VA. I think they want me to help with shifts. You know, a lot of nurses are trying to have one last vacation before the summer is over. It's good money."

"Well, I think that's a wonderful idea!" I said and finally sat down with them. "Better than working for nothing, not that I don't believe in volunteer work, because I certainly do."

"Mom always says that if you pulled all the people out of my school that volunteer it would fall apart."

"It probably would," Jackie said.

"Well, I'm doing my talk on Poe at the library gratis," I said.

"Did you and Deb finally settle on a date?" Jackie said.

"Halloween weekend," I said.

"Well, we'll have to check the calendar, because Mr. Charles over here has to start fifth grade on the twenty-second. At some point we have to go home. That's awful soon to come back if we're coming for Thanksgiving too."

"Not going," Charlie said very quietly.

"Yes, you are, Son."

Hmmm, I thought, what am I missing here?

"Charlie, why don't you and I walk the beach together this morning?"

"Well, okay, but we'd have to go soon because I'm meeting the kids from Greenville to go skateboarding in the parking lot at Fort Moultrie."

"Skateboarding?"

"Yeah, you didn't see it? Guster bought me this awesome skateboard!"

I got up and took their plates, rinsing them for the dishwasher. "Aren't those things dangerous?"

"Mom? When you see Charlie on his skateboard—wearing his helmet, I might add—you'll see that he owns the road."

"Really? Well, then, I can't wait! Drink your juice, darlin'."

"It's weird," Charlie said.

"Well, then, don't drink it," I said. "It's just juice."

"Sorry, Glam."

"It's better with tequila in it anyway," Jackie said and started to laugh. I gave her the hairy eyeball, and she laughed even harder. "I don't know what's wrong with me this morning."

"I think your sense of humor is back in town," I said, "and it's been gone too long. Charlie, go get Stella and Stanley, and I'll be done here by the time you get back."

"I'm outta here!" Charlie said in a burst of energy, and he was gone. "Thanks for breakfast, Glam. The French toast was awesome!"

"What would the young ones do if they couldn't say *awesome* and *sweet*?" Jackie asked. "Although, I gotta say, the French toast actually *was* awesome. Here, give me that towel. I'll dry."

Within the hour, Jackie was on her way to the city, the new darlings of the house, Stanley and Stella, having had their run, were curled up on my porch having their morning nap, and I was walking down the beach with Charlie, heading toward the lighthouse.

"It's probably a good thing that I left the dogs at home," Charlie said. "They're so wild you'd have a hard time controlling even one of them."

"I'm sure you're right. The ocean looks angry today," I said. "Do you know why?"

"Too many fish in there?"

"No, because there's a tropical disturbance down by the Dominican Republic and it makes the water churn. Be sure that you and your friends stay out of the water today."

"Even the gully?"

"No, you can swim in the gully at low tide, but don't put your toes in the ocean. You might get caught in a rip tide and get carried out to sea. It's a stupid way to die."

"Okay. What's a smart way to die?"

"At one hundred and twenty-five years old in your sleep with no pain. And with your hair and makeup done by Hailey from Allure."

"Oh, Glam, you're so silly."

"Glam is clever, not silly. An important distinction. So what's going on with you, young man?"

"What do you mean?"

"Well, this morning at the breakfast table, I heard you mumble something about staying here."

He dug his big toe into the cool sand and, looking very forlorn, drew a circle. "I wish I could."

"I know. I wish you could too. But you can't because you have to go back to school."

"I hate New York."

"You do? Why?"

"Because terrible things happen there. All Mom does is mope around the house, and it's too sad. I don't want to be sad, and I don't want her to be sad either."

"I don't want y'all to be sad either." Oh, Lord, I thought my heart was going to break.

"All we do is think about Dad and cry."

"Oh, Charlie!"

"And I hate my school too."

"Why, baby?"

"Because nobody cares about anybody."

"Oh, sweetheart, even you know that can't be entirely true."

"No. It *is* true. People are jealous of every little thing and the big kids push around the little kids. And the teachers are a joke. They don't do anything about it."

"Oh, my darling boy. Don't you think that the schools here have their fair share of bullies and negligent teachers? Of course they do!"

"Maybe. Is that supposed to make me feel better?"

"Yes. And you know what? If you were here every day, maybe it wouldn't be so special to you? Why don't we get a calendar and let's count the weekends until Thanksgiving and Christmas and Easter and let's figure out how we're going to get you back here for a good long stretch in the summer. I have lots of points on my credit card that I can use for airline tickets so you don't have to take that insufferable drive."

"If you say so. That's better than nothing."

"It's a heck of a lot better than nothing! Now, let's cheer up, all right?"

We reached the rocks near the lighthouse and turned to go back. The eastern skies were forbidding and dark. There was a storm coming, but it would probably just be some rain and enough wind to bring in the hanging baskets and take the cushions off the porch chairs. I wasn't particularly concerned with this squall. It didn't even have a name. When they named the storms and said they were a category 4, that was when I checked my battery supplies and went to the store for water. Other than that, most people in the Lowcountry kept an eye on the weather reports but went on about their business and didn't panic.

We were almost back to my house when Charlie announced that he was stopping off at his friends' house. He wanted to be sure they were all up for the day and said he would be home shortly to pick up his skateboard. I knew he'd be safe, so I said all right and blew him a kiss. Then I burst into tears. He had no idea how desperately I wanted him and Jackie to stay, while I was so glad to see that he was beginning to focus on his own life again and I knew that the time they had spent here had been instrumental in both of them thinking about their lives going forward. And I knew that when they left I would be inconsolable. Absolutely inconsolable. But I couldn't let either one of them see how I felt. If Jackie ever decided to move home, I wanted it to be her decision, not the result of me pushing her into something she'd blame me for later. I also realized how quickly I had become used to them being there. Each day had purpose, and I went from minute to minute, meal to meal, thinking how rejuvenated I felt to have the job of seeing about them. I hardly ever wept except in the movies, but now my tears were coming and coming, the unsummoned and unwelcome little shits. I hated to think what I must have looked like. Who cared anyway? No one. Realizing that no one cared about my tears, I cried all the more. Thank God the beach was relatively empty. I would have hated being caught looking like a doddering old fool.

When I walked over my beach steps, I could see someone on my porch. Who was it? Deb? No. As I got a little closer I could see it was Buster. Great. Old shirt. No makeup. Red nose running like an open faucet, and surely my eyes were bloodshot like hell. Great. Then I thought, Screw it. I don't care what he thinks anyway.

I sniffed hard, wiped my eyes, climbed the steps, opened the screen door, and went inside. He was at the far end of the porch playing with the dogs, scratching them behind their ears. He stood.

"Don't get up," I said.

"What the hell's the matter with you? You been crying? You never cry!"

"Allergies. It's pollen from the sea oats. I get this from time to time." I took off my sneakers and reopened the door, knocked the sand out of them, and left them on the top step under the overhang.

"What the hell did you do to your hair? You cut it!"

"Well, aren't you observant?"

"I thought you knew I liked it better long!"

"It's my hair. Not yours. So, don't concern yourself with it. And speaking of hell? Just what the hell are you doing here?" Stella and Stanley got up and came over to me and licked my legs. Then they took another lick and another lick . . . "Stop licking me, you crazy animals!"

"I brought a hurricane preparation kit."

Nothing short of a nuclear disaster could make the dogs stop licking my legs. I kept trying to push them away, but it was in vain. They were snacking on my new body lotion.

"That's nice. For what? I think that over the past decade I've been able to hold the Salty Dog together in one piece."

"I always loved that name."

"I don't."

"I know. Anyway, Arlene's up to a category three. That's her name. Arlene."

"Great. Every Arlene I ever knew was a raging psychopath."

"Humph. Where's my grandson?"

"He's out there somewhere in the streets of Sodom and Gomorrah with his friends from Greenville, and then the plan is to risk life and limb on that fool skateboard you bought him. Stop it, you silly dogs."

Buster smirked at me and pointed to the dogs. "Don't worry about Charlie on the skateboard. He could give lessons. Whaddya have on your legs? Bacon?"

"*Excuse me!* I'm going inside!"

"I'd wash my legs if I were you!" he called out to my back.

"Oh, stuff it, you old trout!" I hollered to him.

"And you're an old crab!" he yelled back to me. And he was laughing.

11

"I thought so!—I knew it!—hurrah!" vociferated Legrand. . . .

"Come! We must go back," said the latter, "the game's not up yet;" and he again led the way to the tulip-tree.

—Edgar Allan Poe, "The Gold-Bug"

Jackie

I came home from the VA hospital wrinkled, sweaty, and with a part-time job. They needed help, and I guess I secretly wanted to see what it would be like to work there if I ever came back to Charleston. So I told them I'd work Sunday, Monday, and Tuesday from seven A.M. to seven at night. It was just for a couple of weeks, and I knew I'd learn something. You always learned something in a new job—a new treatment or therapy or about new medicines. As much as I loved visiting with my mother, I was beginning to get the itch for some diversion. And I missed nursing. Once it's in your blood it's hard to resist the call to duty. And I was aching to be with veterans. If nothing else, we would understand each other.

I came into the house through the kitchen, and no one was there. So I went from room to room until I found Dad and Charlie on the porch. They were at the trestle table, leaning over a hurricane-tracking chart. There was a pile of colored highlighters and other things scattered around.

"Hey, Dad! What a nice surprise to find you here!" I gave him a kiss on his cheek.

"Well, I brought down some supplies in case this Arlene decides to pay us a visit. I wanted Charlie to know how to prepare for a hurricane. After all, he is the man of the house, right?"

"Yup," Charlie said.

"We made a hurricane checklist. See?" He handed me a legal pad on which he had written a list of things to be sure you had on hand and a list of things to do to secure the house. I noted that it said the skateboard should be in the trunk of the car in case they had to evacuate. "And we've had a nice morning. I took Charlie down to Dunleavy's for a chili dog, and I had a very tasty chicken pot pie. We had a good time, didn't we?"

"Yup," Charlie said. "And now Guster and I are tracking Hurricane Arlene on this map. We got it free at the fire department. About an hour ago it looked like she was headed straight for the Bahamas, but now it looks like she's just holding steady."

"Which might mean she's gathering strength," Dad said. "But if you ask me, I think she's going to make the turn and head up to Cape Hatteras."

"I hope so," I said, looking at the flashlights, hand-crank radio, and bungee cords on the table. I picked up the radio and looked at it. "We used to have one of these when I was a kid."

"Every house should have one," Dad said. "If you lose all your power, you can still find out what's going on."

"Yeah, like an alien invasion! Where's Mom?"

"She went inside to wash her legs about three hours ago," Dad said and winked at Charlie, who covered his mouth to suppress the giggles.

Some people were obviously having a laugh at Mom's expense. And Mom had locked herself in her bedroom.

"Okay, that makes no sense. What are you bad boys talking about?"

"Guster said that Glam had this lotion on her legs and Stella and Stanley went nuts, licking her to death!"

"Your poor mother was beside herself!" Dad said and smiled. "I'm sorry. I know it's not nice to laugh, but you should've seen those crazy dogs just slurping away. Oh, me! It was some sight!"

"Hush, both of you! So what else are y'all doing?"

"Well, we were gonna measure the part of the island where I'm hiding the treasure. I challenged the Greenville kids to a treasure hunt. They're making a map too. Just like in 'The Gold-Bug'!"

"Oh, I don't know how long I can stay, Charlie."

"Stay for supper! Stay for supper! Please?"

"Well, I did bring your grandmother a mess of flounder and some corn and tomatoes. I could show you how to cook fish—if your grandmother will have me, that is."

"I'll go ask her," I said and went inside.

I rapped my knuckles on her door.

"Who is it?" she called out.

"Just me," I said. "May I come in?"

"Enter at your own risk! I'm trying to condense myself into a pair of Spanx. It's not pretty."

Sure enough, there stood my mother trying to yank up a one-piece torture chamber that promised to flatten her tummy and smooth out her thighs and hips—or to cut off her circulation if she didn't get it in place soon.

"Need some help?" I asked.

"Maybe. I'm just about worn out from this fool thing!"

"Yeah, you pretty much have to have a degree in circus contortion to get in these silly things without breaking a sweat. Here. Look here. Get it where you want it on your thighs, and then I can pull it up inch by inch to under your bosom."

"This is so ridiculous," she said. "But it really does make a difference. At least I think it does." She fussed around with the legs until they were straight. "Okay, now let's move this sucker north!"

"Gotcha!" In a few minutes her body shaper was where it was supposed to be and I thought, Well, no doubt they should've sold her one that was at least one size larger. "Um, can I ask a delicate question?"

"Of course!"

"What if you have to use the bathroom?"

"It has a slit, you know, a slit down there."

"Gross."

"Or you can just hold it. I think I'll just hold it if I have to go."

"God, I would. Nasty!"

"I agree. I mean, the slit is one of those concepts that sounds sensible, but in reality? It doesn't live up to its hype."

"I've got the picture. Gross." Who was I to call anything gross? How many times had I used a hand-dug latrine? I picked up the aqua linen shirt and matching trousers that were lying on her bed. "Wow, this is a gorgeous color. Did you buy this yesterday too?"

"Yes, Ms. Donaldson says I should wear one color from head to toe, except for black, which she thinks is too harsh for my complexion. Not sure I agree with that. Now I have to try and re-create my face."

I watched as Mom laid out all the new makeup she had bought, and I could see that she was confused.

"I know I'm supposed to use all the serums and creams first and let them dry . . . now, where's that chart?"

"So I took a job today, just part-time, to make a little money and to help out at the VA. I've got seven A.M. to seven P.M. Sunday, Monday, and Tuesday. Only if it's okay with you, of course."

"Why, sweetheart! That's just marvelous! It will give me a little more time with Charlie, and you can see what's going on around town."

"So you don't mind, then? It might put a cramp in your social life."

"Honey, there's nowhere I'm going that I can't take Charlie."

"Well, we'll see how it goes. You *do* know that Dad's here?"

"I'm aware."

"Did you know he's out there explaining how to track hurricanes to Charlie with this huge chart, and then he's got a crank radio—"

"He's the crank," Mom said.

"Well, you're probably not going to like this, but I need to tell you that Charlie invited him to supper."

"What?" She nearly dropped a whole bottle of facial toner on her rug. "You *must* be kidding."

"Nope. And apparently Dad brought fish and corn and tomatoes and a basket of peaches. I guess he was hoping you'd let him stay too. What do you think? Yes?"

"I think no. No, wait. *Hell* no. How's that?"

"This is going to look awfully bad to Charlie, Mom." I could feel my temper rising. Now I was stuck in the middle.

"Oh, fine. Now you're playing the kid card?"

"Sort of."

It finally dawned on her that she was putting me into a difficult position. It also dawned on her that Dad would see her looking pretty fine in aqua linen.

"Well, maybe I'd be willing to cook, but I'm not sitting at the table with that man."

"Why not?"

"Are you serious, why not? Eleven years of no husband on holidays, birthdays, and God save me, our wedding anniversary, and now he shows up with a sack of fish and I'm supposed to scoot out there like Audrey Hepburn in *Sabrina* and whip up a soufflé for Linus?"

"I think you mean Julia Ormond."

"No, that's a remake, dearie. Although, personally, I do prefer Harrison Ford to Humphrey Bogart. Bogart always looked like he needed a shower and a shave. Except there was one movie where he wore a white dinner jacket and looked very elegant."

"*Casablanca?* Look, Mom, I understand how you feel, but it's going to look very awkward if you don't sit."

"Believe me, if you don't bring it up, they won't even notice. I'm the Grand Facilitator to your father. I just always made things happen, but I'm not happening in them. He never needed a wife. He needed a house-keeper and cook."

I stared at her and thought what an unsatisfying marriage this must have been for her. Was Dad that much of a caveman? I didn't believe that for a minute. At least I could always depend on Jimmy to be sensitive.

"Then why in the world are you still married to him?"

"That's my business. Now, you go tell the old bastard he can stay but he'd better behave. I'm doing this for Charlie. I need to finish getting dressed, and apparently it could take a while. And set up the bar, okay? Scary as this sounds, I might have to drink my way through this."

This cocktail ritual of hers could become habitual and not good for her health. I'd talk to her about it another time. Tonight was not the night for her to go cold turkey.

"Don't worry. The bar will be perfect. And thanks, Mom. This will mean a lot to Charlie, you know, it will show him what being an adult is all about."

"What the hell is that supposed to mean?" She was getting irritated, because my mother seldom cursed unless she was.

"That people can have their differences of opinion, but family is family. And even if you and Daddy did get divorced, he's still Charlie's grandfather. I mean, looking back, don't you think it was a little ridiculous that Daddy couldn't come to Jimmy's funeral because you were there?" I just threw it out there.

"Well, who would you rather have had with you?"

"That's the whole point, Mom. Charlie and I weren't supposed to have to choose."

She looked as though I had slapped her. In the time-honored tradition of families who live in a state of denial, I ignored her, closed her door, and went back to the porch. Like the rest of us, she had to live with the consequences of her decisions. It gave me a certain sense of liberation to tell her she had hurt me. No more eggshells for me. Since Jimmy's death

I had seen many changes in myself—some of them good and some of them based on fears that would most likely never materialize. But one thing was for sure: I didn't feel her separation from Dad was justified anymore. She was exaggerating Dad's abuse and, as usual, playing the part of the martyr. Did I really believe that Dad had never told her "Happy Birthday" or "Merry Christmas" in all these years? No, I couldn't buy that.

And I wanted her to be nice to him. He had certainly shown he had every intention of being nice to her. Maybe the fish, corn, tomatoes, and peaches were his way of wooing her? Come to think of it, all I had done was insinuate that there was a man flirting with her, and here he came like the Magi bearing gifts. And I'm sure in Dad's mind they were gifts. They ain't got no Saks Fifth Avenue up the road in Murrells Inlet.

"You're on for supper, Dad."

"Really? Why, that's wonderful!"

Dad's surprise was all over his face. He had not expected his presence at the table to receive my mother's papal blessing.

"Great!" said Charlie. "Let's go measure!"

"Well, what do you say we do the width today and the length another time? After all, you want to cover a pretty large area."

"I can do the length tomorrow! Let's go!" Charlie was already on his feet, pulling Dad up to stand. "Come on, Guster!"

"Easy there, partner!" Dad said. "If you ever have another baby, could you have one with less energy? For my sake?"

I was so stunned. More children? I sort of lost my balance. But I pulled myself together and hoped that my surprise didn't show on my face and Dad's remark had not registered with Charlie.

"Y'all go have fun! Dinner at six?"

"Don't worry. We'll be back in plenty of time."

I shooed them off the porch and started to set up the bar on the same table by picking up all their markers and so on and putting them back into Dad's tote bag. Another baby? I had no intention of ever getting married again, but what if I did? And if I did, what if I did find myself in the *family way*? How would that make Charlie feel? If I started a new life with someone else, wouldn't Charlie feel out of place? It was true that in theory I could still have more children, but wouldn't that be betraying Jimmy or at least Jimmy's memory? Well, whatever the future had in store for us in that department, it would have to accept Charlie as a full citizen of any new family. We had been through too much together to have anyone try to squeeze Charlie out of the equation by the tiniest millimeter. A new family? Holy hell, marriage and more children were a mind-boggling thing to even consider, and there I was doing just that. Insane.

I dug around in Mom's linen closet for a tablecloth for the bar, something that seemed festive. I put my hand on a colorful table runner that looked like a Mexican serape. That would work. On the floor of the closet were a box of paper lanterns, the kind you string up for a party, and a pair of glass hurricanes that needed a serious spritz of glass cleaner. I looked at it all and thought that even though it wouldn't be dark until well after eight, wouldn't they set a romantic tone when they were lit? After all, Dad was here, and wasn't that a reason for at least Charlie and me to celebrate? Mom could stew all she wanted. I was determined then that Dad would have a wonderful night. And maybe some soft lighting would soften my mother's heart.

There were existing hooks around the border of the top of the porch, probably put there years ago for just this purpose. I hung the lights on them in minutes without a struggle. After I cleaned the table, I put the serape down the center. It looked so great that I wondered why she didn't use it all the time. Well, the answer to that was pretty clear: it had been a long time since she had thought there was much happening in her life worthy of party decorations. But did she have unrealistic expectations of Dad? Was that why they were still apart? At that moment, I thought she did. On either end of the table, I placed the clean hurricanes over two big candle columns, wondering if anyone would catch the connection with the weather. That was probably too much to ask.

I hauled all the liquor bottles out to the table and set them up in perfect rows on the left with mixers and garnishes and glasses on the right with an ice bucket and a wine bucket. I went to dig around the refrigerator and found the cheese ball. Perfect. A centerpiece! It looked great on Mom's smallish round platter that had a design of red branch coral painted all over it. I took an unopened package of crackers and laid them next to the platter. Because the air on the front beach was basically always wet, open crackers at four were soggy crackers by six. Even I remembered that. And in a moment of uncharacteristic artistry, I arranged parsley sprigs all around the cheese ball, giving the platter that certain *je ne sais quoi*. *Je ne sais quoi*, indeed. Who was I kidding? However, it should come as no surprise to anyone that setting up a bar in this family was second nature to us all. I stepped back, squinted my eyes, and gave it an appraisal. To the squinted eye, it looked like a photo shoot from some food magazine. It was more than good enough.

By six o'clock, Dad and Charlie had returned and the three of us were on the porch enjoying a cool drink. Dad had brought in a small cooler from his truck with six cold beers neatly resting inside. I had obviously overstocked the bar, but so what? I'd become so used to carrying all those bottles and the accoutrements back and forth from the liquor cabinet to the porch that I was using the laundry basket for transport instead of making multiple trips.

For a change, I was wearing a cute blouse and a short skirt, hoping it would improve Mom's disposition to see me pay some attention to my appearance. I even had on lipstick. And for the sake of Stanley and Stella's sanity and mine, I did not use my mother's moisturizer on my legs.

Charlie was guzzling a cherry Diet Coke that Dad made for him. They were rocking in their rockers, back and forth, debating what would go into the buried treasure Charlie intended to put together for the Greenville Three. Three candy bars that wouldn't melt? Three comic books? Maybe something old-fashioned like a jump rope? Did anyone jump rope anymore? Dad wanted to know. What about yo-yos? Charlie said that yo-yos don't work that easily, and Dad said he'd show him how to get it going. No problem. That he used to be a champion at yo-yo tricks. Really? Charlie said and ran to get his. Dad promptly showed him how to do a trick he called "rock the cradle," and "walk the dog." Charlie was so excited he could hardly breathe, but alas, even with Dad's careful instructions, Charlie could not make it happen.

I loved being the bug on the wall for them, listening to Dad playing the grandfather and to Charlie just naturally being a kid with his Guster, the giggles, the questions, the innocence, their boundless joy that was so apparent—it was one of those transcendent moments I would never be able to re-create or describe with any degree of accuracy. But my heart was so full and satisfied. I was so grateful to have Charlie for my son. I was so happy that Charlie could bring such happiness to my father and my father to him. It was powerful stuff.

Mom finally joined us, stepping out into the evening air, a vision in aqua trailed by a swirling cloud of jasmine. Dad just stopped talking and stared at her.

"Cat got your tongue, Buster?" she asked, with the tiniest of self-satisfied smirks crossing her face.

"No, I just, uh—" Dad trailed off.

"You think she looks good now? You should've seen her last night, Guster! The old guys at the restaurant were sending her drinks every five minutes! You look great *again*, Glam!"

Well, out of the mouths of babes, just as they say. My attention had been directed at shaking up a batch of Manhattans, and I did not realize what Charlie had revealed until it was too late to hush him.

"Is that true, Annie?" Dad said. "You? Taking free drinks from men?"

"What of it?" She shrugged her shoulders to let Dad know she didn't care what he thought. "Discretion is the better part of valor, Charlie," Mom said, regurgitating one of the better-worn maxims of the Britt clan.

"What does *that* mean?" Charlie asked, looking to me for an explanation.

I leaned in to whisper to him. "It means that when it comes to the business of relationships between people, it's best to turn on the filter between the brain and the tongue before you start talking." Charlie knew he had made an error in judgment. But I wasn't going to let him drown or even wobble on something so slight. "It's true, Dad. The Codgers Committee gave Mom a thumbs-up. Big time. That color is *amazing* on you, Mom. Does anyone want a Manhattan?"

I hoped I had ironed out the wrinkles all around.

"Well, now, I believe I would *love* a Manhattan," Mom said, sounding like a true belle. "That sounds absolutely *lovely*."

"I think I'll just have another beer," Dad said to no one in particular with a trace of annoyance. He reached in his cooler. Clearly, he didn't like the idea of competition.

"How come we never have this at home?" Charlie asked.

"What?"

"Cherry Cokes and party lights?"

"It doesn't work as well unless you have salty air and a cheese ball," I said. I popped open the crackers and heaped a moderate amount of Mom's concoction on one, handing it to Charlie. "Taste this!"

Charlie popped the cracker into his mouth and chewed it up, his eyes growing large. Finally, he said, "Wow. That's awesome!" Then he helped himself to another one. And another.

"Don't ruin your appetite, baby," I said and watched as Dad walked to the other end of the porch.

I could hear Steve's car pulling up. Dad called out to him, "Hey, there, Steve! Come join us for a drink!"

Well, you didn't have to invite Steve Plofker twice. He came bounding up our steps. To be fair, he had to get his dogs anyway. And they, hearing his voice, jumped up from their sleeping spots like two hairy Lazaruses and began yelping *Hello! Hello! Hello!*

Yes, I understood a certain amount of doggy-speak.

"Good evening, everyone! Boy, today was a muggy one, wasn't it?"

"Aren't you in your office all day? I mean, isn't it air-conditioned?" I asked, being a little bitch for no reason other than I liked making him squirm.

"Yeah, like a meat locker," he said without missing a beat. "But when it gets this hot and humid, the air-conditioning just can't do the job. But thanks for your concern for my comfort."

"Right," I said, feeling my neck break into a sweat. "Would you like a Manhattan?"

"Why not?" he said, adding, "I haven't had one of those in years! Thanks!"

"Steve?" Dad said. "You much of a cook?"

"Well, I can burn a steak with the best of them," he said, giving my legs a stealth evaluation while simultaneously scratching his dogs' ears and throwing his head back so they could lick his neck. "Can I help you with something?"

But I saw him looking and knew exactly what he was thinking. If he thought a woman like me would ever wrap my leg around his waist like that little slut had last night, he was cracked in the head. Besides, I wasn't interested. In addition, dog spit on your neck couldn't be sanitary.

"I was thinking that since the ladies look so nice and I promised Charlie I'd teach him to fry fish that if you'd stay for dinner, maybe you'd help me cook. Annie's wearing a new outfit and all. You know . . ."

Steve spun around and looked at Mom, doing a double-take, which did immeasurable good for her ego.

"Wow! Annie! You look like one million dollars after taxes! You cut your hair!"

"I liked it better longer. Long hair is sexier," Dad said. "So what do you say? Want to fry some fish with me?"

Mom and I rolled our eyes.

"Sure! I'd love to!" he said, and I handed him a drink. "Cheers!"

"The hush puppy batter is in the refrigerator," Mom said and then whispered to me when they had gone inside, "They're going to destroy my kitchen. And since when does he think about *sexy* in connection with *me*?"

"Who knows, but he sure was looking at you with *that* look! If they wreck the kitchen, we'll make them clean it up," I said.

"Oh, please. I think we should move dinner to the dining room. The kitchen is going to reek of oil and fish and onions."

"I wouldn't move dinner to make Steve Plofker happy," I said. "And if we go to the dining room, you'll *have* to sit with us, especially now that they're cooking."

"You're right. Let's go make us a centerpiece of herbs and flowers for the table. There's always something in the yard. Besides, I don't want my *short hair* to smell like fish."

"Oh, hell, Mom, let's go help them, or we won't get dinner until Tuesday."

Mom magically arranged handfuls of lavender and rosemary in two conch shells, which, I was later informed by Charlie, were actually whelks. Placed back to back and with votive candles around them, they looked really pretty. It was amazing what you could do with found objects. And, I had to admit, Mom was resourceful.

We slipped in between the men, moving the china from the kitchen table to the dining room. I slipped out to the porch, mixed up another batch of Manhattans, refilled our glasses, and took another beer to Dad. No one objected. I made Charlie a cherry Coke, and he was thrilled.

Charlie was having the time of his life with Mom's deep fryer, dropping in big dollops of the cornmeal batter, cooking them until they were golden brown, and draining them on paper towels. For every three that hit the paper, one went into his mouth. Dad and Steve had two big skillets of fish frying, and discussions about how to season them peppered the air, no pun intended. Mom sliced the beautiful tomatoes onto a base of lettuce on a platter and dropped the corn into boiling water. We melted a stick of butter in a Pyrex casserole dish and placed it in the microwave, an old trick, so that when the corn was done we could roll it around and butter it evenly. Dinner was almost ready. And it was a real Lowcountry feast.

As soon as we sat down and had our glasses in midair to toast, Miss Deb came in the door and straight to us. Her face was awash with distress. Mom practically jettisoned from her seat to her side.

"Get another chair," she said to me, but Dad got up to do it instead.

"Whatever is the matter, Deb?" Mom asked. "Is Vernon all right?"

"I saw the lights on, but y'all are having your supper. I'll call you later."

"Sit!" Dad said. "Sit and have some supper with us!"

He held a chair for her as Steve moved his place setting down the table. Miss Deb sat, but she looked at Mom with her *I'm not so sure* face.

Mom said, "Listen, you have to eat, and we could feed the whole island with what we have here tonight. Now tell us. How's Vernon? Buster, get Deb a glass of wine. Jackie, fix her a plate. Thanks, y'all."

"Oh, I'm sure it's just me. They admitted him for observation. I mean, there's no real reason to panic, but I just have this terrible sinking feeling in my heart that, well, I don't know."

"He's at East Cooper Hospital?" Steve said. "I can look in on him tomorrow morning. Who's his doc?"

I put a full plate in front of her, and she looked at it as if she hadn't had a decent meal in ages. But then, if it's true that we eat with our eyes first, the food was irresistible. Steve poured her a glass of wine.

"Fran Wanat. I mean, Wanat's the best cardiologist we've got in the whole state, and he says not to worry, so maybe I should just relax and have a nice evening with y'all! Right?"

"I know Sharon, his wife. She's darling! Drink up, sister!" Mom said. "Vern will be fine."

The doorbell rang, and I could hear children's voices calling out for Charlie. "Is Charlie home? Char-lieeeee?"

"Can I go to the door?" Charlie asked me.

"Of course!"

He jumped up and ran to the door, returning with the father of the kids from Greenville.

The father, John the Elder, the infamous bankruptcy lawyer, said, "I'm taking the kids up to the Palmetto Grande to see a movie and then out for ice cream. My sister's two kids are coming also. We've got two big SUVs loaded with varmints. Everyone wanted to know if we could invite Charlie. He can stay over with us. The kids have built a pillow fort all over the living room, and I guess we're looking at a night of controlled mayhem."

"Please?" Charlie said. "I'm done with dinner."

His plate was clean. Not a crumb left. Who could tell him no to an invitation like that? I nodded my consent and hooked my thumb toward the door, indicating permission for him to skedaddle.

"Whoa, whoa, whoa! Come around here, boy," Dad said, extracting a stack of cash from his pants pocket and peeling off a twenty-dollar bill. "Don't spend it all in one place."

"Oh, Guster, thanks, but I don't need it. I have a job, you know." He reached into his pocket and pulled out a handful of severely crumpled fives. There must have been six of them. Maybe eight.

Dad smiled and said, "Take the money and say, 'Thanks, Guster.' Okay, Mr. Big Shot?"

"Thanks! Love you!" Charlie snatched the twenty, hugged Dad's neck, blew me a kiss and was gone.

"Send me a text when you get back to the island!" I said.

He gave a thumbs-up and ran ahead to meet up with the kids.

"I'll take good care of him," John the Elder said.

"Oh, I know that. Thanks," I said and followed him to the back door.

"Pray for us," he said. "It's gonna be a long night."

"Oh, you'll have fun. Take pictures of the fort!"

Charlie piled into the car, smiling and happy, soon lost in a sea of adolescent goodwill and smiles. I felt pretty good about just letting Charlie go off with them like that. It never would've happened in Brooklyn. Oh, invitations came in Brooklyn, but there was more advance planning and less spontaneity. Here, doors were open, porch lights were on, and it was just easier all around to be inclusive and congenial. And I wasn't worried for an instant that someone was going to carry Charlie off into the night. I was getting over my paranoia. Temporarily.

I went back inside, and Miss Deb was talking about Vernon. "They just want to run some tests. So they kept him. I mean, they've always sent him home before. So it makes me a little nervous."

"I don't blame you!" I said. "But I feel very sure that if he was in real danger he'd be in an ICU."

"Well, actually, he *is* in the ICU. They want to monitor him overnight. But his EKG was negative, and one of the ER doctors said he thought it might be reflux. Vernon had had quite a bit of salsa and chips while he was watching television."

"There you go!" Dad said. "That's probably it."

"Well, then, you don't have to worry at all!" Mom said. "Isn't that smart of them? I'll tell you, modern medicine! They can perform miracles. Isn't that right, Steve?"

"I see miracles all the time," he said, and he shot me a look that said *doesn't sound good*.

It didn't sound good to me either, but Steve and I didn't know much about cardiology beyond what they teach you in basic emergency care. Maybe he had done a cardiac rotation, but that would've been years ago. And then I saw something that reminded me of active duty in a triage setting in the hills of Afghanistan. Miss Deb began to talk in a higher-pitched tone of voice, totally laser-focused on another topic rather than Vernon, who should have been her only priority.

"I can't believe I sat here and ate all this food and didn't even see that you have transformed yourself into a beauty queen! Annie Britt! What have you done to yourself? You look fabulous!"

"Doesn't she?" I said and smiled.

"I think she looks great too!" Steve said.

"Humph," Dad said. "Annie can go get all the haircuts in the world, but at the end of the day she's still fifty-eight years old."

Silence.

"That wasn't nice," Mom said and got up. "A lady never reveals her age. It's not even necessarily in her obituary. I'll be in my room."

More silence.

"What'd I say that was so terrible?"

"Oh, Dad," I said. This was what Mom was talking about when she said Dad could be sarcastic and insensitive. "It was going so well."

"I don't get it," Dad said.

Deb looked around and then said, "I'll go talk to her." She left the table.

Steve looked from my face to Dad's and back to mine. "Wow! Nine o'clock already? I'd better get the dogs home and settled in for the night. I've got to be at the hospital by seven tomorrow."

"I'll walk you out," I said.

We stood at the screen door on the porch for a minute. The dogs were antsy to get outside, so Steve opened the door and they bounded across our yard to his and sat at his door, waiting. They had acquired a new habit.

Suddenly the paper lanterns seemed out of place, and it made me a little sad. Things had not gone as I had hoped.

"My old man sure knows how to clear a room, doesn't he?" I said, hoping he wouldn't think ill of us.

"He just wasn't thinking," Steve said. "But I'm pretty sure he hurt your mom's feelings."

"Yeah. You're definitely right about that. I've been gone for a long time, and I guess I never realized that he really did things like that. Mom always said he was insulting, but I never believed her."

"Hmmm. What's up with them? Are they divorced or separated or what?"

"Well, they've never done anything legal. I think, you know, the time apart has been mostly a good thing for both of them. But it looks to me like Mom fixed herself up for him and then he shot her down even though—"

"He still loves her," Steve said.

"Exactly. And I think she still loves him. They're grown-ups. They'll have to work it out. Anyway, please let us know if you find out anything about Vernon."

"I will. What a beautiful night! Looks like that Arlene finally blew out to sea."

"Yeah, well, I got another storm brewing in the house."

"Yeah, you do. Thanks for dinner. See you tomorrow?"

"Yeah. Thanks for cooking," I said. "Good night."

Steve Plofker was growing on me.

I went back inside. Dad was washing the dishes with Miss Deb. She handed her dishcloth to me and I began to dry and she went looking for her purse. She said good night to us, but Dad insisted on walking her to her door. One minute he was a prince, the ideal grand-father, and then without warning he opened his mouth and out popped the Devil. I just didn't know what to say to him.

Dad decided to stay for the night on the pretense that he wanted to make things right with Mom in the morning. I agreed, pointing out that in addition, it was dark on Highway 17 and it was getting late. I directed him to Charlie's room, since we had a vacancy for the night. Soon the house was quiet. Order had been restored, Dad was snoring evenly, Mom did not resur-face, and Charlie was safe at his friends' house. My last thought before I drifted off to sleep was that if Mom and Dad ever lost each other before they resolved their issues, they'd sure have an awful lot of regrets.

12

. . . we had fairly unearthed an oblong chest of wood . . . three feet and a half long, three feet broad, and two and a half feet deep. . . . a treasure of incalculable value lay gleaming before us.

—Edgar Allan Poe, "The Gold-Bug"

Annie

It was early morning, and the skies were clear and blue. When storms turned out to sea, the Lowcountry looked washed clean, as though the good Lord was giving all us sinners another chance for redemption. I didn't feel the need for another chance, but I knew somebody who did—the wild animal that was snoring like every hog in hell on the other side of the house. Jackie snored like a lady hog, Charlie snored like a baby lamb, and Papa Bear? I recognized Papa Bear's unforgettable refrain. Maybe I should have the ductwork cleaned. There was definitely something off kilter on that side of the house, because I'm sure I never snored.

The kitchen, by the way, glistened from a thorough scouring, and all the garbage had been taken out. Lucky for him. Well, even though Buster had shown very badly last night, it surely had been wonderful to have everyone around the table. That's what my life lacked. My family and friends around my table. And I needed more fun.

I was dressed in my walking clothes because my plan was to get out of the house before the old bastard got up expecting waffles and eggs. I called Deb's house and got their voice mail. Then I called her cell phone and got voice mail again. That wasn't right. The hair on the back of my neck stood up on end, and a chill ran through my body. I began to panic because my instincts told me something was dreadfully wrong. I grabbed my purse, ran down the back steps, and jumped into my car, headed for East Cooper Hospital.

I drove there as fast as I could with the single purpose of getting there on time. On time for what? I knew for what. I could feel Deb's terrible pain before I even got there. I could hear her in my mind praying for mercy. I begged God to change things but I knew in my heart that the worst had already happened. I knew it even before I pulled into the parking lot, jumped out of my car, and ran to the main entrance.

She had said he was in the ICU. I found its location on the information board and barely got onto the elevator as the heavy doors were closing. I could feel my heart slamming against my ribs, and I was out of breath. Upstairs, I saw Steve in the hall with his arm around Deb and Deb's shoulders were heaving. I ran to her side.

"Oh, God! Deb? What's happened?"

"He's *gone*, Annie. Vernon is dead."

"Oh, my poor dear friend! I am so, so sorry!" I put my arms around her, and she wept and sighed and wept and I wept with her. "Tell me what happened. Please, tell me what happened."

Steve ran his hands up and down his cheeks and sighed deeply. "He had what they call the widow maker. Even though all his tests were clear, he had a sudden rupture of plaque in his arteries which caused a massive heart attack. They tried *everything* to revive him, but unfortunately, the doctors couldn't. It was the same thing that killed Tim Russert."

"Oh, God. I remember that. This is so unfair. Just so unfair."

"He was getting dressed to come home," Deb said. "He was coming home, Annie." She began to sob.

I had never seen my friend in such a state of distress. I was distressed too. I'd loved old Vernon, even though he rarely left his La-Z-Boy to be with us for a meal or a movie. He was less like the big, brawny, can-do husband and more like Deb's personal, very lovable, big old pussycat. I had known him for as long as I'd known her, and because Deb and I saw each other every day, I knew everything about him. I still could not comprehend that I was standing there in the hall of the ICU reeling from the news of Vernon's death because death was incomprehensible anyway. And Deb was just a complete emotional wreck.

"How can this be?" she kept asking over and over.

"I don't know, darlin'. I just don't know," I said. What else could I say?

I turned to see Buster and Jackie standing there. One by one, they scooped Deb into their arms and hugged her. I heard Buster say, "Oh, my sweet friend, I'm so sorry." And our poor Jackie, well, Jackie knew Deb's pain better than she ever would have wanted to know it.

Steve turned to me. "I called your house right before you got here. Jackie answered the phone and said you weren't home. How did *you know* to come?"

"If I told you, you'd never believe me."

"Try me," he said.

"Okay. I could hear Deb wailing—in my head. This is the Lowcountry, Steve. That's how life goes around here."

"You're *that* connected?"

"No, we're *all* that connected if you know how to listen."

"I'd love to learn," he said.

"I don't think there's anything to teach. You just have to tune in and listen."

I drove Deb back to her house but only after the head nurse gave her a few minutes alone in the room with Vernon's body. There was nothing I had ever seen more profoundly sad than watching Deb, my friend of over thirty years, lean over her husband's lifeless body, push his hair away from his forehead, and kiss him there with all the tenderness any woman could possibly have. The only thing more gut-wrenching was remembering the day I'd watched my daughter do the same thing. Deb did not know yet where her heart was headed. I did. Jackie did. But few would unless they had lived through the experience themselves. It was just so horribly sad.

Steve had to do rounds at the hospital and go to his office and see patients, but he promised to check on us as soon as he could. So I gathered Deb's things up and threw my arm around her shoulder, and we left in my car. Buster and Jackie were right behind us, Buster driving Deb's car and Jackie in hers.

I turned off the radio. This was no time for music. Not yet. Not even Michael Bublé. It was time to try and shore Deb up, because there was a lot to be done and I knew I would be the one to see her through. In fact, I *wanted* to be the one.

"So, Deb? I don't want you to worry. I'm going to be right by your side every step of the way, okay?"

"Thanks."

"You up for a few questions?"

"Sure."

"Do you want me to make phone calls?"

"God, yes. I don't think I can do that. Not right now."

"It's okay. Just give me your address book. Jackie and I can take care of that."

She nodded and again said, "Thanks."

"And do you have a preference of Stuhr's or McAlister's?" They were the two most popular funeral directors in town.

"McAlister's, I guess. But it doesn't matter really."

"I'll see who's free. And do you know if Vernon had a will and life insurance?"

"Yes, there's a will and there's life insurance. The originals are in the safety deposit box at the bank, but I have copies at home."

"That's good enough. And would you like me to call the rectory at Stella Maris to arrange a funeral Mass?"

"I think Vernon would have loved that. But everything he wanted is spelled out in his will. You know Vernon. Or *knew* him, I guess I should say now. He has been waiting to die for years. He bought our plots at Mount Pleasant Memorial to celebrate our twentieth wedding anniversary."

We had a small gallows humor chuckle then.

"Yeah, God, that was Vernon all right," I said. "A practical man if ever there was one."

"Well, it wasn't very romantic. He was a good man, but not very romantic," she said and sighed from the bottom of her soul. "I'm so tired I could sleep for a week."

"That's why I'm asking you these things now. I'll get the ball rolling, and you get a nap. By tonight your house will be crawling with people. Where's your sister?"

"Hawaii. You know, we still aren't speaking. We haven't really spoken since Momma's funeral."

"Well, you and I both know she shouldn't have grabbed that amethyst ring for herself. It was supposed to be yours." I'd heard the story of the ring a hundred times. "People are so greedy. They forget it's a serious sin to take something that doesn't belong to them."

"It's called stealing. That ring will never make her happy."

"Let's hope. Should I call her?"

"Sure. But she won't come."

"Yeah, but she's your only sister. She should be told."

"Whatever you say. You're more of a sister than she ever was. Oh, Annie. I can hardly even think right now. I can't believe he's gone. I mean, just like *that!*"

"I know. I know. That's why I'm here. It's too terrible."

We arrived at her home, and Buster hurried over to help her out of the car, up the steps, and into her house. Deb wasn't even sixty, but on that morning she was moving like she was one hundred years old.

We went directly to her room. She handed me an accordion folder from a shelf in her bedroom closet. "The will, the insurance policy, and the deed for the cemetery plot are all in there. And here's my address book. The library and faculty list is in the back. I'm just going to shut my eyes for a few minutes."

"Don't worry. I'll come and ask you if I need anything. For now, you just rest."

She climbed into bed. I turned on her ceiling fan, closed her blinds, and pulled the door quietly behind me. I went to the kitchen, where Buster and Jackie were standing by the sink.

"What can I do to help?" Jackie asked.

"Get an inventory of the liquor and wine and mixers. You know people on this island drink like all forty. Make a list, and then maybe you'll go to the store, Buster?"

"Sure, no problem."

"Then you and I have a lot of phone calls to make. Is Charlie okay?"

"Yes. I spoke to him a few minutes ago. He's just going to spend the day with his friends. He's fine. The last thing he needs is more exposure to death."

"I agree. Okay, good."

I sat down at the kitchen table, attempting to read the insurance policy, and Buster sat down next to me. "Should I make a pot of coffee?" he asked.

"I don't see why not," I said, as evenly as I could.

"Listen, about what I said last night?"

I took off my reading glasses and looked at him with the most imperious face I had. "Yes? What about it?"

"Well, I just want you to know that I think you look really pretty and you'll probably be even prettier when you're eighty."

"Is this your way of apologizing?"

"Yeah. Yes. Yes, it is."

"Apology accepted. Now, why don't I make coffee and you read this darned thing. I hate all this legalese. I am always so afraid of missing something."

"Sure. Hand it over."

"And there's his will too."

"No problem."

The coffee was brewing in minutes, and I realized my stomach was growling. We all needed breakfast. But there was no time to stop and go to the grocery store. I found a loaf of bread and started making toast. There was peanut butter in her pantry, and there were some bananas on the counter. It would suit us just fine. I lined up three plates and thought about who to call first. The funeral home, I decided. They would help us write the obituary for the newspaper. And they sold everything else we needed.

"Hey, Buster? Look at Vernon's will. Did he specify what kind of a casket he wanted or any other details he wanted covered at his funeral?"

"I don't know. Let me see here . . ."

I put a cup of coffee in front of him and a plate of food. He took a sip of the coffee. "You still make the best coffee on earth. Thanks."

"Well, thanks, Buster. I can't believe Vernon's gone."

"Yeah, it is unbelievable. Well, would you looky here—"

I took the will from Buster and read the passage he pointed to. Vernon wanted a simple wood casket, but he wanted Johnny Cash's "Ring of Fire" to be played at his wake.

"Oh, my God! Is he crazy?" I said. "We can't do that!"

"He was as crazy as a bedbug. It's what the man wanted, but I say let's let Deb decide this one. What do you think? Was he worried about going to Hell?"

"Only if sloth could send you there, bless his heart."

"You are too much, Annie," Buster said, smiling and shaking his head.

Jackie came into the kitchen with a legal pad. "Do I smell coffee? Here's the list." I took it from her.

"How are they set for booze?" Buster asked.

"Thanks," Jackie said when I handed her a mug. "It depends on what you count as booze. If you count sambuca, Campari, crème de menthe, Baileys, amaretto, pomegranate liqueur, and Marsala wine as liquor, then they're in good shape. If you're looking for vodka, scotch, gin, and, I don't know, maybe rum? We have to go to the store."

"Vernon was a beer man," Buster said. "I'll bet there are five cases of Budweiser in the refrigerator under the house."

It didn't meet code to have a refrigerator at flood level, but most people I knew had a refrigerator or a freezer or both under the house along with their bicycles, golf cart, boat, lawn mower, kayak, and of course, their cars. If a hurricane hit that flooded the island, a rusty old refrigerator loaded with beer would be the least of our problems.

"I'll go look," Jackie said.

By noon Deb was up and in the shower and we had notified everyone who needed to know. All that was left to do was to take Deb over to McAlister-Smith to choose the casket and find the clothes to lay him out in. In his will he had specified a black shirt and black pants, like his hero Johnny Cash.

"What's up with this Johnny Cash fixation?" Jackie asked when we told her about the music and the clothes.

"Vernon was a man who had very specific tastes," Buster said. "You know? I think the only live concert he ever went to was back in the seventies when Johnny Cash played at County Hall. It just stayed with him, I guess. I mean, he used to tell me about that concert all the time. He loved Johnny Cash."

"Everybody loves Johnny Cash," Jackie said. "Even me."

"Yeah, but heavenly days, would you want 'Ring of Fire' played at your wake?" I said. "Probably not."

"You're right. I'm going down to Café Medley to get sandwiches," Jackie said. "I'll be back in a flash."

"I'll take a turkey on whole wheat," Buster said. "Do you need cash?"

"No, I got lunch covered. Mom?"

"Anything's fine for me. I'm not fussy."

Jackie left, and then it was just Buster and me alone in the room. We were doing just fine together. Did that mean anything to him? Not wanting to bring up the subject of our weird relationship status, I turned to the sink to wash up the cups and plates from the morning. He broke the silence.

"Annie? Does Deb know about this?"

"Does Deb know about what?" Deb said.

"Hey! She's up!" I said. "Did you get any sleep?"

"Believe it or not, I did," she said.

"You might want to look at this," Buster said and handed her Vernon's will.

"You want coffee?" I asked. "I just made a fresh pot."

"Sure. Thanks. I need my glasses," she said.

"Take mine," I said. I took them from the top of my head and slid them across the table.

"Thanks. Now let's see . . . *what*? Did y'all *see* this? Was he out of his *mind*?"

Then she started to laugh and laugh and laugh. Her laughter was so welcome that we laughed with her. Had Vernon done this so that Deb would laugh her head off, or had he been serious? I asked her and got the wrong answer.

"Oh, no! He was as serious as he could be! He always said he was going to do this, and I didn't believe him!"

"So we have to do it," Buster said.

"Wait!" I had an idea. "It doesn't say that it has to be a Johnny Cash CD playing with Johnny singing, does it?"

"No," Buster said. "It just says he wants that song played at his wake. Why?"

"What if it was played by a chamber quartet?"

Their mouths dropped open, and they stared at me.

"Brilliant!" Deb said. "How much would it cost?"

"Annie? You are a genius!" Buster said. "Don't worry about the cost. He left you two hundred and fifty thousand dollars in life insurance."

"He did *what*? Let me see that!" She looked at the amount of the policy and gasped. "Holy God. I can't believe it. When did he do this?"

"I don't know," Buster said.

"Wonderful!" I said. "The bank is open and decorum has been restored! I'll call my friend who plays viola with the South Coast Symphony. And what if they played other music too, like 'I Walk the Line' and 'Green, Green Grass of Home'?"

"Absolutely!" Deb said. "And who said they couldn't play 'Amazing Grace'?"

"No one! And maybe just some pretty music like Vivaldi's *Four Seasons* or Handel's *Water Music*?"

"You ladies sure know how to make lemonade out of lemons," Buster said.

"It's what women always do, Buster," I replied. "I'm calling Dawn Durst right this minute."

"That seems to be the case," he said. "Just be sure they don't play that song 'A Boy Named Sue.'"

By five that afternoon all the arrangements were made. Still at Deb's house, we had a stocked bar ready and a huge platter of fruit and cheese on the dining room table in case someone wanted to nibble. As predicted, the old islanders began to arrive at dusk, bringing casseroles, hams, and pies, and of course, Marshall Stith brought one of his infamous coconut cakes, which rendered all others to the shadows of ineptitude. Everyone had a lovable story about Vernon and heartfelt words of sympathy for Deb. The wake would be the next day and there would be even more people, Deb's friends from the school, friends from church, and, of course, Vernon's friends from SCE&G, where he had worked his whole life until he retired at fifty-two.

Just as we thought, Deb's sister, Anita, did not come. She sent flowers instead. The next day Deb and I were at McAlister's and it was the dreaded appointed hour to view the body.

"Who put a tie on him?" Buster asked. "He wouldn't be caught dead in a tie."

"Apparently he would," I said, deadpan.

There lay Vernon's body, dressed in black, with a black tie neatly knotted under his collar. Considering he was as dead as a doornail, he looked rather chic. For a dead person.

I helped Deb up from the prie-dieu and took her around to see all the beautiful flower arrangements that had been arriving all day. The framed happy pictures of them together that surrounded the room would remind everyone that Vernon and Deb had had a long happy marriage.

I didn't want Deb focusing on Vernon's body. She might begin to weep. Corpses in open caskets were beyond grotesque anyway. I hated when people said, "Oh, look what a good job they did on Mabel! She looks just like she could sit up and talk to you!" Please don't sit up, Mabel, I'd think, please don't. But Vernon had wanted an open casket, so that's what he got.

Deb had been holding herself together remarkably well. And she'd asked me to try and help her from being too maudlin. Wiseacre humor was my secret weapon of the hour.

"I'm sure the salesperson at Belva's misunderstood your sister, Anita, Deb," I said. "No one sends flowers this dinky and cheap for the funeral of an immediate family member."

"You're so wicked! But you don't know Anita," Deb said. "I'm surprised she sent anything at all."

The chamber musicians arrived, set up, and began to play. The music was beautiful, the wake lasted until nine o'clock, and no one, except Monsignor Ben Michaels, said a word about "Ring of Fire," which I heard played at least twice.

" 'Ring of Fire'? Are we concerned about Vernon's immortal soul?" he whispered to Deb and me.

"Oh, no, Father. I'm sure Vernon died in a state of grace," Deb replied. "He wouldn't hurt a fly."

"Well, I anointed him with the last rites, but I'll say an extra novena just in case," he said.

"Thank you, Father," I said. "You never know. It can't hurt, and it might do some good."

"Have you been ill, Mrs. Britt? We haven't seen you at Mass in a long time."

"Me? Oh, no. I'm fine. I've been traveling. You know my daughter lost her husband?"

"Yes, I was very sorry to hear it. And it's a relief to see you looking so well. I hope we'll be seeing you at Mass more often, Mrs. Britt."

I nodded and gave him a tight-lipped smile, thinking, You sanctimonious old fart. He had almost no idea what went on in my life, but he didn't mind reprimanding me in front of my friend and whoever else might have heard him. How did he know I hadn't taken up the One True Cross over at Christ Our King Church in Mount Pleasant?

The day of the funeral was a blur. While we were consumed by our mutual desire to get Deb through this ordeal with the least amount of pain and suffering, it would be a lie to say that I was not distracted by Buster and three new tropical storms that were brewing near the British Virgin Islands. Buster kept saying not to worry, he had a close eye on them. Saying he had an "eye" on a potential hurricane should give you some idea of Buster's deep sense of humor.

He had been staying over in the guest room, only scooting back and forth to Murrells Inlet once for a dark suit and a few other things. He had been especially charming, and, God knows, he had been more helpful than I ever remembered him being. I kept fantasizing that he would try and sneak back into his/my bedroom, but if ever there was a wrong time to patch up our relationship, this was it. And just because he was being so congenial after one minor screwup, it didn't mean he wanted to move home. I tried not to think about what had become of us, but every time I saw him with Charlie or heard him laugh or caught his eye, well, the truth was my heart ached a little, not just for him but for us.

Jackie said she would allow Charlie to come to the church if he wanted to, but I encouraged him to stay with his friends.

"Bring him to the reception at Miss Deb's afterward. There'll be lots of other children there."

"Yes, that's a better idea. I'm not so sure I can handle this myself," Jackie said. "But I've known Miss Deb since the day I was born. I have to go."

"You just lean on me, sugar," I said.

"You can lean on me too," Buster said.

It seemed impossible, but we were acting as a family, all of us at once. And it hadn't happened in so long, I was almost terrified to make much of it because if Buster and Jackie realized it too, what ground we had gained might be lost. Somebody might get nervous and head for the hills. Maybe it was the death of Jimmy that had been the catalyst, and now, with the shocking loss of Vernon, we were thrown together again. I thought about what Jackie had said when she reminded me that I wouldn't let her father attend her husband's funeral. She was right. I had been a very foolish woman to be so prideful. I owed them more than I had been giving.

But wait. Weren't women always made to feel like they never gave enough? And didn't your family always want more? Well, right now Deb was my priority and I was determined to see her through. We could calculate the balance of my taking versus my giving at a later date.

I don't have to tell you that the graveside service was surreal. Anyone who has ever stood over open ground and watched a loved one lowered into it knows the wretchedness that comes over you. I watched as Steve, Buster, and the other pallbearers performed their duty with unbelievable dignity and respect. I was so proud of them.

I've been to scores of funerals and graveside services, and I know this much: the family or the person who has suffered the loss needs you there. I cannot fathom how unbearable it must be to go through a burial alone. When my mother died, the scores of people who came to the services or brought food or sent cards—well, it just made all the difference in the world to me. It made the worst day of my life bearable. Hopefully, all the people who turned out to honor Vernon's life made it easier for Deb.

Finally we left the cemetery, and soon we were back at Deb's house for the reception. As predicted, the suffocating rooms were overflowing with children and adults, the dining room table groaning under the weight of all the food and drink. The bereavement committee brought platters and bowls of mouthwatering fried chicken, red rice, potato salad, green salad, and rolls, and it all disappeared right before our eyes as though David Copperfield were behind the curtains working his magic.

Deb was exhausted. We were all exhausted. When the last person left, Steve and Jackie took Charlie home. Buster and I stayed to help Deb do a final sweep of the house for glasses and napkins. I filled a plate with food for her dinner, covered it with plastic wrap, and slipped it into the refrigerator. I put away everything that remained in the dish rack, and Buster took out the last bag of garbage. We found Deb sitting in her living room, looking at pictures of Vernon in a scrapbook.

"How are you doing, sweetheart?" I asked her.

She closed the album and looked up at us. "All things considered? I think I'm . . . well, I'm okay. I'm doing fine."

"Would you like us to sit with you for a while?" I said.

"No, y'all go on home. I think I need some downtime, you know?"

"Absolutely," Buster said. "Now, you know, we're just a few houses away. All you have to do is pick up the phone."

"Thank you. Really. I don't know how I would've managed without both of you," she said.

"I'll call you later," I said, and we left.

On the way home Buster kept clearing his throat.

"You warming up to sing an aria?" I asked, teasing him.

"No, I just wanted to say something to you and I'm having trouble finding the words."

"Oh, just spit it out, Buster." I was about to get a lecture. I could feel it in my bones. I had committed some transgression that he couldn't allow to pass without a critique. "Since when do you worry about hurting my feelings?"

"No, you've got it all wrong. I was going to say how much I admire the kind of friend you've been to Deb in the past few days. The tone you set made me be a better friend to her too. For Vernon's sake. And yours too. I mean, you did so much to organize everything and it all worked out so beautifully, but it was a helluva lot of effort on your part and I just, well, I wanted you to know that. I saw how you put your heart into everything to make it easier on Deb. It was a very generous thing you did, Annie. Very generous and kind."

"It's what friends do for each other, Buster."

"What the hell happened to our friendship, Annie?"

We came to the bottom of the Salty Dog's steps and stopped.

"Oh, Buster. Listen, I haven't changed. The kind of thing I did for Deb that you tell me you so admire is the same thing that drove you crazy enough to run you out the door eleven years ago."

"Well, then, I was a horse's ass eleven years ago."

"You might still be one for all I know. Although you do seem to be showing some signs of improvement."

13

The chest had been full to the brim. . . . All was gold . . . with a few English guineas. . . . The value of the jewels we found more difficulty in estimating. There were diamonds . . . rubies of remarkable brilliancy . . . emeralds . . . sapphires . . . an opal. . . . a vast quantity of solid gold ornaments;—a prodigious golden punch-bowl. . . . We estimated the entire contents of the chest, that night, at a million and a half of dollars . . . it was found that we had greatly undervalued the treasure.

—Edgar Allan Poe, "The Gold-Bug"

Jackie

It was early Wednesday and raining like the dickens. We were catching the outer bands of rain from one of those tropical storms. The others had turned to squalls and thankfully fizzled out. The nameless one that remained was one of those storms that didn't have enough wind to do any real damage, but the standing water it would leave in its wake would provide breeding grounds for millions of mosquitoes. And frogs. Great. That was the thing about hurricanes and tropical storms, they left town in the same fashion that a stubborn old dowager would leave a cotillion, slowly saying good-bye to her minions, returning for one last waltz, finally leaving for parts unknown, maybe to dissolve into nothingness or to simply find another party, gather steam, and raise a little more hell.

I was in the kitchen making brownies and watching *Today* on television. The weather in New York was much more appealing. It was dry and sunny, no humidity. I got a little homesick for Yankee territory then because as much as I was not obsessed with my looks, I hadn't had a decent hair day since we had arrived.

Mom appeared all dressed and smelling very good. Some mischief was afoot, because since when did she put on cologne at seven in the morning?

"Morning, sweetheart!" she chirped and gave me a peck on the cheek. "Do I smell chocolate?"

"Yeah, I'm making a batch of brownies for Miss Deb. I thought I'd go around to her house and sit with her for a bit, maybe go for a walk on the beach if it ever stops raining."

"Honey, you're so sweet to do that, but you know she's got a house filled with cakes and cookies."

Wasn't it just like good old mom to remind me my efforts were ill conceived and unnecessary?

"So she can freeze them. I didn't know what else to do, and I'm not going over there empty-handed. You taught me that."

"Yes, I did. Now, can I make you some breakfast?"

"Actually, I made a pot of grits and I was going to scramble some eggs. Where are you going all gussied up this morning?"

"Up to Murrells Inlet with your father. He has to get some things. He asked me if he could stay for as long as you and Charlie were here, and I said, yes, but only in the guest room. No muffky-poofky, *if* you know what I mean."

"I see." Did I need to hear that, especially at this hour? "Eggs?"

"Why not?" she said. "I'll make toast."

"Great."

I scrambled eight eggs because as soon as I had four in the bowl, Dad and Charlie appeared. We had a fast breakfast together, and Dad and Mom stood up, scraped their dishes, put them in the sink, and ran water over them. They seemed nervous for some inexplicable reason.

"Wow, it's really pouring," Charlie said, looking out the window. "Maybe I should take an umbrella to walk the dogs?"

"I would. There's a big one in the hall closet," I told him. "Hey, Dad? Y'all be careful on the road, okay?"

"Now you sound like me," Mom said.

Charlie found the umbrella and zoomed over to Steve's. Mom put on her raincoat and tied a scarf over her hair and under her chin.

"Do I look like Sophia Loren in that fifties movie, what's the name? It was shot in Italy?" she asked.

"Spitting image," I said.

"Let's go, Glam!" Dad said, calling her by her nickname for the first time.

As they hurried down the steps to Dad's car I had the distinct feeling that I wasn't getting all the facts from those two.

I cleaned up the messy kitchen and took the brownies from the oven, and the smell of them brought Charlie from the hammock to my side. He was riveted to Steve's e-reader and "The Gold-Bug."

"Think I could have one?" he asked.

"Of course! When they're cool, I'm going to slice them and arrange them on a paper plate. Miss Deb won't even guess that a couple of them are missing. The plan was to go over and see her for a bit. What about you?"

"Well, I'm not going anywhere in *this* weather," he said, saying it just like Jimmy used to when it was foul weather in New York. I was so surprised. It could've been Jimmy talking. Jimmy could have been right there in the room.

A little later I knocked on Miss Deb's door, and after what I thought was a prolonged amount of time, she answered.

"You busy?" I asked.

"Lord! Come in out of this weather! You'll catch pee-neumonia!"

It was a curious pronunciation, but the one we always used to make children laugh.

"I brought you some brownies," I said, stepping inside.

"Well, come on in and let's have one. I just made some tea."

Her kitchen table seemed to be the hub of her house as the porch was of my mother's. I took a seat and folded back the plastic wrap on the brownies. She put a glass of iced tea in front of me.

"Sugar?" she asked.

"Nah, I'm sweet enough," I said.

"That's what your momma always says."

She was right. Here was yet another sign that I was metamorphosing into the Mother Fly.

We squeezed a lemon wedge into our glasses and toasted to the general state of the world, picked up a brownie, and took a bite.

"Mmmm!" she said. "So good!"

"Thanks. Duncan Hines. So? How are you, Miss Deb?"

She leaned back in her chair, inhaled and exhaled, and said, "I'm okay. I'll tell you one thing, when something like this happens? You sure find out in a hurry who your friends are."

"You're telling me?"

"Yeah, we should start a club for girls in our boat."

"Some club *that* would be," I said, sounding like authentic Cobble Hill. "United Widows? What a bummer."

"To be sure. So, Jackie, how are *you* doing?"

"Oh, I'm all right, I guess. I mean, this has been a great visit, especially for Charlie. I think that being around my parents has helped him so much. He's smiling all the time. Dad bought him that crazy skateboard, you know."

"Yep, I've seen him whipping up and down the streets. He's a little hot shot!"

"He sure is. And Steve's dogs have taught him a lot about responsibility and all that."

"Steve's a sweetheart and a true gentleman. You know, your mother and I used to tease each other about him, because he's single and so handsome."

"Yeah, he's a prince." She looked at me funny. "No! He really is!"

"I've seen you two sparring!"

"Oh, he just likes to kid around."

"Not unless he's gay. Men don't just fool around."

"Humph. She did tell you he wears boxers, didn't she?"

"How in the world do you know *that*?" She started to laugh.

"Because *I'm* the one who took the picture of them! You didn't know that? Somebody owes me money."

"What? Your momma is such a liar! She told me *she* took the picture!"

"Well, she didn't."

"Isn't that just like her? Where is she today? I should've heard from her by now. But with this rain, we're not walking today."

"She went up to Murrells Inlet with Dad."

"Really?"

"Yep. Dad's staying for as long as we're here—but in the guest room."

"I see. The guest room. And why?"

"You're asking me? Maybe because he snores?"

"Humph. Listen, between you and me? I think the spark's still there."

"I think so too, but that's their business. Anyway, I love both of them and I want them to be happy. However they work that out is okay with me."

Miss Deb looked at me and arched one eyebrow. "Really?" she said.

"No. Actually, since I've been here and before Dad came back? I've seen things I'd rather not know were true about her. Number one, she's been really lonely. I think she sits on that porch at night and talks to herself, drinking cheap wine until she can't see straight."

"Well, you're right about the wine. It is cheap. But I don't know about how lonely she is."

"I do. And I think her fascination with Steve ran deeper than yours."

"Maybe. But it was just good clean fun. I think it's your father she truly loves."

"Yeah, I'd like to think so. But he really hurt her. She's been so pissed at him for so long I don't know if they can patch it up and then stay patched up when Charlie and I are gone back to New York. Anyway, I can't see why they live separately. They need each other."

"You're right. May I ask you something that's really none of my business?"

"Why not?"

"Why on earth are you going back to New York?"

"Miss Deb, all due respect, I belong in New York. I have a house and a job waiting for me at the VA hospital there."

"I don't know about all that. Let me show you something."

She got up and went to her desk where all her papers were. Then she put a pile of sympathy cards in front of me. They were all from Charlie. I looked at them. One had a huge cross on the front, another had a flying seagull . . . he had drawn, colored, and signed them. I didn't know what to make of them.

"I cannot fathom how deeply he must still be grieving for his father. If he had made one card, I would've said, Okay, isn't that sweet. But eight? It's too much, Jackie. He hardly knew Vernon. This isn't normal."

"No, it can't be."

"That boy needs to be with family, your parents especially, and all of us."

"Jesus God, what do I do about this?"

"Talk to him. And, you know what else, Jackie?"

"What?"

"You need to think about your future, maybe getting married again, for your sake and for Charlie's sake too."

"Oh, please! I'm not ready for anything like that."

"I'll admit it's a little soon, but don't rule it out."

"And what about you? Have you thought about getting married again?"

"Oh, honey, nobody wants a woman my age."

"Don't say that! That's terrible. You're an amazing vibrant woman!"

"Yes, I am, and I don't like it, but the odds are simply not in my favor. But you're young enough to have more children and have a whole family again. Don't be afraid of getting back in the saddle."

"Oh, Miss Deb, I wouldn't even know where to begin."

"If you don't know where to begin, where does that leave me? I was married to Vernon for over thirty years. Just like your mom and Buster. We used to double-date in high school."

We talked a little more, and then I went back to the Salty Dog. My heart was heavy over Charlie's excessive acts of sympathy. He had unnerved Miss Deb, and I was unnerved too. Maybe he wasn't doing as well as I'd thought.

I found him on the floor of the porch, wrestling with the dogs and laughing. It even seemed like the dogs were laughing. And for some reason it all seemed mentally healthy enough to me.

"You ready for some lunch?" I asked.

He stopped and sat up. Stella and Stanley continued to lick his face and hands. Maybe I'd break down and get him a puppy when we got home.

"Yeah! I'm starving!"

"You want to make a tomato sandwich, or what do you feel like?"

"I feel like a taco! Can we go to Taco Bell?"

"No, but we can go to Juanita Greenberg's!"

"What's that?"

"It's good. Trust me. They have tacos."

"Olé! Ándale, ándale! Arriba, arriba!"

"Where'd you learn that?"

"On *Sesame Street* when I was about three."

"Go wash your hands ten times and let's go. And be sure to use soap!"

I had a taco salad with shrimp, and Charlie had traditional tacos. Of course we shared guacamole and chips.

"It's not raining," Charlie observed.

"Surely the skies are out of water for the day. What do you think?"

"Hope so. That was so good, Mom," Charlie said on the way home. "Thanks!"

"You're welcome!" I said. "I enjoyed it too."

"Hey, you know what? I have to buy stuff for the treasure chest. Where should we go for that?"

"CVS? They have everything else in the world."

We turned into the parking lot at the CVS on Coleman Boulevard, went inside, and began digging around in the toy aisle.

"What about yo-yos?"

"Yo-yos suck," he said with all the gravity of an old man commenting on his own fatal illness. "Maybe Guster can make them work, but I sure can't."

"Please don't say *suck*. Or those bounce-back paddle balls?" I said. "That could be fun, you know, have a contest to see who can whack it the most times in a row?"

"Yeah, plus they won't melt in the ground. And maybe some comic books? And, I don't know, some packs of gum?"

"How come we have to do a triple chest and they only have to do a single?"

"I know. I thought about that. Good thing I have a job."

"I think I can cover this, Charlie. You save your money for college or something."

We loaded up the basket with what Charlie wanted to buy and stood on line waiting to pay. There was a jar of single long-stemmed red silk roses wrapped in cellophane on the counter. Charlie took one out and put it in his basket.

"Who's that for? Glam?"

"Oh, no. It's for Miss Deb. You know, to let her know we love her?"

"Put it back," I said. "Right now."

"But I have my own mon—"

"Did you hear what I said? Put it back."

"Why?"

"We'll discuss it in the car." I could feel my pulse starting to go out of control, another sign of The Reincarnation of Annie Britt's Nervous System.

We paid the cashier and left. We got into the car, and I started the engine. Charlie wasn't speaking to me. He was staring out the window.

"Listen to me. When I was over at Miss Deb's this morning, she showed me all the sympathy cards you made for her. I'd like for you to explain to me why you thought it was necessary to make *eight* sympathy cards. Look at me when I'm talking to you, young man!"

He turned to face me, and tears were streaming down his face. His jaw was as tight as a New England clam. He was plenty pissed.

"When Dad died? You got a billion cards! I just wanted to make sure she got enough. That's all."

"That's all?"

"Yeah, that's *all*."

I yanked two tissues from the box I kept in the car and handed them to him.

"Wipe and blow," I said. "I'm a terrible mother. I apologize. I hadn't thought of that." I choked up, and a few tears spilled over. I pulled a tissue from the box for myself.

"It's okay. You're not a terrible mother. You're a great mother." He blew his nose and looked at me. "Does Miss Deb think I'm weird?"

"No. She thinks you're a sensitive and caring young man. For the record, so do I. And so does everyone else. We're all just a little concerned about how you're adjusting to life without your dad."

"It sucks. Sorry, but it does."

"You know what? You're right. It sucks."

"Don't you miss him?"

"Not an hour passes that I don't think of him, Charlie."

"But being here makes it easier, doesn't it?"

It was the continuing campaign to stay rearing its impossible head.

"I think this has been a great getaway for both of us," I said, hoping he'd realize we were headed back to New York very soon.

Later I thought about that conversation over and over and came to believe a couple of things were happening. First, Charlie realized his dad wasn't coming back, and that alone was a horrible truth. And second, though it was an awful struggle for him, he was dealing with it as a ten-year-old boy might. An adult would never jam another adult's mailbox with sympathy cards, but a child might. Maybe he was doing better than I thought, certainly better than I'd thought before I talked to him.

When we got home, Mom and Dad were there. Mom found Charlie a big shoe box to use for a treasure chest, and they covered it in aluminum foil. They put all the surprises inside and rewrapped the entire thing in plastic wrap.

"There's booty in there!" Mom said to him and wiggled her eyebrows.

"Glam! You know what booty *means*, don't you?"

"Don't *you*?" she said, and I swear to you, her eyes twinkled as she watched him make a horrified face, loving the fact that she could make him laugh, that they had a secret joke. "Now let's finish that cryptogram."

"And I'll help you finish that map," Dad said, from his rocker, where he had been absorbed by a sports magazine.

It's a funny thing about a good porch overlooking the ocean. It was great in hot weather when you needed shade. It was good when it rained to be close to nature but stay dry and safe. It was soothing in the dark, or it could be a place to whisper secrets late at night. So the proximity to the ocean meant we should wipe down the windows every day—so what? The truth was that we didn't do it on a daily basis. And since I'd been home we'd cleaned the windows only when company was coming or when we noticed the windows were streaked with salt. We'd been so busy with one another and every other thing that we had ignored them. And Mom, who had always been a stickler for the cause of their cleanliness, hardly seemed to care. The rest of us didn't care either. What had come over us? It had to be something good.

Later on that afternoon, when the cocktail hour was nearly upon us, I had completed my most important task of the day. The lights were restrung, the serape spread across the trestle table. Bottles, glasses, ice, and garnishes were in place to begin another night of family festivities. Instead of a cheese ball we had a bowl of boiled peanuts.

Mom had made a huge pot roast with potatoes and carrots. It was resting in her Dutch oven on top of the stove, and the aroma from it made my mouth water. Of course there was a steamer of rice. My folks had to have rice for gravy. The kitchen table was set. We'd eat when we felt like it. There was no reason to rush.

I was waiting for Mom to return from Miss Deb's. She'd gone over under the guise of discussing her Poe lecture, but the real reason was to check on how Miss Deb was doing. Dad and Charlie had gone down to the area of General William Moultrie's grave site to bury the treasure.

I was going onto the porch when I heard Steve's car pull up. He was probably going to come over to get his dogs. I had come to like Steve. Actually, I should say that I had come to hold him in some esteem. I admired the regard he had for Charlie and the fact that he had been such a rock for Miss Deb in the minutes following Vernon's death. And he had been a pallbearer, which seemed to me to be an awfully difficult role to perform. He was really nice to my parents. And he was good with his dogs, kind and affectionate. Funny, I had not wanted to be his friend, and I wondered then if I'd ever had a friend who had more to offer than he did. I could not recall the name of a single one. And he was a doctor. We shared a passion for lessening the suffering of others.

"Hi!" I called out to him as he approached our front steps. "How was your day? Come to liberate the kids?"

"Good! Thanks. Yeah, my hairy kids. Did they behave themselves today?"

I held the screen door open for him, and he came onto the porch. Stella and Stanley jumped up and ran to him. He leaned down, talked some baby talk to them, and scratched their ears. They sank to the floor, and he rubbed their tummies simultaneously. They were overcome with happiness to have him back home.

"They're such great dogs it's ridiculous. I was even thinking I might get a dog for Charlie when we go home. He's so attached to yours. So am I, sort of."

"Good dogs make a house happy. Hey! The house is awfully quiet. Where'd everybody go?"

I told him and added, "They'll be back soon. Would you like a glass of vino? Or a beer or something else? A vodka gimlet?"

"A gimlet? Really?"

"No? Don't like gimlets?"

"Um, it's not that. It's the onions. They're sort of gross."

"Yeah, they are." Why had I suggested a gimlet? I hated those sour little onions too.

"I think a glass of wine would be just the thing. Can I open the bottle?"

"Sure! Thanks. Ever since that night when Mom got busted by Miss Deb for drinking wine from a box, we've had bottles. Not award-winning bottles, you can be sure, but bottles with corks."

"Well, that's a step up for sure." He smiled at me, and I smiled right back. "So I understand you've been taking shifts at the VA. How's that going?"

"Really good. Really good. I just wanted to check it out, you know?"

"And I'm sure they need the help."

"Well, I have this small advantage of having seen what happens over there—in Afghanistan, I mean. So when these guys are a bit messed up emotionally in addition to their physical injuries, I know why."

"Here you go. Cheers!"

"To Stella and Stanley!" I said and thought, Well, that was a pretty idiotic thing to say. Toasting dogs? Really? "Steve? May I tell you something personal? I'd like your opinion."

"Of course. Shall we sit?"

"Let's." We sat in two rockers, and I took a deep breath. "So today . . ." I told him about the cards at Miss Deb's and the rose, and he was quiet for a few minutes. "What do you think?"

"I think he's telling you the truth about why he made so many cards. Charlie's an extremely honest and well-intentioned kid. Child psychiatry isn't my specialty, as you know. I have a friend who's a pediatric shrink who I like a lot. I could run it by him to see what he thinks. But my guess is that he just needs more time to pass. You know, that first birthday without him, the first Christmas, and so on."

"That makes sense."

"I think the accepted wisdom is that most times a child will heal on roughly the same timetable as the adults around them because they take their lead from their parents. My best advice is to keep him talking about it. You know?"

"Yeah, we talk a lot. It's been rough for both of us."

"I know that. I could see it from the first moment I met you. It probably doesn't help to say this, but I went through all of this when I lost Catherine."

"So that's her name! I keep meaning to ask you. She was so beautiful!"

"Now, how would you know that?"

"Because the first few mornings Charlie came over to get your dogs, I went with him. He was a little nervous. I saw all the pictures on the wall and assumed it was her. How did you get through it? The grieving, I mean."

"Well, the normal ways. I buried myself in work. I ran a marathon. I went to every movie that came out. I did everything I could to keep her out of my head."

"Yeah, that's one reason I'm working over at the VA."

"I figured as much. And then I kept going to the cemetery, even though I knew it wasn't healthy, but I'd go there anyway and talk to her and cry like an idiot."

"Crying doesn't make you an idiot," I said.

"I know that, but anyway, one day I woke up and decided my tears weren't going to bring her back and it was time for me to start living again because that was what she would want me to do. So now I live for her and for me. Every day. That's what I do. I live for two."

"That's really a completely brilliant idea."

"Well, I don't know how brilliant it is, but it seemed to make me feel a lot better. By the way, I've got the mug you left in my bedroom."

I knew my face turned scarlet because I could feel the heat.

"I won't ask why you were in there." He waited for me to offer some response, and I didn't say one word. So he cleared his throat and smiled. "Look, I don't know. Maybe you should tell Charlie to imagine that he's living for his dad too?"

"I will sure think about that." In the next breath I let my shields down and asked him about that slut I'd seen him with. "So you can tell me to mind my own grits, but who was that girl I saw you with on your deck a few nights ago, right before Vernon died? Is she someone important?"

"Who? You mean that crazy blonde?"

"Yep, the nice lady who wrapped her leg around your waist." I giggled.

He started to laugh. "You're funny. Do you know that?"

"On occasion. But you didn't answer my question, did you?"

"She's this girl I dated once or twice who's calling me all the time. She just broke up with her boyfriend, and she wanted some company. I was just trying to be nice. That's all."

"Really?" I was on my second glass of wine, and my tongue was as loose as an overdone lasagna noodle. "You sure looked like you were being *awfully* nice! From where I stood, that is."

"What are you saying, Mrs. McMullen? Are you maybe a little jealous of her?"

"Don't be absurd. That kind of cavorting in the moonlight isn't my thing!"

"I'll bet it is. I'll bet you can cavort with the best of them. Not today and not tomorrow, but soon, cavort again you will. Yoda sees all and knows all."

"Yoda. Tell Yoda to kiss it."

"Yoda would love to."

14

Ah, hereupon turns the whole mystery; although the secret, at this point, I had comparatively little difficulty in solving. My steps were sure, and could afford but a single result. I reasoned, for example, thus: When I grew the scar-abœus, there was no skull apparent on the parchment. When I had completed the drawing, I gave it to you, and observed you narrowly until you returned it. You, therefore, did not design the skull, and no one else was present to do it. Then it was not done by human agency. And nevertheless it was done.

—Edgar Allan Poe, "The Gold-Bug"

Annie

Since Jackie went to work so early, I got up Sunday morning with the birds to make her an egg and some toast. I walked her down the back steps and picked up the newspaper at the bottom of our driveway as she backed out. I waved good-bye, and she waved back to me and I thought, Lord, please bring my daughter and my sweet Charlie home to me permanently. Then I thought, Well, hells bells, as long as I'm praying I may as well go to church. I had this theory that praying in church sort of put your petitions on a scud missile to Heaven, like giving them a priority delivery. I certainly did not agree with everything about my church these days, but I still believed in its basic tenets. So I went inside, poured myself another cup of coffee, and went to my bathroom to fix my face.

I could hear the rhino sawing wood through the walls. Did I really want to live with that again? Maybe. But was he asking to come back? No. I looked in the mirror at myself and tried to see past all the reminders of fifty-eight years of living. My eyebrows were turning white. I wondered if he would be more anxious to come back to me if I was forty-eight years old instead. I could not be certain, but I suspected the answer was a lousy, inequitable, damn-Madison-Avenue-to-hell *yes*. Hide my soapbox on *that* topic, or we'll be stuck here forever.

I put on my new aqua linen trousers and shirt with my choker of freshwater pearls and brushed my hair. Well, screw it, I said to my dressing room mirror, I look good for my age and that's the best I can do.

When I got to the kitchen, Charlie was there, drinking a glass of milk and eating a banana.

"Well, good morning! Why are you up so early, baby? You don't have to work today. It's Sunday."

"I know, but I'm used to getting up now. Does that make sense?"

"Yes! Of course it does! Your body has its own alarm clock or something like that. Hey! I'm going to Mass. Want to come? I'll take you out for breakfast afterward?"

"Deal! Just gotta brush my teeth."

Charlie zoomed out of the room and was back before I could find my car keys and sunglasses.

"Let's go," I said.

During Mass, I caught the monsignor looking at us and I would've stuck needles through my eyeballs rather than acknowledge him, so I did that thing where you sort of glaze over and let your attention drift elsewhere. After Communion, Charlie was kneeling, and I noticed that he seemed to be praying so fervently that it worried me. I put my arm around his shoulders and gave him a squeeze. He looked up at me with those eyes of his and smiled, but I could see his little heart was filled with sadness. I knew without asking that the larger part of any sadness he might be feeling had to come from missing his father. The rest? Who could say? Maybe he was remembering the funeral. I would talk to him over breakfast and try to gauge how he was handling his life. Life is a struggle, I would tell him. Some days are better than others, and every person's life is bittersweet, filled with joy and pain.

As true as all those sayings might have been, they really didn't help. Pancakes helped. Running down the beach with a couple of happy dogs helped. Having friends helped. Mainly the best help was diversion for the short term and the passing of time in the long term. I had buried enough people in my life to know that was the absolute truth.

We arrived at Page's Okra Grill in Mount Pleasant, and the place was crawling with families just out of church. The men who'd served as ushers still had on their navy or seersucker blazers, and the rest of the men were in shirtsleeves. The ladies of my ilk wore sleeveless sundresses no matter the state of their upper arms or a nice linen outfit that covered the sins. The young people dressed as though they had no respect for the sanctity of the occasion of worship, but don't get me started on that either. Church is no place for shorts and jeans, even if one attends the twenty-eighth splintered-off sect of some minuscule, hardly-heard-of Protestant church that holds its services in a barn. Sorry. You're going to worship the Lord? Dress for the occasion, please. And brush your hair. Anyway, no one had asked me to establish a Sunday-morning dress code for all the Christians of the world, so I'd just keep that nugget to myself.

"What looks good to you, Charlie?" We were finally seated in a booth for two and going over the menus.

"There are so many choices! Have you ever had a western omelet, Glam?"

"Yep, I have, and that's the best way I know of to eat eggs, except for a Swiss cheese and mushroom omelet. Unless, of course, you're talking eggs Benedict with extra hollandaise sauce on the side. And a Bloody Mary. Made with Zing Zang. Why?"

"Zing Zang? What the heck is that?"

"It's a spicy mixture grown-ups use to make Bloody Marys. You don't need to know that for another decade, I hope. The waffles here are good too. But you should try the western omelet if you like chopped-up green peppers."

"I love them."

The waitress, whose name tag read LIBBY, stopped at our table. "Coffee?" she asked.

"Please," I said, "and iced water."

She put a mug down in front of me and filled it. "And for you, hon?"

"Chocolate milk?"

I looked at Charlie, thinking I had not offered him chocolate milk since he'd been here.

"It's Sunday," he said. "Why not go all out?"

Libby and I exchanged smiles.

"Too precious," Libby said. "I'll be right back to get y'all's orders."

I stirred my coffee and looked at my beautiful grandson. What a great gift he was to all of us. It was so wonderful to have a young person like Charlie in my life to shape and guide.

"Did you hear my question, Glam?"

"Oh, I'm sorry, sweetheart. My mind was a thousand miles away. What did you say?"

"I said, if it doesn't rain this afternoon, we're going to have our treasure hunt!"

"Well, I know, and I'm so excited for you! Do you think they will make it really hard for you to find?"

"I don't know. Probably. Those kids can be pretty diabolical."

"Fifty-cent word," I said. "Good one."

"Thanks. I just think the whole thing was such a great idea. I wish we could've found disappearing ink like they had on the cryptogram in 'The Gold-Bug.' "

"We could probably find it on the Internet. Too bad we didn't have more time. Next time! Right? There's always a next time."

Libby reappeared with Charlie's chocolate milk. "So, what's it gonna be, young man?"

"I'd like the western omelet with French fries and ketchup."

"Sounds good. And for you, ma'am?"

"Oh, I think I'd like an egg-white omelet with Swiss cheese and mushrooms. No potatoes. No toast."

"Yeah, I'm always on a diet too. Not that it ever lasts. Son? You want a biscuit?"

"Sure!"

"I'll bring you two," she said and left.

"So, Glam? What's up with you and Guster? Is he moving back in?"

I nearly choked. Is this how his generation communicated respectfully with their grandparents?

"Why on earth would you ask such a question?"

"Well, because I think you need to have someone around the house. I mean, I can do things like take out the trash and change lightbulbs that are too high for you to reach. I like climbing ladders. And I can wash the car and cut the grass."

"Sweetie, you already do many of those things to help me, and I appreciate it so much."

"Yeah, but if I stayed and went to school here, it would be so much better for all of us. Don't you see? I mean, what's going to happen to Stella and Stanley if I have to leave? They'll die from loneliness!"

So will I, I thought, so will I.

"You know, Charlie, I think you have to do what your momma wants you to do. She's your parent."

"You don't know how awful it is to live in Brooklyn compared to here."

Libby put our food in front of us. It looked delicious. "Y'all enjoy!" she said and walked away.

"May I have the ketchup, please?" he called after her.

She turned back to us and slid the bottle across the table. The ketchup bottle had been right in front of us all along.

"If it was any closer it woulda bit your little nose off! Ha ha!" she said, and Charlie rolled his eyes.

I was sorely tempted to roll mine.

"Listen, Charlie, if your momma wanted to stay, she'd be welcome, just as you are, and I think you know that. But she has to make that call, not us. And whatever she decides, we have to honor it, right?"

"I *really* don't want to go, Glam."

"I know, sweetie. I wish you didn't have to, but I'm afraid you will. Look, once you get home and start school, time will fly. You know it will! And before you can whistle Dixie, Thanksgiving will be here and you'll be back! Right?"

"You don't understand."

"What don't I understand?"

"Our house *smells* like Dad. Everywhere you look there's a *picture* of him or *something* that reminds you of him. When Mom gets back, she's going to get depressed *all over again*. I don't think I can take it, Glam. I really don't."

What he really meant was that *he* would get depressed. I would have to speak to Jackie about putting away pictures and mementos and maybe even repainting so the rooms smelled fresh? Maybe Buster and I could buy them a new sofa so the old one wouldn't remind him of sitting there with Jimmy watching television. Oh hell, I didn't know what to do. I'd ask Buster.

"I'll speak to your mother," I said. "Now let's eat. There are starving children all over the world."

We finished up our breakfast, which was delicious beyond description, paid the bill, and went home. When we got there, the house was empty. Jackie was at work. And I found a note on the kitchen table from Buster that he and Steve had gone to the fish and tackle store to buy Charlie a rod and reel.

Charlie looked at the note and said, "Awesome! Meanwhile, can I go see Jessee, Johnnie, and Jojo? Pleeeeeease?"

"Sure! Go have fun! But if you leave their house to go *anywhere* else, you must call me, okay?"

He gave me a thumbs-up, grabbed his skateboard and helmet, and was gone.

I called Deb. "You busy? Want to go for a walk?"

"Great idea. I need it. I've been doing nothing but eating since the funeral. I feel like a slug."

"Meet you at my beach steps in ten minutes?"

"Puuur-fect," she said and hung up.

I changed my clothes and pulled on my sneakers, wondering what there was to be done about Charlie. I knew how Jackie felt. I had not moved a single picture of Buster in all the years he'd been fishing. Well, to be honest, I should say "since he had left me," but I had told myself it was temporary so many times that now it was! And those pictures marked happier times: Jackie's wedding, our vacations, and so on. Who wouldn't want to be reminded of an occasion that gave you pleasure? So I could easily understand why she didn't put pictures away. Still, I'd have a chat with her. And Buster.

Deb was waiting for me, and in record time we were off and walking.

"So do I look bloated?" she asked.

"Of course not! If you feel bloated, eat asparagus. Or drink hot lemonade. You know that."

"I know, I know."

"But here's the twenty-four-million-dollar question."

"What?"

"Do I look like I had sex?"

She stopped dead. *"WHAT?"* She started to laugh, and so did I. *"With who? Buster?"*

"Hush! Someone will hear you! Yes, with Buster! Who else? The freaking milkman?"

"Oh, my heart! Oh, my God! How did this happen? Where? I swear to God! I can't breathe! I have to sit down!"

"Stop! Keep walking. You're drawing attention to us! If anyone heard us, they'd think we're as crazy as hell. So remember yesterday morning I went up to Murrells Inlet with him?"

"Jackie told me. You'd better tell me every single *word*, Annie Britt. Don't you dare leave out one thing!"

"I'm not! So, we went out to lunch at this crazy place called Drunken Jack's, and it was pouring rain to beat the band, remember?"

"Remember the rain? Are you kidding? It was a good day to build an ark."

"Truly! Well, since it was raining, we decided to get some Bloodys and fish po'boys. He had three and I had two, and we were completely snockered. I *never* drink vodka, as you know. Nasty. Anyway, somehow we got back to his rental house, but I knew I *had* to have a nap. He sure couldn't drive back to the island without a nap, so we crawled in the bed. Before you ask, yes, there is a second bedroom, but the bed was covered with laundry, which figures. We took off our clothes, because who gets in the sack with all their clothes on? Then everyone would say, 'Oh! It looks like you slept in your clothes!' So we nodded off, and when we woke up an hour or so later, nature took its course!"

"Well, that's interesting, but did nature take his *time*?"

"Yes, nature took his time, you nosy Nellie."

"So was it, I mean, you know . . . would you do it again?"

"I don't know. Maybe."

"Annie Britt, don't lie to me."

"Okay, I'd do it in a heartbeat. Anyway, he's staying in the guest room for as long as Charlie and Jackie are here."

"I heard that from your daughter. May I ask why he's in the guest room, you daggum fool? He's your husband!"

"Because he snores like a beast."

"Actually, I made Vernon sleep in our guest room when he snored. God, that man shook the house."

"They all do. It's amazing. Anyway, I wanted to tell you I know about Charlie's cards. Jackie and I discussed the whole thing. Jackie asked Charlie, and he said the reason . . ." I told her Charlie's explanation, and she nodded.

"Children just see the world differently," she said. "And they react differently than we do. I'm really glad there was nothing more to it. What a sweet child."

"Thanks but I'll tell you what . . ."

"What?"

"That sweet child *really* doesn't want to go back to New York."

"Look, shut my mouth and call me Aunt Fanny, but I think she should stick around for a while too. At least one semester. But she tells me she already has a job lined up for herself at the Brooklyn VA."

"She does?" I felt my heart sink.

"Yes. You know? I mean, why can't she see that her loss is bringing the rest of her family back together again? It's as plain as the nose on *my* face!"

"Because she's a knucklehead. A truculent, short-sighted, self-involved knucklehead. And she's so wound up in her own grief she doesn't know what to do! Maybe her father can talk to her and get her to listen. I don't know."

"Well, if you give the old man a little more lovin', I'll bet he will!"

Deb started to laugh again, and so did I. In fact, we laughed off and on the whole way home. Who had ever heard of anything as stupid as hiding the fact that you're screwing your own husband? It was one of those crazy family stories you hoped your grandchildren remembered to tell when you were long gone—under the right circumstances, of course.

I invited Deb to sit on the porch with me for a while. Charlie's treasure hunt was set to begin within the hour, and I was aching for a cool drink. I was pouring iced tea for us, and Charlie came through the back door.

"Hey, Glam! Guster back?"

"I just came in myself. Haven't seen him. Want a cold drink of water or iced tea? It must be a thousand degrees out there today."

"Decaf?"

"Your mother and her decaf business! Don't you know that all those children in China drink tea all day long and they wind up at Harvard and MIT?"

"Maybe I'll just take water, then?"

"How about watered-down iced tea?"

"Sweet!" he said.

"Oh, honey, did you want sugar?"

"No, Glam, *sweet* means *awesome*."

I handed him the glass. "Well, I'm glad you cleared that one up for me, because I never would have figured it out. That's for sure. Miss Deb's on the porch. Go say hello."

"Sure! Then I'm going to wait on the back steps for the Greenville Three."

"Sounds like a good plan," I said, and a few minutes later I followed him out to the porch.

"Thanks," Deb said when I handed her a glass. "So Charlie tells me he's already buried his treasure. And that you helped him make a cryptogram like Poe's. It sounds like an awful lot of effort went into this, Charlie."

"Yeah, it did. But I think it's going to be worth it. I can't wait to see their faces when they get the crypto-gram! Think I should give them a pencil?"

"Yes! Of course! Just make sure it has a big eraser!" I said.

We drained our glasses pretty quickly. Then, as I debated getting up to refill them, I heard the back door slam. I jumped. Buster knew how I felt about slam-ming doors. Maybe Steve did it. He probably didn't know about me and slamming doors. In any case, the men were back.

"You might want to go see what Guster brought home, Charlie."

"And, darlin' child? Could you refill our glasses?"

"Sure!" Charlie took our glasses and went inside. "Guster?" he called out.

"In here, Charlie! Come see!"

"You don't want to go say hello?" Deb said.

"You mean, get up again? I'm too pooped to pop. Besides, now that I've allowed him to enter the Magic Gate, shouldn't he come to me?"

"Magic Gate? Oh, girl! You are too funny!"

Moments later, the door opened, and there came Buster with our tea, this time with lemon and sprigs of mint.

"Why, thank you, Buster! We are so parched! Aren't you parched, Deb?"

"Like the Sahara," she said and giggled.

"I'm going to be on the steps with Charlie and Steve waiting for the other kids. Want me to call you when they get here?"

"That would be perfect! I just need to sit for a few minutes. We walked quite a distance and in this heat? Mercy!"

"You just need fluids," he said. "All right, then. You ladies hydrate."

When she was sure that Buster was out of earshot, Deb said, "You collapsing camellia! You are so terrible!"

"Not terrible. Just naughty enough. And only some of the time. All women are a little naughty sometimes."

"True. And he did bring us tea."

"Because he wants to visit the Magic Gate again. What did I tell you?"

"Well, with Vernon gone, it's going to be a helluva long time before anybody tries to gain access to mine."

"Listen," I said, thinking of how lonely my best friend was bound to be and soon, "the Gold Key in the Magic Gate is never a perfect fit, and at our age? The whole mess is overrated anyway."

"Really? You really think so?"

"Well, darlin'? It was the first visit to the Gate in over a decade. We're both a little rusty. But we laughed like hell and had a good time, so I guess who cares?"

"You do realize Jackie would have a stroke if she ever heard her mother talking like this?"

"You do realize that Jackie thinks her parents have plastic mounds where their genitals are supposed to be, like Barbie and Ken?"

"Oh, my God! You are so funny! Come on, let's go wish Charlie happy hunting."

Actually, the intimate encounter between the Golden Key and the Magic Gate had been as sweaty and exciting as it was twenty years ago. I didn't want Deb to think she would be missing out. But truly? I had been shocked by the electricity of the event. Did I say that the right way?

Just as we arrived on the back steps, the Greenville Challengers screeched to a halt on their bicycles.

"You guys ready for the challenge of your life?" Charlie asked. He was so excited, his voice just bubbled with anticipation.

"Yeah! Bring it on!" they said.

"Okay! On the count of three, we swap maps! Ready? One! Two! *Three!*"

Paperwork changed hands, and moments later they were off, racing in different directions. Charlie had thought he would take the dogs, but in the last moment he agreed with Buster and Steve that navigating his skateboard with two frisky dogs on leashes might be too much.

"I told him he'd wind up hanging up in the branches of a magnolia tree!" Buster said.

"Or a ditch with a broken leg," Steve added.

"Well, that surely did the trick! Shall we sit on the porch and have a cold drink?"

"Why not? It's hotter than the hinges on the back door of Hell," Buster said. "Come on, Steve, let's get us a beer."

And that's how we passed the next few hours. Talking, telling stories, doing the island thing of just letting an afternoon pass with no thoughts of supper or what the next day would bring. Just as the tide turned and the island cooled down for the evening, Charlie came in with a whole bag of loot, mostly comic books and candy, but he had dozens of mosquito bites all over his arms and legs. It didn't dampen his spirit one iota. He had solved their map, and he wondered if they had solved his.

"Don't go anywhere, young man," Steve said. "Let's cover those bug bites with something so they won't itch, you won't scratch, and you won't get some disgusting infection! I'll be right back."

"Yeah, please, 'cause I'm already itching like craaazy!"

Steve rushed over to his house and came back in minutes with a tube of medicated gel. "Here, just put dots on each bite and tap it in just a little."

Charlie did just as Steve said, and soon he was making the sounds boys make to indicate relief.

"Awwwww! Gaaaaa! Awwwww!"

"Better?" Steve asked.

"I'm gonna live! Hey, Glam? Can we have burgers for dinner, and will you teach me how to make onion rings?"

"Sure! I've got a dozen burgers in the freezer just waiting to be wanted. And there's a bag of onions in the pantry."

"Yay! Hey, Guster? Will you take me down the island to see if we see them near Fort Moultrie?"

"Sure, let's go!"

They left, and I turned to Steve. "I've never seen Charlie happier."

"And why shouldn't he be? He has an entire island for a playground and a chorus of adults who can't do enough for him."

"I wish we could talk Jackie into staying down here with us. Charlie sure wants to, but, well, Jackie has other ideas, I suppose."

"I could talk to her if you'd like," Steve said.

I replied, "And what would you say? I'm afraid she has to come to this on her own, Steve. That's the kind of person she's always been. We just keep trying to make her see by example and not so many words. She has an audio-processing disorder."

"What the heck is that?" Deb said.

"It means she doesn't listen to almost anything we say."

Steve nodded. "I think I see that. So we have a difficult task ahead and not much time to accomplish it."

"That sums it all up just right," I said.

Jackie rolled in around seven thirty. We had the grill fired up, and Steve and Deb had commandeered the dinner with Charlie. Buster was bartending. Buster and I asked her how her day had gone. She said it had gone really well. Charlie bubbled over and over about his treasure hunt and how he really had those Greenville kids going and that he had to help them follow his map but in the end they all loved it and had a wonderful time, except for his bug bites but don't worry, Steve took care of him. Steve poured her a glass of wine and handed it to her. How was your day? he asked. And she said, Great, just great. That's wonderful, he said, really it is.

For the first time in a long time we just took our plates out to the porch and held them in our laps. It was the end of another scorching hot day, punctuated by a simple supper, laughter, goodwill, and all of it flavored with the salty breeze of the sea. I had not been so happy in years. Neither had the Salty Dog.

15

"But I have just said that the figure was not that of a goat."

"Well, a kid then—pretty much the same thing."

"Pretty much, but not altogether," said Legrand. "You may have heard of one Captain Kidd . . ."

—Edgar Allan Poe, "The Gold-Bug"

Jackie

I had to drag myself out of the bed the next morning, but once I got into the shower and stood under the water I started to wake up. A good showerhead is a gift from God. I toweled off and put on a clean pair of scrubs. It was already after six. I'd have time to make a cup of instant coffee in the microwave and then hit the road. I'd grab breakfast in the cafeteria at the hospital. To my surprise, Mom was in the kitchen, cooking.

"Morning! What are you doing up so early?"

"G'morning! Well, sweetie, I knew you wouldn't have time to cook, so I thought I'd make you an egg.

Poached eggs on toast okay for you? There's coffee. Help yourself. And gimme a smooch."

I kissed her cheek and took a mug from the cabinet. "Mom, you really don't have to do this, you know. I can get my own breakfast." I filled my mug and went looking for the half-and-half, finding it behind a container of watermelon cubes. "Is this melon local?"

"Yep. Johns Island. I'm aware you can cook. But I was up anyway."

"How come?" I dumped some melon into a bowl.

"I don't know. Just have a lot on my mind, I guess."

"We're out of half-and-half." I poured the last of it into my mug and stirred it around.

"There's another carton in the refrigerator downstairs."

"That second refrigerator is pretty handy, isn't it?"

"Yes, it surely is."

She put the plate of eggs and toast in front of me, and I thought, Wow, I'll miss *this* when I get home. "This looks so good. Thanks, Mom."

"My pleasure," she said. "I'm going to get my shower. See you tonight!"

"Okay! Have a good day!"

I ate quickly, rinsed my plate and slipped it into the dishwasher, grabbed my keys, and headed for the car. Driving over the causeway, I began to have this nagging feeling that I was being set up. Even last night, everyone had been like Oh, how was your day? Can I get you more wine? Tell me what happened to you today. Blah blah blah. Something in my cynical mind told me they were all in cahoots with one another to get me to stay here and not go back to New York. I know that sounds awful to say, but I could smell a trap and my instincts were never wrong, which was why I was still alive. The truth was in their eyes.

I got to work, and my favorite nurse, Mary Stevens, was on duty.

"Hey, Mary, how are you this morning?"

"Well, two of my triplets have the stomach flu and the third one just broke out in chicken pox even though she had the vaccine. Thank God John's home."

"You should take them over to my mother's house. She's got the Mother Teresa gene gone wild, and it's always itching for a new cause."

"Momma driving you a little crazy, is she?"

"All right. I shouldn't say this because it will make me sound like a brat, but here's the poop. My husband dies; as you know, my little boy is depressed, so I'm at my wit's end with that, and I bring him down here."

"Okay, you've told me all this. What's next?"

"Well, Mom's got this big house on the front beach that has this gorgeous view and all that and the next-door neighbor is eight years older than I am, he's a widower and a doctor and really hot—"

"Yeah, this sounds like a tragedy waiting to happen . . ."

"And my father, who hasn't lived with my mother in over ten years, suddenly reappears and is *so* nice to my son, as is the doc next door. They take him to a RiverDogs game, they take him fishing, the doc hires him to take care of his dogs, they plan this crazy treasure hunt based on Poe's 'The Gold-Bug' that my mother is helping him read on the doc's e-reader, he makes friends with some kids from Greenville and goes swimming every day."

"Yeah, this sounds terrible. Go on . . ."

"So my dad buys Charlie this really great skateboard and my mom teaches Charlie how to make hush puppies and onion rings, and the doc takes care of Charlie's mosquito bites."

"So what's the problem?"

"Charlie's as happy as a pig in mud, and he doesn't want to go home."

"Who's doing all the laundry?"

"Oh, my mother, of course!"

"And the meals?"

"She is. I mean, I got up at six this morning, and there's my mother, poaching eggs for me."

"Wow. That's a hell of a crime. So what are you going to do about it?"

"It's a trap! Can't you see that?"

"Um, actually no. Let's see now, beachfront house, gorgeous available man next door who's obviously not stupid or broke—he's got ideas on how to help you cope, I suspect? I mean, only because he's been through the same thing and misery loves company?"

"That's right."

"And you're their only child and Charlie's their only grandson and they want y'all to stay and live with them? Probably rent free?"

"Well, probably. I mean, I could help."

"Let me tell you something, sugar. I've got ten-year-old triplets and my husband's in construction. You might have heard there's a slump in building new housing?"

"Yeah, of course."

"Yeah, well, we'd give anything to have a setup like that. Especially to have grandparents in our children's lives. And you know what else?"

"What? Look, Mary, I know I sound like a jerk. My family's wonderful, but my husband's buried in New York. I just can't leave him there."

"Jackie, honey, I mean this in the nicest way possible. Your husband is in Heaven. His *remains* are in New York. There's a big difference."

"You're right, I know you're right. But I'm just not ready to walk away yet, you know? I mean, there's the house and so many memories tied to every board and nail that holds it together. We brought Charlie home from the hospital there. We celebrated all our birthdays and had Christmas trees there. You know what I mean? How can I just leave that all behind?"

"You'll come to that point when you're ready to move on, I guess."

"Yeah, and I just feel like my family is pushing me to do this against my will by using Charlie as a weapon."

"Or—and consider this one carefully—they just happen to adore both of you. Maybe you don't want to share? And didn't you bring him here to help him get over his depression? Sounds like it's working to me. Anyway, I have to deliver meds. We can talk later."

Mary was right about everything, of course. But there was still something to be said about comfort levels, and I was desperately uncomfortable with the idea of remaining in my mother's house indefinitely. And what of Charlie? Was I being stingy? Maybe a little. Was I worried that if they loved Charlie so much, he would love me less? Somewhat. Was I worried that their affection would undermine my authority? Wasn't that already happening?

I went through the rest of the day performing all my duties, administering classified pain medicines, updating charts, talking to the doctors, preparing patients for surgeries, seeing that they were comfortably settled in their beds postop, and doing everything I could to see about our patients overall well-being. My shift seemed to pass so quickly because the VA was a very busy place and all the staff was stretched to capacity. But I loved it. When I walked out of there at seven o'clock, I always felt like I had done my job well and that I had done people some good.

Driving over the Cooper River Bridge was the highlight of my commute back to the beach. I remembered the old bridges and how when I'd lived at home as a girl, how dangerous they'd seemed. Then years later, after I'd left, the city had had a team of engineers assess the bridge's stability. When all the reports had come in, work had begun immediately to replace them. It turned out they *were* dangerous. But still, there was nothing like a drive over the new bridge or the old rattletrap bridge with the windows wide open to make you feel like you were flying in the clouds. I just loved it.

I decided to stop by Whole Foods and bring home some finger foods for snacks, although when I looked at my watch, I was pretty sure my folks and Charlie had already eaten supper. So we'd use them tomorrow.

Maybe I'd buy some blueberries and I'd ask Charlie and Dad to teach me how to make ice cream, so we could make it together when we got home. And when we got home, maybe I could find a safe park in Brooklyn near the house where Charlie could skateboard to his heart's content without me breathing down his neck. Since we'd been on the island, his expertise had mushroomed as though he had wheels growing from the soles of his feet. I knew those parks existed; I'd just always been too busy to find one near us. But if I could help Charlie expand on some of his newly acquired skills back in New York, maybe he would be happier about going home. He wanted more freedom. There had to be a way to make that happen for him and at the same time satisfy myself that he would be safe.

I rolled my cart down the vegetable and fruit aisles. There was corn from Johns Island and tomatoes. I picked up a dozen of each. Then there were peaches from Aiken and Estill, known for their sweetness. I put eight into a bag. All that Dad had brought were long gone. Next I picked up a quart container of blueberries and moved on to the cheese section. That was where I traditionally lost my mind. A block of Gruyère that had been aged for twelve years went into the basket along with a wedge of Huntsman. Then I took a brick of French goat cheese in a very expensive looking tiny box made of the thinnest balsa wood you can imagine. And lastly I had to have a small round of Explorateur. Three kinds of crackers, a bottle of cornichons, a bottle of Dijon mustard, two pieces of different pâtés, and a baguette later, I made it to the checkout line. The cheese section was to me what a good butcher section had been to Jimmy. It was where he had bought steaks or veal chops when he felt like we needed a splurge. For us all of those gourmet items had been too expensive for an everyday meal, and even if we could've afforded them for every day, even with all our exercise, we would've weighed five hundred pounds if we'd indulged that often. It was another tradition I wasn't ready to relinquish. Special-occasion food shopping. I imagined then that I'd have to shop with Charlie and let him choose the meat for us. He'd probably like that.

There was very little traffic, so I was home in no time, pulling up in our driveway just as Steve pulled up in his.

"Hey, there!" I said. "You're getting home kind of late, aren't you?"

"Yeah, I had a kid over at St. Francis who had her tonsils out and then broke out with a first-class case of chicken pox. Poor kid. I just wanted to have a look at her. I play golf on occasion with her grandfather Charlie Way, and he called me, so I went. You know, a favor."

"Well, that was awfully nice."

I opened the back of my SUV and pulled out the shopping bags.

"I'm that kind of guy. Besides, he's done a million really nice things for me. Here," he said, "let me help you with that."

I handed him the bags. It had been forever since anyone had treated me like a member of the fair sex. He should've seen me wearing camouflage with fifty-five pounds of gear on my back. He'd never lift a finger for me again. But it was sort of nice, actually. The feminist in me was not insulted in the least.

"Thanks! So how'd she look?"

"Awful. But she'll be better tomorrow and even better the day after."

I looked up at the house. The porch lights were on. I hurried up the steps and held the screen door open for him.

"You're awfully fit, you know."

I looked him square in the face and said, "Yes, I know."

"You ever go kayaking?"

"Yeah, right down the middle of the East River. In between the tugboats. And the Staten Island Ferry."

"You're such a wise guy sometimes. If you were a nicer girl, I'd take you over to Shem Creek and let you borrow one of mine."

"I'll get to work on my people skills right away."

We were both smirking, testing the edges of friendship. There was something happening, because I could feel a twinge in the bottom of my stomach.

Mom and Dad were in the kitchen, sitting at the table. The table was still set, minus one.

"Hi, sweetheart! How was your day?" Mom asked.

"Great," I said.

"Here, I'll take that," Dad said to Steve.

Steve put the bags on the counter and asked, "Everybody all right?"

"Yeah, just waiting for Jackie so we can polish off some leftover pot roast," Dad said. "Did you eat, Steve?"

"No, but I'm good. I've got a fridge filled with sushi."

"Sushi? That's sissy food, no offense." Mom shot Dad a death-ray look. "No, I'm serious! I don't know how you make a meal out of that stuff!"

"It can be really delicious," I said.

"Humph. There ain't but one way to eat fish in my book. Fried. Except for sometimes baked and stuffed with crab. Or in chowder."

"Dad's a real gourmand," I said and giggled. I started unpacking the groceries I had brought home. "Where's Charlie?"

"Charlie ate. He's off on his skateboard," Mom said. "I told him to be back by dark."

"Okay. Anybody want a little cheese and crackers? A little duck liver pâté?" I was already putting it all on a plate. Steve looked at it like he'd die if he couldn't have some.

"Steve? Why don't you open a bottle of wine for you and Jackie? It's in the refrigerator on the door. Annie and I are enjoying our second very small martini."

"Slowly," Mom said. "Very slowly."

"Yeah," I said and handed him the corkscrew. "Slow is a good idea. The last time I had two martinis, I woke up naked with my jewelry on."

"Jackie!" Mom said. "You shouldn't tell a thing like that!"

"Why not? I thought it was a riot," I said. It was slightly odd for me to tell that story, but I knew there was something in me that wanted Steve to think I could be a wild child.

"Um, excuse me for being on the other team, but I agree with your daughter," Steve said and laughed as he pulled the cork. I could read his mind—*wish I had been there*. Aha.

"Glasses?"

I handed him two from the cabinet. There was no bar set up that night, which was probably wise, but it had not stopped my parents from finding their way to the olives.

"Well, it's about the most reckless thing I ever did in my life." I pushed aside a place setting and put the platter of cheese and crackers on the table.

"Right," Steve said and clinked the side of my glass. "She carried a loaded rifle through the hills of Afghanistan, but two martinis were her undoing."

"Oh, please. I was with my husband, and we went to a Christmas party where everyone was drinking martinis. It was stupid, I'll admit, but not especially risky. Try the Huntsman, Dad."

"Which one is the Huntsman?"

"It's the cheddar with the stripe of blue cheese in it. But here, I'll fix you some."

I cut a chunk, put it on a cracker, and handed it to him. He ate it and made a yum-yum sound.

"Pretty good, huh?"

"Very good," he said and turned to Mom. "Can I make one for you?"

"Why that would be so sweet, Buster! Isn't he darling?" she said to me.

Mom was tighter than a tick. She must've been. Dad might have been too. But I knew one thing, they needed fresh air. And at least she hadn't resurrected her red lipstick.

"Yeah, *darling* was just the word I was looking for," I said and laughed. "Why don't y'all go sit on the porch?" I picked up the cheese board and handed it to Steve with my eyebrows as arched as I could arch them. He got the message. "I'll join y'all in a few minutes. I just want to wash my hands and get out of these scrubs."

"That sounds great," Steve said. "Besides, I have to get the kids home at a decent hour. School night and all that."

"No! Stay!" I blurted out. I don't know why I said that, but I did. "There's tons to eat."

"Well, all right. I'll stay, then. Thanks."

Dad pulled Mom up from her chair, and they left the room arm in arm doing the wibble-wobble as they went. Nothing like a couple of shots of good gin to motivate Cupid.

"Make them eat cheese so they don't get tanked," I whispered. "I'll be out there ASAP."

"Got it," he whispered back.

I ran to my room and dug through my closet. I had a clean red linen shirt and a pair of white capris. They'd have to do. So I threw off my scrubs, brushed out my ponytail, put on my change of clothes, and slipped on a pair of sandals.

I hurried back to the kitchen and checked the pot roast. Thankfully, there *was* plenty for everyone.

I added another place setting to the table, and as quickly as I could I went to the porch to join them. Dad was holding court, reciting "Casey at the Bat," which he did only when his blood alcohol level was beyond the legal limit. Maybe he'd been sipping some beer before they started shaking the shaker. My parents had too much to drink only when they were nervous, and what in the world did they have to be nervous about?

Steve was thoroughly amused. Mom was shaking her head in disbelief, as she had not had the privilege of hearing Dad's dramatic presentation in years. And Charlie, who had returned and somehow slipped by me, was completely enthralled.

"Ten thousand eyes were on him as he rubbed his hands with dirt; Five thousand tongues applauded when he wiped them on his shirt. Then while the writhing pitcher ground the ball into his hip, Defiance gleamed in Casey's eyes, a sneer curled Casey's lip."

Dad was quite the living room actor, reciting his favorite poem with all the accompanying movements, rubbing his hands on his shirt, sneering, and so forth.

"Oh, hello, sweetheart!" Mom said. "Come join us!"

"Oh, now, Annie, you've made me lose my place," Dad whined. "Charlie? What was the last line?"

"A sneer curled Casey's lip!" Of course, Charlie sneered the most exaggerated sneer he could muster, and everyone was charmed.

"Ah!" Dad said and continued his rendition until the final line was delivered: "But there is no joy in Mudville—mighty Casey has struck out!"

Charlie clapped and jumped up and exclaimed, "Oh, Guster! That was wonderful! Can you do it again?"

Mom and I groaned. Then Dad realized he was hogging the mike and sputtered, "Another time, Charlie. In fact, I can teach it to you, if you'd like."

"Dinner's ready," I said, and we all went inside to the kitchen.

Somehow pot roasts improve with a little age on them, and the one we had reheated was no exception. It was delicious, and there wasn't enough left to feed the ants.

"This was wonderful," Steve said after wiping up the gravy on his second serving with a piece of bread. "Absolutely just like my mother used to make."

"And it was my mother who taught me to make it!" Mom said, not wanting a good pot roast to add to her age.

"Well, I'm going to say good night because I have early appointments in the morning. See y'all tomorrow, and thanks again!" Steve was standing by then and went around the table to give my mother a hug and shake Dad's hand. I got up to walk him to the door and get his dogs.

"See you tomorrow! We'll wash up the dishes, Jackie," Dad said. "Come on, Charlie, help your Guster and Glam put the quietus on this mess, and I'll tell you all about Mudville. There's a big dispute over where the real Mudville is . . ."

As soon as we stepped onto the porch, Stella and Stanley got up and ambled over. I could tell they were worn out. The heat was getting to everyone, even the dogs.

"You know, Charlie has just loved taking care of them," I said.

"Yeah, I think I got the better end of the deal, though," he said.

"How's that?"

"Well, if Charlie didn't have the dogs over here every day, I wouldn't have the excuse to see you."

"Just what are you saying?"

"Whoa, whoa! I'm not asking you to slow dance, okay? I'm just saying it's nice to have someone to talk to who's been through the same horror show."

"Oh, I'm sorry. God, why am I so touchy?"

"I don't know the answer to that one. So have you decided when you're going back? That's some awfully long drive, isn't it? What is it, like eighteen hours?"

"Yeah, it's really terrible. Probably the end of next week."

"I'll give you my e-mail. Let me know when y'all are coming back."

"Why?"

"You know, you've got the wrong attitude here. I'm a nice man."

"You are. I don't know why I'm suddenly so bitchy. I was just thinking today or maybe it was yesterday, I can't remember. Anyway, I was thinking about what a great guy you are. Just so you know and don't go get a fat head over it, I was a little jealous when I saw that cheap tramp with you on your deck. There, I've said it, and it doesn't matter because I'm leaving anyway."

"Really? Tell me the truth, why *are* you leaving? Your family is here, not in New York."

"Isn't your family in Ohio? You don't live with them, do you?"

"My family isn't like yours. They're stuffy and humorless. I got born into the wrong family, I think. Now, your parents? I am completely crazy about your parents. They're like the two coolest people I know."

"That's because they're not your parents. I couldn't live with them. Especially my mother. I'd lose my mind. I mean, I left here years ago to make my own life."

"Well, whatever you say. But I wouldn't leave the Lowcountry if you gave me the south of France and threw in Napa as a bonus."

"Really? Why?"

"Because it speaks to me."

"Seriously? Are you crazy?"

"Maybe, but probably not. You've just forgotten how to listen, and I've just learned."

"Really? So what's it saying?"

"Hmmm, I don't know if you want to hear it."

"Oh, please. Do I strike you as Nurse Sensitivo?"

"Hardly." He looked at me for a moment. "Okay, the Lowcountry is saying that I have a beautiful young woman before me with a lot of living left to do but she's too unhappy to live like she should. And, it's saying that happiness is a choice—"

"Oh, come on—"

"Wait! There's more. And maybe her misery and some convoluted concept she has about what she thinks independence is, is more important to her right now than anything else. Maybe she thinks that if she stops being moody and unhappy her husband's spirit will fly away forever. To be happy would be like him dying all over again, except now she'd be the one killing him."

"Jesus God, Steve, that's pretty heavy."

"Yeah, well. Life's heavy. Anyway, I gotta go. We both have to get up at six. Thanks for dinner."

"Sure," I said and watched him leave and cross our yard to his. "Anytime." My words were absorbed into the damp night air.

With the way I tossed and turned, you would've thought I was sleeping on a bed of rocks that night. I kept dreaming about Jimmy. When Mom saw me in the morning she tried to hide her surprise, but I knew I looked awful. I filled a mug with coffee, wondering how many cups it would take to get my motor into gear.

"Didn't sleep so well, honey?" she said.

"No, I kept dreaming about Jimmy. It's the first time I've dreamed about him."

"I've got oatmeal and fresh fruit this morning. How's that?"

"Great." She put a bowl in front of me. It was slow-cooked steel-cut oatmeal sprinkled with brown sugar and blueberries. The campaign continued in earnest. "Wow."

"You're welcome. So what happened?"

"He was on this boat in the distance—"

"Crossing over the River Jordan—"

"No, really, Mom. You want to hear this or not?"

"Sorry."

"Anyway, suddenly we were at this funeral, I don't know who died, but Jimmy was holding a baby and he turned to me and put it in my arms."

"Boy or girl?"

"I don't know. Girl, I think, but I don't know why."

Mom stood there looking at me with this funny smile.

"Okay, you've consulted your Lowcountry inner witch doctor. May we have the interpretation, please?"

Dream interpretation was my mother's specialty, taught to her by her mother and to her mother by her mother. But looking for signs in the Lowcountry always produced wonders.

"That's Jimmy telling you he's fine and to go on with your life."

"If one more person says that to me I'm going to scream!"

"Don't look at me. He's your husband, not mine."

16

Here Legrand, having re-heated the parchment, submitted it my inspection. The following characters were rudely traced, in a red tint, between the death's-head and the goat:

53‡‡†305))6*;4826)4‡.)4‡);806*;48†8¶60))85 ;1‡(;:‡*883(88) 5*†;46(;

. . . "These characters, as any one might readily guess, form a cipher—that is to say, they convey a meaning; but then, from what is known of Kidd, I could not suppose him capable of constructing any of the more abstruse cryptographs. I made up my mind, at once, that this was of a simple species— such, however, as would appear, to the crude intellect of the sailor, absolutely insoluble without the key."

—Edgar Allan Poe, "The Gold-Bug"

Annie

Jackie left for work and I sat at the kitchen table, waiting for Buster to mosey out of his cave. Deb and I had decided to suspend our morning walks as long as

Buster was there because I wanted to have breakfast with him. I was taking our marriage out of storage and, sort of but not completely, trying it on for size.

"If you feel like walking, call me."

"I will," I said.

But more important, I was going to have a granddaughter. Oh! I was so happy! Who would be the father? Would she get married? She had better get married, or I'd take off my belt and wail on her little fanny. Wait, no, I wouldn't. I had not worn a belt in years. I wasn't sure I even owned one anymore. But I told Deb the story of Jackie's dream. She understood and agreed with me.

"That girl sure is a spitfire! May I just speak as one Lowcountry old salt to another? Don't you just love it when people think they're actually in charge of their lives?"

"Yes, ma'am! Makes me laugh. You see, she's forgotten that in the Lowcountry, the hand of God is alive and well."

I had no intention of telling Buster the news. Over the years, every time I had told Buster something from a dream meant thus and so was going to happen, he'd told me I was crazy and looked at me like I was one of the old witches from *Macbeth* stirring the pot. And when that predicted event came to pass, he'd harrumph that it was merely coincidence. Well, there were too many coincidences to be coincidences, okay? So Jackie's remarriage and daughter-to-be would remain my secret, but maybe I'd start to crochet a pastel pink afghan and just let him wonder why. Wouldn't that be fun?

"G'morning, Mrs. Britt, how did you sleep?"

Buster was up and poised for his morning hug. Because there was no one around to take our picture and put it up on Facebook, I gave the old bear a full frontal, arms around the neck, the whole nine yards. He did not object.

"Coffee?" I asked.

"Sure," he said and released me. "What's for breakfast? Something smells very good."

"You're smelling brown sugar. Sit, I'll get you a bowl."

I scooped out a generous serving of oatmeal, gave it the full garnish, including a pat of butter, and put it on the table before him.

"Thanks. I didn't know oatmeal could be so . . . well, so dang pretty!" He smiled at me, and I thought he was still handsome, in an appealing rugged weather-beaten kind of way.

He was probably living on cornflakes, and cooking oatmeal probably never occurred to him.

"Thanks," I said and handed him a mug of coffee.

"Is Charlie up?" he asked.

"No, but it's time for him to go get the dogs. I'll go wiggle his foot."

"You mind if I make some toast?"

"Gosh, no. Help yourself to whatever you want."

I heard Buster grunt as I left the room. It wasn't a grunt of disapproval; it was one that sounded like *Well, how do you like that? I can help myself!* Don't read too much into it, I thought.

I opened Charlie's door quietly and peeked inside his room. The only movement was the gentle turning paddles of the overhead fan and the rise and fall of Charlie's back. He was sleeping on his stomach; his torso and one leg were on the bed and the other leg was in midair, hanging over the floor. At some point he had kicked the covers off, and the leg of his pajama bottom was pushed up to his knee. He was a study in boyhood, and if I'd been an artist I would've set up my easel right there.

"Charlie?"

"Huh?"

"Time to get up, sweetheart. Gotta go get the dogs. And breakfast is ready."

" 'Kay. I'm coming."

Was it possible that he had grown overnight? He rolled out of bed and walked past me, headed for the bathroom. It seemed that his bottoms were too short.

When Charlie came back with Stanley and Stella and settled them on the front porch, we all sat down at the table. Buster announced that he was going fishing and did Charlie want to come along? I said that I would like to come along too, and they looked at me like I had just said Barack and Michelle were coming for dinner or some kind of crazy thing like that.

"Why can't *I* fish with y'all too?" I said, feeling a little defensive, but one of the things I'd told myself is that if we should ever flirt with a reconciliation, I would try to find out what it was about fishing that held such an attraction for him and thousands of other men.

"No! Of course you *can*! You just never *wanted* to go fishing before!" Buster said.

"Well, where are you going to fish?"

"I was thinking Breach Inlet," Buster said.

"Wonderful! Can we stop at Thomson Park for a few minutes?"

"What kind of Thomson Park?" Buster said.

"I like parks," Charlie said.

"No, no. Not that kind of park. Buster, I'll bet you a dollar that you never even heard about Colonel Thomson, did you? Because the whole site is pretty new. I just learned about him myself."

"What is it? More historical markers?"

Buster was highly skeptical about combining a fishing trip with history or anything that smacked of a nonrecreational event. I knew him. I could see disillusionment on his face.

"Don't worry, sweetie," I said, "if it's boring, I'll bait the hooks!"

"I want to see that!" Charlie said. "Glam touch a live wiggly thing? No way!"

"Way! Glam's not afraid of bait! And this park is not like those boring plaques along the highway," I said. "It's an inspiration. No lie."

"We'll see about all that," Buster said.

"Charlie, why don't you go run the dogs? I'll clean up the kitchen and get dressed. And Dr. Hemingway? Prepare your mind to be boggled by how many fish I bring home."

"Yes, but are you going to rise to the challenge of cleaning them?" Buster said.

"Absolutely not! Nasty! That's a boy job. I cook them. That's my job."

"I'm gonna go get everything together," he said, kind of laughing to himself. "Is my cleaning table still under the house?"

"Well, yes, but it's been repurposed as a potting table for my plants," I said.

"What?"

"I guess you can just move everything to the ground and hose it down."

"Oh, fine. I leave the house for a little bit, and my cleaning table becomes a home to begonias and geraniums."

"A little bit? How's eleven years? Should I have made it a shrine?"

"Humph. Well, I'll just go see about it, then . . ."

"Well, you just go on and do that!"

What did he think? That his slippers were still tucked under his side of the bed and his reading glasses were still on the end table next to his favorite chair?

Even the newly allegedly mellow Buster could be exasperating.

Buster knew a spot on the back of the island where you could throw a cast net and catch shrimp. He intended to use live shrimp for bait. Yikes. I wasn't so sure that I felt comfortable about stabbing them with a hook and murdering them in cold blood, although I suspected they didn't even have blood, and if they did, it wasn't red or warm. In any case, Charlie had never thrown a cast net, and he was excited to try it. I had my camera ready because there was nothing more beautiful than a young boy throwing a net, set against the long green marsh grass and the brilliant blue of the Carolina sky. My camera was the size of a deck of cards, making it extremely easy to carry in a pocket (which was why I ever used it) and it's the most high-tech gizmo I owned.

Buster began to give Charlie a lesson. "You see, Charlie, you really need three arms for this, but since we only have two, we use our teeth to help. Watch this."

Buster took his net, which was only about forty-eight inches in circumference and stretched it out between the full breadth of his arm span.

"See? You hold it like this. But you take the middle point in between your teeth like this." He demonstrated.

Then he took the net out of his mouth; it had surely seen better days and had been in God only knew whose mouths. I was certain that it had never been washed and that it had to be infested with germs.

"I think catching bait with a cast net is a feat better accomplished by males of the species," I said.

Charlie, who now held the net between his teeth, started to giggle. He looked at me and said, "Gross, huh, Glam?"

"Yes, gross. Just remember to let go with your teeth," I said, "or it might pull your teeth out."

"For real?" Charlie looked a little horrified.

"Aw, Annie! Don't go scaring the boy! I've been throwing cast nets since I was half his age."

"Is it true, Guster? I just grew these teeth, you know. They're new."

"Sort of. Look, I'll tell you what. I'll throw it a few times and you watch. Then if you want to do it, you can give it a try. Watch the timing, okay?"

I pulled out my camera and got ready. Just as Buster sent the net flying across the water, I snapped a picture. Perfect! Buster pulled the net back in, and it had a few shrimp inside.

"See these little guys? This is what shrimp look like before they get their stupid little heads snapped off."

"Wow! Cool! Look at them jumping around!"

"Well, they prefer water to land, so let's put some water in that bucket, pick them off the net, and drop them in."

Charlie was mesmerized by the whole process. And pretty soon, with Buster's guidance, he was handling live shrimp and throwing the cast net like he'd been doing it all his life too. Within a short period of time they caught plenty of bait. Best of all, I had wonderful pictures to show Jackie. It was so thrilling to witness the patience Buster had with Charlie and just as amazing to witness Charlie's utter joy at discovering something new that he could now do with very reasonable proficiency for a boy of his age.

"Charlie?" Buster said. "If a man can fish? In this part of the world, he can feed himself and feed his family. It's important to know how to do these things. Very important."

Charlie nodded his head in agreement, Buster ruffled Charlie's hair, and we went back to the car.

Buster started the engine, and as we backed out from the oyster-shell road, I could hear the water sloshing around in the bucket.

"What if that water gets on the floor of your car, Buster? It's going to smell pretty funky."

"Ah, Annie, real men don't worry about that kind of hoo-ha, do they, Charlie?"

"No, sir, especially when the floor of the back-seat has these rubber containers that the bucket's in." Charlie started to laugh.

"Now, don't go telling all my secrets, Charlie, or Glam-ma will know too much!"

"Humph. Disrespectful naughty boys," I said, pretending to be offended. "Let's park right over there by Thomson Park."

We did and we unloaded all the fishing gear, letting it rest beside the side of the SUV. The Breach Inlet Bridge was only steps away. We walked over to the tiny park that had been erected to the memory of Colonel Thomson and all the men who had fought with him.

Charlie and Buster looked at the weather-protected placards that told the basic story of the Battle of Breach Inlet, and I could see they were thoroughly uninterested.

"Okay, guys! Listen up! Now! Imagine this! It's June twenty-eighth, 1776. You've got the American patriots on Sullivans Island and the British army on the Isle of Palms. There're over three thousand Brits and *less than eight hundred patriots*, and we kicked their butts. I mean, *kicked* their butts the whole way back to Buckingham Palace!" God, I missed teaching history. "Right here! Right where you all are standing!"

"No way," Buster said.

"Really?" Charlie asked.

"I never heard those numbers," Buster said.

"On this very sandbar. Yep. Right here. Try to envision it. Can you imagine? No wonder Colonel Thomson's nickname was 'Danger'! Yep, that's what they called him. Y'all want to drop a hook in the water now?"

"Wait a minute. Why didn't they have more men to fight?" Charlie asked.

"Yeah, and how'd they win against odds like that?" Buster asked.

I had them right in the palm of my hand. "Because they outsmarted Major General Henry Clinton every step of the way. They had a few other things working for them too. Number one, part of Thomson's troops were Indians and excellent fighters in nontraditional ways. *And* all the men were very good shots *and* the hot summer didn't bother them one bit. Clinton's men came over here, in *June*, mind you, dressed in big heavy wool uniforms, they had to sleep on the beaches, the alligators and snakes scared the devil out of them, and they were just eaten alive by mosquitoes."

"Worse than I was?" Charlie said.

"Even worse, Charlie, even worse. But the main thing besides great leadership and knowing the terrain better than the British guys was that the American patriots had a real passion. They wanted their freedom more than anything else in the world, and they were willing to die fighting for it."

"Wow," Charlie said.

"Wait a minute," Buster said. "Where the hell were General Moultrie and all those guys while this was going on?"

"Oh, come on, Buster! You know perfectly well where they were!"

"Yeah, I know, but I want you to tell our boy here."

"Okay, they were at the other end of the island fighting another battle. You see, Charlie, in those days, this end of the island was all wilderness. There were no houses or anything. It was like a jungle. So, the other battle for Sullivans Island was fought with the British navy, and General William Moultrie was down the island in charge of that."

"Tell him the best part, you know, about Parker," Buster said, egging me on.

"Okay, but very briefly. You see the plan was that Admiral Sir Peter Parker and his nine Birtish ships would wipe out Fort Moultrie and then General Clinton's men would swarm the island, wiping out anyone who was left. But Thomson, who fought against Clinton in this very spot, pushed back Clinton's troops. So the British navy never got the ground support they were hoping for. And General Moultrie was focused on a couple of the ships in particular and one of them was the *Bristol*. That's the one Admiral Parker was on. So don't ask me how they did this, but one of Moultrie's men shot Parker in the region of his backside and Parker's fanny was exposed all through the battle."

"*WHAT?*" Charlie yelled, he was getting so excited.

"And his leg was hurt too, but who cares about that?" I added, but Charlie was already gone to heaven on the tidbit about Parker's butt. I couldn't blame him. I had not had a class of kids in all my years teaching who didn't lose it when they heard the Parker story. "But anyway, it was the Americans' passion for freedom that carried the day in both battles. And better leadership. Now can we go catch a fish? I'm starving!"

"How come I never heard any of this stuff in school?" Charlie asked.

"Oh, I'm sure they'll give it to you eventually. Pretty exciting, huh?"

"Wow, I'll say," he agreed.

"And your Glam has a way of making it all come to life," Buster said and smiled at me.

Lord, I knew this man too well to think it was a random compliment. He was gunning for a ticket to the Magic Gate in the Master Suite. Uh-huh. I knew him better than I knew my own name. Maybe I'd let him pay a visit. *IF* he was very sweet.

We walked out to the bridge and across it a little ways.

"What are we going to catch, Guster?"

"Oh, we might get us some spottail bass or some trout. They're running pretty good this time of year. Let's just see. Can I bait your hook, Annie?"

"If you insist," I said and was grateful that I didn't have to put those darling little shrimp on my spit. Privately in my head? I gagged at the thought.

We stood by the railing on the bridge and fished until we had plenty of catch and the sun was becoming too much to bear. When Charlie pulled in his third trout, which had to be at least twenty inches long, we decided it was time to give it up for the day.

"This fishing rod is lucky, Guster! Thanks again!"

"It's easy to cast, isn't it?"

"Smooth as silk!" Charlie said, barely able to contain his enthusiasm each time he got a strike. "Ooh! Y'all! I got a whale on the line! I swear it's a whale!"

"Don't swear, darling! Let Guster help you!"

And of course, Buster would help him reel in his fish and get it off the hook.

I had caught two lovely bass. Buster caught one. We had enough fish to have a party. We gathered our gear and began to make the short walk back to the car.

"We can give a fish to Deb," I said.

"And Steve," Buster said.

"And I can make bouillabaisse. Bass is perfect for that."

"What the hell is that?" Buster asked, and I was reminded that he despised anything that smacked of pretension. And in his mind *anything* French would meet that criterion, maybe even including Brie.

"It's a French seafood stew," Charlie said. "Aunt Maureen and I love it. Every time Mom got deployed she'd take me to this place called La Bouillabaisse. Just me and her."

"See?" I said.

"Really? What's in it?" Buster said.

"Tomatoes, fish, onions, garlic, I don't know what else. I can look it up on the Internet if you want. Want to make some?"

"If you learned how to make it, wouldn't your aunt Maureen be delighted?" Charlie got a peculiar look on his face and I asked, "What is it, honey?"

"I thought you understood," he said. "I can't go back there."

"Why not?" Buster asked.

"Because it will be a disaster."

"I have to talk to you about this, Buster," I said. "I need your help."

I looked at Buster, and his eyebrows were knitted in that old familiar way that showed his concern.

"Come here, Charlie," he said, dropping the bucket of fish to the ground by his SUV. He kneeled down to look Charlie straight in the eyes. "What can I do to help, son?"

"Let me stay," he said and began to cry. "Please let me stay."

Buster stood up, put his arms around Charlie, and hugged him for all he was worth.

"Oh, dear," I said and dug in my pocket for a tissue. "Here, sweetheart."

"Come on, buddy," Buster said. "There, now. Let's go home and make some sandwiches and talk about this. It's lunchtime. We'll figure something out."

Well, wasn't that just like Buster to tell Charlie we'd figure something out? What? Just what did he think we could figure out to solve *this*? It was Jackie's call to make, not ours.

Charlie climbed into the backseat of Buster's SUV, and we were home in a few minutes.

"All right, young man. It's time to clean the fish. You gonna help me?"

"I guess so."

A very somber Charlie and a deeply concerned Buster took the bucket of fish under the house, and I climbed the steps to the house.

"Tomato sandwiches all right with y'all?" I called out to them.

"Yeah, God, it's too hot to eat anything else," Buster called back. "Thanks."

The very first thing I did was wash my hands. Please! I had touched the handrails of a bridge and a fishing rod, and I felt so sticky that if I didn't have to make lunch I would've hopped in the shower. Actually, my hopping days were behind me. Now I stepped cautiously into the shower.

The second thing I did was take Buster my largest rectangular Pyrex dish, in which he could put the cleaned fish. It was like the old days. He would bring me beautifully cleaned and filleted fish, and I would figure out what to do with it.

"Thanks," he said and smiled at me. "Feels like old times."

"You're welcome," I said, thinking, Well, it's not. There's been a lot of water under the bridge in all these years. Then I looked at Charlie. "You okay, baby?"

"Yeah, I guess. Boy, cleaning fish is a messy business, isn't it?"

"Well, yes. I think I would faint if I had to cut the head off a live fish."

"Well, they're not exactly alive," Buster said. "They're sort of stunned."

"Okay, well, I'm going to go back upstairs and make lunch. Y'all come on up when you're ready."

"Will do," Buster said. "We won't be too long. Right, Charlie? Hand me that knife, please."

When Buster and Charlie came inside for lunch, the table was set for three. A platter of tomato sandwiches cut in half was in the middle with a bowl of potato chips and a smaller bowl of pickles. I had a pitcher of iced tea, of course, and a small bowl of lemon wedges. But I had a new beverage for Charlie: the Arnold Palmer.

Half iced tea and half lemonade. Surely Jackie couldn't object to that. And, most important, I had rinsed the remaining guts off the fish before I let them near my Big Chill refrigerator.

"I'll just cover this with plastic wrap and put it in the fridge for now," I said. "We're going to have an amazing supper."

Buster washed his hands at the kitchen sink and encouraged Charlie to do the same, which he did. That simple act of washing hands together, the sight of their backs at the sink, well, it was a diamond-sharp example of why grandparents loved being grandparents. The little boy who feels so much and knows so little yet about the world and about life, standing next to the older man who would love to show him everything he knows that's of value and worthy of pursuit. And most important, it's as though they both know that time is the enemy, working against them, so the time they *do* have together is so cherished.

We sat down, and I passed the platter of sandwiches around. I had made a fast recipe for basil mayonnaise in the blender and used it instead of the store-bought goop.

"Wow," Charlie said. "This is really good, Glam."

"Yeah, it really is, Annie. I've missed your basil mayonnaise. Nothing like it."

He was on his best behavior, and I suspected that the closer we got to nightfall, it would improve even more. By bedtime I might have Prince Charming on my hands.

"Thanks, guys. So you liked fishing, did you, Charlie?"

"Yeah. I wonder if Edgar Allan Poe could fish."

"Probably. I mean, it's not that hard," Buster said. "But who knows?"

"Well, that's an interesting question to ask, because I'm pretty sure the answer is no. The early part of his life was spent in urban environments and in boarding school in England. Then he attended the University of Virginia, got tossed out, joined the army, and arrived here on the island. It was in November of 1827, I believe."

"Using a fake name," Charlie said, taking a bite of a pickle. "Edgar Perry, right?"

"That's right. Anyway, his job was to order and organize all the food and supplies they needed for the whole fort. It wasn't exactly like being a general, but he did such a good job handling his duties that he was promoted to sergeant major. But there's no evidence he caught the fish they ate."

"Annie? Since when do you know all this about Poe?"

"Well, darlin'? I've had a lot of time on my hands in the last few years, haven't I?"

"Hmmm. Yeah, I reckon so."

"Charlie, I hope you and your momma can be here when I give my talk at the library."

"Me too!"

"What talk?"

"Well, Deb wants to raise some money for the library, so she asked me if I'd give a talk on Poe. Listen, he was a real interesting character."

"Was he ever!" Charlie said.

"You don't know the half of it, Charlie. Come back and see me when you're eighteen! Anyway, so, she's going to ask her volunteers to make some sandwiches and cookies and whatever, a punch bowl of something, I guess, and charge a little admission. Hopefully, it will work."

"Well, put me down for a front-row seat," Buster said.

"Really?" I said, a little surprised because I had thought Buster would never be interested in Poe.

"Yeah, really. I'm real proud of you, Annie."

"So am I, Glam. Now if y'all could just figure out a way I can stay here, the world would be awesome."

"What's the *real* problem, Charlie? Just spill it," Buster said.

Charlie told Buster basically the same things he had told me, and Buster shook his head.

"Do you want me to talk to our daughter?" he asked.

"I've wanted to ask you to do that. Yes, please, talk to her."

Buster reached over and patted the back of Charlie's hand. For some reason it gave me hope.

17

". . . Acting on this hint, I made the division thus: 'A good glass in the bishop's hostel in the devil's—twenty-one degrees and thirteen minutes—northeast and by north—main branch seventh limb east side—shoot from the left eye of the death's-head—a bee-line from the tree through the shot fifty feet out.'"

"Even this division," said I, "leaves me still in the dark."

"It left me also in the dark," replied Legrand, "for a few days; during which I made diligent inquiry, in the neighborhood of Sullivan's Island, for any building which went by the name of the 'Bishop's Hotel' . . ."

—Edgar Allan Poe, "The Gold-Bug"

Jackie

"So you caught this fish *yourself*, did you?" I asked Charlie over dinner that night.

"Yep, and that sucker was a real fighter too. He really gave me the devil, didn't he, Guster?"

Charlie had developed a beautiful golden tan, and because of all the sun, he was sprinkled with freckles that made him even more adorable. He was also beginning to adopt a lot of my dad's sayings, such as "He gave me the devil" and "that sucker." Ah, family.

"Yep. But Charlie reeled him in," Dad said. "I'm real proud of our boy here."

"Nothing like fresh fish," Mom said.

"I like it better fried in flour and milk," Dad noted.

Mom cleared her throat to express her annoyance. I couldn't blame her if she was a trifle irked. Even to the casual observer it would have seemed that all she did was put one meal on the table after another and every morsel was always fresh and as delicious as she could manage. Even since Charlie and I had been here, who could even calculate the hours she'd spent thinking up, shopping for, preparing, serving, and cleaning up after meals alone? The kitchen, the table, the porch, the island. That was just about the entirety of her world.

Was I more satisfied because my world was larger? The answer, which had been an unequivocal yes when I had arrived with Charlie in tow, was disintegrating into something I recognized as the cobwebs of confusion. I had no idea how life would be when we returned to New York. Rather than my looking forward to it, it had become a terrible dreaded challenge to be faced.

My mother was so very proud of her meals and the tables she set. It seemed that since I'd been home she'd gone to even more effort than I could recall from other visits. No, this was a lovely world of her own imagining and carefully manifested by her hand alone. All day long and through the night she did everything in her power to make it inviting to us and pleasing to all our senses. It was all hers. I'd even go so far to say that she would be justified to claim some partnership with the ocean, the breezes, and the beach itself. How she took care of her family and friends was deeply important to her. And Dad, who never gave things like what made Mom tick a thought in the world, dropped these little cherry bombs. I'd talk to him. *I like fish fried in flour and milk.* If he could see, indeed if they *both* could see, what went on in Afghanistan, they'd be so grateful to God to have a family, food, friends, and most of all the freedom to enjoy them in safety.

"Yeah, we all love the crunch of fried fish batter, but we'll live longer if we eat our fish cooked this way," I said. "And it's better than the fish in Tikrit."

"I expect *that's* true," Mom said.

"I never had fish in Tikrit. But I sure ate a lot of goat. When I was lucky enough to get it. Mostly we ate really skinny chicken."

I gave Dad the hairy eyeball.

"Good grief!" Buster said and paused, his faux pas sinking in. "Annie? This fish is actually delicious. And I've heard goat can be tasty too."

"Tastes like chicken!" I said.

"Does it really?" Mom asked.

"No, but that's what we told ourselves." I laughed. "No one goes to Afghanistan for the food."

The fish in question was just grilled, with lemon juice, olive oil, and fresh thyme. Naturally, we had the two staples that came with a fish dinner: grits and salad. But no hush puppies. Despite Dad's protestations that fish could be vulcanized into worthiness only when cremated in a cast-iron skillet swimming with heart-clogging, bubbling-hot grease, he was enjoying it immensely, literally gobbling it up. We all were.

"I'm just feeling kind of hangdog about not really teaching Charlie how to fish until today. I mean, when he was little we went crabbing and sometimes he'd help me reel one in, but today I was fishing with a young man, not a kid."

"Oh, come on, Dad, you used to take him out in the boat with you all the time," I said.

"Guster is right, Mom. Today was different, the real deal. I've grown up a whole lot since the last time we went fishing. Can I have some more grits, please?"

"Of course you *can*, but *may* you?" Mom said and passed the serving bowl to him.

"She means you should say 'May I have some more grits?' instead of 'can,'" I said and wiggled my eyebrows.

"She is the cat's mother," Charlie said.

"No inside jokes," Dad said, pretending to be dour. "No, our Charlie here has learned how to tire out the fish by letting him run with the line to really sink that hook in his cheek. And then, just like those fellas on the fishing channel, he slowly reeled him in."

"Yup! That's what I did. Hey, Glam? Is there a book about the battles on Sullivans Island?" Charlie said.

"Oh, sweetheart, I'm sure there are many!" she answered. "I'll bet there are some right here in this house."

"Why don't you run a search on Dr. Steve's e-reader?" I said.

"Awesome idea! I'm gonna do that *right* after supper!" Charlie said.

"*After* we do the dishes!" I said, leaning back and taking a look at him. It did seem like he was growing up right in front of my eyes. "So, kiddo, what sparked your interest in the history of the island all of a sudden?"

"There's a new small park at Breach Inlet dedicated to Thomson from the Revolution," Mom said. "We stopped for a quick visit before we went fishing from the bridge."

"Yeah, Mom, you can't believe what went on right here on this island! There was this English guy—"

"I still can't believe you went fishing, Mom. It's way out of character for you."

"As long as I have your father to bait the hook and remove the catch, fishing is something I actually enjoy. Sort of."

"Exactly my point! Gotta be hard to really fall in love with the sport."

"So, Mom? This guy, Peter Parker—"

"It wasn't that unpleasant; it was just too hot today, I think."

"*Mom!* I'm trying to tell you about this guy Parker—"

"Sorry, sweetheart. Sometimes you have to wait your turn. But tell me. I want to know all about Peter Parker."

For the next ten minutes, Charlie regaled us with his interpretation of the Battle of Breach Inlet, Parker's bare backside, and the value and strength of passion. He was becoming quite the animated storyteller, and it was pretty obvious he was fueled by my mother's renowned lust for history.

"They *won* because of their *passion*, Mom. It's *important* to have a passion in life." He looked at all of us from face to face. "Isn't it?"

For a moment, that brief moment between processing the question and offering some reply, I saw my parents ask themselves if there was anything about which they were still passionate. I also saw them give each other a bashful half smile.

"It certainly is, Charlie," Dad said.

"Passion keeps you alive, Charlie, and it also lets you *know* that you're alive! If you don't have strong feelings for something, you simply aren't living!" Mom said, trying to win the Emmy for Best Actress in a Drama. "Don't you agree, Jackie?"

I thought about it for a minute and how loving Jimmy so passionately had broken me apart and how loving my country and freedom had led me to a place where I wasn't so sure my passion for it served anyone well.

"Yes, but passion can be dangerous too," I said.

I was thinking of the Taliban and how women were less valuable in that society than a skinny cow or a goat. And even with all the efforts the world has made to improve the status of women in cultures like Afghanistan, girls and women were given away in compensation for crimes of passion to the families against whom the crimes of passion had allegedly been committed without the benefit of any kind of tribunal of justice. The women were enslaved and beaten and sometimes died for lack of nourishment. In the best cases they were sometimes released. And if they weren't released and didn't die, they were made to bear children against their will and were made miserable for the rest of their lives by constant beatings, berating, and deprivation. And the rest of the world seemed to be turning a blind eye to it all, because even when we got involved, and even when we put our lives on the line, nothing seemed to change very much.

"What are you thinking about, Jackie?"

"Oh, I guess that passionate love is very exciting, but political passions . . . well, they can lead to a lot of senseless suffering. You know . . ."

My parents looked from my face to each other's and back to Charlie's, avoiding what I implied. In my mother's house, nobody liked to talk about this war. The American Revolution and the Civil War were popular topics, but the one their only daughter was fighting was taboo.

"Well, I think what Charlie learned today is that without the passion of all the American soldiers on this very island we'd be singing 'God Save the Queen,'" Mom said. "Isn't that right, Charlie?"

"Yeah, Mom. You're missing the point, maybe? This is a lesson in how to win when the odds are like totally way against you."

"Hmmm," I said. "Okay, soldier, let's get these dishes cleaned up. Mom, thanks for another great meal."

"Wait! I've got peach pie! Doesn't anybody want pie?"

Of course we did. Eventually the dishes were done and we dispersed like tiny beads of mercury, each to his own favorite perch.

After Charlie downloaded *The Short History of Charleston*, which he wanted to read, he decided to turn in. I guessed that the heat of the day had got the best of him. I said good night to my boy, reminded him he had to repay Steve, and he promised he would.

"I've got so much money I don't know *what* I'm gonna do with it," he said.

I had to smile at that. "We can open a savings account. How about that? Or you could buy your ever-loving momma a Porsche?"

"I don't have *that* much money!"

"Oh, okay." I leaned over him and kissed his forehead. "I'll be right here if you need me, okay?"

I went to join my parents. I kept asking myself, If they can get along this well, why aren't they together?

It was so heartening to have our tiny family under one roof. And to think that all I'd had to do was mention that another man was flirting with Mom to get Dad to spring into action. I should've rattled his cage years ago.

Dad was in the living room, standing in front of the television, watching the Weather Channel.

"Where's Mom?"

"On the porch. I just wanted to check the weather. This time of year you can't be too vigilant."

"So what's happening?"

"Another storm, and I don't like the looks of it."

"Why's that?"

"The eye's already over a hundred miles wide. And it's slow-moving."

"I don't know what that means, but the tone of your voice says it ain't good."

"No, it ain't. Let's just keep watching it. They're saying that if the winds gain strength to a category three, they're going to delay school openings in Charleston, Berkeley, and Dorchester Counties."

"When does school open?"

"Next ten days or so. I don't know why they're saying that now. Seems premature. But maybe the authorities know something we don't. Maybe there's a string of storms coming behind it. Come on." He clicked the remote, and the television screen went dark. "Your momma's out there all by her lonesome."

"Gosh. I don't remember that kind of precaution before."

"Me either. Probably because of Katrina and all . . ."

"Yeah. Maybe."

Mom was on the porch, rocking and sipping on a nightcap of some strain of "O Be Joyful."

"Come sit!" she said.

"I think I am going to go and get myself a little splash of something. Freshen your drink, Annie? And can I get you something, Jackie?"

"I'm fine," I said.

"I'm fine too, Buster. Thanks."

Daddy slipped back inside the house, and as soon as Mom figured he was beyond hearing us she said, "Hasn't he been great?"

"Yeah, he sure has."

"I almost don't mind him being here, but I wish he'd wait until we were away from the table before he says something stinky about the meal."

"I'm convinced he doesn't mean half of what he says, Mom. But! To his credit, as soon as he's made to see that he's being rude, he backs off and apologizes. Look on the bright side. Maybe he's retrainable."

"Wouldn't that be something? Old dog? New trick? Anyway, he's being awfully sweet."

"Yeah, he is. I think he got around us and realized he's lonely up there in Murrells Inlet in his creepy old bachelor pad."

"Really?"

"Yes, ma'am. And I think being around Charlie has been wonderful for both of them."

"I agree with you on that one for sure."

"Right? I need to talk to you about us leaving too."

"Oh?"

"Yeah, wonderful as all of this has been, Mom, and it has been so great, with these storms coming and all, I'm just thinking that we'd better get out of here. It's a long drive, and I don't want to get caught in some evacuation traffic snarl for hours. Remember that hurricane about ten years ago when people sat on I-26 for like twenty hours?"

"Who could forget that? But there's no rush, is there?"

"Well, there's a pretty terrible storm headed this way. Dad sure seemed concerned about it."

"Really?"

"Yeah. I think that tomorrow I'll start packing our SUV and keep up with the news and then we can decide. But one way or the other, it's probably time, like we say down here in the Lowcountry, to think about fixing to go on and get ready to do something about getting a move on."

"That's such a funny saying, but it's true. We say that all the time. Or some variation."

"I have to get Charlie ready for school, and there's a lot to do. A million forms to fill out. And I don't know if I told you this, but I have a job at the Brooklyn VA waiting for me. I hope so, anyway."

Mom was silent for a few moments, and then she said, "Deb told me about your new job." As if to say *I heard it from her, not you, thanks a lot.*

"Look, Mom, I know you want me to stay. In many ways I'd like to stay too. But now is not the time. For some reason, I just feel very strongly that Charlie and I need to go back and get back on that horse again. Otherwise it sends him a message that we weren't strong enough to really make it on our own. To face our reality. You understand that, don't you?"

"And this storm is giving you the impetus to get up and begin the trek early?"

"Yeah. Dad said the eye was over a hundred miles wide. That's huge, I guess. And it's slow-moving. That's not good. It makes me nervous."

"Nervous? You're nervous about something? Since when?"

"Seriously? This year taught me how to worry and wring my hands like no other."

"Humph. Here's the problem. When you start running from trouble? It confers with the devil on how to find you twice as fast. Listen to your Nervous Nellie mother."

"Well, I hope you're wrong about that. I really do."

Dad rejoined us and took his place in a rocker across from us that he had turned around to face us.

"Well, Buster, it looks like our girl is leaving us."

"Is that so, Jackie?"

"Only for a short period. I'll be back at Thanksgiving. If you'd like us to come, that is."

Of course both of my parents said *oh yes, please come* and *maybe you should think about flying next time* and *we can help you with tickets*, and on and on they went. Dad even said that if I wanted to drive for whatever reason I had, he would fly up to New York and help me drive home. And that if we got lonely, they could come for a visit. I didn't know if they meant that they would visit together or separately, but it didn't matter. It was their sentiment that so touched me. I thought I was lucky then to have two parents who understood so well what I needed to do for Charlie and for me.

They seemed to be fully supportive until Dad said, "You know, Jackie, there's something I want to talk to you about. It might mean something and it might not, but I think it's worth bringing to your attention."

"What? Of course! Tell me."

"I've had a few occasions to talk to Charlie about going back to New York, and you know he's not too thrilled."

"He's a kid," I said. "And every day here is like Christmas for him."

"Yes, I know, and your mother and I agree with what you say and your plan and all that. That's not the issue. Charlie thinks that your house in New York is too sad, that everywhere he looks there's a reminder of his dad. He's afraid that you're going to sink into a depression if you go back."

"Which means *he* will, not you," Mom said.

"Oh, great. So what do you think? Of course there are pictures of Jimmy all over the place. Why wouldn't there be?"

"We understand, and we don't disagree with you," Dad said. "But for him it might be too much. I'm no expert on this. That's for sure."

"He says the house even smells like Jimmy," Mom said. "Maybe a fresh coat of paint and new slipcovers for the sofa might help? I don't know, Jackie."

"Who *does* know?" I remarked and sighed for all I was worth. "I'm glad you told me this. At least it gives me a clue to what might set him off again. God, our life is so upside down."

A month ago I would've flown into a rage at what they were saying, and now I was taking it more in stride.

"Not really, baby. You still have your momma and daddy. All you have to do is squeak, and we'll be there."

"I appreciate that more than you can imagine."

"But she's right, Annie. Jackie and Charlie are looking at some big changes," Dad said. He was quiet for a few minutes. "So tell me, Jackie, how do you feel about not going back to active duty?"

My military career was the hot button we had so carefully avoided pushing for years. But now that it appeared to be safely and finally behind me, my father apparently felt it was all right to ask about it.

"That's such a complicated question, Dad, because it's not like I have much of a choice." I thought about it for a minute and then said, "You know, my unit was all about humanitarian aid. The women I met wanted to know what they could do to improve their lives, become a little more independent financially, provide a healthier life for their children—the normal things women want. We helped them but in small ways. I sometimes wonder if we really made a measurable difference to them."

"Well, of course you did, but I don't know how you'd measure such a thing anyway," Mom said.

Were we actually having the discussion I had hoped for all these years? It appeared we were.

"I guess by how much business they did? I mean, we helped them figure out how to set up a cooperative with women in other villages, to sell things they made, you know, like knitted hats and scarves or little boxes decorated with bits of turquoise and coral. For that you would just add up the sales and track them year to year."

"You sound frustrated," Dad said.

"Probably because I am. I mean, there were a lot of things that went on that I can't talk about because they're still classified."

"Oh, honey! Your father and I don't want you to tell *one word* you're not supposed to tell, do we, Buster?"

"Of course not." Dad cleared his throat and drained his glass.

"Look, at its most basic, the problem is trust. The Afghanis trust the Pakistanis but the Iraqis don't trust Americans or *any* of the other guys and nobody trusts the Taliban. How do you get all these guys to the table to negotiate a lasting peace? Good luck. Never mind changing the way they treat their women and children. *And* never mind drug trafficking. It's a mess. So you wonder, after you've witnessed every atrocity you can imagine, if you did any good."

"And what have you decided?" Dad asked. "Surely you must believe our troops have done an awful lot of good for the people."

"Oh! Without a doubt! But as a humanitarian, I'm always looking for something more. I think this is what I took away from my experience. Those women live under an oppression that is nearly indescribable, *but* when I show up and the other men and women in my unit show up and we take their hands and look into their eyes, they *know* that *someone* out there in the rest of the world understands their plight. And that *however* we can do it, we *want* to make it better for them."

"Well, that's a great reward, Jackie. I mean, that has to be very satisfying, don't you think so, Buster?"

"Of course, but I think I understand Jackie's frustration. I imagine that when you leave you're just not sure if things will really change for the better. Is that it?"

"Yep. That's the core of it, for me anyway. Listen, when you're with a bunch of women who would be thrilled to have the *least* of our privileges, it stops you in your tracks and makes you think about how profoundly grateful you are to live in this country. And it is your most fervent wish, I mean, *very most fervent* wish that you being there has at least given them some hope."

"Hope that change will come?" Mom asked.

"Yep. Hope that change will come," I said. "But it's almost futile."

"My word, darlin'. That is so sad."

"Your mother and I are so proud of you, Jackie. I don't think we've ever told you that often enough. You're a brave young woman. Very brave."

"Thanks, Dad."

"She gets that from my side of the family," Mom said.

"Naturally," Dad said.

Of course we all laughed, but I was grateful for the darkness so my parents couldn't see the tears that were running down my face.

18

"That is a question I am no more able to answer than yourself. There seems, however, only one plausible way of accounting for them—and yet it is dreadful to believe in such atrocity as my suggestion would imply."

—Edgar Allan Poe, "The Gold-Bug"

Annie

It was not a beautiful day. The skies were overcast, as though the world was huddled under a giant soup bowl of thick gray oatmeal. We were about to get a taste of what menace Mother Nature had tucked deep inside her pockets. Hurricane Candace was going to wreak havoc on the Lowcountry. I could feel it in every last one of my bones.

Deb and I decided to take a walk despite Buster's residency in the Salty Dog. I guess I was getting so used to him being around that I finally felt like it didn't matter if I left him for a bit. I went out for groceries, didn't I? And Lord knows, my cholesterol needed some exercise. Besides, he was fully occupied, determined to clean the waffle iron with an old soft toothbrush, and afterward he planned to tackle the toaster oven, which was all but a lost cause it was so pitted from the unavoidable salt air. I don't know what had come over him lately, but our division of labor had certainly flip-flopped from the old days. Basically now, if I cooked, he cleaned. He said it wasn't fair for me to do all the work. Well, hells bells, *I* knew that! What took *him* so long to reach spiritual enlightenment? But I wasn't going to point it out. It didn't always pay to be right. But he was surely acting like he lived here again, and that was something over which we were going to have to have a little Come to Jesus Meeting.

I just smiled pleasantly and said, "Thanks, Buster! I'll be back in an hour. Are you sure it's okay?"

"Of course! Go! It's good for you!" he said, adding that I should give Deb a squeeze for him.

I was telling Deb how Buster had refashioned himself into a domestic god while we hurried down the beach on a very high tide, trying to avoid the water that rushed to shore.

"Well, Lord love a duck, will wonders never cease? I can just see him scrubbing away," she said.

"Honey, you should've seen him going to town on that grill! The darn thing looks brand new! And now some man over at Haddrell's hardware sold him some cedar planks that you soak in water and then you grill fish on them. Suddenly he wants to grill fish. Probably because Jackie told him it was healthier."

"Well, she would know."

"Absolutely."

"They don't catch on fire? Those plank things?"

"No, because they're saturated with water. You soak them overnight."

"My word. What's next?"

"Truly. But you ought to see him jockeying for Grill King. He gets out there with Steve, and they're comparing techniques on whether or not to flip steaks only once or over and over. And what kind of dry rub to use on ribs. All kind of fool mess. I swear, some men will argue about anything."

"Because their whole life is one big fat stupid contest. That's one thing I sure do miss about Vernon. He never argued about anything."

"Yeah, he was a pussycat."

We were quiet for a moment then because I knew she was thinking about him and I didn't want to interrupt that private communion or whatever was going on inside her head. But I couldn't hold my tongue until the cows came home, so I finally spoke.

"So the stupid storm's definitely coming, and Jackie's definitely leaving."

"Is one related to the other?"

"Well, *of course* they are! She wants to get out of here ASAP. Besides the storm, Charlie has to go back to school and she's got to get him ready, but, boy oh boy, does my little grandson ever have a hot temper? Whoo boy!"

"He's still pitching a fit? Charlie? That sweet child?"

"Yeah, that angel. Like I never saw in my whole life! Jackie was putting some things in the back of her SUV this morning, and Charlie was arguing with her until I thought he was going to explode! It was a good thing I got up early to make waffles. Otherwise they might have really gone at it. I went out there and said, 'All right, you two! Enough is enough! Besides, the waffles are getting cold, and Charlie? I made you chocolate milk.'"

"And then what?"

"Well, I told him he had to obey the Fourth Commandment. He simply has to! Finally they came to the table, but Charlie wasn't too happy."

"Poor thing. I don't blame him, do you?"

"Let's turn around." We had reached a point where the beach was all but nonexistent at high tide, so we turned and began walking back. "Blame? I don't think there's blame to be laid anywhere on this one. But I think that if Jackie was the kind of girl who was more easily reabsorbed into the bosom of her own family instead of being so bloody independent, things might be different."

Deb rolled her eyes at me as she had for years whenever she thought *anything* I said smacked of pretension. I simply had a love of the language, and that's significantly different from being a Miss Fancy Pants.

"Well, Annie, you know I love you like a sister, but she's too old to live with her momma and her daddy. I mean, she's a woman of the world."

"Humph. Some world she made for herself."

"Annie! It's not her fault Jimmy died!"

"I'm aware, but a high-risk life can carry high consequences."

"Okay."

"But never mind all that. Here's the thing about her. She was in a war, a *real* war. You *know* she saw men, women, and children die right before her eyes, but she won't talk about it. And you can't tell me she wasn't changed inside her heart and mind by what she saw. And then her husband dies, not just *dies* like a normal person would but in a terrible fire! You can't tell me she isn't plagued by visions of it every single day and night. But she still won't talk about him except in the most general terms. I just think she needs to stay with us longer."

"You might be right, but it's still her call."

"Yes, I respect that. After all, if she thinks that returning to New York is the best thing for her and for her son, she should do it. I'm just saying that I disagree. Nobody can hold all that pain inside forever."

"She doesn't tell you *anything* about her experiences in Afghanistan?"

"Nope. She only talks about whether or not she made a measurable contribution to the lives of the people. She's worried about the *value* of her own performance. What about the horror show she lived in for months and months?"

"You know, Annie, some people can handle trauma better than others. They're able to compartmentalize. Medical professionals are certainly on the top of *that* list."

"True."

"Think about it. What would be completely unnerving to you or me is an everyday no big deal to her. And who knows? Maybe she didn't really witness anything that was so awfully horrible."

"Well, I'll give you one for my nerves compared to hers. I'm a total sissy and proud of it. But war is war, and that war in Afghanistan isn't like the others. There's no battlefield per se. Everywhere is a battlefield. There are no rules. You can't trust anyone, not even children. Between suicide bombers and land mines, you'd have to be a nervous wreck every minute. Jackie may not ever want to talk about it. I read the papers and I know what goes on over there. It sure isn't like the Battle of Breach Inlet. Or even the Civil War. Or even Vietnam. Anyway, I just wish she'd open up a little more. About Jimmy too."

"Maybe she will in time. Or maybe she never will. I mean, I talked to her a little about staying, and she's very determined to go back north. I'll bet you a dollar that one reason is because she feels like that's where Jimmy is and she doesn't want to leave him."

"That's ridiculous. Jimmy McMullen is in Heaven with Vernon sipping on a Budweiser."

"Probably, but I know how she feels. I've been out to the cemetery a couple of times just to make sure Vernon's marker is swept and all that. Listen, this has to be awfully hard for her. Losing Vernon has been awfully hard for me."

I stopped and grabbed Deb by the arm. "I know, darlin'. I think about Vernon and Jimmy every day, and I pray for them all the time."

"I do too."

"Listen, Deb? I have to tell someone this, and you're my best friend."

"What? You can tell me anything."

"Their visit has been so important to me. For the first time in years I have had my whole little family together. And it was so good for *all* of us. I felt like a *mother* again. Do you know what I mean? It's *killing* me to let them go back. I'm afraid we'll all fall apart and go back to some fractured version of our old selves. What will I do if that happens? I just don't think I could stand it." I was on the verge of some very serious tears.

Deb all but laughed at me, and I couldn't imagine what she thought was so funny.

"Oh, Annie Britt! I could just kiss your face!"

"Why?"

"Don't you see, my dear sweet friend? You can't undo the good you've done. You do so many nice things day and night for everyone that they flock to you like a moth goes to the flame. No one is going to stay away from you for too long. And if they do? Then they're a damn fool."

"Oh, God, Deb! Do you really think so? It's just that I'm so nervous that they're all going to leave me and never come back! And I know it was a tragedy that brought us all together and then Vernon's death made us even closer. This might sound terrible, but I've been so deeply happy for the first time in I don't even know how long. I just don't want it to end."

"Quit your worrying. Listen to me. Quit your worrying."

"And now there's this awful storm! What's her name?"

"Candace. What a ridiculous name for a hurricane. Since when is there anything sweet about a hurricane?"

"I just don't like the thought of Jackie and Charlie driving in high wind and heavy rain."

"Listen to you! There's not even one drop of rain on the ground yet, and you're already thinking the worst!"

"You're right. My nerves are acting up again. Listen, I want you to come for dinner tonight. It's the proverbial Last Supper. They're leaving in the morning at the crack of dawn."

"Should I bring a pie?"

"What do you think?"

By six o'clock that night, all the shutters on my house, Steve's house, and Deb's house had been closed. And Buster, bless his heart, had gone to Lowe's and bought a generator for the refrigerator and the kitchen lights in case we lost power. Everyone's porch furniture, except ours, had been brought inside, hanging baskets had been taken down, and while we worked like beavers to prepare our homes for the worst, we stayed glued to the Weather Channel on television. It appeared to me that the one-eyed evil Candace was headed directly for Sullivans Island.

Earlier, around four o'clock, I'd parked in my driveway and there was Buster, holding the ladder for Steve. Steve was pulling the shutters together and flipping the latches to keep them closed. I was coming in from the grocery store with four cases of water, a case of protein bars for emergencies, and steaks for dinner. Red meat was always designated for dinners of importance.

"The Piggly Wiggly was a madhouse!" I said. "People were grabbing for bread and milk like the Apocalypse is coming."

"I expect it was crazy. Lowe's was crazy too. People piling up sheets of plywood to cover windows and I don't know what all," Buster said. "This darn Candace has everybody all worked up."

It was true. People in the checkout lines had panic all over their faces. I said, "Well, Buster? What if the storm blows up to Cape Hatteras or out to sea? All this worry and work for naught?"

"Then we'll open the shutters and rehang the hammocks. I'd rather us be safe than sorry."

"You're right, of course. And you and Steve are awfully good to help Deb get her house ready too."

"Just trying to help out where I can."

"Still. It's really nice of y'all to do it."

When I passed behind him, I could see he was smiling, even from the back of his head because his ears moved in a certain way when he did. I remembered then that I had always loved that, the fact that his ears moved but also that he smiled so honestly and with his whole face. It was one of his many endearing qualities that I had almost forgotten.

I also noticed as I unloaded my trunk that Jackie's SUV was almost completely packed. I wondered how the squabble with Charlie was going. I would find out as soon as I went inside. The house was quiet. I went to Jackie's room and peeked in. She was lying down, probably trying to get rested up so she'd have the strength for the long drive. I didn't want to disturb her, so I closed her door gently and went to find Charlie, who was in his room lying on his bed reading.

"These puppies are going to miss you," I said and patted his comforter. "If they start yelping in the night, what should I do?"

No answer.

"Well, Charlie baby? Are you going to talk to me?"

He looked up at me with those blue eyes of his right through those bangs that needed another trim, and I thought I might burst into tears. Charlie had been weeping, because his eyes were bloodshot, but his jaw was set like a steel trap. Charlie McMullen was pissed off in purple, paisley, plaid, lavender, and puce. I had never seen him so upset.

"Glam? I'm so mad at her I could *kick* something. I just want to *kick* something!"

"Oh, come here to me," I said. "I know just how you feel. I really do."

I put my arms around him to give him a hug, and he was almost rigid. I rubbed his back like I used to do for Jackie when she was a little girl, upset about something, and eventually she would relax. After I made a whole lot of little circles on his back, Charlie finally sighed and leaned in against me.

"She just doesn't understand I'm not kidding. I mean it."

"Who's she? The cat's mother?" I said and finally got a smirk if not a smile.

"Right. Can't you talk to Mom?"

"Charlie. I will. But I have to tell you sweetheart, I don't think it's going to do much good. She's pretty determined to get out of here ahead of the storm. And the storm looks like it's going to be a pretty nasty one."

"Then shouldn't we all be together? I mean, should you and Guster be alone?"

"What do you mean? That we're too old and frail to handle a little wind and rain?"

"No, I just—"

"Well, if and when the storm hits and starts going really crazy, I'll try to remember to bring Guster in the house." Then I laughed a little and finally got a real smile out of him. "I think the plan is for Dr. Steve and Miss Deb to ride out the storm with us."

"So if something happens you have a doctor here?"

"No, so that we'll have four people to play cards or Monopoly! Now, do you want to help me get dinner on the table or what?"

"Okay." He slid off his bed and followed me out of the room.

From the corner of my eye I saw him wave a fist at Jackie's door and thought he might be very angry with his mother, but I was actually glad to see he had a temper. If there was anything that had bothered me about Charlie's behavior since he'd been here, it was that he seemed to have turned into a bit of a Goody Two-shoes. I'd told myself he was so well behaved because he had been traumatized and then depressed over losing his father and perhaps he didn't want to add anything more to Jackie's burden. He had seemed like a little old monk just going through the motions of saying and doing the right thing. The very fact that he allowed himself to lose his temper meant that he was coming back to normal. He was healing and wasn't afraid that a disagreement with his mother would upset her. He cared about himself again. As much as I disliked the fight, I took every other aspect as a good sign.

"Why don't you set the dining room table, Charlie? And since we're having steaks, let's use my bistro dishes. We can use my grandmother's plates for dessert."

For the rest of the time I would use every opportunity to tutor Charlie on the details and the minutiae that made what seemed to be an ordinary existence sparkle like a diamond. Always save the best for last. And when my granddaughter arrived on this earth, I'd do the same for her.

Soon we were enjoying our last happy hour on the porch, paper lanterns and all, and watching the ocean charge in toward the beach as the storm grew nearer. Despite the hurricane and the fact that Jackie and Charlie were leaving me, I had tried to set a cheerful stage, except for my outfit, which was a long purple linen tunic over purple shantung silk capri pants with a long chunky necklace made of very large black and red plastic beads and my red strappy sandals. It was somber but not morose. And not that anyone *really* needs to know this, but by the mercy of the Virgin Mother, I didn't need Spanx for this ensemble to hang right.

The skies were ominous but not so terrifying. However, the waters of the Atlantic were churning and darkening. Each incoming wave roared, pounded the shore, and then whooshed in, leaving a trail of silvery foam when the ocean pulled back to do it all over again. We had witnessed this panorama so many times before, and all the noise from the exploding surf was exciting, not particularly frightening. This was merely Candace's calling card. Candace herself had yet to arrive.

"Come on up here, Dr. Steve, and let us buy you a drink!" Buster called out.

Steve slipped through the oleanders and came toward our house just as the rain began to fall. He was wearing a summer parka with a hood, probably because he wanted to share grill duty with Buster.

Buster and I were sipping light gin and tonics with lots of lime. Charlie, still forlorn, was on his second cherry Coke, and Jackie was drinking weak decaffeinated iced tea. The hors d'oeuvre that night was a platter of peel 'n' eat boiled shrimp with a tangy tomato-based cocktail sauce. Of course I had soaked washcloths in strong lemon water, wrung them out, rolled them up like little sausages, and placed them in a sweetgrass basket on the table. Shrimp prepared and consumed in this manner were better enjoyed in your mouth than remembered all night long on your hands. They were the same towels I used for oyster roasts, bought by the dozen for a pittance. And though wet naps got the job done, they didn't offer nearly the same cachet as a cool scented cloth. Like ants, wet naps are for picnics. My opinion.

"What can I get for you?" Buster said to Steve.

Steve quickly looked to see what each of us was having and said, "Y'all drinking gin and tonics?"

"Yes, indeedy-do we are," I said and thought, Oh, aren't you slick tonight, Annie?

"Well, I think a gin and tonic would hit the spot. Thanks. You look very nice tonight, Annie."

"Why, thanks, Steve," I said and looked at Buster.

"What?" he asked.

I rolled my eyes at him, thinking that getting a compliment out of this man required a crowbar.

"So what do you think about this storm?" Jackie asked Steve, which I thought was interesting as they hadn't even said hello yet.

"I think there are still so many variables that we don't really know. Hopefully it takes a hook to the east and misses us completely!" he said. Buster handed him his drink. "Thanks, cheers! So, Miss Jackie? Here's to a safe trip back to Brooklyn and to your swift return."

Even in the fading light, I saw Jackie blush and thought, Well, good! She is a little sweet on him and maybe that will bring her back to us even sooner.

"Thanks, Steve," she said.

"Stella and Stanley are going to miss you, Charlie. But don't worry, I told them to expect you back by Thanksgiving." No reply from Charlie. "Hey, why so glum, chum?"

If he could say "Why so glum, chum?" I didn't feel so bad about "Yes, indeedy-do." It only meant that our inner dorks were comfortable around each other.

"I don't think it's safe to travel in a hurricane," Charlie said.

"Of course it's safe to travel or your mother wouldn't make the trip," Buster said.

"I'd never take a risk with you, Charlie," Jackie said. "You should know that."

"Whatever," he said.

Charlie had renewed his fervor for his DS and was deeply involved in a game that killed aliens on a foreign planet in another solar system. Normally, I might have encouraged him to put it away, especially since it was his last night with us. But his mood was so dark that I decided to be silent on the topic. Especially since Jackie didn't seem annoyed by it. Suddenly he got up to go inside the house.

"Where are you going, son?" Jackie asked.

"I just have to check something. I'll be right back." He left the porch and, sure enough, didn't let the screen door slam behind him.

Just a few minutes later, the screen door opened. "Anybody home?" Deb had come in through the kitchen, and she strode out onto the porch.

"Hey, Miss Deb!" Buster said. "Can I fix you a drink?"

"Oh, sure! Whatever y'all are having is good for me. So are we having a hurricane party? Getting ready for Candace?"

I had always loved and would always love that she felt so welcome that she could just glide through my door and make herself at home.

"Ready for her to turn out to sea," I said and gave her a hug.

"I brought a chocolate pecan pie I made for Charlie. It's in the kitchen. And it looks fabulous, if I say so myself!"

"That's so sweet of you, Miss Deb!" Jackie said. "Charlie is sure gonna miss your pies!"

"Well, then, you'll just have to bring him back all the time so I can fatten him up! Now, Buster? Are we really worried about this silly hurricane or what? It looks pretty bad on the news."

"No, but I think it would be a good idea for all of us to be together until it passes," Buster said. "What do y'all think? I mean, Deb, if you're over there in your house all by yourself, all we're gonna do is worry about you. You too, Steve."

"That's true," Steve said. "I think it's a great idea. We can just lock up our places and wait it out."

"Oh, Buster! You are too sweet!" Deb said. "Hey! What about your house up in Murrells Inlet?"

"The landlord battened down all the hatches. Besides, the only thing I've got up there is some fishing tackle and my Green Egg. It would take a helluva lot more than a hurricane to damage that thing!"

I said, "Y'all? Buster's got a generator all ready to flip on that will keep the refrigerator cold, and we have the grill. What do you say? I think our house has weathered more hurricanes than almost any house on this island."

Did I say *our* house?

"That's probably true," Jackie said.

"I was thinking of a Scrabble marathon," I said.

"Well, Mom? That's sure better than Twister!"

Jackie started laughing, and when I recalled what Twister was I started to laugh too.

"Come on, let's get dinner going," I said. "The steaks are all seasoned and waiting on the counter, and I'm sure the potatoes are done by now."

On the way into the house, Buster took my arm to let the others go ahead. "We'll be right along," he said. "I just want to have a word with Annie."

"No problem," Jackie said.

"I'll get the grill fired up," Steve said.

I thought, What in the world?

"Listen, Annie, this hurricane is supposed to make landfall around four in the morning, and it's headed straight for somewhere between here and Myrtle Beach. It's a category three right now. The winds are over a hundred and twenty miles an hour. Could go much higher."

"Oh, my God, Buster! That's terrible!"

"Remember it stalled around the Bahamas yesterday? It picked up steam. It will probably slow down a lot if it passes over any piece of land, but if it rolls in as predicted, I don't think I want Jackie and Charlie on the road until it dies out."

"Absolutely not! I agree one hundred percent!"

"And listening to the National Weather Service, it looks like the rest of this hurricane season is going to be especially active."

"Good grief!"

"What I'm saying is that I'd like to stay here and make sure everything is all right. You know, I want to know that you're safe and the house is safe and all that."

"And all that?"

"Ah, hell! You're not gonna make this easy, are you?"

"Make *what* easy, Buster?"

"I want to come home, Annie. I still love you. So much. I want to come home. I do. Really."

I looked into his beautiful eyes, his bottom lids lined in red from age and all the deep crow's-feet around the sides of them from hours in the sun. I still loved him too. My heart was screaming, Yes! Come home! Stay with me! But my mouth had other words in mind.

"You finally sick of fishing?" I asked, and sorry, I couldn't help the self-satisfied feeling that caused the corners of my mouth to turn up in a smile.

He smiled back, turned his head to one side, and squinted his eyes, looking at me suspiciously as though I'd asked him if he'd like to jump off the Cooper River Bridge.

"Don't go crazy on me, Annie. I didn't say anything about giving up fishing."

"Hmmm. I see."

"Well?"

"Well what?" I looked at him squirming around and thought, Oh, all right. "Oh! I get it! You want an answer right now?"

"Are you saying you don't love me anymore? Is that it?"

"Buster? I've never loved anyone *else*. You know that."

"How am I supposed to know that?"

"Because I'm *telling* you so, and now I'm gonna *show* you!" I took his face in my hands and gave the old codger the kiss of a lifetime.

When I let him go, he said, "Wow! Whew! Annie? I promise to pick up my fishing gear and not leave stuff lying around. Okay?"

"That's good enough for me. Now let's go feed these people! You talk to Jackie, and I'll dress the salad."

"I like the way you do business, Mrs. Britt," he said and gave me a light slap on my backside.

"What? You old fool! There'll be no funny business in front of the kids! Is that clear?"

"Yes, ma'am! Loud and clear."

Steve was out in the rain under an umbrella with the steaks and Deb was slicing the baguette, dropping chunks of bread into a bread basket.

"You got butter on the table?" she asked.

"No, it's in the fridge," I said. "I'll get it." I reached into the refrigerator, put my hand on the butter dish, something I thought I could probably do in the dark, and handed it over to Deb. It was remarkable how many simple things in my life had become habitual, like where I kept my butter dish and how I folded my towels and how I made my bed. I liked my habits because they made me feel like I had some control over my life. And now Buster was coming home. So far, and that would be approximately ten minutes into it, I liked the idea. A lot.

Jackie and Buster came into the kitchen from the living room. They decided they would watch the storm track carefully and figure out what to do about her departure as the night went on.

"Look, if I leave tomorrow afternoon instead of early in the morning, it really doesn't matter too much. So I agree. Let's watch and wait."

"I'm gonna go help Steve before he ruins our dinner," Buster said and winked at me as he passed by. "It's almost dark, and the rain is really starting to come down."

"What's he winking about?" Jackie said.

"Oh, was he winking? I thought he had a gnat in his eye," I said.

"Humph. Ain't no fool like an old fool," Deb said.

"What does that mean?" Jackie said.

"It *means* your father has expressed a desire to fully resume his marital status."

Jackie and Deb stopped dead and looked at me as if to say, *Get off your high horse, Queen Victoria, and speak to your subjects like a normal person.*

I returned the look, and finally we laughed.

"Okay," Deb said, "I'm thinking when this storm passes, *somebody* better be getting their old bahunkus over to the florist to buy a gargantuan bouquet for my best friend!"

"And *somebody* better be buying my pretty momma some really decadent chocolate!"

"And what about Crogan's?" I asked. "Don't you think *somebody* should find something sparkly in a little velvet box for his unbelievably loyal and *extremely* patient wife?"

"Here, here!" they chorused, and we picked up three random glasses to clink and then we shared a very silly fit of giggles. But in the next moment we stopped when the wind gave a good long howl all the way around the house. "We'd better get the chair cushions and everything off the porch. I think we can just lay it all down on the living room floor."

The three of us hurried out to the porch and began gathering up everything as quickly as we could. The paper lanterns had already come down from the hooks and were in shreds from banging against the porch railings. The hammock was doing a crazy dance in the wind, and it took Deb *and* Jackie to get it down. We began bringing in rockers one by one, and in just the short period of time that we'd left the porch after having one drink until then, we were getting wet as the strong winds had the rain blowing sideways. Suddenly we had a hurricane on our hands. If this was the outer band, what would the weather be like by four A.M.?

"Where's Charlie?" I shouted to Jackie. "He could hold the door for us!"

"I'll get him! He's in his room. *Charlie? Come help us, son!*"

It seemed a little ridiculous now that we had waited so long to empty the porch, but who knew the storm would become so furious that quickly? Nonetheless, we continued our job while we heard Jackie screaming over and over for Charlie.

"Maybe he's outside with Buster!" I called out to her.

"Maybe he went to get the dogs!" Deb yelled.

It wasn't five minutes later that we all realized the horrible truth: Charlie was gone.

19

"It is clear that Kidd—if Kidd indeed secreted this treasure, which I doubt not—it is clear that he must have had assistance in the labor. But, the worst of this labor concluded, he may have thought it *expedient* to remove all participants in his secret . . ."

—Edgar Allan Poe, "The Gold-Bug"

Jackie

"Okay," I remember saying, "we have to put our heads together." My heart was racing so fast I was short of breath. "I found this note on his pillow. It looks like he climbed out of his window. The fire escape ladder was hooked to his windowsill, and the window was open."

"That explains why no one saw him," Steve said.

"Why would he do such a thing?" Dad asked.

"He's ten," I answered.

We were all standing in the kitchen, except Mom, who had collapsed into a chair. Miss Deb had her hand on Mom's shoulder. Dad and Steve had come in from the rain and were dripping water all over the floor. The steaks piled onto the foil-covered platter would have to wait a while. It was odd what registered when a trauma happened. For me everything came into sharp focus. My mother obviously had the opposite experience. I wasn't even sure she could hear us.

"Let me see the note," Dad said, taking it from me.

The note read, "Mom, you can go back. I'm staying here. I have plenty of money and protein bars. Don't worry. I'll be fine. Love you. Charlie McMullen P.S. Sorry."

"He took the protein bars? I just bought them this afternoon!" Mom said and we ignored her.

"He can't have gone that far," Dad said, handing the note to Steve. He stepped out onto the back porch and then came back inside. "My cast net is gone."

"Is he planning to live off the land? Did he take his skateboard?" Steve asked.

"I'll go look," I said.

"I'm calling the police," Dad said.

"For what?" I asked.

"Because," he said, "they'll be patrolling the island all night, and if they spot a little boy they'll know where to bring him."

"Right," I said and hurried around the house to see if I could find Charlie's skateboard. It was nowhere to be found. His clothes he had been wearing all day were in a pile on the floor of his room. What I had laid out for him to wear on our trip was gone.

I heard Dad on the phone. "Ten years old. Charlie McMullen. He's almost five feet tall, black hair, blue eyes." Pause. "Yeah, he was wearing shorts and a T-shirt."

"No, he changed his clothes!" I said. "Dad! Tell them he was wearing long jeans, a navy-and-gray-striped T-shirt, and sneakers. And his windbreaker, it was red! And he took his RiverDogs baseball cap."

"Did you hear that?" Dad said. "Okay. Yeah, this is Buster Britt. Yeah, Britt. We're up at twenty-eight and a half. Yep, the Salty Dog. Thanks. Much appreciated."

"What did they say?" I said.

"The dispatcher said for us to sit tight and don't go looking for him in this weather. It's too dangerous to be outside. They're sending a patrol car to us right away, and the others will be on the lookout for him."

"That's it? No manhunt? I mean, we've got a kid on the loose in a *hurricane* and the four policemen we have on this island are all we have to find my *only* child? Screw that! I'm outta here!"

I turned to go get my purse, and Steve followed me to my room.

"I'm going with you," he said. "Grab Charlie's dirty clothes."

"For what? I don't need any help."

"*Yes, you do!* Don't argue with me. I'm bringing the dogs. They're Boykins, remember? They'll be able to smell Charlie a mile away!"

"Oh, God! I hope so!"

I found my purse, ran to Charlie's room and scooped up his T-shirt and shorts, and hurried back to the kitchen.

"I need a flashlight, Dad," I said. He put the one he was holding into my shaking hands.

"I'm gonna get the dogs and their leashes," Steve said. "My car or yours?"

"Let's take yours. He might run if he sees mine." Besides, I was trembling too hard to drive.

Steve rushed out the door.

"Be careful, honey," Dad said. "I'm gonna walk the beach with my big flashlight."

I nodded. "Good idea. Thanks."

"Start with the house where that Greenville family is staying," Mom said from her fog. "I'm going to say a rosary now."

I didn't comment. What was the point?

"I've got my cell," I said. "Call me if you hear anything."

I zipped up my own windbreaker, pulled the hood around my head, and tightened it.

"Where else would he go?" Miss Deb asked.

"Maybe the forts? Be careful, Jackie," Mom said. "Put a hat on. It will help keep the water out of your eyes. By the door . . . on the hook." I took her old canvas bucket hat and pulled it down on my head. "For God's sake, please be careful!"

"I will," I said and hurried out the door, down the steps, and across the yard. The rain was coming down so hard it hurt.

Steve, struggling with Stella and Stanley, clicked the remote from his back steps to unlock his car, and I jumped in. Stella and Stanley hurried up into the backseat and Steve got in, starting the engine as quickly as he could.

"Let's go to the Greenville house first," I said.

"Which one is it?"

"It's on Atlantic Avenue, around Station Twenty-seven." It was only a short distance. "That's it, on the left."

It was easy to see that it was unoccupied. The shutters were closed. There were no lights, no cars, no signs of life. "They must have evacuated," Steve said.

"Yeah, let's go over to Middle Street and then go over to Poe's. He loves Poe's Tavern."

Middle Street was a ghost town, and to my surprise, Poe's was locked up tight as a drum.

The gas station was the only business still open. Steve turned in there and stopped. "You stay here. I'll be right back," he said and hopped out, leaving the engine on and the windshield wipers still furiously wiping away.

I watched him go inside, and then I turned to Stella and Stanley, giving them a good whiff of Charlie's clothes. "Listen, you two, we gotta find my boy. Please help me. Please help me."

They whined and yelped as though they understood me. I prayed that they did, with all my heart I prayed.

I felt ill, as though I might have a stroke or that I might die. I could feel my life draining away. I didn't know what was happening to me. I began to pray harder. *Please, God, please don't take Charlie away from me. I don't think I can live without him. But if you have to take him, please take me too. Because I can't live . . . I just can't.*

The door opened, and Steve jumped in his seat as fast as he could, slamming the door. "Oh, God, look at you," he said.

He reached into his glove compartment and pulled out a pack of tissues. Apparently I had been crying and I didn't even know it.

"Thanks," I said and wiped my face. "Anything?"

"Yeah, the woman in there said a kid matching Charlie's description was here about half an hour ago. He bought a hot dog and smothered it in ketchup."

"That had to be him! Did she see where he went? Did he say anything?"

"Yes, but nothing very useful. She said to him, what are you doing out in this kind of weather? And he said he just felt like a hot dog. She said he stood there and ate every bite, said thanks, and left by the front door. And that he paid with a very wadded-up five-dollar bill."

"Well, that helps nothing. Except that it was thirty minutes ago. He couldn't be too far away. Let's try Fort Moultrie. He could hide a million places in there."

"I agree."

I called home. Mom answered. "The police are here," she said. "They want a picture of Charlie."

"Just give them the most recent one. Mom, tell the officer that Charlie stopped by the gas station and ate a hot dog."

"Why would he do that when he knew we were having steak?" Edith Bunker's mother was my mother's maternal grandmother's sister.

"Well, Mom, I guess he preferred a hot dog. We're going down to the forts now. Is Dad looking on the beach?"

"Oh, yes. And I'm here with Deb. Be careful. The wind is fierce."

"I'm not coming home until I find Charlie. Call me if you hear a single thing, okay?"

"Of course!" Then she whispered to me, "I think the policemen are a little annoyed that you didn't stay home like they said you should."

"Really? Ask them what they would do and remind them that I'm an army nurse, okay?"

I hung up and continued staring out the windows, scanning every street, yard, and side street for anyone outdoors who might resemble Charlie. But of course no one was outside, even on the porches. We had an old family tradition, like many islanders, of sitting on our porch to watch storms, especially thunderstorms. But when the wind topped fifty miles an hour, we took down the hammocks, turned over the rockers, and went inside.

The wind was howling like thousands of demons breathing down our necks, and the flooded streets were already littered with debris. Palmetto fronds ripped from trees flew by us while the trees themselves bent this way and that, caught in the growing strength of Candace. Garbage cans rolled across the streets, crashing into curbs, their contents spilling everywhere. Lightweight porch furniture that had not been secured became airborne, flying into neighbors' houses and trees. Blown-out porch screens flapped in the wind like laundry on a clothesline. And all the while Steve struggled to keep his SUV steady, the streetlights flickered. I just hoped and prayed we'd find Charlie before the island lost power.

"This is horrible," I said. "It's my worst nightmare come true."

"We're gonna find him, Jackie. I know we're gonna find him."

We pulled up outside of Fort Moultrie. Steve said, "You got Charlie's clothes?"

"Yeah, right here," I said and handed them over to him.

"Okay, let's make a run for the front entrance. You ready?"

"Let's go," I said and opened my door. I had to push against it to get out because the force of the wind was right on us. The flashlight was tucked tight under my arm. Steve opened the back doors, and somehow by the grace of God, he got his dogs out. He began to run with them toward the entrance, and I was right behind them. When we got there we stopped, out of breath, and leaned against the wall, breathing hard.

"Okay," Steve said and held Charlie's clothes under their noses. "Now go get Charlie!"

I turned on the flashlight and aimed it down the tunnel. Stella and Stanley took off running like I'd never seen them go. I was amazed.

"I used to do a lot of bird hunting before my wife died. The dogs are trained to search and retrieve."

"Even in a hurricane?"

"I had to pay extra for that, but yes."

It was a stupid joke, but I knew he was trying to get me to calm down. We needed to think of where else Charlie might be if he wasn't holed up in one of the many tiny rooms or niches in the fort. Minutes later the dogs were back. Charlie wasn't here. My heart sank. Steve was disappointed too.

"What else was Charlie involved with this summer? I know he did an awful lot of skateboarding. And he played with those kids a lot."

"Yeah, and he got all excited about the Revolutionary War battles that were fought over here."

"Wasn't he reading something by Poe?"

"Yeah. 'The Gold-Bug.' I thought it was too mature for him, but he really got into it. He made a map for a treasure hunt and actually had a hunt with those kids. He loved it. And I had to peel his Poe's Tavern T-shirt off his back to wash it. He like lived in it."

"Jackie, I've got it. Goldbug Island. He's on Goldbug Island. Come on, we've got to hurry."

"Oh, God! But there's no shelter there except the clubhouse, and I'd bet my life that it's locked up!"

"We can worry about that when we get there. Come on. Grab my hand."

This time we were running right into the wind, and it was only because he held me so tight that I even stayed on my feet. Mom's hat went flying to kingdom come, and the rain felt like needles on my face. Thank God we didn't have far to go. When we got to the car, Steve got the dogs in the car first. Maybe because they had a lower center of gravity, they were able to better withstand the wind. I climbed in on his side and crawled over the console. It took a stevedore's strength for him to pull the door closed.

"Okay, now," he said. He threw Charlie's clothes into my lap and started the engine.

We got as far as Dunleavy's Pub and were just making the left when a patrol car appeared behind us.

"Sullivans Island's finest appears to have an interest in us," he said.

We continued on toward the Ben Sawyer Bridge and saw there was a roadblock. We slowed down and rolled to a stop. A police officer approached Steve's side of the car and indicated by twirling his finger that he should roll down his window. He did, and the officer shined his large flashlight into the car.

"Can I see your driver's license, sir?"

"Of course." Steve pulled his wallet from his jacket, removed his license, and handed it to the officer.

The officer read Steve's name and handed it back to him.

"I'm sorry but you'll have to turn around, Dr. Plofker. Can't go over the causeway. It's flooded. Too dangerous."

"Officer? My little boy is missing. We're pretty sure he's on Goldbug Island."

"You that McMullen kid's mother? I heard about that on our radio."

"If we could just go over the bridge and down to the island. We're not trying to go to Mount Pleasant or Charleston."

"I'm sorry, ma'am. Too dangerous. My orders are no one crosses the bridge."

"Officer, I'm an army nurse. I did six seven-month tours in Afghanistan. My husband just died. I can't lose my son too. Please . . ."

"Jeez. That's awful. Afghanistan, huh? I was with the 101st Airborne Special Troops Battalion."

"The Screaming Eagles? They were on my post."

He stood back and looked at me for a moment. "You realize you'll be taking your life into your own hands out there?"

"Until three months ago, that's what I did for a living," I said.

"Just be careful," he said.

"Thank you, Officer," Steve said and raised his window. "I thought you only did three tours."

"*Only?* Never use the word *only* when you're talking about that hellhole. I needed to impress him. The Screaming Eagles have a reputation for eating their young. Raw."

"Let's go get Charlie."

"He's *got* to be there."

We inched over the bridge and made the right turn onto the steep hill that would lead us down to the island. The weather was getting worse by the minute. Trees and limbs were down, and pools of water were everywhere. The island was going to be completely flooded as soon as the tide came in. Anything that wasn't nailed down was going to float away and never be seen again.

Then we encountered our next problem: the gate to the island was locked. But even from there I could see that a large tree had come down on the clubhouse. What if Charlie was in there? What if he'd gotten hurt?

Steve stopped there and asked, "What do you want to do? Either I can crash the gate and buy them a new one when the storm passes, or we can make a run for it."

It wasn't like an iron gate at a prison but more like a simple metal bar, probably aluminum, that crossed the drive like a triangular-shaped cattle gate.

"You call it."

"Okay, I'm going for it. I'm turning off your air bag, but back up your seat as far as you can just in case. And if mine pops out, slash it with this."

He handed me his Swiss Army knife, and I backed up my seat as far as it would go.

"Ready?"

"Yes."

He backed up the car about fifty feet and then slammed the gas pedal to the floor.

BAM!

We easily broke through the gate, and Steve's air bag didn't deploy. He ignored that detail and drove as close to the clubhouse as he could go, splashing through water and driving around fallen limbs.

"Give me Charlie's shirt again. And you wait here."

He opened his car door and let the dogs out. I would do no such thing. I got out of the SUV, and my first thought was that I was going to blow away. The wind had to be close to a hundred miles an hour. Maybe more. What would it be like by four A.M., when the eye was supposed to pass over us? I could see him screaming at me, but the wind was so loud I couldn't hear what he was saying. Stella and Stanley had already taken off running, and don't you know they stopped where a huge branch from an uprooted live oak tree had crashed through a large plate-glass window of the clubhouse. I was hanging on to the handle of the door of the car, and Steve inched his way around to get me. I crouched down and began to make my way to him like a duck.

He pulled me up and put his arm around me; we dropped our heads down and struggled toward the window. The dogs were barking wildly. Steve pulled them back from the shattered glass and looked in.

"Go back!" he screamed to them, and they took off toward his Expedition.

Next, without a word, he pulled off his jacket, wrapped it around his hand, and broke away enough of the remaining glass to make a hole large enough for him to pass through. Then he climbed the branch and jumped inside. I was right behind him with my flashlight. We scanned the room, and there was Charlie, lying on the floor near the door. I thought my heart would jump out of my throat.

"Charlie!" I screamed and began running to him.

Somehow Steve got there first and turned him over. He began giving him little slaps on his face to bring him around. A ceiling fan had fallen on him and knocked him out.

"Come on, Charlie, speak to me. Come on, boy. Your momma's here, and she wants to talk to you."

"Charlie? Sweetheart?"

"Careful, I think that wrist might be broken," Steve said.

Charlie's eyes fluttered and he groaned.

"Baby, open your eyes and talk to me," I said.

"Momma," he said in a whisper. "I'm so sorry."

I helped him sit up, kissing him all over his head and wiping away blood. Steve took his own jacket and made a sling out of it. "Let's put your arm in here, son," he said. "Gently, gently."

He called him "son" not in a territorial way but in an endearing way. I didn't even bristle. At that point I was weeping with joy. Even Steve was crying. Charlie began to cry too. His forehead was cut, and he had numerous superficial cuts on his hands. Even if his wrist was broken, it would heal. Clearly it wasn't a compound fracture. It would all heal.

"We need to get him to the ER," Steve said.

I was sitting on the floor, leaning against the wall, with Charlie across my lap.

"Well, we can't stay here, but we can't go over the causeway," I replied. "Can we take him in the morning when the storm's over? I mean, you're a doctor and I'm a nurse. Can we just take him home and patch him up until daylight? We can wake him up every hour, you know, to watch him for a possible concussion?"

"You're absolutely right. We can absolutely do that. How's that wrist, Charlie?"

"Hurts," he said.

"How's your head?"

"Hurts."

"Okay, Charlie, we're gonna have to get you out of here. If you can walk to the window, your momma can pass you through to me and we can get you home. You game?"

"Yeah," he said.

"You know it was Stella and Stanley who found you?" Steve said.

"Really?"

"Yeah, but it was you, Steve, who figured out Charlie was here," I said, and I knew I'd be grateful to him for the rest of my life.

We fought our way back to Steve's SUV, where the dogs were lying patiently in the mud underneath his vehicle, waiting for him. He got them out and into the backseat and lifted Charlie up to my lap in the front seat. There was mud all over the car, and we were all soaking wet. This man was as good as gold. We went back over the Ben Sawyer Bridge, stopping to tell the police that we had Charlie, and they were happy that we did. They'd call off the search, they said.

"Mom?"

"Yes, sweetheart?"

"Am I in trouble?"

"No, sweetheart. No."

I called home, and Mom answered the phone. "We found him!" I said.

"Oh! Praise God! Deb! Call Buster! Jackie and Steve found Charlie! Where are you?"

"We're on our way home," I said, and I meant it in every sense of the word.

Epilogue
Annie's Parting Words

It might have been the end of October, but everyone was still talking about Hurricane Candace. People were complaining about how long their insurance companies were taking to pay and how many more jillions of bugs we had and how the beach still didn't look right and on and on. Please. I had no complaints. I had my family under one roof, and that was *all* that mattered to me.

The Salty Dog had sailed right through our visit from Candace except for the paper lantern lights, my doormats that I had completely overlooked, that must have flown away like Frisbees, and beach sand that was so pervasive that it seemed like it was even in our hair. Buster and Steve had become quite the team and were so helpful during the cleanup, taking charge of the outside. They went to Lowe's together and rented a power washer and blasted the salt and leaves and sand from the outside walls and porches of our houses, including

Deb's. The men reopened the shutters, Jackie, Deb, and I rehung the baskets and hammocks and set the rockers in a row, and we were as good as back in business. Charlie's wrist, which had a Colles' fracture, whatever that means, was in a splint that prevented neither running down the beach with Steve's dogs nor some mild skateboarding. His explanation for running away was that he had been following his passion. After a lot of stern talking to, Charlie agreed that he would indulge in his passions only with his mother's permission until he was twenty-one. In the days and weeks that followed the hurricane, I had worried that Jackie would blame me for lighting a fire in Charlie that had led him to believe he could go against the odds like the American patriots during the Revolution and somehow stay without her sanction. She didn't blame me even once. She was so grateful that Charlie was all right, she couldn't think of another thing.

Halloween was Monday, and Charlie was excited. He wasn't sure that he wasn't too old to go trick-or-treating, but he was going to give it a try because his new school (that he professed to adore) was having a Halloween parade. Jackie and I had put together a dark suit, complete with an elaborate bow tie, a fake mustache, and a stuffed black bird sewn to his shoulder. He was, you guessed it, Edgar Allan Poe.

And speaking of Uncle Edgar, the moment of my talk had arrived. We were all gathered at the Island Club. Deb had decorated the ceiling with at least seventy-five hanging black birds made from construction paper. Charlie had helped her cut them out, and Buster had helped her suspend them from the ceiling with transparent fishing wire and some gummy fixative that didn't damage the paint. Then she'd used rolls and rolls of orange crepe paper strips to create some kind of curtain that would never make it to the pages of *Southern Living*, but I said not one word about that. Bless her heart, she had turned her bloomers inside out to make the day a success.

Believe it or not, the event was sold out. I think that spoke more to our resident population's devotion to our library than today's Nervous Nellie speaker. In any case, the ladies on the committee made beautiful brownies, yummy-looking cookies, and all kinds of little tea sandwiches. There was a punch bowl of pink lemonade. Charlie was enjoying his fourth cup. The plan was that Deb was going to welcome and thank everyone, introduce me, and then I was to rattle on about Edgar for approximately thirty minutes. We would wind it up with questions that I prayed I knew how to answer. The event had already raised close to a thousand dollars. And the best news of all was that

Aunt Maureen was here. Well, "best news of all to some degree" is probably the better way to phrase it. She wasn't much of a conversationalist and she was a teetotaler, which what can I say that you don't already think about that?

Ever since Jackie had decided to stay for a while, she'd felt like she owed something to Aunt Maureen, and I agreed. She owed her a lot. So Buster whipped out his credit card, and the next thing we knew Maureen was living large in the Lowcountry on Sullivans Island, supposedly for a mere ten days. Last Sunday I took her to Mass at Stella Maris, where she promptly fell in love with Monsignor Ben Michaels. He just gushed all over her to the point where she could barely breathe. But she did.

"He's such a lovely man! And so refined!" she said with stars in her eyes. "I wouldn't mind joining the Ladies' Altar Society. As long as I'm here, of course."

"Why not?" I said and thought, Oh, please, no.

She was thinking of staying longer, forever maybe, she said. I thought, Now what? Should I do a needlepoint pillow about fish and visitors? But I knew it was this island. I'd seen the sultry nights and salted breezes of Sullivans Island turn the most dedicated type A city slickers into laid-back islanders. But Maureen? Was she the cross I would have to bear to let the good Lord justify giving me so much other happiness? Well, if she was then I would.

People began taking their seats, balancing paper plates on their knees and holding their cups. I could feel my nerves acting up. I got the shakes. I hated public speaking. It terrified me. But I had practiced my talk so many times that I thought it *might* be possible to deliver it even if my adrenaline-pumped brain was screaming for me to run like hell for the door.

"You all right, Annie?" Buster asked. He was standing with me, waiting for the ordeal I was to endure to begin.

"Oh, I'm just a little nervous, that's all."

He took my hand and patted the back of it. "Well, you shouldn't be."

"And just why not?"

"Because you're the most beautiful girl in the room. That's why." He leaned over and gave me a kiss on the cheek.

"Oh, you—" I said and thought, Wow, what a few visits to the Magic Gate can do for a certain old salt's attitude. Yes, he was reinstated in my/our bedroom. Besides, I needed the guest room for Maureen and all her sensible shoes.

I turned around, and Jackie and Steve were at my side.

"I just wanted to wish you good luck, Mom," Jackie said and kissed my cheek.

"Thanks, honey, but I'm a little nervous, you know?"

"Nah, listen, if old Father Ben Michaels can let his fiery brimstone fly from the pulpit and no one throws tomatoes, you've got this thing nailed. You were *made* to do this! Who's more entertaining than you?"

"Jackie's right, Annie," Steve said. "Everyone's here to have a good time. Just pretend that we're all on your porch and it's happy hour!"

"My God! That's brilliant!"

And that's just what I did.

After she thanked the immediate world, Deb introduced me like I was new in town and I stepped up to the mike with my notes and my cup of lemonade. People clapped politely. I was shaking in my shoes.

"Thanks, Deb. Would everyone please raise their cups and repeat after me?"

To my utter astonishment, they raised their cups.

"To the glory that was Greece . . ."

They repeated every word.

"And the grandeur that was Rome!"

Again they repeated the line verbatim.

"Cheers!" I said and put my cup down. They said and did the same. "Those two lines are from one of

Edgar Allan Poe's most beautiful poems he ever wrote, 'To Helen.' However, her name was actually Jane. Jane Stanard, to be exact. Mrs. Stanard, who had an eerie resemblance to Poe's mother, was unhappily married, which drove her to depression, then to being put away in some ghastly, dark, dank, dirty institution, where she eventually went completely insane and died. This is only one example of Poe's poor judgment and bad luck when it came to the women in his life and the bad luck he brought to them. Nonetheless, it's a great poem and those two lines are a toast we still hear thrown around Poe's Tavern all the time. One hopes."

The audience laughed, and I thought, Okay, maybe this is going to be all right. I can do this! So I went on with it, gaining a little confidence every time they laughed in the right places and when I heard them say "Hmmm" or whisper "How about that?" to a friend when I told them something about Poe's life that wasn't common knowledge.

I ended my talk with a quote from Poe's obituary published in the *New York Tribune* by one of his many enemies, Rufus Griswold.

"It said, 'Edgar Allan Poe is dead. He died in Baltimore the day before yesterday. This announcement will startle many but few will be grieved by it.' Griswold continued to say terrible things about Poe for the rest of his days, including starting a rumor that Poe slept with his mother-in-law." Standing in the back of the room, Deb pointed to her watch. "Oh! Goodness! Well, I could go on forever, but I think my time is up, but I just want to say thank you to everyone who came out to support the Edgar Allan Poe Library and I hope y'all had a good time."

People clapped like it would bring money down from the skies, and I was so surprised I started to laugh. That's when I noticed that Steve and Jackie were holding hands and smiling at each other the way people in love do.

"Now I'd be delighted to try and answer any questions."

I answered questions for a while, and when they began to slow down, I wound things up by thanking them again. There was, incredibly, more applause. I could hardly believe it. I was so relieved that it was over I thought I'd just go home, chug a box of wine (just kidding), and fall into bed for the night. But it was only four thirty in the afternoon. Too early. Jackie, Steve, Maureen, and Buster came to where I stood cleaning up my papers. Charlie was already outside running around.

"Mom, you were wonderful! I didn't know you *knew* so much about Poe. I learned a lot!"

"Thanks, sweetie. Could you tell I was a wreck?"

"Gosh, no," Buster said. "You were terrific. What do you think, Steve? Time for a beer?"

"Sounds great!" Steve said. "Maybe we have time to throw a hook in the water before dark?"

"I'll meet you back at the house," Buster said.

"You were very entertaining and enlightening," Maureen said as though there was a whole lemon stuck in her mouth.

"Why, thanks, Maureen. What do y'all say we go home and start thinking about supper?"

"Dinner's ready," Maureen said, unaware of the Lowcountry distinction between dinner and supper. She'd learn. "I made lasagna. It's Jimmy's recipe. Charlie loves it."

"Is there enough for Deb too?" I asked, a little surprised that she had felt it was all right to just move into my kitchen.

"There's enough for twenty people," she said and bounced her head up and down as if to indicate that the rest of her body agreed with her mouth. Saints preserve us, she didn't have one ounce of grace or poise. "While you were down here hanging crows and getting this place ready, Steve took me to the Piggly Wiggly. I've been cooking all afternoon."

"Well, thank you *so* much! Isn't that *grand*, y'all? That was *so* kind of you!" Inside, I was *dying*. Who goes into another woman's kitchen and makes herself at home like that? It was not like she was my *blood*. Be quiet, nerves, I told myself. With Jimmy gone, who else did she have in New York? No one. The rest of her relatives were a thousand years old. "Jackie? Why don't y'all go back home with Maureen, and I'll stay here to help Deb close up."

"Sure," Jackie said. "Anybody seen Charlie?"

"He's running around in the parking lot," Buster said. "He's fine."

"You're having supper with us, right?" I said to Steve.

"Of course! If you'll have me."

"*Please*. Don't even think otherwise."

They left, and Deb and I finally had a moment alone. "Whew!" I said. "So was it okay?"

"Annie," she said and dropped her hands to her sides. "You were a pip, girl. You had a hundred people in a trance."

"Oh, please. Well, I had fun too. Let's clean this up and get out of here."

We worked like devils with the rest of her committee, disposing of cups, plates, napkins, food, and all the decorations. When I got home at six, I was filled with trepidation. As I came in through the kitchen door, I could not believe my eyes. The kitchen was immaculate. The smells of garlic and tomatoes were mouthwatering. The dining room table was set so beautifully, I couldn't have done it better myself. And best of all, the trestle table was all set for cocktails. Maybe old reliable Maureen wouldn't be so bad to have around after all.

When we got to the table the conversation was all about the sights Maureen should see all around Charleston. Until Maureen put a plate in front of each of us. The food was so gorgeous and fragrant we stopped talking.

"Put a blessing on it, Buster, and make it snappy," I said, and Charlie giggled.

Buster blessed it, and we began to eat a meal that transported us to another realm. I had never had lasagna like this. Never.

"Glam?" Charlie said.

"Yes, *dah-lin*?" I was feeling very southern for Maureen's benefit.

"Why did Edgar Allan Poe sleep with his mother-in-law?"

Gulp, I thought. I saw Jackie, Buster, Maureen, and Steve snicker in unison.

I replied with a straight face, "Well, it was just a nasty rumor that he did. But *if* he did, it would only have been because they were so terribly poor they had to sell Edgar's bed and it was very, very cold. But I don't believe it ever happened."

"Okay. Can I have some more lasagna, Aunt Maureen?"

Whew, I thought.

"Of course you can, Charlie. Do you want to help yourself? Or do you need me to help you?"

"I can do it," he said.

"Tell me what's in this lasagna, Maureen. It is simply out of this world." If she stayed too long, I'd be as big as a cow.

Maureen actually smiled at me, and I thought, Actually, she isn't all that homely when she smiled.

"The secret is béchamel sauce made with skim milk and nutmeg, and I use turkey and pork instead of beef. I use béchamel instead of ricotta. It cuts the calories in half."

"Well, praise God for that!" I said and laughed. "Okay, let's get serious here. *What else* can you make?" How a woman who looked like Ruth Buzzi's little-old-lady character from *Laugh-In* could cook like a certified angel was the conundrum of the day.

"Just about anything French or Italian. I know I'm Irish, but who wants to eat corned beef and cabbage? Or blood sausage? I'd rather eat pasta dishes like scampi Fra Diavolo. Isn't that right, Charlie?"

"Yup. Aunt Maureen makes wicked scampi, which is really shrimp."

"I don't know what the heck scampi Fra Diavolo is, but I'm gonna bring you five pounds of shrimp tomorrow!" Buster said, and we all laughed.

What I didn't know that night was that we'd eat and laugh our way through the holidays and well into 2012. When Easter rolled around and Jackie appeared with a diamond on her left hand, Buster and I wept with happiness. Charlie was so glad he could barely contain his excitement.

When I asked him what he thought about having Steve as his stepfather, he said, "He's a really good guy and he saved my life and he has dogs. So the dogs will be mine too! Plus I think my mom really likes him."

"I think so too."

Maureen, true to her reputation as The Stalwart One, went back to Brooklyn, put Jackie's home on the market, and said a special novena to St. Joseph that it would sell. She even buried a statue in the backyard, explaining to us that there was no front yard to use as recommended, only cement sidewalks, and she didn't want to go to jail for defacing public property. "Monsignor Michaels says the Lord will understand and grant me a special dispensation."

The poor, poor well-meaning, generous-hearted woman was dead in love with a celibate priest. But by Memorial Day, when a rumor began to float around that he had asked to be released from his vows, Maureen blushed and stammered every time we brought it up. Like my mother used to say, God rest her soul, there's a lid for every pot. Still, I think my mother would have been flabbergasted like the rest of us.

Jackie continued nursing at the VA hospital. Deb and I continued our morning walks. Buster and I ended our evenings on the porch, rocking, listening to the ocean, looking up at the stars, and chatting about the day's events. Sometimes I'd have my crocheting on my lap, and no one had the courage to ask me who the dainty pink blanket was for, especially Jackie. That made me laugh to myself.

Every night Maureen retired early, presumably to coo on her new cell phone with Ben, as he was now known. I had to give her credit. She was the least obtrusive houseguest I'd ever had. That inconspicuousness gave Buster and me the porch.

"I guess Jackie will be moving my mother's quilt next door soon," I said.

"Yeah, this time it won't be so complicated for us to go for a visit."

"Very funny, Mr. Britt."

"Thank you, Mrs. Britt. But don't you love the way she actually defers to him once in a while?"

"Yes, I do. It's because she respects him, especially since the moment they rescued Charlie. I think that was the clincher. It's when she finally let her guard down."

"Took long enough, but everything happens when it's supposed to, I guess."

And I'd agree with him on that too.

"We've got it good, Buster," I'd say on so many nights.

"Yep, as long as you don't start fussing around and driving me crazy again," he'd mumble, trying to get a rise out of me.

As always, I took the bait, but nowadays, it was all in fun. "Oh, hush, you old carp! I'll tell my nerves to come over there and take a bite out of you!"

"No! *You* hush, you old . . . what did I call you last night?"

"Last night? Let me see. Hmmm. I think I was a flounder, or maybe that was Tuesday night?"

"You never gave up on me, did you, Annie?"

"No, I never did. Or Jackie or Charlie. And I never will."

"We're a family again because of you, Annie. You know that, don't you?"

"It helped that you all cooperated," I'd say and smile. "It's also because you're a fabulous man, Buster Britt."

Then we'd reach out across the darkness to each other just to have a connecting touch and we'd remark on what a marvelous state contentment was. For all of the differences between us, Jackie and I always agreed on one thing: a good woman's heart knows no bounds. And love is the most powerful and wondrous gift in the world. Yes, it is.

Acknowledgments

Actual porch lights became an inspiration for this story because I have always loved the idea that folks left their porch lights on when they were still pleased to receive a random visitor after dark or because they were waiting for someone's safe return. And I grew up on an island with a lighthouse, whose powerful beam existed for the sole purpose of guiding boats and ships into port safely. Light has always been a symbol of welcome, anticipation, and safe harbor.

The other inspiration for this story stemmed from the fact that Edgar Allan Poe once called Sullivans Island home. I had read most of Poe's work but didn't know who the man himself really was. I couldn't wait to find out. The very first thought that came to mind as I began to read about Poe was that everyone seemed to want to claim him—Boston, Baltimore, Charlottesville, and of course, Sullivans Island— but during his lifetime very few people seemed to love him.

Just as the true nature of Dorothy and DuBose Heyward's characters had been a puzzle for me a few years ago, it seemed that James M. Hutchisson had been asking himself the same question about Heyward and then Poe. If you want to know more about the real life of Edgar Allan Poe, you *must* read James M. Hutchisson's book *Poe* (Jackson: University Press of Mississippi, 2005). I found it to be an engrossing read and an invaluable source of fascinating information. It shed new light on Poe, helping me gain a much deeper understanding of this very complicated, brilliant man and his quirky, truculent personality. So, Professor Hutchisson, just as I thanked you for your wonderful work on the Charleston Literary Renaissance and the life of DuBose Heyward, I thank you now for your irresistibly delicious biography of Edgar Allan Poe. And Matthew Pearl's work on Poe entitled *The Poe Shadow*, which you should also read, led him to the extremely interesting theory that Poe did not die from rabies or poor lifestyle choices but from a brain tumor, which I think makes an awful lot of sense in light of the details. Thank you, gentlemen, for your excellent work.

Robert Rosen? Where are you, bubba? Step up and take a bow! It is my old pal Robert who is the masterful and witty pen-swinging gentleman behind a small but value-packed volume called *A Short History of Charleston* (Charleston: University of South Carolina Press, 1997). I can't remember anything I've written without consulting the pages of *ASHOC*. To enhance a visit to the Holy City, I suggest every tourist should buy a copy of this fine work and read it.

I'm always looking for books on the Lowcountry that might teach me something new, bringing stacks of them home to ponder. In my travels I stumbled on another wonderful book, perhaps not as well known as the Hutchisson, Pearl, and Rosen books but no less helpful or interesting. If you want to amaze the children in your life or be the new "it" girl (or boy) on the beach party circuit, pick up a copy of *1001 Questions Answered About the Seashore* by N. J. Berrill and Jacquelyn Berrill (New York: Dover Publications, 1976). If you own a beach house, you should own this book.

Special thanks to my dear friends Adrian Shelby and Ed Bindel for leading me to their gracious cousin Lieutenant Colonel Jocelyn Leventhal of the U.S. Army, who enlightened me on day-to-day life in Afghanistan. And to Tammy M. Finney, MSN, RN, SHCH, CWC, of the Ralph H. Johnson VA Medical Center in Charleston, South Carolina, for her important information and insights.

Thanks to Christian Georgantonis of Douglas Manor, New York, for the idea to make the Nintendo DS the favorite gaming device of my character Charlie McMullen. And thanks and smooches to my childhood pal, former mayor, and island king Marshall Stith, for getting the skinny on the windows of the Goldbug Island Clubhouse's manager extraordinaire, Thomas Smith, and his help in lining up the cameos for some Station 22 favorite patrons: Mark Tanenbaum, Larry Dodds, David Kenney, Mike Richardson, Johnny Disher, Bill Roettger, and Steve Reeves. These excellent specimens of genteel islanders are no more in the habit of sending drinks to women than the man in the moon, at least, not to my knowledge. They appear in these pages in the name of good clean fun. And many thanks to my sweet friend Dawn Durst for fictionally providing the music for Vernon's wake, and to my dear friends Fran and Sharon Wanat, many thanks as well.

And to Margaret Donaldson, many thanks for your support of the Lowcountry Open Land Trust, a mighty worthy cause. Ms. Donaldson will happily transform your home or place of business, but sorry, not your persona. But Hailey Nagel of the Allure Salon in Charleston, who walks through this story as herself, can help you out—especially if you have oxidized beach head. Or if you're on the beach—Sullivans

Island, that is—you can call Julie Nestler at Beauty and the Beach and she'll take care of you just like she does Annie Britt. And to Mike Veek (Go, RiverDogs!), thanks for appearing here, and I hope you never get poison ivy, but if you do, call George Durst or Duke Hagerty, not Steve Plofker. Steve Plofker is our great pal in Montclair, and he is not a dermatologist but a generous supporter of the Montclair Art Museum. And I hope his wife, the one and only Bobbi Brown, thinks I painted a fair picture of Steve's sweetest side. She should rest assured that Steve's not messing around with Jackie McMullen in real life, only in this book. Jackie's here because, well, because she's one of the finest women I've ever known and I thought she'd get a kick out of being a leading lady.

I'd like to thank my wonderful editor at William Morrow, Carrie Feron, for her marvelous friendship, her endless wisdom, and her fabulous sense of humor. I am blowing you bazillions of smooches from my office window in Montclair. And to Suzanne Gluck, Alicia Gordon, Eve Attermann, Claudia Webb, Cathryn Summerhayes, Tracy Fisher, and the whole amazing team of Jedis at WME, I am loving y'all to pieces and looking forward to a brilliant future together!

And to the entire William Morrow and Avon team: Brian Murray, Michael Morrison, Liate Stehlik,

Adrienne Di Pietro, Tessa Woodward, Lynn Grady, Tavia Kowalchuk, Seale Ballenger, Ben Bruton, Leah Loguidice, Shawn Nichols, Frank Albanese, Virginia Stanley, Jamie Brickhouse, Rachael Brennan, Josh Marwell, Michael Brennan, Erin Gorham, Carla Parker, Donna Waikus, Rhonda Rose, Michael Morris, Caitlin Rolfes, Gabe Barillas, Deb Murphy, and last but most certainly not ever least, Brian Grogan: thank you one and all for the miracles you perform and for your amazing, generous support. You still make me want to dance.

To Buzzy Porter, huge thanks for getting me so organized and for your loyal friendship of so many years. Don't know what I'd do without you!

To Debbie Zammit, seems incredible but here we are again! Another year! Another year of tuna salad on Mondays, keeping me on track, catching my goobers, and making me look reasonably intelligent. I know, I owe you so big time it's ridiculous, but isn't this publishing business more fun than Seventh Avenue? Love ya, girl!

To Ann Del Mastro, George Zur, and my cousin Charles Comar Blanchard, all the Franks love you for too many reasons to enumerate!

To booksellers across the land, and I mean every single one of you, I thank you from the bottom of my heart, especially Patty Morrison of Barnes & Noble, Tom Warner and Vicky Crafton of Litchfield Books,

Sally Brewster of Park Road Books, and once again, can we just hold the phone for Jacquie Lee of Books-A-Million? Jacquie, Jacquie! You are too much, hon! Love ya and love y'all!

To my family, Peter, William, and Victoria, I love y'all with all I've got. I'm so proud of you and so grateful for your understanding when deadlines and book tours roll around every year. As always, just for being who you are, my heart swells with gratitude and pride when I think of you, and you are never far away from the forefront of my mind. Every woman should have my good fortune with their family. You fill my life with joy. Usually. Just kidding.

Finally, to my readers, to whom I owe the greatest debt of all, I am sending you the most sincere and profound thanks for reading my stories, for sending along so many nice e-mails, for yakking it up with me on Facebook, and for coming out to book signings. You are why I try to write a book each year. I hope *Porch Lights* will give you something new to think about and somewhere new to try. There's a lot of magic down here in the Lowcountry. Please come see us and get some for yourself!

I love you all and thank you once again.

HARPER LUXE

THE NEW LUXURY IN READING

We hope you enjoyed reading
our new, comfortable print size and found it
an experience you would like to repeat.

Well – you're in luck!

HarperLuxe offers the finest in fiction and
nonfiction books in this same larger print size and
paperback format. Light and easy to read, HarperLuxe
paperbacks are for book lovers who want to see
what they are reading without the strain.

For a full listing of titles and
new releases to come, please visit our website:

www.HarperLuxe.com

SEEING IS BELIEVING!